AI

'But if I get married, ...
be just as badly off as I am now! I'd have no money of my own. I'd still have to do what someone else wanted all the time. And all the men round here are going to be just like Mr Chesil when they're older. I'm not going to spend the rest of my life checking the linen and counting preserves. I'd rather die!'

The maid studied Amaryllis' flushed, accusing face for a long moment before saying casually, 'There are other ways.'

'Other ways? What other ways?'

'You could sell your favours, as they say.'

Amaryllis stared at her. 'You mean, like Betty in the village? But, Bella — it's terribly wrong! Mamma says . . .'

Bella looked at her impassively. 'Hasn't done your mother much harm.'

'But she's married!'

'You think they do it differently, do you?'

'But being married's different! That's not selling it!'

'Oh, no. Of course it isn't,' said Bella. 'You just *give* it away. And everything else.'

Amaryllis was silent for a moment. Then she said doubtfully, 'I'm sure it must be wrong . . . but, how much would I get?'

Priscilla Jenkins

AMARYLLIS

ARROW BOOKS

Arrow Books Limited
17-21 Conway Street, London W1P 6JD

An imprint of the Hutchinson Publishing Group

London Melbourne Sydney Auckland
Johannesburg and agencies throughout
the world

First published by Hutchinson 1982
Arrow edition 1983

Made and printed in Great Britain
by The Anchor Press Ltd
Tiptree, Essex

ISBN 0 09 930840 1

One

With the exception of Amaryllis Vaughan, everyone in Shropshire approved of the marriage and it seemed as if they had all come along to witness the ceremony. The pews were filled with the families of every substantial landowner for three valleys round and the villagers crowded into the gallery had counted no fewer than fourteen carriages drawn up around the churchyard.

It was generally agreed that Mrs Vaughan had done very well for herself, remarrying at her age. It was not easy at the best of times for a widow of forty-five to establish herself again, and when all the first husband had left behind him was a ramshackle old house and a nineteen-year-old daughter it was almost impossible. If Mrs Vaughan had not been such a plump, pretty, respectable woman, she could not have done it. But after two years of widowhood it was all settled. Captain Vaughan had been an odd sort of husband, very unpredictable at times – to put it no worse – but William Chesil was a sensible, straightforward man who knew how to look after a woman. Mrs Vaughan would be able to rely on him.

It was a little soon, to be sure. Only two years . . . Surreptitious glances were cast at the memorial tablet above the Vaughan pew. Carved by the local mason in a style twenty years out of date it read:

In Affectionate Remembrance.
Captain Titus Vaughan, late of Monksedge in this parish.
Born 1793. Died 1834.

Beneath this simple inscription the mason had chiselled a

funeral urn and beneath the urn, penned up resentfully in the family pew, sat Miss Amaryllis Vaughan, only daughter of the above.

A fly came in through a broken window pane and buzzed around her bonnet. Amaryllis hit out at it with her prayer book and returned to the disgusted contemplation of her future stepfather, standing by the altar rail.

'Dearly beloved . . . gathered together . . . reverently, discreetly, soberly,' began the clergyman.

Amaryllis, braving disapproving glances, looked over her shoulder at the congregation. The men's hats were placed devoutly on the pew beside them, the women's eyes were lowered, but few of them were paying much attention to the clergyman's words. They had heard them so often before.

'Marriage . . . for the procreation of children . . .'

They caught that. Sly looks were exchanged. 'Small fear of that at forty-five,' they murmured to one another behind their hands.

'As a remedy for sin and to avoid fornication . . .'

Amaryllis's gaze returned to her stepfather's sturdy frame. His face was turned towards her mother and she could see the ripple of sandy hair, the pallid eyes and the chin receding into the thick neck. Why, oh why had her mother done it? Amaryllis thought that if she'd had any warning of the engagement, she would have stopped it somehow. But it had never occurred to her that anyone could wish to marry William Chesil. She'd always taken care to be out whenever he called at Monksedge, leaving her mother to entertain him alone.

The bride looked admiringly up into the groom's face and Amaryllis sighed in exasperation. There was no getting away from it; her mother really seemed to like the man. She'd been so pink-faced and excited this morning, she hadn't noticed Amaryllis's sour looks. She was such a fool, she even liked Henry Chesil and only a besotted future stepmother could do that. It was not that one could *dis*like Henry exactly. He was so nondescript it was hard to keep your mind on him at all. He would hover around anyone with an ounce of vitality like a moth round a candle flame. He was probably doing it now. She stole a glance round her bonnet to where Henry sat alone in the Chesil pew. When she was a child she used to stick out her tongue at him. It would be bad enough having to live with the Chesils – she couldn't stand being stared at by Henry as well.

'For mutual help, society and comfort . . . ' droned the clergyman.

Amaryllis gave him a vicious glance and studied her shoes.

In a pew on the other side of the aisle, a dark man yawned behind his hand. Country weddings were not his style; he'd been a fool to come to this one. It was his debts that were to blame as usual. He'd only just got out of London in time. And here he was in Shropshire, bored to death, with nothing better to do than waste an afternoon at church. He gave the congregation a cursory glance. Commonplace, damned commonplace. Thyrza Vaughan was a pretty woman of course, and there was a certain pleasure to be had from the sight of Titus Vaughan's wife remarrying – and such a clod too. He dwelt on the thought maliciously. He'd had the last laugh on Captain Vaughan. . . . He looked at Thyrza again. Pretty, yes, but no style, none of these provincials ever had. Thank God she'd had the sense to avoid orange blossom at her age. There was a daughter too, wasn't there? He looked idly round the church. Yes, that was definitely the Vaughan daughter. Her face was soft and rounded like her mother's but those ripe lips were all her own. Pearl ear-drops set off the warmth of her skin and her hair was a strange gilt shade, as if her mother's yellow curls had been dipped in silver. Her figure was obscured by the side of the pew. Not that it mattered much. The way women's dresses were made nowadays, there was precious little to see. Titus Vaughan's daughter . . . Amaryllis bent down to retrieve a fallen glove and he caught a glimpse of a white neck.

'Wilt thou love her, comfort her, honour and keep her, in sickness and in health?' the clergyman was asking the bridegroom.

Mr Chesil seemed to have no doubt about his abilities. His responses were loud and firm. It was the bride's turn now.

'Wilt thou obey and serve him?' the clergyman began.

Amaryllis still studied her shoes, her expression concealed by her bonnet.

'With this ring I thee wed, with my body I thee worship . . . ' Mr Chesil was repeating obediently after the clergyman. Amaryllis thought that she could just imagine his body: fat and pursy and smelling a little stale. The vows over, the psalms began. Amaryllis's gaze wandered up the aisle to where her mother still stood before the altar, and then back along the pews again. Suddenly, she noticed the dark man sitting with bowed head staring down at his closed prayer book. Amaryllis had seen him from a distance on several occasions and knew at once who he was: Lord Vanbrugh, the owner of one of the largest estates in Shropshire. She stared at him. What on earth was Lord Vanbrugh doing at her mother's wedding? She was sure he couldn't be a friend of the Chesils.

The psalms came to an end and the clergyman mounted the pulpit and opened his address. Lord Vanbrugh raised his head and Amaryllis was able to see his face in profile. His brows were narrow above a straight nose and his sensual mouth was in strong contrast to the spare line of his jaw. His skin was smooth and well cared for; he displayed none of the broken veins and wind-coarsened cheeks of the country squires around him. He was smiling sourly, amused by the clergyman's inanities. Amaryllis leaned forward, hoping to get a better view of his face. As if his attention had been attracted by the movement, he turned in her direction and their eyes met.

Amaryllis knew that her mother would tell her to look down at once, but he was staring at her – why shouldn't she go on staring back? She wanted to look at him and for once she was going to do what she wanted. Her eyes held his in a hard impersonal gaze. For a full minute Amaryllis and Lord Vanbrugh stared at one another, while the clergyman's voice droned on above them – 'Wives, submit yourselves to your husbands as unto the Lord . . . for the husband is the head of the wife . . . '

Two

Chesil House had been built shortly after its owner's first marriage, his wife's dowry providing a substantial part of the cost. The house stood foursquare at the end of a short drive. Five windows ran along its upper storey and four along the lower, neatly bisected by the door which was supplied with a triangular pediment and a pair of pilasters. It was to Chesil House that the bride and groom returned after a fortnight in Worcester. They were warmly welcomed by Henry and the next morning, as soon as the horses were rested, the carriage was sent over to Monksedge to collect Amaryllis and Bella, her maid.

Amaryllis had no wish to go to Chesil House, but Bella's expression persuaded her to get sulkily into the carriage where she spent the journey in silence. The sight of William Chesil, standing at his door to welcome her, provoked an outburst of resentment, and it took all Bella's warnings to make Amaryllis smile at him.

This reluctant good behaviour continued until her stepfather suggested that the young people might like a turn at shuttlecock and battledore. While their children played this unenlivening game on the lower lawn, Mr and Mrs Chesil seated themselves on a bench in front of the house to observe the match, their view framed by groves of meagre saplings which Mr Chesil assured his wife would soon grow to be a fine stand of timber.

'A handsome couple, my dear,' he said complacently, watching Henry and Amaryllis running about on the lawn.

'Henry's such a nice young man,' replied his wife. 'Amaryllis is a lucky girl. It was good of you, William, to take her.'

'I couldn't get you on any other terms, eh?' said Mr Chesil jovially.

'Oh, William! What nonsense!'

'Well, well, it's only right she should come. I like to do the proper thing you know. Besides, we make quite a nice little family together. It's a pity that servant woman had to come along of course. Bella? Was that the name? Still, I daresay she'll make herself useful in some way or other.'

'Oh William – if only I hadn't promised Titus I'd keep her! But he made me *swear* to do it.'

'I understand.' He patted her hand soothingly. 'There's a few shillings from the Monksedge rents. They'll cover Bella's wages. But *I'm* going to take care of Amaryllis. Her food won't amount to much, but she'll need pretty dresses and so on. I'm going to make sure she wants for nothing.' Mr Chesil was comfortably aware that he was shining by contrast to Amaryllis's father, who had left her with no income to speak of.

'I don't know what we've done to deserve such kindness,' said his wife. He gave her an affectionate peck on the cheek. 'You must let me be the judge of that. Besides, little Amaryllis will pay it all back one day, eh? But we've talked about that already.'

'She *is* rather headstrong,' said Mrs Chesil doubtingly.

'She needs a father's hand, that's all. Nearly two years, isn't it, by now? And you couldn't manage all on your own, now could you? Don't you worry about it any more.'

Despite Mr Chesil's optimism, down on the lower lawn Amaryllis was beginning to lose her temper. Hampered by her long skirts, she was no match for Henry who was having to hit the shuttlecock very slowly to enable her to give him a game at all. At last, in running to parry a faster stroke than usual, she tripped over her skirt and fell to the ground. Henry hastened to help her up, asked her anxiously if she was hurt and picked up the battledore she had flung to the ground in her irritation, but Amaryllis stalked up the lawn to the terrace, announced that she was going to walk round the shrubbery and departed. Henry, looking as guilty as if he were to blame for her ill humour, sat down beside his stepmother with an awkward smile.

Mr Chesil looked after Amaryllis rather uneasily. She was a hot-tempered little thing. He hoped she wasn't going to be difficult – though he'd soon put a stop to any nonsense, of course. She was a bit too like her father for comfort. The fellow had never really fitted in. Take that time at the Hunt Dinner when he'd pulled the chair away just as old Bennet was sitting down. Vaughan hadn't laughed at all, though the other fellows had roared. Funny how you didn't forget these things. After all these years it still rankled. Come to think of it, he'd been thicker than need be with the last parson too – a fellow whose sermons had been a bit much for a plain man to stomach. Not that Vaughan had ever turned up at church, of course. Oh no, he kept to himself and when he did entertain it was always some London fellow, as odd as himself. A resentful flush crept into Mr Chesil's cheeks.

He glanced at his wife, placidly talking to Henry, and reminded himself loyally that there was something of her mother in Amaryllis too. She owed her looks to Thyrza, no question about that. She was a pretty little thing. He'd felt quite proud of her at the wedding when he'd seen her sitting there in church in her new bonnet. But give him her mother any day. Thyrza was the sort of woman you could be sure of. Just the sort of wife he wanted, and at her age not much fear of children to encumber the estate. He'd look after her – he'd buy her a new workbox, next time he was in Shrewsbury. Hers was rather shabby. Yes, a new workbox, one of the good ones inlaid with mother of pearl. He could more than afford a few luxuries now that he had her annuity. A pretty poor fellow Vaughan, to leave her with no more than she'd brought him, and that servant business was the outside of enough. If that Bella woman hadn't been so ill-favoured . . . As it was, he had his suspicions. And Amaryllis – she was only getting that tumble-down house Vaughan had inherited. Hardly worth a penny. Vaughan had added nothing to the estate. Content to idle away his time on his army half-pay. Mr Chesil turned to look in the direction of the shrubbery. No sign of Amaryllis yet. Better leave it for the moment. He'd heard somewhere that nineteen could be a difficult age. If his little Eliza had lived she'd be just twelve. He pushed away the memory of two thin loving arms and turned to speak to Thyrza.

The next few days made it clear to Amaryllis that life at Chesil House was governed by an unvarying routine. Her mother appeared quite contented, but it chafed Amaryllis unbearably. At Monksedge, she and her father had led a casual existence, eating when it pleased them, sleeping when they wanted to. Here at Chesil House, Amaryllis woke up in the morning knowing exactly what the day ahead contained. After breakfast she was expected to go for a ride but even that was not the same as it had been at Monksedge. At Chesil House Henry always escorted her on the safe rides he considered suitable for a lady. He had fixed ideas of what a lady was or was not capable of, and thought it only gallant to adhere to them in spite of Amaryllis's objections. She soon discovered that Henry was happiest trotting along a lane, giving her simple pieces of information about the number of sheep on a hill or the kind of crops in a field. From time to time he would ask her about Monksedge, and though she had never given it a thought when she had lived there, now that she was imprisoned in Chesil House she felt a desperate loyalty towards it. She described it with an enthusiasm which quite bewildered Henry, who had always thought of it as a rather run-down old place. Black and white timbering was very old-fashioned and the land was only fit for sheep-runs.

After her ride, Amaryllis would come reluctantly down to the drawing-room. Her mother was seated on the sofa in her best lilac satin, receiving wedding visits by her husband's side.

'Yes,' Mr Chesil would reply to the visitors' congratulations, 'Yes, I can safely say that I've drawn a prize in life's lottery.' He would draw his wife's arm through his and look proudly down at her while Amaryllis glowered in a corner.

On the third afternoon she absented herself from the drawing-room, but at dinner that evening she was told to be present in future.

'I want our friends to see us together now that we're all one family,' said Mr Chesil reproachfully. 'Henry was with us all afternoon. It looked strange you know, to have no daughter there when the son was able to be present. We had to make excuses for you.'

'I never saw visitors at Monksedge.'

'No doubt. But at Chesil House we do things differently.'

Amaryllis gave an impatient sigh and as a last resort looked to her mother.

'That's right, Amaryllis. Here we do as your new father says,' said Mrs Chesil, smiling at him.

After dinner, the family sat in the drawing-room as usual, while Mrs Chesil worked at her embroidery and Mr Chesil looked at the paper, occasionally reading out items of interest about crop yields or the price of wool. To Amaryllis this was the worst part of the day. She sat immobile, staring at the clock, willing the gilded hands to move faster round the painted face, irritably aware of the snip, snip of her mother's sewing scissors, Mr Chesil's heavy after-dinner breathing and Henry's mild gaze upon her. She was becoming heartily tired of Henry. It was bad enough having to ride with him, but she was beginning to notice that wherever she was, sooner or later Henry would be there too. She shifted in her chair, turning away from the clock to study the stuffed pheasant in the glass case so that Henry would only be able to see the back of her head.

Her stepfather eyed her over the top of his newspaper, noting her green muslin dress with disapproval. No evening gown – he'd have to change that. He liked his family to dress for dinner. That fellow Vaughan – bringing her up like a pauper! Her hair too – that was not as he liked it. He didn't care for those ringlets, they were untidy somehow. He'd have a word with Thyrza about it. Not that *she* was to blame of course. It was obvious that Miss Amaryllis had had it all her own way for far too long. Twisted Papa round her little finger, and of course Thyrza had had to do what her husband told her – hard though it must have been for the poor little woman. What was wrong with the girl? Sitting there with her hands in her lap. Had she no work to do? Thyrza was always busy with some pretty trifle. Just at the moment she was embroidering him a pair of slippers and very nicely too – now that was an idea. . . .

'Nothing to do, Miss?' he asked, adopting the jovial tone he tried to use when speaking to Amaryllis. 'You ought to have something to do, you know. Here's an idea: why not embroider a pair of slippers for young Henry here?'

Henry reddened.

'I can't embroider,' said Amaryllis flatly. 'Papa said it was a waste of time.'

Mr Chesil had to remind himself that it would be most improper to criticize Amaryllis's father in front of her.

'Well, it seems a pity to sit idle. No music either, have you? We'll have to do something about that!'

Amaryllis sat tapping her foot resentfully and made no reply.

After a while, Mr Chesil put down his paper and began to play backgammon with his wife. Henry took a seat near the board and watched the game. Amaryllis's only occupation was to glance at him impatiently from time to time, amazed that anyone could be content with such a tedious pastime. At last, when Mrs Chesil had allowed her husband to defeat her three times, they went to bed and Amaryllis's torment was over. After a fortnight of such evenings, she knew every flower on the drawing-room curtains and every wreath on the carpet. Even in dreams, the ticking of the clock haunted her, and she played endless games of backgammon with Henry Chesil in echoing drawing-rooms, where pheasants gazed beadily down at her from bookcases with empty shelves.

Three

The servant, Bella Hoxton, had arrived at Monksedge one summer morning six years earlier. Dressed in a dusty bonnet and shawl, she had appeared unannounced and unexpected and, when asked where she had come from, she had simply jerked her finger in the direction of the drovers' road. Amaryllis had looked at Bella in surprise; for the drovers' road ran, broad and green in her child's imagination, all the way from Wales to Smithfield meat market in London, with no carts or mail coaches to give you a lift in between.

Captain Vaughan had asked Bella if she had met with any trouble on the way, but Bella had folded her arms and answered, 'I can take care of myself.' Looking at her, it was easy to believe her. She was over six feet tall, and wore her rough brown hair skewered into a knot. Her black dress did little to conceal the gauntness of her frame, and when she began to work at Monksedge there was something grotesque in the sight of her bony hands busying themselves with a lace petticoat or an embroidered nightdress.

Bella was treated with respect by everyone, not simply on account of her size. There were many unexplained circumstances connected with her sudden arrival in Shropshire, and no one knew quite where she had come from or what she had been doing there. Her belongings, brought with her in a large cotton handkerchief, only added to the mystery since she had nothing but a few articles of clothing, a Dutch teapot and a wax mourning portrait of Princess Charlotte. When Amaryllis had been unusually good, Bella would sometimes show her these treasures, but she never explained how she came by them, or by the golden gypsy earrings which she always wore.

If Bella's origins were mysterious, so too were the means by which she had obtained employment at Monksedge. As far as Amaryllis was able to tell, she had simply presented herself at the back door and asked to see Captain Vaughan, and from that day on her position had been unassailable. But Amaryllis's mother had not been pleased about it. Normally placid and even-tempered, anything out of the ordinary made her peevish, and in Mrs Chesil's world servants came properly recommended, for a month's trial.

Life, as Mrs Chesil understood it, was a set of clearly defined rules. As long as you lived according to these rules, all would be well; your neighbours would respect you and you would respect yourself. The only time she had ever strayed from the prescribed path was when she had married William Chesil a little, a very little, before the accepted period of mourning had elapsed. But the match had been so suitable in all other respects that she had allowed herself to be persuaded. William had assured her that it would be all right, and since he was to be her future husband she had thought it proper to obey him. Obeying your husband was certainly one of the rules. It was there in the marriage service and even poor Titus, who had been so casual about other things, had set some store by it.

Mrs Chesil had to admit that obeying her husband had not always been easy. She had not enjoyed her life at Monksedge very much. How could she be expected to run a proper home with Titus in and out at all hours and that woman queening it over the kitchen? Then there was Amaryllis. Mrs Chesil knew a wife should never neglect the education of her daughters but whenever she told Amaryllis to take out her sampler, the naughty girl would ask her father if she had to. When Amaryllis had reached the age of fifteen without being able to play a note or set a stitch straight, she had warned Titus that the girl would never get married without accomplishments. But he had laughed, in what was really a very coarse way, and said, 'She'll get married, never fear.'

No, thought Mrs Chesil, obeying Titus had not been easy. She had even gone so far as to ask the clergyman, privately of course, if he was *sure* a married woman had to obey her husband. But the clergyman had been quite certain of it, and since he himself was a married man, he must know. Dear William, though, only wanted her to do what was right. Think how good he had been about Amaryllis. She had warned William how unwise poor Titus had been about her upbringing and he had quite understood. He had even agreed to have that wretched Bella at Chesil House. She only hoped Amaryllis appreciated how kind and indulgent her stepfather was being, but she rather doubted it.

In this, Mrs Chesil was quite right. Amaryllis, after a particularly tedious evening in which Mr Chesil had insisted on a family game of whist, was sitting in her nightdress while Bella put curl-papers in her hair.

'I can't stand it!' she said vehemently.

Bella had heard this same statement every night for a week and merely answered. 'You've got to stand it.'

'I can't stand it and I won't!' said Amaryllis, between her teeth.

'You've no choice.'

'I'll go back home to Monksedge.'

'On your own, I suppose,' said Bella sarcastically.

'Oh, you can come too.'

'I can, can I? And who'll pay my wages?'

Amaryllis played with the hairbrush. 'We've paid you six years' wages, Bella. I should think you'd be willing to throw in a year or two for free.'

Bella smiled grimly at this suggestion, twisted and pinned the last curl-paper and went across to the wardrobe to take out a nightcap.

Amaryllis watched her for a few moments and then said crossly, 'Oh very well! I'll pay your wages. There must be some money somewhere.'

'Oh must there,' said Bella, threading ribbon in the nightcap.

'Papa managed all right.'

'With his army half-pay which is gone now he's dead and with your mother's annuity which is gone now she's married.'

'Oh, I'll get her to give me some of it,' said Amaryllis airily.

'It isn't hers to give. It belongs to her husband now she's married again. So does Monksedge till you're of age. Your mother was to hold it in trust for you.'

'Oh Bella! I hadn't thought of that.'

Bella looked at her crestfallen face with gloomy satisfaction. 'No. Very likely not. So let's have no more nonsense about your going back home. Mr Chesil would never allow it.'

'Oh Bella, he's so *awful*! And Henry's almost as bad!'

Bella shook her head and made no comment. She fitted the nightcap onto Amaryllis's head and gave her a push in the direction of the bed. Amaryllis climbed between the sheets and said despairingly, 'I can't wait until I'm twenty-one. I want to go home *now*!'

Bella sat down and folded her arms. 'What makes you think you can go home then either?'

'What do you mean?'

'That old house has a couple of fields and a bit of rough grazing. It might keep you of course, if you're willing to live on turnips and do the digging yourself.'

Amaryllis gazed at Bella in dismay. 'You mean – I'm as poor as that? I've got no money at all?'

'Oh, it's not as bad as it might be, if you're sensible. Mr Chesil's willing to feed and clothe you. You'll be all right, so long as you stay here. But if you know which side your bread's buttered you'll do your best to please him.'

Amaryllis was horrified. Having to live with Mr Chesil was bad enough; to be provided for was intolerable.

'I can't bear it!' she wailed. 'It would choke me! I *won't* be grateful! It's his own fault. If he hadn't married my mother, I'd still be perfectly happy at Monksedge, living on the annuity. Just because he's got his greedy hands on it makes no difference. It's not as though he's done anything to deserve it!'

'Deserve it or not, it's his and he doesn't have to spend it on you.'

Amaryllis clenched her fists. 'I've got to get away from here.' She thought for a moment and then said hesitantly, 'Couldn't I – get work of some kind?'

Bella sniffed. 'The only work for a lady, which I suppose you are when all's said and done, is governessing.'

'Yes?' said Amaryllis hopefully.

'They wouldn't touch you. You've none of those accom-

plishments your mother was always on at you a
can't sew, you can't embroider, you can't play the

'So I can't be a governess,' said Amaryllis tragi

'Don't sound so sorry about it. Working all the hours
sends for twenty pounds a year – you'd never stand it.'

'Well I can't stay here, Bella. You can make up your mind to that!' Amaryllis pulled the covers up over her head and buried her face in the pillow.

She thought long and hard that night, and on the following morning her face had lost its sullen expression and she no longer contradicted her stepfather at every turn. Mr Chesil was very pleased with the change. He always enjoyed breakfast nowadays. It was so pleasant to come downstairs and find his wife smiling at him from behind the coffee-pot in her flowered chintz gown. And now Amaryllis had a smile for him too.

What a nice picture mother and daughter made together in the lamplight last night. He had managed to persuade Amaryllis to start a handkerchief for Henry – easier than slippers for a beginner, so Thyrza had said – and she had been showing the girl how to embroider his initials in a little wreath of laurel leaves. They had had a good laugh about these initials – H.O.C. – and by coincidence hock was Henry's favourite wine! Henry was pleased about the handkerchief too. Anyone could see he was very taken with his stepsister, and there was nothing against it in the table of affinities – he'd had a good look during Matins last Sunday to make sure.

Over the next few days, Amaryllis's good behaviour continued. She was determined to leave Chesil House without delay, but she had no idea how to set about it. Her talk with Bella had sobered her greatly. For the first time she had been made to realize that food and shelter had to be acquired from somewhere, and hers came from Mr Chesil. At this point, a less determined woman might have resigned herself to fate, but Amaryllis was not to be so easily beaten.

She had so little experience, that was the trouble. She'd been to Ludlow often enough and she'd once spent a month with her aunt at Cheltenham, but this did not amount to much knowledge of the world. She had to get money; money was the key to independence. People did make money, plenty of people had it, the question was how? Perhaps her stepfather knew the answer. She would ask him at breakfast the next morning.

She chose her moment carefully, waiting until Mr Chesil had finished his first cup of coffee and had complimented his wife on the devilled kidneys.

'Tell me, how do people like us make a living?' she asked, looking innocently at him across the table.

Mr Chesil looked back at her in surprise. Really, he never knew what she was going to say next. 'Well now, let me see . . . Ladies usually marry someone with enough money to look after them, or perhaps their fathers provide for them,' he added, reddening slightly. This was treading on delicate ground.

'Oh, not just ladies,' said Amaryllis quickly, 'How did you get your money for instance?'

Mr Chesil was flustered by this very direct question. 'Well, er, I inherited it I suppose; the land I mean, most of my income is from agricultural rents. I've added a bit now and then with what I've saved and I hope to leave young Henry here rather more than I inherited. . . . That's the way these things work you know. . . .'

'But if you hadn't inherited any land. What would you have done then?'

'Don't worry your stepfather with questions, Amaryllis,' put in Mrs Chesil. 'William, your coffee's getting cold.'

'Oh yes, thank you dear. Henry – you'll tell Amaryllis what she wants to know while I drink my coffee.'

Henry, conscious of Amaryllis's interested gaze, determined to put things as clearly as he could. 'Well now, the first thing you need is your capital.'

'Capital?'

'Yes. A lump sum you know. Something to start off with.'

'And how,' inquired Amaryllis patiently, 'do people *get* this capital?'

'They might inherit it, or work very hard and save it, or have a bit of luck of some sort, or sell something.' Amaryllis privately thought that this sounded vague but she nodded encouragingly.

'And when they have it,' Henry went on, 'they buy a business with it, or a bit of land, or they lend the money to someone, and then they can live on what we call the income from the capital, in other words the profits of the business or the rents from the land or the interest on the loans and so on.'

'But you have to have your capital to start off with?'

'Oh yes, you can't do without that.'

Amaryllis thanked him and sat looking extremely thoughtful, paying no attention to a discussion of the archery contest Mr and Mrs Chesil were giving that afternoon.

The archery contest was the first party the Chesils had given since their marriage, and cards of invitation had been sent to everyone who had attended their wedding. Amaryllis had a new dress for the occasion and its design had cost Mrs Chesil much time and thought. She often worried about her daughter's appearance. Gowns with narrow sleeves and full skirts, finished off at the neck with a prim white collar, looked decorous enough on other girls. So too did the close-fitting bonnets that half blinkered the wearer. But on Amaryllis they had quite the opposite effect. Her face had none of the demure fragility currently in vogue, and her mouth was far from the little pouting pink bud displayed in the fashion plates. Mrs Chesil finally decided on a white muslin dress for the archery contest. White muslin always looked fresh and youthful. If only Amaryllis remembered to suck in her lips and pinch her cheeks before coming downstairs she would do well enough. Unfortunately Amaryllis, going up to her room to dress for the party, had her mind on other matters. Standing in her chemise to wash herself in a bowl of rainwater, she said, 'Bella! I need capital.'

'Capital! Whatever next, I wonder?'

'No, that's right, Bella. I was talking to Henry at breakfast. Capital's what gentlemen need to make a living.'

Bella looked at her with grudging admiration. 'You're a stayer, I'll say that for you. I could have sworn you'd give in after a week or two. Are you serious after all then?'

'Of course I'm serious!' said Amaryllis, drying herself vigorously with the towel Bella handed her.

'I thought it was just one of your whims. Come over here and I'll do your hair.' Amaryllis followed Bella to the dressing-table and sat down in front of the glass.

'The trouble is, I don't know how to get hold of any capital. Could I sell Monksedge, do you think?'

'No takers,' said Bella. 'No land to speak of and the house isn't grand enough to let on its own.'

'There must be *something* I can do.'

Bella, her mouth full of hairpins, brushed some of Amaryllis's ringlets to the top of her head and secured them in a small coil. Then she pointed to Amaryllis's reflection in the mirror and said, 'There's your capital, my girl. It's all you've got. Make the most of it!'

'Get married, do you mean? I suppose I could. But to whom?' Amaryllis thought for a moment and then said, 'You know Bella, there really isn't anyone.'

Bella went to the window, twitched aside the curtain and looked down on the party already gathering on the lawn. 'Hundreds of them,' she contradicted her. 'You could have a nice home – just like your mother,' she added glumly.

Amaryllis looked very thoughtful. 'I suppose it *would* mean I'd get away from Chesil House,' she said, without much enthusiasm.

'Yes, you'd do that right enough.'

'But if I get married . . . my husband will own all the money, won't he?'

'It's law.'

'He'll have Monksedge and everything.'

'True.'

'But I'd be just as badly off as I am now! I'd still have no money of my own. I'd still have to do what someone else wanted all the time. And all the men round here are going to be just like Mr Chesil when they're older. I'm not going to spend the rest of my life checking the linen and counting preserves. I'd rather die!'

Bella studied her flushed, accusing face for a long moment

before saying casually, 'There are other ways.'

'Other ways? What other ways?'

'You could sell your favours, as they say.'

Amaryllis stared at her. 'You mean, like Betty in the village?'

'In a manner of speaking.'

'But Bella – it's terribly wrong! Mamma says . . . '

'Ah, does she now. She would, of course.'

'Well, it *is* wrong, isn't it?'

Bella looked at her impassively. 'Hasn't done your mother much harm.'

'But she's married!'

'You think they do it differently, do you?'

'But being married's different! That's not selling it!'

'Oh no. Of course it isn't. You just *give* it away. And everything else.'

Amaryllis was silent for a moment. Then she said doubtfully, 'I'm sure it must be wrong . . . but, how much would I get?'

'You're a lady. You can charge a lot. Especially the first time.'

'The first time?'

'You know well enough what I'm talking about. It would *be* the first time I suppose?'

'Of course it would!' said Amaryllis, flushing indignantly.

'Well, you could ask anything from five hundred to a thousand pounds even, if you play your cards right. A genuine virgin fetches a good deal.'

'A genuine one?'

'Mostly they're fake. Sewn up again. Or a bit of broken glass and there you are.'

'And are the men taken in?' asked Amaryllis, only half understanding.

'When they want to be. Never mind that nonsense. You think about what I've said.'

'And do you think I could really do it?'

Bella shrugged. 'Stranger things have happened.'

The stables at Vanbrugh were clustered round a cobbled yard, and their only ornament was a tarnished weathercock.

They were reached through a triumphal arch which concealed the modesty of the buildings to which it gave access. Just inside the arch, Lord Vanbrugh was seated astride his black mare, looking down at his sister Georgiana, who was standing by the mounting block.

'So you won't come with me, then?' he asked casually.

'I can't imagine why *you* should want to go,' said Georgiana. 'Commonplace squires with more money than sense. What *do* you want to visit them for?'

'My dear Georgiana, I'm in no position to be exclusive. Compared to Chesil, I'm a pauper.'

His sister sighed wearily. 'Oh Anthony – *more* debts?'

'Prison – unless I accept Saville's offer for St James's Square.' His mare shied at one of the doves strutting about on the cobbles and Georgiana put out a thin hand to soothe her.

'You'll have to sell then,' she said evenly, 'Though it had better be postponed until after my contracts are signed. I should have liked to be married from our town house, but I suppose that can't be helped.'

'Not unless you want to see an execution levied on the cake. You'd better reconcile yourself to this sort of thing. Mayo's not the richest of men and his character hardly inspires one with confidence.'

'He's got enough money to live in London, at any rate. I'm in no position to complain,' said Georgiana bitterly. 'I can't pick and choose with my poor little dowry.'

'True. No one exercising the faintest degree of discrimination could possibly have chosen Mayo.'

'Nonsense, Anthony. Lord Mayo is very popular with women – or had you forgotten?'

'If I had, you've made it your business to remind me.'

Georgiana smiled. 'Perhaps it was a little tactless of me, taking Mayo.' She glanced at the stable clock. 'Your friends will be waiting for you.'

'So they will. I must be off.' He rode out through the archway and Georgiana walked away to where her own horse was waiting.

By the time Lord Vanbrugh arrived at Chesil House the archery contest was already being described as a great success, although the weather was disappointing. The heavy white sky had a deadening effect, muffling sound so that the voices of the archers on the lower lawn could not be heard by the guests drinking wine on the terrace. The grass was dotted with smiling groups of people, strolling about in the vicinity of the targets, but taking care not to stray into the shooting area which Henry Chesil had marked out that morning with little fluttering flags.

Lord Vanbrugh, riding past in the direction of the stables, looked at them all with distaste. Georgiana had been right of course. A clutch of country squires and their dowdy wives. No sign of the girl with the gilt hair. Where the devil was she? He hadn't come all this way just to see Chesil and his middle-aged bride.

When Lord Vanbrugh returned from the stables, there was still no sign of Amaryllis. His host, flushed with wine and congratulations, bustled over and led him to Mrs Chesil's side, where he paid the usual compliments and listened without interest to her replies. There was a pause until Mr Chesil recollected that an archery contest was in progress.

'I wonder how the shooting is getting on,' he said, peering at the targets. 'Ah yes, it's Maria's turn – my niece, Miss Harris – a very nice little markswoman . . . '

'Your stepdaughter, Miss Vaughan, does she shoot?' asked Lord Vanbrugh.

Some of the good humour left Mr Chesil's face. 'Er, no,' he said awkwardly. 'Is our little Amaryllis known to you then?'

'I saw her at the wedding. She lives with you here, I suppose?'

'Of course. A sweet girl, a real addition to the family,' said Mr Chesil with determined heartiness. 'My son Henry is very taken with her. Between ourselves,' he brought his face rather closer, but failed to lower his voice, 'between ourselves, I think they'll make a match of it. She's no income to speak of, poor little thing, but we'll overlook that. It would be a neat enough thing for the estate. This whole valley would be Chesil land.

It's always been a dream of mine.'

Lord Vanbrugh, not particularly interested, happened to glance up at this point. He was rewarded by the sight of Amaryllis standing just behind her stepfather's chair with a look of fury on her face. He was about to speak when, seeing his eyes upon her, she turned and fled back into the house.

Amaryllis dashed upstairs to her room, slammed the door behind her and threw herself on her bed. Her clenched fists beat the counterpane. 'Marry Henry! I'd rather die! How *dare* he! How dare he! And to tell a complete stranger! "No income to speak of, poor little thing!"' she mimicked savagely. '"Monksedge would round the estate off nicely." Not if I can help it! He shan't have it! He *shan't*!'

It took Amaryllis a long time to work off her fury but at last she sat up, pushed her hair back off her hot forehead and began to think. That man down there with her stepfather – he was Lord Vanbrugh, who had stared at her so in church. What's more, he must have money; she'd never seen it but she knew that Vanbrugh was huge, the largest house for thirty miles round. She would try and persuade *him* to buy her virginity. She couldn't stand another week in this hateful house and he offered the only means of escape. No one else she knew was rich enough. Plenty of people lost their virtue. It wouldn't be so bad. Better than staying on at Chesil House, at any rate. She was sure Lord Vanbrugh would agree to it. Why had he stared at her like that, if he didn't want her? She'd go and talk to him at once, before she changed her mind.

Four

Lord Vanbrugh was lolling in a chair, drinking his second glass of wine, when Amaryllis came towards him across the grass. He watched her approach with interest, thinking that she looked even better at close quarters. Lulled by the charming picture she presented in her muslin dress and frilled summer hat, he forgot her fury of half an hour earlier. He also failed to notice the determined set of her soft red mouth.

The bell for luncheon sounded just as Amaryllis reached Lord Vanbrugh's chair and he offered her his arm across the terrace to where the dining table stood covered with a white cloth. Amaryllis smiled at him as he held her chair.

'We haven't been introduced,' she said, lowering her gaze demurely as he sat down beside her.

'No, but since I know you're Miss Vaughan and you must know who I am, it's not necessary, is it?' he said indifferently.

'I suppose not,' said Amaryllis, rather taken aback. 'Did you have a pleasant ride over from Vanbrugh?' she asked, thinking that she had better say something.

'Not really. The weather is oppressive.'

There seemed no answer to this. Amaryllis smiled rather anxiously and wondered how to give the conversation a more intimate turn. To her relief, Lord Vanbrugh did it for her.

'I saw you at your mother's wedding, didn't I? You were sitting just across the aisle from me.'

'That's right,' said Amaryllis, pleased to find his memory so exact.

Lord Vanbrugh turned to allow a servant to fill his glass. 'You were wearing a blue silk gown. It became you admirably.'

Amaryllis was pleased with the way his voice lingered over the compliment. It looked as though he was going to do some of the work and she could relax a little. He didn't smell either – that was another point in his favour. Amaryllis glanced at her stepfather's flushed face at the head of the table and told herself that she had much to be thankful for. She'd better say something again or he might start speaking to the woman on the other side of him. But what on earth was there to talk about?

Amaryllis found that she was uneasily watching the strong white fingers grasping Lord Vanbrugh's wine glass. With an effort, she looked away from them, stiffened her resolve with another glance at her stepfather and asked Lord Vanbrugh if he had visited Chesil House before.

He shook his head. 'And you, Miss Vaughan, you used to live at Monksedge, didn't you?'

'Yes. It was my father's house. It's mine now,' said Amaryllis, unable to resist a jealous look at Mr Chesil.

Lord Vanbrugh caught the look and suddenly remembered her furious face an hour earlier. He eyed Amaryllis sharply but found that she was smiling at him, her face shadowed by her hat. Dimly conscious of some undergame, Lord Vanbrugh drank the rest of his wine. The consciousness receded.

Looking covertly at him, Amaryllis decided that Lord Vanbrugh was heaven-sent. She didn't like him much, it was true, but this was hardly the time to worry about trifles. She supposed she would have to get him on his own after luncheon. She had no very clear idea of how she was going to go about the delicate task ahead of her, but she was pretty sure it would require privacy. She probably ought to kiss him. Amaryllis looked at Lord Vanbrugh's sensual mouth and felt a qualm of uncertainty. She told herself that she would just have to trust to instinct. People seduced each other all the time. It must be easy.

Lord Vanbrugh meanwhile, drinking a great deal of hock, was surprised to find that he was enjoying himself. Amaryllis was not bad – not bad at all. And he was so bored at Vanbrugh that the prospect of the tepid little flirtation she was likely to allow him was almost appealing. Besides, there was something about her that made him half suspect she might be amenable to more . . . After all, she was a Vaughan, not a Chesil. He couldn't remember when he had last felt so aware of a woman. He turned to gaze at her again and Amaryllis gave him an encouraging look out of her dark eyes.

As the meal drew to its close, Lord Vanbrugh grew conscious of a pleasant feeling of irresponsibility. Life, he decided lazily, could have its way with him for the afternoon. He sat watching a heavy bee drone past, one arm hanging loosely over the back of his chair. Such was his lassitude that, when Amaryllis whispered to him to meet her in ten minutes by the swing at the back of the shrubbery, he showed no surprise but smiled gently and agreed, his eyes still on the droning bee.

When Lord Vanbrugh, rather later than he had promised, made his way through the shrubbery, he found Amaryllis waiting for him, seated on the swing, her skirts wafting out on either side of her. Apart from the occasional burst of clapping which floated up to them from the lawn, they might have been alone in the garden. Lord Vanbrugh said nothing but leant against a tree and gazed at Amaryllis. Well pleased at this attention, she began to swing gently to and fro, her skirts rustling as she passed. Lord Vanbrugh found himself staring fixedly at her pink satin slipper, lightly kicking the ground amid a froth of white lace petticoats. Gradually it penetrated his clouded brain that she was showing more of her ankles than respectable women deemed proper. In fact, now he came to think of it, her whole behaviour from the moment he'd first seen her had not been what respectable women deemed proper. An impatient bee blundered into Amaryllis's skirts and lost itself in the folds of muslin. She shook it free and smiled at Lord Vanbrugh.

He reached out and began to push her. As she swung, the ends of her sash fluttered back to caress his wrists. She tilted her head to smile at him again and her gilt curls fell over his hands, warm and clinging. Lord Vanbrugh stopped pushing and the swing came slowly to a halt. Amaryllis turned and lifted her face towards him, her heart beating with excitement and self-satisfaction. He looked at her warily for an instant and then he took her in his arms.

To her considerable relief, Amaryllis found that seduction

was easy. She had no difficulty in responding to Lord Vanbrugh's kisses. In fact, in the heat of the moment, she almost forgot whom she was kissing and why she was doing it. With renewed self-confidence, she pushed Lord Vanbrugh away a little and smiled at him triumphantly.

'You've had a man, haven't you?' he said eagerly.

'No, not yet.'

He removed his arm with a disappointed air. 'You kiss as though you had.' He turned abruptly away and said over his shoulder, 'I'm not going to apologize. You led me on and you know it.'

'Yes, I did.'

Lord Vanbrugh passed a hand over his forehead and muttered, '*What* did you say?'

'I led you on. I wanted,' said Amaryllis, pausing to select the right words from half-remembered shopping transactions, 'to give you a sample of the goods.'

Lord Vanbrugh gazed at her, mystified. 'I beg your pardon?'

'My virtue,' said Amaryllis impatiently.

'Your virtue?' he repeated woodenly. 'My good girl, have you any idea what you're talking about?'

'Of course I have. I must say, I didn't think I'd have to spell it out to you. I'm offering you my virginity – for a price, naturally.'

He stared at her. 'What price?'

Amaryllis thought quickly. Bella had said she might get a thousand, but Lord Vanbrugh was so rich, he must be good for a bit more. And she knew that her asking price ought to be higher than the one she expected to get, to allow for a bit of hard bargaining. That was the way the farmers at Shrewsbury market always did it. She took a deep breath and said out loud. 'Two thousand pounds.'

Lord Vanbrugh had had a lot to drink but he still recognized a large sum of money when he heard it. 'Two thousand pounds! That's ridiculous!' He looked frowningly at her, wishing he had drunk less. 'What do you want all that money for?'

Amaryllis was quite happy to tell him. 'It's my capital. I've no money of my own and I want to get away from Chesil House.'

'Two thousand pounds is a great deal of money . . . ' he began.

'Yes. It has to be to produce sufficient income.' Amaryllis's dark brown eyes gazed appealingly up into his. 'My virginity and I'll live with you for a month as well.'

This additional inducement worked powerfully on Lord Vanbrugh's clouded intelligence. The thing was now an undoubted bargain. God, she was ravishing . . . He was damned if he was going to let this chance slip. Two hundred, two thousand, what did it matter? He'd no idea where the money was to come from in either case.

'Done!' he said, giving her a proprietorial kiss.

Amaryllis said firmly. 'That's a contract then.' Lord Vanbrugh was about to kiss her again, when she added, 'How are you going to pay me? I'd like cash in advance.'

He laughed. 'No doubt you would.' His brain began to clear a little. The money. God knew where it was going to come from. Saville's payments for the London house were already earmarked three times over. He began to wonder if he hadn't been a little rash. He'd given his word and would have to abide by it, but perhaps . . . He looked down into Amaryllis's determined eyes and went back to reckoning up his assets. Great Aunt Sophia was still living in the Gloucester house. His credit was no longer any good at the moneylenders. There was only . . . Yes, Pembroke Street, by God! He'd give her Pembroke Street and to hell with it! That would put paid to Georgiana's spite. He'd be damned if he'd have Mayo in the family – damned if he was going to be humiliated by his own sister. Titus Vaughan's daughter too – there was a certain poetic justice about it.

'It won't be cash,' he said out loud. 'I'm giving you houses.'

Amaryllis started to protest, and he said hastily, 'It'll be much safer than carrying all that money about. You'd be robbed the minute you set foot outside Chesil House. I'll let you have the deeds as soon as my man sends them to me. The houses are all freehold. They're in London; in Pembroke Street.'

Amaryllis looked suspiciously at him. 'How do I know they're worth two thousand pounds?'

'You have my word on it.'

'No, I've a better idea. We'll ask my stepfather. He knows a bit about London property. You describe the houses to him and ask him what he thinks they're worth.'

He shrugged. 'If you insist. It's not necessary.'

'Let's go and find him now,' said Amaryllis.

Mr Chesil watched them complacently as they walked towards him across the lawn. It was good of Lord Vanbrugh to come; he didn't often mix with the local gentry. He'd never expected him to accept the invitation. It had only been sent out of politeness.

'Well, my lord, we shall soon have a winner,' he said, pulling forward a couple of chairs. 'The contest is nearly over.'

Amaryllis and Lord Vanbrugh sat down.

'Is Miss Harris going to win?' asked Amaryllis.

'I think so, I think so,' said Mr Chesil earnestly.

'A charming property you have here,' said Lord Vanbrugh. 'You built the house yourself, I believe?'

Mr Chesil agreed that he had and began to describe the sort of bricks he had used.

'Clearly you're well informed on the subject of property,' said Lord Vanbrugh, cutting him short. 'Tell me, have you any houses in London?'

'No, but my widowed sister has some property there. I travel up to town now and then, to keep an eye on it for her. She looks to me for advice in such matters.'

'Ah, then I wonder if you could advise *me*,' said Lord Vanbrugh. 'I have a row of four houses in Pembroke Street, near Leicester Square, built about a hundred and fifty years ago. Rather run down now, perhaps, but fine town houses in their day. One of them has a double frontage. How much do you think I should ask for them?' He gazed at Mr Chesil, blandly inquiring.

Mr Chesil put the tips of his fingers together and said thoughtfully, 'I should be inclined – without, of course, having *seen* the property in question, I should be inclined to say . . . The double's a multiple let I suppose? Yes, I feared as much.

Well now, what do you say to three hundred pounds apiece and five hundred and fifty for the double, assuming it's in worse repair than the others?'

Amaryllis did a quick calculation and drew in her breath sharply. She darted a furious glance at Lord Vanbrugh, who hastened to retrieve the situation.

'One thousand four hundred and fifty? Oh come, my dear sir, with the greatest respect, my man of business put them at two thousand at the very least . . .'

Mr Chesil looked uncomfortable. Unwilling to offend his guest, he said hastily, 'Ah well, in that case, I daresay I may have been a little overcautious. Not having seen the properties, you understand, the state of repair is almost impossible to estimate. Your man of business will no doubt have a much better idea of the values.'

Lord Vanbrugh smiled graciously. 'I shouldn't have troubled you with the matter. Ah – I believe the archery is over,' and he nodded towards the lower lawn. Mr Chesil made his excuses and hurried away to distribute congratulations.

Amaryllis drummed her fingers on the table, her nails making sharp, angry clicks. Lord Vanbrugh gazed serenely at the summer landscape.

'Rather a difference don't you think – five hundred pounds?' said Amaryllis between her teeth.

He turned his head. 'Five hundred and fifty,' he said, kindly correcting her arithmetic. 'Surely you're not going to pay any attention to your stepfather? He clearly didn't know what he was talking about.'

'I disagree. I thought that at *first* he talked excellent sense.'

'He agreed with my estimate in the end.'

'He would have agreed with any figure you cared to mention. That much was obvious.'

He shrugged. 'If you don't like my terms . . .'

Amaryllis had no intention of letting him slip through her fingers at this stage. She thought quickly, determined not to give way without forcing some concession.

'I certainly don't,' she said coldly, 'but I am prepared to be reasonable. I'll accept the houses at your valuation, providing you pay me one hundred pounds cash – in advance. We had a contract,' she added, as he started to protest, 'and you tried to cheat me.'

'Oh, very well,' said Lord Vanbrugh, reflecting bitterly that he'd have to sell his watch the next time he was in Shrewsbury. 'I'll send the money round by my coachman tomorrow. My carriage will be waiting for you at the bottom of the lane as soon as it's dark.'

'You mean – I'm to come to you tomorrow?' asked Amaryllis. Her palms suddenly felt damp at the prospect.

'Of course. There's no reason to wait, is there? I'd take you now if I could, but I've got to get rid of my sister. What's the matter? Have you changed your mind?'

Amaryllis summoned up a bright smile. 'No, no,' she said airily.

Five

The moment the last guest climbed into his carriage, Amaryllis rushed into the house and upstairs to her room, calling for Bella.

She was laying out Amaryllis's evening dress and paid no attention.

'I've done it, Bella, I've done it!' cried Amaryllis, triumphantly.

'Done what?' said Bella, without interest, as she shook out a flounce.

'We're leaving tomorrow! Lord Vanbrugh's agreed to everything!'

'What did you say?' For once, Bella showed surprise. She sat down heavily and stared at Amaryllis. 'Lord Vanbrugh! I don't believe it.'

'It's *true*,' Amaryllis insisted.

'Well!' said Bella, 'Well! You're a quick worker and no mistake!' She looked sharply at Amaryllis. 'Cut price I suppose. How much?'

'Two thousand pounds!' said Amaryllis grandly.

'Two thousand!' Bella was horrified. 'I said *one*, if you're lucky. He'll never pay that much. He was making a game out of you,' she added resignedly.

'He *wasn't*. He couldn't keep his eyes off me. He was quite besotted!'

'Drunk, you mean.'

'Well, yes,' Amaryllis admitted, abandoning pretension. 'But not too drunk to remember he's given his word.'

'But will he keep it?'

'I'll make him keep it!'

'Two thousand pounds!' Bella looked at Amaryllis with reluctant admiration. 'However did you manage to persuade him?'

'Oh, it wasn't difficult. I just got him on his own after luncheon and . . . explained it to him. I could see he was hesitating, so I threw in a month of my company as well. That seemed to decide him.'

Bella shook her head. 'He sounds like a bad lot. Didn't he try and warn you off?'

'No, of course not. Why should he? *I* was the seducer,' said Amaryllis proudly.

'I don't doubt it, but he must be thirty-five if he's a day *and* he's been a widower ten years. Whereas you're only nineteen and his host's stepdaughter into the bargain.'

'What does it matter? It's his money that counts.'

Bella sniffed.

'Don't be such a wet blanket,' said Amaryllis impatiently. 'I've been very clever, haven't I? We're leaving tomorrow. So hurry up and dress me for dinner and then you can go and pack.'

'Stand *still,*' said Bella. She worked in silence for a moment or two, undoing the tiny pearl buttons at the back of Amaryllis's dress. Then she said thoughtfully, 'This money – come to any arrangement, did you?'

Amaryllis explained that Lord Vanbrugh was paying her in houses. 'They're in London, so we'll have to go there the minute we leave Vanbrugh.'

Bella looked very uneasy. 'London? I don't think I want to go there.'

'Well, it can't be helped, so you'll just have to put up with it. He didn't offer me anything else.'

'These houses of yours – where are they?'

'In Pembroke Street, near Leicester Square.'

'Pembroke Street,' Bella repeated it slowly to herself. 'So Lord Vanbrugh's got a sense of humour, has he?'

An hour later, Lord Vanbrugh was dining with his sister. Conversation was intermittent until the second course, when Lord Vanbrugh announced that he had made arrangements for Georgiana's departure to Gloucester on the following morning. She contained her anger at this news while the servants were present, merely pulling her bracelets irritably up and down her thin arms while she talked of other things.

'It's too bad of you, Anthony,' she said, when dessert was on the table and the doors had closed behind the servants. 'I resent the way in which you order me to leave Vanbrugh whenever it suits your convenience.'

Lord Vanbrugh took a peach from the dish before him. He shook his head. 'In that case, you shouldn't have been born a girl and fifteen years too late.'

'I know this house belongs to you . . . '

'Then you'll appreciate that I intend to do as I please in it.'

'You must be the most selfish man alive,' said Georgiana. Lord Vanbrugh finished his peach, wiped his fingers on his napkin and smiled to himself.

'Will you be staying on at Vanbrugh for a while?' Georgiana inquired.

He nodded and poured himself another glass of wine.

'You are expecting a visitor, no doubt?'

Lord Vanbrugh nodded again.

'A lady perhaps?'

'No, Georgiana, *not* a lady.'

His sister looked contemptuous. 'I understand you, I suppose. What I *don't* understand is how you're going to pay for it.'

Lord Vanbrugh smiled again, less pleasantly, and made no reply.

Amaryllis was unable to eat much dinner the following evening. She was so quiet that her mother made no protest when she pleaded a headache before the meal ended and escaped upstairs to her room.

Bella was already there, hastily packing Amaryllis's wardrobe into two large bundles.

'You'll have to carry one,' she said. 'I've a box to manage. You write a note to your mother. She'd better be told what's become of you. We don't want any search-parties.'

'No, I suppose not. But what on earth shall I say?'

'The truth. Start writing. There's no time to spare.'

Amaryllis seized pencil and paper and wrote hurriedly,

Dear Mamma,

I have gone to London where I expect to make a good deal of money. Tell Mr Chesil I shall return when I am of age to take back Monksedge and the accumulated income and the interest on it.

Your loving Amaryllis.

'A very businesslike last sentence,' Bella commented. 'Your mother will have a fit when she reads that.' She folded the note and placed it on Amaryllis's pillow. Amaryllis paid no heed to her.

'My dress is rather crushed,' she said, smoothing down her amber-coloured skirts. 'Are you sure this gold locket looks right? I shouldn't wear my pearls instead?'

'He won't be noticing what you wear,' said Bella impatiently. 'Come over here and let me put on your cloak. Pull the hood up – that's right!'

Amaryllis stood still while the cloak was tied on and then wandered uneasily away again.

'I wonder what sort of a night it is,' she said, pinching out the candles and going over to the window.

'Drat the girl,' muttered Bella. 'I can't see what I'm doing.'

Amaryllis was about to draw the curtain when she heard the dining-room door opening downstairs and her mother's voice saying, 'I'll just go up and see how Amaryllis is before tea.'

'Quick, Bella,' gasped Amaryllis. 'Hide the bundles! She's coming up!' Bella dragged them hastily into a closet while Amaryllis lit the candles, pulled off her cloak, bundled it under the bed, and seated herself before the mirror just as her mother mounted the last stair.

She sat, resting her forehead on one hand as her mother entered the room.

'How are you feeling, Amaryllis dear?' asked Mrs Chesil. 'We were all worried about you, so I came up to see how you were.'

Amaryllis murmured that she would be better in the morning.

'Perhaps a cold compress would help?'

Amaryllis, looking at her mother's face, felt suddenly guilty. What would her mother think when she found out the truth? Perhaps she needn't go to Vanbrugh, perhaps if she could just explain to her mother how she felt . . .

Heavy steps were heard on the stair. 'How is little Miss Amaryllis?' inquired a fatherly voice outside the door.

'Oh, there's William,' said Mrs Chesil, turning away from Amaryllis. 'How kind of him to ask after you. I'm just coming, William!'

Amaryllis set her jaw. 'I don't need anything,' she muttered sulkily, 'I'm just going to bed. I'll be quite well after I've had some sleep.'

'Very well, dear. I'd better go now. It's time for William's tea.'

Amaryllis waited until she heard the drawing-room door closing behind her mother and then she sprang to her feet, retrieved the cloak from under the bed and flung it on again.

'Let's go, Bella,' she said. 'Quick, before they finish tea.'

Clutching their bundles, they went downstairs. They walked fearfully on the edge of the treads, but the house had been soundly built and no creaks betrayed them. Down in the hall a line of light showed beneath the drawing-room door and Henry Chesil's voice could be heard, reading aloud from the newspaper. Amaryllis crept across the hall to the door of the dining-room on the far side. She carefully turned the handle, entered the room, and beckoned to Bella to join her. The shutters were still open and the room was moonlit. It was easy for them to make their way over to the window without making a noise. They raised the sash, lowered their bundles over the sill and then climbed out onto the terrace.

The great house at Vanbrugh had been built of grey stone in the Palladian manner. The central block had an imposing portico and the wings were decorated with crumbling pilasters and a classical frieze. But the only parts of Vanbrugh visible to

Amaryllis, in the inadequate light of the carriage lamps, were a flight of steps and the bases of two stone columns, soaring up into the darkness.

The carriage door was opened by a manservant, who looked at Amaryllis indifferently and then led her up the steps into a shadowy hall, where the only light came from the candelabra he held in his hand. With Bella close behind her, Amaryllis followed the man up a wide stone staircase. At the top of the flight he crossed a landing, pushed open a heavy door and stood aside for her to enter.

Much to her surprise, Amaryllis found herself, not, as she had expected, being welcomed by Lord Vanbrugh in a drawing-room, but standing solitary in a vast and deserted bedchamber. Intimidated by its magnificent dimensions, she was obliged to summon up all her courage before she could ask the servant to bring up the luggage and find a bed for her maid. The man bowed and left the room and Amaryllis took off her cloak, and laid it down on a massive marble side table. She looked doubtfully at the bed which loomed up before her in the centre of the room, its canopy surmounted by dusty scarlet plumes.

'It looks very old,' she said nervously.

Bella went over to investigate it. 'Well, the sheets are clean enough, at any rate.'

Amaryllis got up and wandered across to warm her hands at the small fire burning beneath the stone mantelpiece. Above it hung a Venetian mirror framed in glass blown into fantastic shapes of shells and flowers. The mirror was mottled with age and gave a strange silvery reflection which drained things of their colour.

'I'd better undress you,' said Bella, seeing a washstand in one corner of the room. She dipped her finger in the ewer. 'This water seems to be warm. Where's that man got to with those bundles?'

'That sounds like footsteps now,' said Amaryllis.

'I thought Lord Vanbrugh would be here to receive me, Bella. Do you suppose I won't be seeing him till tomorrow?'

'He'll visit you tonight, if I know anything of men.'

Amaryllis did not have long to wait. She had undressed and was seated in her nightgown in front of the fire, when the door opened and Lord Vanbrugh strode into the room.

'Good,' he said, giving her a quick glance, 'you're ready, are you?'

He stopped abruptly as he noticed Bella. 'Who the devil's this?'

'She's my maid.'

'*Your maid*? Good God, you don't need a maid! You're not on a visit!'

'I know I'm not!' said Amaryllis, recovering her poise. 'But I need her and she's going to stay!'

'Well, never mind that now. There's one thing I want to make absolutely clear. You can give me back that hundred pounds, get into my carriage and go straight home, or you can stay here and lose your virtue; the choice is yours. But if you decide to stay, I'm not having you screaming that I've seduced you just because you don't like what you get. Understand?'

Amaryllis stood up. 'I understand, and I'm going to stay.'

Lord Vanbrugh looked at Bella. 'Does your mistress know what I'm talking about?'

Bella nodded. 'She knows.'

'Right.' He turned back to Amaryllis. 'Well, what are you waiting for?'

'*I've* got something to say first,' announced Amaryllis. 'So far, all I've got out of this is that hundred pounds and I'm warning you, here and now, that if you cheat me out of the rest of it I'll . . . I'll put a viper in your bed and watch it bite you!'

'Oh you will, will you? Well, let me tell you, young woman, I'm not in the habit of cheating people!'

'That's not been my experience!' Amaryllis retorted.

Bella retreated silently to the door and left them to it.

Six

The next morning, Amaryllis opened her eyes on the tattered silk linings of a set of strange bed curtains. She stared at them, puzzled, for a few moments. Then, remembering all at once where she was, she turned on her side and found herself gazing at an empty pillow. There was the smell of coffee in the air mingled with the scents of dust and bed linen.

'So you've woken at last, have you? I thought it would take the last trump to do it.'

Amaryllis sat up, holding the sheet close to her chin with one hand and pushing her tumbled hair back off her face with the other. Lord Vanbrugh was sitting by the window in breeches and riding boots, eating breakfast from the worn silver tray on the table beside him.

'Help yourself,' he said. 'I always eat in here when I'm alone.'

Amaryllis was about to point out that he was not alone when some instinct warned her to keep silent. She looked about her for something to wear.

'Take my dressing-gown' said Lord Vanbrugh irritably. 'It's around here somewhere.'

Amaryllis climbed gingerly out of bed, found the dressing-gown and put it on. It was still warm from its previous wearer but it was much too large for her and trailed along the floor. She dragged a chair over to the breakfast table, sat down and poured out a cup of coffee. Her companion pushed a plate of ham in her direction and then returned to his breakfast and paid her no further attention.

The next five minutes passed in a silence broken only by the clink of china. Then Lord Vanbrugh put down his cup, yawned and said abruptly, 'I'm going out. I don't know when I'll be back but I expect to find you here when I return.'

Amaryllis made no reply. She began to spread butter on a roll. Lord Vanbrugh looked at her for a moment. Then he came over to her. He put his hands on her breasts and caressed them for a moment or two. Then he seemed to lose interest and left the room without another word. Amaryllis continued to eat her breakfast with a scowl on her face.

A few minutes later, Bella came into the room. 'I saw he'd gone. What was it like?'

'Boring,' said Amaryllis savagely. 'I feel sore.'

'Well, what did you expect – a night of ecstasy?'

'He hardly spoke to me! I might have been a piece of furniture for all he cared!'

'He did warn you . . . '

'Is *that* all you can say? He treated me like dirt – he only touched me when he had to – and when he'd finished all he said was, "It wasn't worth two thousand pounds!"' Amaryllis seized Lord Vanbrugh's discarded cup, smashed it against the wall and burst into tears of fury.

Bella suppressed a smile. 'I shouldn't waste tears on it, if I were you. He's paying you, isn't he? Through the nose too. Show him a smiling face – he'll be less likely to cheat you at the end of it.' She picked up a petticoat. 'It's nearly midday. High time you were dressed. The sun's shining. Why don't you go out into the garden?'

When she had finished dressing, Amaryllis marched out of the room and down the stairs, her heels ringing on the stone treads. At the bottom, the vast hall lay deserted. A faded tapestry sagged against the wall above the empty fireplace and the air felt dank and chill. Wondering if she and Bella were the only human beings in the house, Amaryllis hesitated for a moment until the sound of servants' voices in the distance reassured her. Then she crossed the hall to the entrance doors, pulled them open and stepped thankfully out into the sunshine.

She found herself standing beneath the portico, looking out

on a weed-choked drive which curved away between the trees to the distant road. Amaryllis descended the steps to ground level and followed a paved walk which led her round to the other side of the house. Here a lawn sloped gently to a small lake in the valley bottom. The lake was fed by a stream which cascaded down the opposite side of the valley among rocks and trees, and on its far bank there stood a little pillared temple, reflected in the water.

Amaryllis decided to go and look at the lake and wandered out across the lawn towards it. The grass was longer than it should have been and the slope was white with daisies. Down by the lake there were buttercups and a seat of stained marble shaded by a grove of trees. Amaryllis seated herself and turned to look back at the great house on the hill above her.

How still it seemed. Most of the windows were shuttered. Surely there should be someone about: maids at work, gardeners busy in the grounds? A plume of smoke rose from one of the many chimneys, but otherwise there was no sign of life. Still convinced of Lord Vanbrugh's wealth, Amaryllis blamed the silence and decay on his shameful neglect of his duty. She thought sulkily that Vanbrugh was almost as hateful as its owner.

Amaryllis began to feel very sorry for herself. She stared desolately out across the lake, feeling herself adrift in a friendless world. Tears rolled slowly down her cheeks and for a fleeting moment she even wished herself back at Chesil House. Then Bella's words came back to her. 'He's paid for it, hasn't he?'

Amaryllis's natural optimism began to revive. He was certainly paying for it. It was a business contract, her first, and she'd definitely had the best of the bargain. Let him be as rude as he liked, she'd outsmarted him. Amaryllis wiped her eyes on the sleeve of her dress. In four weeks' time she'd have her money and need never see him again.

She jumped up and wandered through the grove of trees along a winding path which led her back up the side of the valley. The sun filtered down through the bright summer green of the leaves and she forgot Lord Vanbrugh in the happiness of the moment. Halfway up the hill, she came upon a clearing where a marble Diana with a crescent on her brow posed gracefully with her bow and quiver, flanked by white foxgoves. Then she went on up the path, listening to the cuckoo calling on the other side of the valley. She wondered, with a mixture of guilt and defiance, what was happening at Chesil House. Her letter must have been found that morning, but no one would know where she had gone for several days. Vanbrugh was thirty miles away from Monksedge and news travelled slowly in rural Shropshire. And once they found out (if they ever did), that she'd left home to become Lord Vanbrugh's mistress, they wouldn't want her back. She was safe so far as the Chesils were concerned. Her mother would be upset – but it served her right for marrying that dreadful man!

At the top of the path the trees thinned and Amaryllis came out at the corner of the west façade. To her right were the house and the lawn, to her left a leaden satyr stood at the entrance to a paved terrace, bordered by ilex trees. Amaryllis turned and walked along it to a wrought-iron gate at the far end. The gate creaked as she pushed it open and left rust on her hands, but it gave access to an orchard with the young fruit just showing beneath the leaves. The mossed tree trunks stood knee deep in buttercups and in their centre stood the small chipped statue of a goddess, its lichened hands outstretched.

Amaryllis crossed the orchard to another gate at the far side and found herself at the back of the stable yard. She followed a strong smell of horses round to the front and entered the stables through the main arch. A groom gave her an appraising look and touched his hat half-heartedly. Amaryllis nodded to him and was about to go over to where a grey mare looked out of her stall, when Lord Vanbrugh rode in.

'You've found your way here, have you?' he said over his shoulder as he dismounted. 'I'm dining shortly. Come back to the house.'

Amaryllis was by no means sure that her company was required at dinner, but she changed into the amber dress she had worn on the previous night and told Bella to put up her hair. These precautions proved wise. An hour after they had entered the house together, Lord Vanbrugh strolled into the bedroom.

'It's time for dinner,' he said. 'This way.'

Instead of offering Amaryllis his arm, he dug his hands in his pockets and strode off to the dining-room, without looking to see if she was following him. He did not speak again until halfway through the meal.

'Well, what did you do today?' he asked casually, 'Walk round the park?'

'Some of it, I went down to the lake and came back along that path through the woods, past the statue of Diana.'

'Ah yes. The virgin goddess,' he said unpleasantly. Amaryllis gave him a fierce look and he laughed. 'What did you think of my gardens?'

'There are a lot of statues in them,' said Amaryllis, without interest.

'Hundreds of them. My grandfather brought back a ship-load from Italy and scattered them everywhere. Far too many: Pomona in the orchard, Diana in the glade. He wanted to put Priapus in the kitchen garden but my grandmother stopped that. She said the maids were troublesome enough already.'

'Priapus?' asked Amaryllis unguardedly.

'The god of gardens.' He made a crude gesture and added caustically, 'I'm glad to see you can still blush.'

Amaryllis soon discovered that large tracts of the house were kept locked and shuttered. Lord Vanbrugh spent much of his time in the library or in the series of well-lit saloons where his pictures were hung, while Amaryllis sat in a small room on the second floor, its windows peering out between the columns of the portico.

'It's just about presentable – if you keep the curtains drawn,' Lord Vanbrugh had said when showing it to her, but Amaryllis was pleased with it. The walls were painted with faded garlands of flowers and flying birds and it was furnished with ivory-coloured chairs upholstered in threadbare brocade. On wet days, Amaryllis and Bella spent much of their time there, reading the books which Amaryllis smuggled out of the library when Lord Vanbrugh was absent. She took anything which seemed relevant to her future life in London: old maps, guide books and manuals on estate management and the proper ordering of accounts.

'Listen to this Bella,' Amaryllis said one day, dirtying her dress against a volume bound in mouldering calf. '"Pembroke Street: this handsome thoroughfare was named for the Earl whose town residence adorns the north side of the street". . . An earl! Think of that! It sounds very grand . . . "Conveniently situated for persons wishing to visit the Mall and the coffee houses . . ."'

'And just when was that book written?' inquired Bella.

'I don't know, it doesn't say . . . A hundred years ago perhaps?'

Bella jerked her head. 'That book's a waste of time. Fashions change; you'll see.'

'Oh Bella! The Earl of Pembroke's town house.'

'Houses are like horses. They get old and useless and end up in the knackers' yard. You won't find many earls in Pembroke Street nowadays. Old-clothes dealers, yes, any amount of pickpockets and washerwomen – but not earls.'

Amaryllis hunched her shoulders. 'How do you know? You haven't even been there!'

'I know the area,' said Bella forbiddingly.

Amaryllis's relations with Lord Vanbrugh continued hostile for the first three weeks of her stay. The first day set the pattern for the rest. After preserving an irritable silence at breakfast in their bedroom, Lord Vanbrugh went off to the stables. They met again at dinner where, now and then, he would make some abrupt remark or cutting comment. He would also inspect Amaryllis across the candle flames, his eyes narrowed in an appraising stare he did not trouble to conceal. Now that his face was familiar to her, Amaryllis had no desire to stare back and she would sit, ignoring his scrutiny, her eyes on one of the portraits that covered the walls.

One morning at the beginning of the fourth week, Amaryllis awoke first and lay gazing up at the canopy until a movement beside her warned her that her companion had also returned to consciousness.

'Go and see what the weather's like,' said an ill-humoured

voice. Amaryllis climbed reluctantly out of bed, crossed to the window and pulled back a corner of the curtain.

'It's pouring with rain.'

'Oh God. It *would* be.'

'Are you getting up? It's nearly breakfast time,' said Amaryllis, glancing at the clock on the mantelpiece.

'No, I am not. I loathe this place when it rains. Come back here.'

'Do you want to do it again?' asked Amaryllis, regarding him without enthusiasm.

'Get back into bed when you're told!'

Amaryllis returned, lying down on the extreme edge of the bed. Lord Vanbrugh reached out and pulled her roughly over to the middle.

'It's time you learnt that a whore's first duty is to cultivate at least the *appearance* of enthusiasm.'

'I'm not a whore!' snapped Amaryllis.

'You're not only a whore – you're a very expensive one. And you're giving me a damned bad service for my money.'

'I do what you want,' she said indignantly.

He raised himself on one elbow and looked down at her. 'Do you?'

'You bought a virgin, didn't you? What did you expect?'

'Damn it, you're supposed to look as though you're enjoying it! That doesn't take much effort does it? You don't need experience for that! Moan a little, kiss me – that sort of thing. You know perfectly well what I mean. You acted the part well enough before you got here!'

'So did you!' Amaryllis retorted. 'Why should I kiss you? How often do you kiss *me*? You don't even *speak* to me half the time. You just grab me and get on with it!'

'I *don't*. I . . . Damn it! Why the hell should *I* justify my actions! I'm the one who's paying for it!'

'You paid for my virginity and my company for a month. You never said anything about enthusiasm. I'm not doing this for pleasure, you know.'

'Thank you!' he said furiously.

'You've treated me like dirt ever since I got here. Why *should* I pretend I like it?'

'I'm *paying* you that ludicrous sum of money – that's why! You cheated me into it and now . . . '

'I *didn't*!' exclaimed Amaryllis, outraged.

'Don't act the innocent with me! I was drunk and you know it!'

'It made no difference! You wanted me right from the first. You couldn't keep your eyes off me!'

He laughed sarcastically. 'Oh yes. I was desperate for you, I suppose. Frantic with lust. For a little nineteen-year-old provincial? You *must* be joking.'

'You did want me!' said Amaryllis uncertainly.

He shrugged. 'I always womanize when I'm drunk. You happened to be the nearest, that's all. But since you're here, I might as well take advantage of the fact.'

He pulled loose the ribbons of her nightdress and his mouth came down on hers. Despite her anger and resentment, Amaryllis felt herself beginning to respond.

Seven

'I'll show you over the house this morning,' said Lord Vanbrugh after breakfast. 'It's so wet, there's nothing else to do. We'll start downstairs. Just wait a minute while I get the keys.'

Amaryllis was interested at first, but as she was conducted from one room to another, each more dank and cavernous than the last, her enthusiasm waned. She looked in concern at the patches of damp on papered walls and at the mildewed flesh of the gods and goddesses disporting themselves across the ceilings. There was very little furniture, and what there was stood islanded in seas of faded carpet, under dusty shrouds. Holes in the plaster showed where chandeliers had been wrenched out and pale patches on the walls revealed the loss of paintings. Niches stood empty and the rain pattered against uncurtained windows.

Amaryllis pulled her shawl more tightly round her shoulders and glanced dubiously at Lord Vanbrugh.

'In a bad way, isn't it?' he said. He led the way into a great ballroom, which occupied the whole east wing of the house and was supplied with a marble floor and an abundance of tarnished gilding.

'We overreached ourselves here.' said Lord Vanbrugh wryly. 'You're wondering why the place is falling down about our ears like this? There isn't the money to repair it. This house has been the ruin of us. The land was mortgaged twice over to build it and we've never recovered since.'

He crossed to a window and began to fling back the shutters, letting in a grey, watery light which revealed a full-length portrait at the far end of the room. 'There's the culprit. My grandmother, Roxana, Baroness Vanbrugh in her own right. In my family the title can pass through the female line in default of male heirs. It's a good portrait, isn't it? Painted by Gainsborough when she visited Bath.'

Amaryllis looked up at the painting. It depicted a lady in a silver satin dress. Her cloudy hair was pale with powder and there was a crimson ribbon at her neck. She stood in a commanding pose against a stormy sky.

'You've inherited her eyes and chin,' said Amaryllis, turning to compare her companion with the portrait.

'I've also inherited her extravagance. Not that my spending compares with hers. No estate could stand the burdens she put upon Vanbrugh. People said the architect must have been her lover to persuade her to build so prodigally. They were wrong of course – she didn't need persuading. Her husband designed the gardens – they were expensive too. He had the Temple of Flora built for her birthday. There's a statue in it that's said to look like her. She used to take tea there on summer afternoons with her chaplain in attendance and a tame poet or two to read admiring verses to her.' Looking up at the portrait, he said suddenly, 'We'll do the same. Before the temple falls down from old age and neglect. I'll arrange it as soon as the weather clears. There's her tea service somewhere about; the old-fashioned kind with dishes instead of cups and saucers. I'll tell the servants to find it.'

The rain continued until well into the following morning, but by eleven o'clock the sun had come out and the sky was clear of clouds. Amaryllis had not taken Lord Vanbrugh's tea drinking scheme very seriously and was surprised when he came into her room and told her to be ready at three.

'But you can't possibly wear those modern clothes,' he said, frowning at her dress. 'They won't do at all. Come along. We'll find something more suitable.' Taking her hand, he pulled her out of the room and up the stairs.

'Where are we going?' asked Amaryllis, panting slightly as they mounted a fourth flight.

'Up to the attics. There are trunks of old clothes up there. We're sure to find something that will do.'

He unlocked a door and revealed a long, low-ceilinged room coated with dust and cobwebs. The atmosphere was hot and airless and a small scurrying sound suggested that they had disturbed a mouse. Lord Vanbrugh walked over to a window and forced it open with considerable difficulty, since the frame was warped with years of disuse. Amaryllis crossed the room to a great heap of trunks, her slippers disturbing little clouds of dust as she went. She chose the largest trunk and lifted its grimy lid to reveal a pile of dresses, cut to a fashion half a century old. They still smelt faintly of the lavender and orris in which they had been stored, though the odours of damp and decay were stronger. Excitedly, Amaryllis began to burrow down amongst the layers of silk and satin and gauze, flinging dresses out onto the floor until there was a great mound of mildewed finery beside her.

Near the bottom of the trunk she came across a scarlet satin ball dress. She brought it out into the light, and then, holding it against her, began to parade up and down the dusty attic.

Lord Vanbrugh laughed at her. 'You remind me of Georgiana, she used to come up here as a child . . . That dress won't do for our purposes though. Here, let me have a look.' Catching some of Amaryllis's enthusiasm, he seated himself astride a hat box and began to toss through the heap of dresses, heedless of the lace frills dragging in the dust.

'Wear this,' he said at last, holding up a gown of primrose silk. 'It's not as old as most of them – perhaps it was my mother's.'

'Let me see!' cried Amaryllis eagerly, discarding the scarlet satin and dropping down on her knees beside him. Lord Vanbrugh threw the dress across to her and opened a battered chest, which was full of pasteboard boxes. He ripped off their lids and shook out delicate ivory fans painted with Chinese mandarins or wreaths of violets or shepherds in little Italian landscapes. Amaryllis seized one and began to fan herself.

'What's in that trunk over there?' she asked, pulling it towards her. The lid came away from its rotting hinges. Amaryllis pushed it to one side, and reaching into the trunk lifted a layer of tarnished silk to uncover a row of masks staring up at her, the relics of some long-past revelry.

Lord Vanbrugh held one up laughing, and then began to hunt through the trunk, bringing out painted masks, gilded masks, masks of satin or thick black velvet, and Venetian masks shaped like fantastic moths and exotic butterflies. He ranged them about him on the grimy floor and Amaryllis picked one up and put it on. Lord Vanbrugh followed her example. Then they looked uneasily at each other.

'You seem different,' said Amaryllis distrustfully, 'all mouth and chin.'

Lord Vanbrugh made no answer for a moment. Then he said, 'I don't like you in a mask. I can't see your expression. Though I daresay I can guess at it.' He fell silent again and sat gazing fixedly at Amaryllis.

'Don't stare at me like that,' she said, shifting under his gaze. 'You look as if you hate me.'

His eyes dropped. 'Hate you? Of course I don't hate you. Don't be absurd.' Ripping off his mask, he reached out and dragged her down against him, among the dusty dresses.

When Bella had ironed the primrose silk dress, Amaryllis went up to the bedroom to put it on, followed by Lord Vanbrugh.

Bella eyed him sourly. 'It's a flimsy bit of a thing,' she said, holding the dress up to the light.

'That's right,' said Lord Vanbrugh. He turned to Amaryllis. 'You'll have to get rid of your petticoats. It's supposed to cling to your figure.'

Amaryllis looked at the dress without enthusiasm. 'Aren't you going to leave the room?'

Lord Vanbrugh lounged into a chair. 'Don't be a fool, Amaryllis. You've nothing left to hide.'

He made no further comment until she was standing, shivering slightly, in the primrose dress.

Then he looked at her admiringly. 'You know, you'd make quite a passable whore – if you'd only put a little effort into it.'

Out on the lawn, the sun was shining and the grass was warm. Amaryllis felt light and floating without her heavy petticoats, and her curls waved in the breeze. The temple had a pillared front which was open to the sky and inside it stood the statue of the goddess, with flowers carved in her marble hair. Amaryllis and Lord Vanbrugh took their seats and a servant arranged the china on a lacquered tray. With solemn ceremony, Lord Vanbrugh made the tea in a round earthenware pot and after a suitable pause, poured it out in porcelain dishes, fragile as shells.

They sat in silence, sipping their tea. Amaryllis gazed out between the columns of the temple at the sunlit landscape and the still waters of the lake.

'The ivy is strangling that pillar,' she said presently. 'You ought to have it rooted up before it cracks the stone.'

'Oh, leave it alone,' said Lord Vanbrugh carelessly. 'This place will be a ruin soon enough. What does a year or two's difference matter?'

'You can't be *that* poor.'

He laughed. 'Oh, can't I!'

'Well, you have horses and servants and things, and there's the houses you're giving me.'

'All done on credit. And the houses I'm giving you weren't exactly to spare.'

Amaryllis felt a little guilty. 'You could always sell something.'

He looked amused. 'Could I indeed? And what could I sell?'

'Oh anything, furniture, paintings, the statues in the park . . . '

'The furniture at Vanbrugh is a little thin on the ground. My parents sold the good pieces before I inherited the place. In my turn, I've sold the pictures, except for a few favourites I'm keeping as insurance against the worst. I got rid of most of the statues years ago, though that was no great sacrifice – there were far too many of them. There used to be a whole pantheon of gods and goddesses along the ilex walk. I sold them to pay my tailor's bill, and got rid of a job lot of fauns, dryads and centaurs at the same time.'

'Well, never mind,' said Amaryllis. 'My month's nearly up. At least you won't have me to keep any more.'

'Ah, yes, I was going to talk to you about that,' said Lord

Vanbrugh casually. It's all right. You can stay longer if you like.'

'Yes, but I want to go.'

Lord Vanbrugh's face was expressionless for a moment. Then he said, 'You'd better have these, then. They arrived this morning.' He drew a greasy packet of deeds out of his pocket and threw them across to her. Amaryllis caught them eagerly, undid the tape and spread them out in front of her. She found them largely incomprehensible, but she made out the words 'Pembroke Street' on most of them and said she was satisfied.

'I should think you are,' said Lord Vanbrugh dryly, watching her as she pored over the creased parchment. She was going then. Nothing surprising in that, he supposed. She couldn't have made it clearer that it was the money she was interested in. He wondered bleakly what she might be like with a man she was attracted to – if such a man existed. Lord Vanbrugh felt dimly aware of something missed. Perhaps he could have made a better thing out of it; if he'd been less angry and she'd been less ungracious.

Lord Vanbrugh yawned and, closing his eyes, leant back in his chair.

Amaryllis tied up her deeds, got up and wandered outside. The servant was stretched out asleep under the trees and the afternoon was hot and still. She went down to the lake's edge and trailed her fingers in the water. Looking back, the temple seemed frail and melancholy, almost overwhelmed by the dark woods. Lord Vanbrugh called to her to come and have more tea and she returned to the temple, pulling a length of convolvulus from a laurel bush as she passed. She wandered across to the statue of Flora and idly wreathed the real flowers round the stone ones in the goddess's carved hair. Lord Vanbrugh poured out the tea and handed a dish to Amaryllis.

'Complete the offering, pour a libation and make a prayer to the goddess: whatever you most wish for.'

Amaryllis took the dish and poured a trickle of the golden liquid over the statue's marble feet.

'My capital,' she said unhesitatingly.

* * *

Three days later, Amaryllis's month was up. Some pictures from Lord Vanbrugh's London house had arrived by carrier that morning and he went down to supervise their unpacking as soon as breakfast was over. This left Amaryllis free to help Bella with the final preparations for their departure. The London coach was to pass close to Vanbrugh at midday and Amaryllis was in a fever lest they should miss it. Reasoning that Lord Vanbrugh would never feel the loss, she had taken one of the trunks from the attic, and Bella had packed it on the previous evening. Fidgeting with excitement, Amaryllis waited until Bella was ready, and then they put on their bonnets and cloaks and went downstairs to take leave of Lord Vanbrugh.

He was standing in the hall with two of the servants, surrounded by pieces of packing case and piles of wood shavings. One painting had already been unpacked and stood propped up against a pillar. Lord Vanbrugh turned when he saw Amaryllis and said, 'Are you going then?'

Amaryllis said that she was.

He shrugged. 'Very well.'

He looked at Amaryllis, her face determined under her bonnet. She'd be back in tears on the next coach, of course. These little affairs never ended that simply unless one dealt with professionals. Amaryllis was certainly as rapacious as a professional, but he'd assumed that when he grew tired of her he'd have to introduce her to a new protector. He looked at her again and felt a stab of compunction.

'You'd better give me a receipt for those deeds. There's a desk in there,' and he pointed to the morning-room. Having got rid of Amaryllis, he scribbled the address of his man of business on a piece of packing paper and handed it to Bella with a significant look. She could go to Bentley if things got desperate. Bella opened the paper, read its contents and nodded approvingly at Lord Vanbrugh before stowing it away. Amaryllis came back and gave him the receipt.

'We're leaving now,' she said. 'Goodbye.'

He made no answer, but nodded carelessly and stared at his painting as Amaryllis and Bella left Vanbrugh without a backward glance.

Eight

Looking at London from the windows of the coach, Amaryllis's first impression was one of blackness. Soot-blackened buildings, streets dark with dirt, men in black frock coats carrying glistening black umbrellas, crossing sweepers' naked feet coated with jet black mud and black hansoms moving at a funereal pace beneath a leaden sky. The city seemed endless: an interminable uniformity of dark brick façades, roofed with slates and topped with chimneys belching smoke upwards to form the pall of fog over the city. Sometimes a newly built house stared out from the rest, its bricks still yellow as if a leprosy had bleached the blackness of its neighbours; sometimes a warehouse or a sombre church broke the monotony; and once Amaryllis looked down on a railway cutting gouged out across the face of the city, leaving here a church denuded of its chancel and there a garden half cut away with the roots of its solitary tree left grasping at nothing.

Eight o'clock struck from many churches.

'We must be nearing the City,' said Bella.

Their fellow travellers began pulling off their nightcaps, folding up their travelling shawls and worrying about the placing of their baggage. Their preparations were premature. As the coach neared its destination, the traffic became so thick that you could have stepped out of a first-floor window and crossed the street over the tops of the carriages, avoiding the omnibuses stranded like whales in the midst of the smaller vehicles. The coach slowed to a walking pace and the passengers fretted, looking irritably out of the windows. At last, some twenty dragging minutes later, the coach swung under an arch into the yard of the Bull and Mouth Inn, and the journey was over.

The yard swarmed with people. Ostlers, porters, hawkers and loungers all surged forward as the passengers got down. Amaryllis had no sooner set foot on London soil than she was surrounded by a clamouring crowd offering her oranges, almanacs, cures for rheumatism, betting slips, violets and a beggar's blessing. Dazed by these attentions, she looked round for Bella, who was telling a porter to take the luggage inside. This seen to, Bella rescued Amaryllis and piloted her through the yard to the inn. Here, by way of contrast, they found it hard to get any attention paid to them at all, but at last Bella's forbidding expression secured them a room and the promise of breakfast.

Half an hour later, breakfast had still not arrived and there had been no answer to Amaryllis's pulls on the bell. Feeling faint with hunger, she got up and put on her bonnet again.

'Come on, Bella, I'm not waiting any longer.'

Bella nodded. 'Another coach has come in. They're all busy in the coffee room. We could eat down there,' she suggested.

Amaryllis had had experience of coaching-inn meals on the previous day. 'I want a proper breakfast,' she said crossly. 'We'll go somewhere else.'

Once out in the street, Amaryllis and Bella were caught up in a silent, soberly dressed crowd. It was heading eastwards and of necessity Amaryllis and Bella turned that way too. All about them were men with shuttered faces, eyes fixed firmly on the ground as if bent on some inner goal. Some seemed wide awake, others half asleep, but they all moved forwards at the same brisk pace, their feet ringing on the pavement. As Amaryllis looked at them, her own pace slowed and the man behind her almost cannoned into her.

'Admiring the view, are we?' he asked sarcastically.

'Walk faster and mind where you're going,' said Bella in her ear. 'People haven't time to stroll around. They've got to get to work.'

Amaryllis obediently walked faster. Her quickened pace seemed to speed up her reactions. For a brief, exhilarating moment she was conscious of the city spreading out around her, crammed with life. It began to rain and the wet brought out the alien scent of London; sour smells of soot and dust; rank odours of sewage and decay; wet cloth, leather and horses and the occasional fragrance of oranges and tobacco.

'Here we are at last,' said Bella suddenly, and taking Amaryllis's arm, she propelled her out of the moving column, through a door with 'Bankside Coffee House' engraved on its glass panel, and into a low-ceilinged room with a sanded floor.

It was simply furnished with two rows of tables flanked by high-backed settles which had been placed at right angles to the wall to form partitions. Each table was covered with a clean white cloth, a heavy cruet stand and some breakfast china, and a waiter with a long apron stood at the far end of the room by a kitchen hatch which was giving off warm smells of coffee and fried ham. There were a good number of customers seated at the tables, their hats on the racks above them, their umbrellas dripping in the tub by the door. Many of them were reading newspapers on long wooden poles, and at Amaryllis's entrance, they all lowered them and stared at her.

Amaryllis lifted her chin, marched towards the nearest vacant table and sat down, followed by Bella. After a shocked silence the waiter advanced, pausing beside their table as if he had just happened to come to a halt in that particular spot and any other would have done as well. His eyes looking glassily ahead, he muttered out of the corner of his mouth, 'It's no good, Miss, you'll have to go.'

Amaryllis looked at him in surprise. 'Why?' she demanded.

'No ladies, Miss,' came the muffled reply.

'Oh, that's all right,' said Amaryllis crisply, 'we don't mind. We're much too hungry to worry about any of that.'

'My gentlemen customers . . . ' the waiter began.

Bella sighed, took out her purse, produced a shilling and laid it down next to the cruet stand. The waiter eyed it mournfully and shifted a little to conceal it from the general view. 'Coffee,' said Amaryllis firmly, 'and cream and fried ham and poached eggs and kidneys and hot rolls and butter and marmalade . . . ' She looked inquiringly at Bella.

'A pair of herrings, *with* butter and toast and a pot of tea – strong, mind,' said Bella.

'And herrings and tea for my maid,' Amaryllis finished.

The waiter gave no sign of having heard her but since he scooped up the shilling and disappeared in the direction of the kitchen, Amaryllis felt fairly confident that her order would be filled.

Sure enough, the waiter soon returned with a pot of coffee and a jug of cream. He shot out a hand and slid them onto the table as he passed as surreptitiously as possible, but his actions were observed and there was a disapproving rustle of papers from the gentlemen customers.

Amaryllis, intent on her coffee, paid no attention at first, but when she had drunk her first cup she felt sufficiently restored to look about her. One or two customers were still giving her disapproving glances, but most had returned to their newspapers. The chief exception was a pink-cheeked young man at the next table who, after craning round the edge of his settle for some time, finally knelt on the seat and peered over the top straight at Amaryllis, sitting opposite.

'Why is that vulgar young man staring at me?' she asked Bella, very distinctly.

The young man took offence at this description. 'Vulgar, am I? Vulgar! And I suppose it isn't vulgar, coming into a public coffee house, as bold as brass . . . ' He was about to continue when Bella turned and gave him a look which caused him to disappear behind his settle with the speed of a subsiding Jack-in-the-box. The waiter, who had been observing this passage with disfavour from the safety of the kitchen hatch, now came forward, slid a teapot onto the table and disappeared again.

'Tell me, Bella,' said Amaryllis, passing her the cream jug, 'if women aren't supposed to eat in coffee houses, where do they eat?'

'Depends on the women,' Bella answered, pouring strong brown tea. 'Working girls buy a slab of bread and a mug of what passes for coffee at a street stall. But ladies eat at home. They never go to public eating houses.'

'But what do they do about food if they're not at home?'

'They always are at home – their own or someone else's. Ladies don't work except as governesses. I've told you that before. They can eat at hotels sometimes, if they're travelling on long journeys.'

'Then why didn't you take me to a hotel?'

'Because you're not going to be a governess. You've got to get used to men's company and men's ways if you want to be independent, and they'll have to get used to yours. This coffee house, for instance; they're all in a state about you now, but have your breakfast here often enough and they won't even notice you . . . '

When Amaryllis had cleared her plate and the remains of Bella's herrings had been removed, Amaryllis poured herself a fresh cup of coffee and said briskly, 'I think we should go and take a look at Pembroke Street this morning. I'd like to introduce myself to my tenants. We ought to look for lodgings too. It'll be cheaper than a hotel, won't it? But we'll start with Pembroke Street.'

'That depends on whether you want to be businesslike or not.'

'Of course I do.'

'Then don't go and visit your tenants out of the blue. They won't know you from Adam. The first thing to be done is to go to the previous landlord and get *him* to introduce you to the tenants.'

Amaryllis had to admit the sense of this. 'But the previous landlord was Lord Vanbrugh – we can hardly go and ask him.'

'Not him, his agent,' said Bella patiently. 'You don't suppose Lord Vanbrugh collects his rents himself, do you? It's all done for him.'

'But we don't know where his agent lives.'

'Yes we do. His lordship gave me the address. It's a Mr Bentley in Warwick Street, not far from here.'

'He gave *you* the address? Why didn't he give it to *me*?'

Bella shrugged. 'I don't know. I didn't ask for it, if that's what's worrying you.'

The journey to Warwick Street was uneventful since, to Amaryllis's surprise, the pavements were now almost deserted.

'Where are they all?' she asked, looking about her for the crowds.

'At their offices by now, back in the City,' answered Bella.

'There won't be another rush till eleven, when their wives and daughters go out shopping – but you won't see *them* in this part of town.'

Mr Bentley's office was situated in a dingy building in an even dingier street. He looked disapprovingly at Amaryllis and started when she took off her bonnet and revealed her shining hair.

'Yes, Miss Vaughan, Lord Vanbrugh *has* informed me of the transfer,' he said in tones which implied a strong doubt of his employer's sanity. 'I'm instructed to hand over to you all relevant papers, schedules, leases and so on. The keys I don't have at present. They are in the possession of a Mr Yardley who collects our rents, but I'm expecting him at any moment if you would care to wait . . . ah, here he comes now . . . Miss Vaughan, Mr John Yardley,' said Mr Bentley, telegraphing unutterable things to him with his eyebrows.

Mr Yardley came forward and shook Amaryllis's hand. He was a thickset man of about thirty, with brown hair tightly curled like a ram's fleece.

'You'll have come for the keys to Pembroke Street. I'm afraid I haven't got them with me at the moment. Rent day's not till Friday.'

Amaryllis's face fell. 'Couldn't someone be sent for them? I did want to see the houses today.'

'Certainly. But if you can wait until this afternoon I'll be able to show you round the properties myself. It'll be easier if I'm there to introduce you to the tenants.'

'Oh yes, thank you,' said Amaryllis gratefully, committing the term 'properties' to memory. She looked at Mr Yardley rather doubtfully, finding it hard to place him. He spoke with a strong London accent, which he made no attempt to conceal, but his language was educated and direct. His clothes were those of a gentleman, though unpretentious in cut and material, but his heavy boots were more appropriate to an artisan. He appeared to be a rent collector, but he had been formally introduced. Amaryllis was puzzled.

Mr Bentley, meanwhile, had been ferreting about in various drawers and came forward with a bunch of papers in his hand.

'If you're ready, Miss Vaughan, perhaps we could complete the purchase?'

Amaryllis had no idea what he meant and looked inquiringly at him. 'There are certain documents to be handed over on these occasions,' he explained unhelpfully.

Amaryllis tried hard to look comprehending.

'Value, I understand, has already been received,' he said with a reproving cough, 'and the deeds are consequently in your possession. But since the transfer was very *informal*, there are certain additional matters to be settled. I have here the fire insurance agreement which covers the properties until December. No doubt Lord Vanbrugh has already required reimbursal of a suitable proportion of the premium?' and he looked at Amaryllis over his glasses.

'I don't think so,' said Amaryllis uncertainly. 'He never mentioned it.'

Mr Bentley sighed. 'In that case, abiding by Lord Vanbrugh's letter of instructions, I shall have to hand the policy over to you without further ado. Most irregular!' he muttered crossly. 'I shall inform the company of the change of ownership. You will want to see the receipts for the latest payment of parish rate.'

Amaryllis doubted this but she took the pieces of paper. They seemed quite incomprehensible and she returned them with speed.

'Mr Yardley has the schedules of tenancies, repairs and so on . . . and I think that's everything,' said Mr Bentley with evident relief.

'Yes, I'll bring them with me this afternoon,' Mr Yardley volunteered. 'Perhaps we could meet here, Mr Bentley. At two o'clock, if that's convenient for everyone.'

Nine

Amaryllis was very subdued as she and Bella walked away from Warwick Street.

'What did you think of Mr Yardley?' she asked Bella.

'Hard to tell, at first. He keeps himself to himself.'

'He was a lot more helpful than Mr Bentley though, the sour old misery!' said Amaryllis, still sore at having her ignorance exposed.

'He wants to keep his rent collecting job. Only natural.'

'I liked the look of him. I think I'll keep him on for a bit.'

'It'll cost you ten per cent of the rents in commmissions,' Bella warned her. 'I could collect the rents for you just as well. I'd like to see the tenant who could put one over on me!'

'Yes, I know. But you've no experience in managing property, Bella, and I hardly understood a word Mr Bentley was saying. We need someone on hand who can advise us. Let's keep him on for a bit till I've found my feet.'

When they returned to Mr Bentley's office at two o'clock, they found Mr Yardley waiting for them with a sheaf of papers and a bunch of keys. Mr Bentley did not put in an appearance, but Amaryllis caught sight of him through an open door, sitting at his desk in the inner office, stirring a very large powder into a very small glass of water. Mr Yardley greeted Amaryllis calmly, showing no sign of the fact that he had been suffering from considerable confusion of mind about her. He was well aware of the nature of her relations with Lord Vanbrugh and though he did not approve of them, such affairs were too common in London to be afforded more than a passing shake of the head. But Amaryllis herself was not at all what Mr Yardley had expected.

Lord Vanbrugh's tastes did not usually run to innocent country maidens, however inviting. A grim suspicion that Amaryllis had been wantonly seduced in one of his Lordship's fits of boredom began to grow in Mr Yardley's mind. It would certainly explain the size of her endowment. Two thousand pounds was a colossal sum, even by Lord Vanbrugh's standards. Conscience money, said Mr Yardley to himself. His sympathies aroused, he had failed to join in Mr Bentley's strictures on Amaryllis and had come along this afternoon prepared to be as helpful as possible.

'We'll walk to Pembroke Street,' he said when he had handed Amaryllis the papers. 'It's not far – just south of Leicester Square, near the back of the new Gallery.'

Amaryllis agreed to this and then said tentatively, 'Before we meet the tenants, perhaps I could establish whether you would be prepared to continue collecting the rents?'

'I should be glad to. My present arrangement is ten per cent of monies received.'

'I'll continue that. We'll shake hands on it then.' Her gloved hand met his and clasped it formally for a moment.

'Do you collect rents for any other properties?' asked Amaryllis presently as they walked down Warwick Street towards Glasshouse Street.

'A few, but I'm really a builder by trade. I have my own workshop down by the river – over near Somerset House. I came into the rent collecting business by way of house repairs.'

'Have you done any repairs in Pembroke Street?'

'Oh yes, I know the properties pretty well by now.'

'Good. I shall look to you for advice then. I mean to take an active interest in my properties, Mr Yardley.'

Their route took them through several drab streets which clearly came to life after dark. House fronts were covered in garish signs advertising alcohol and dancing and only such buildings as might be revealed by the gas-lamps were in good repair. Looking down as they crossed the road, Amaryllis saw an opera glove and a trampled cigar lying side by side in the gutter, mute relics of the previous night. They reached a grubby square and turned a corner.

'Is Pembroke Street much further?' asked Amaryllis.

'This is Pembroke Street,' said Mr Yardley.'

Amaryllis felt sick with disappointment. Pembroke Street was just as drab as its neighbours. It had the same dull brick façades, the same splintered paving stones, the same sordid gutters. Looking at it, Amaryllis wanted to cry.

But it was not, after all, so very bad. The street was wider than most and the houses had four shabby floors in place of the more usual three. One of them, in the centre of the terrace, was twice as wide as the rest, with a balcony and a pillared façade. There were no broken windows or gaping roofs, no tattered washing flapping in the foul air from an open sewer – only a sad, drab, down-at-heel feeling. The paintwork in the street was old and faded, and the roofs had a speckled look suggesting that slates were replaced parsimoniously, one by one. There were no trees, but here and there a pot of straggling greenery stood on a window ledge.

'Which properties are mine?' asked Amaryllis, bringing out the term with a casual air.

'Numbers Nine to Twelve. These over here,' said Mr Yardley, leading the way down the street. 'That large one with the pillars is sometimes called Pembroke House after the Earl who built it. It's in rather a bad condition, I'm afraid.'

Amaryllis looked at it without enthusiasm. The double front door had a battered appearance and the columns were chipped at the base as though they'd been gnawed by giant rats. The roof was in a particularly bad condition and several slates appeared to be holding on by willpower alone.

'We'll start at Number Nine,' said Mr Yardley. 'The tenant is a Mrs Dixon, a very respectable woman who takes in lodgers. She's developed quite a connection in the City.'

Amaryllis thought that Number Nine looked reasonably well cared for, with a polished knocker and clean steps. The house had the air of providing decent accommodation with no extras. The door was opened by a very plain maid and the smell of roasting mutton floated out to them. Mrs Dixon appeared almost at once, her stout figure bundled into a green plush dress which gaped slightly at the seams.

'Miss Vaughan? Pleased to meet you. The new landlord? Well, what a surprise! Are you a relation of Lord Vanbrugh?'

Mr Yardley gave Amaryllis a reassuring glance. 'Miss Vaughan purchased the property.'

'I only wish I could do the same,' said Mrs Dixon, failing to notice Amaryllis's guilty blush. 'Well, Miss Vaughan, this is a respectable house and I make sure it stays that way. Some of my gentlemen are a bit young, it's true, but their references are good – and there's very little high spiritedness on *my* premises.'

Amaryllis was a little surprised at the earnestness with which Mrs Dixon spoke.

Number Ten was not as well kept as Number Nine. The knocker was dulled and the hall was covered in grubby panelling from which the paint was peeling. The lower floors were occupied by a shipping clerk's widow, who gave Amaryllis a very doubtful look when she learned who she was. Daunted by this reception, Amaryllis escaped as soon as she could and followed Mr Yardley upstairs to the third floor where he unlocked a door.

'Here we are,' he said, standing aside for Amaryllis to enter. 'These rooms have been empty for a couple of weeks as the tenant defaulted. We had to levy execution on the furniture for the unpaid rent. I didn't relet, since I knew you'd be taking over.'

Amaryllis entered the room and looked about her. A grubby striped paper covered the walls and an old racing calendar had been glued on to it in place of a picture. A dead plant sat in the corner in a cracked pot and the floor was covered in stained felt which even the bailiffs had rejected. The windows were grimy and there were cigar stubs on the sills. The next room was in a similar condition and in the third room, at the back of the house beside the stair well, a broken blind hung drunkenly at the only window which looked out over a shabby back street.

The upper floor repeated the three rooms below, the largest one containing, besides mouse droppings, the signs of slovenly cookery. Amaryllis retreated downstairs, returning to the room they had entered first. She stood staring thoughtfully out of the window, telling herself that she couldn't afford to live in hotels for ever. She *had* to come here; it was the obvious place. But it was so sordid and poky and disgusting. She hadn't escaped from Chesil House only to end up in a back slum! Amaryllis stared dismally down at the cigar stubs on the window sill. Gradually her common-sense began to fight back. She told herself that dirt and bad drains were all that was really wrong with the place and they could be put right. If she wanted to improve her properties and increase her rents, she'd have to live here and learn her trade at first hand – or leave the place to rot as Lord Vanbrugh had, while she dragged out her life in cheap lodgings, never getting any richer.

Amaryllis lifted her chin. 'I'd like to live here myself,' she announced. She looked Mr Yardley squarely in the eyes. 'I've not much money and I'll have to buy all my furniture. I can't afford anything expensive. Could your men do a simple repair and redecoration job?'

'We could certainly do the repairs and one of my men can turn his hand to painting if it's nothing elaborate.'

'It won't be,' Amaryllis assured him. 'I just want the walls painted, and the floors sanded and waxed.'

'We'd better have the sweep in too,' said Bella, pointing at the pile of soot in the fireplace, 'and broken glass in the skirting. There's rats without question. What about water and gas?' she asked, knowing that Amaryllis would overlook these details.

'There's no gas,' Mr Yardley admitted, 'but there is running water – right up to the top of the house,' he added proudly.

'Oh, we can do without gas for the present,' said Amaryllis. 'We never had it at home, did we, Bella? But if there's water . . . then we could have a water closet!' she cried, forgetting modesty in her enthusiasm. Mr Yardley had tactfully refrained from mentioning the primitive sanitary arrangements under the stairs but the stench had revealed their presence without the need for words.

Startled by her reference to matters most women would blush to mention, Mr Yardley merely nodded. Then he said hastily, 'There is just one other thing, Miss Vaughan.' He coughed and looked away from her out of the window. 'This is not a bad street, as streets go in London, but the area is – not very quiet. I expect you know what I mean. I strongly advise you to stay indoors after dark and never go out alone in the daytime – if you wish to avoid unpleasantness.'

'Is it dangerous?' asked Amaryllis quickly.

'No, not dangerous, not in the daytime, but unpleasant,' and he turned and led the way downstairs, his manner suggesting that delicacy prevented him from being more explicit.

Ten

Leaving Number Eleven till last by common consent, Amaryllis and Mr Yardley walked on to Number Twelve, followed by Bella. The ground and first floors of the house were occupied by a doctor and a lawyer respectively, who were both out at work. The upper floors had been let to a Miss Forrest, who proved to be only a year or two older than Amaryllis. Her furniture was brand new, she was fashionably dressed and she paid the same rent as Mrs Dixon for less than half the space. Amaryllis was inclined to be friendly to such a profitable tenant, but Miss Forrest was so quiet and self-effacing that she soon gave up the attempt. While they were talking, Mr Yardley stayed by the window, looking down into the street. Amaryllis, hearing the sound of laughter floating up from the pavement, glanced out herself in time to see two girls in vivid red shawls leave Number Eleven and walk away down the road, arm in arm. Almost as if this was a signal he had been waiting for, Mr Yardley turned back from the window and suggested that they move on.

Amaryllis approached the door of Number Eleven with distaste. It was covered with filthy fingermarks and the steps were littered with rubbish which was heaped against the rusty railings. Once inside, she found herself in a hall much larger than the modest entries of the other houses. As she began to mount the staircase she was assailed by a battery of smells, composed of a solid undertow of damp and drains, overlaid by vinegar, stale cooking, tomcats and various other components Amaryllis was not at all anxious to identify. The stairs were far from clean and she held up her skirts to keep them out of the dirt, wrinkling her nose with disdain.

The first door they came to was marked 'H. Maybird: Piano Tuner', but there was no reply to Mr Yardley's knock. Facing it, across the landing, was another door marked 'Salisbury: Instruction in Drawing' which was opened by a pale woman wrapped in a darned shawl. Behind her, Amaryllis glimpsed a high-ceilinged room containing a few shabby bits of furniture standing about in forlorn little groups, separated by stretches of empty floor. There were a number of medicine bottles on the windowsill and a small black kettle steamed on the brick hearth which had been built in the centre of the huge stone fireplace.

'My brother is out and I am not well,' said the woman, coughing slightly as she spoke. 'Perhaps you could return when he is able to be here?'

'Of course, Miss Salisbury,' said Mr Yardley kindly. 'I just wanted to introduce you to Miss Vaughan, your new landlord.'

Miss Salisbury seemed too ill to show surprise at this news but she put out a thin hand for Amaryllis to shake, managed a smile and then retreated to her fireside, coughing as she closed the door.

Going up the next flight of stairs, the scent of vinegar became so strong that even the smell of the drains was defeated and Amaryllis was forced to hold her handkerchief to her nose. Mr Yardley seemed immune. He hammered on a door and called out his name.

'I can't come out!' shouted a female voice. 'I'm doing my pickles!'

'It's Mrs Clay,' Mr Yardley told Amaryllis. 'She lives here with her husband. Is Mr Jenner in?' he asked, through the door.

'Not him!' shouted Mrs Clay. 'He's out working for once!'

'Never mind,' said Amaryllis quickly. She was half-stifled by the reek of vinegar. 'Let's go on up to the next floor, before we suffocate.'

On the third floor landing there were strange plucking sounds and a strong scent of turpentine vied with the vinegar. Amaryllis's eyes began to water and she looked despairingly at Mr Yardley.

'We're nearly finished,' he said. 'It doesn't always smell as bad as this. He listened for a moment. 'Yes, it sounds as if Mrs Canning's in. She's a midwife; and very much in demand.'

Bella looked up sharply.

Mr Yardley knocked on the door and it was opened by a small, neat, tough-looking woman. She stood there, peering at them in the gloom of the landing, her arms folded over her print dress. A cloud of vapour and the dank, flat smell of a boiling wash billowed out from the doorway behind her.

'Come on in, do,' she said, trying to wave away some of the steam.

Amaryllis went forward into the room and was slapped smartly in the face by a wet sheet. When she had disentangled herself she saw that the room was hung across with line upon line of drying washing. The furniture was draped with it, so that it was impossible either to sit down or move about. Amaryllis stood still, uncertain of what to do, while Mrs Canning shifted a couple of shirts, got up on a chair and peered out over the lines of washing.

'Meggy!' she cried, 'get that canary! He's about here somewhere, drat him . . . there, there, over by the quilt.'

There was a frantic cheep, a fluttering disturbance in a pillow case and a small girl emerged from the line of washing, clutching a bundle of damp feathers which she deposited in a cage. Mrs Canning got down off her chair and offered a hand to Amaryllis.

'Mary Canning's my name,' she said. 'How do you do? Miss Vaughan is it? A pleasure – and nice to see you too, Mr Yardley, of course. Phew! It's hot in here, isn't it? Come and say hello to Miss Vaughan, Meggy, and then open the windows and let some of this steam out.' The small girl made a curtsey, her hair clinging damply to her knobbly forehead.

Amaryllis was smiling at her, when a sudden shriek tore the air, followed by an anguished wailing, as if all the cats in London had gone into mourning at once. Amaryllis started violently and dug her nails into her palms to keep from crying out.

'There goes Mr Fry again,' said Mrs Canning tolerantly. 'Awful din, isn't it? He mends violins for a living. You get used to the noise. I can't complain, not with my youngest setting up a bawl at two in the morning when she's teething. You'll like to see her, won't you? I'll go and get her.'

She dived beneath the sheets again and returned with a sleeping baby. Amaryllis stared at it, unable to believe anything could sleep through that frightful noise. Mrs Canning was on the point of waking it up out of politeness, when she caught sight of Bella, standing on the landing. She gave a cry and almost dropped the baby, only retaining her grip on it by instinct.

'Bella Hoxton! Bella Hoxton! Turning up on my doorstep after all these years! Well I never . . . ! She sat down on a pile of damp vests in her agitation. 'Just like you too, to stand there like a stock and say nothing. Well, well, well.'

Bella had been trying to shrink into a patch of shadow. She now came forward into the light.

'How are you all, Mary?'

'Fit and well,' said Mrs Canning. 'You too, Bella, I hope? Better than when I last saw you, at any rate . . . To think of coming across you again like this. I can't get over it! Promise you'll take tea with me soon. Any time you care to call – you'll always find a welcome . . . You *will* come? There's so much to talk about . . . But I must stop running on while Miss Vaughan's here.' She turned to Mr Yardley. 'Anything else I can do for you?'

'No, I don't think so. We'll just call in on Mr Fry on our way out. It's getting late,' added Mr Yardley with a worried look at his watch.

'Well, I won't keep you. You'll be taking Miss Vaughan back to wherever she's staying, of course?'

'Of course,' said Mr Yardley, as he crossed the landing to Mr Fry's door.

Amaryllis lingered a moment. 'Did you live in London?' she asked Bella. 'Before you came to Monksedge? Is that where you knew Mrs Canning?'

Bella nodded. 'But I'll answer no more questions – so don't waste your breath asking them.'

They followed Mr Yardley into a room hung with violins which glowed in the sunlight like new chestnuts. Mr Fry sat on a table in the window, his legs folded up under him like an elderly grasshopper. Tools hung from a rack above his head and pots of varnish and tubs of resin were ranged along the shelf above the empty fireplace. The room was spotlessly clean.

'Come in, come in and close the door behind you,' said Mr Fry testily. 'I can't stand dust. It ruins the surface of my varnish.'

When introductions had taken place, he gestured about his room. 'There you are, look as much as you please. It's all I have. No bedroom, no kitchen. I sleep under the table and eat in the chop house in Coventry Street . . . And now I've work to do. Good day to you. Call again.' And he returned to the violin he was varnishing.

As they went down the darkening staircase, Amaryllis heard the front door bang and another door open and close.

'Who lives on the ground floor?' she asked. 'We haven't seen it yet, have we?'

A faint line appeared between Mr Yardley's brows and his hand came up to smooth his tight brown curls. 'They're out, I think.'

'No they're not,' Amaryllis insisted as she descended the last flight. 'I heard someone come in just now.' She crossed to the nearest door and rapped smartly on it, ignoring Mr Yardley's protest.

'Who is it?' called a shrill female voice.

'It's Mr Yardley,' he said before Amaryllis could reply.

'I'm not going to be evicted, am I?'

'No, no,' said Amaryllis hastily.

'Not going to put up the rent?'

'No,' said Amaryllis, less certainly.

'Oh well, no need for a chat then is there? Sorry not to come out but I'm dressing. See you on rent day, no doubt.'

'Is anyone else in?' asked Amaryllis hopefully.

'No – not at this hour! They're all working by now – like I should be if I wasn't so late.'

'We won't trouble you any more then, Miss Cook,' said Mr Yardley hurriedly, turning away and holding the front door open for Amaryllis, who was obliged to leave without solving the mystery.

Eleven

A fortnight later, Amaryllis moved into Number Ten. Even Bella, running a grudging finger over the paintwork, admitted that Mr Yardley's men had done their work well. But although they were fresh and clean, the rooms were very bare, since Amaryllis could only afford the minimum of furniture. The dining-room was empty and the bedroom contained a bed and very little else. Amaryllis's toilet articles were crowded onto the windowsill and her clothes were stored in the old leather trunk she had taken from Vanbrugh. It had been cleaned and polished, but not all Amaryllis's scouring could remove Lord Vanbrugh's crest, stamped on the front.

The parlour seemed almost luxurious by comparison and Amaryllis was proud of it. It was furnished with a sofa and two chairs upholstered in a green sprig pattern, a tea table, and a cabinet displaying a set of flowered china. There was a square of Turkey carpet on the floor and in a corner of the room stood a second-hand rolltop desk in which Amaryllis's deeds and schedules had a good deal more room than they needed. Her one extravagance was a window box full of scented flowers, sweetening the stale air from the street. There was no clock but, as Bella pointed out, to buy one would have been a waste of money with St Martin's striking the quarters for free.

One afternoon at the end of her second week in Pembroke Street, Amaryllis sat in the parlour, waiting for a visit from Mr Yardley, who was coming to tea and bringing the first month's rent money. Since she had asked him to deduct his bill for decorations and repairs from the total, the actual sum handed over would be negligible but she felt the occasion was important none the less. Amaryllis looked round the room with a satisfaction that surprised her, remembering the very different emotions with which she had first seen it.

It was the furniture that altered matters. On her first night in Pembroke Street she had hated the place. She had gone to bed by the light of a candle stuck in a chipped saucer, and had crouched under the covers, listening fearfully to the alien night sounds outside her window: the screech of cats, the wail of babies, laughter, yells, the sound of blows and falling furniture, and through it all the distant roar of the street life swarming past Pembroke Street from Leicester Square out into the Haymarket. To add to her misery, there were occasional scrabblings and scurryings in the wainscoting and faint sinister scratching sounds from the other side of the wall, and once the running feet and gasping breath of a hunted man in the street outside, followed by the shouts of his pursuers.

As Amaryllis lay there, staring at the shadows on the ceiling, she was visited by the dreadful realization of her own stupidity. She had cut herself off from her family and friends and thrown herself at the first man who had come her way. She must have been mad: quite mad. She was all alone in London, except for Bella, and who knew what her intentions were? If Bella left her she could die here and no one would know or care. Tears of loneliness and fear began to pour down Amaryllis's cheeks. A carriage went past, its lamps sending strange shadows across the ceiling. A dog howled, and then yelped as someone cuffed it. Unable to bear her thoughts any longer, Amaryllis got out of bed and crept into the parlour and across to the window.

She pulled up the blind and looked out onto the street. It was silent and deserted and the windows of the houses opposite stared blankly back at her. A solitary drunkard staggered into view and, heedless of her gaze, relieved himself against a lamp post. The dull roar of the great city reached her faintly from the end of the street. Realizing there was no comfort to be had from staying up, she stumbled wearily back to bed and cried herself to sleep.

But the next morning, Amaryllis remembered, she had

woken up to sunlight and the sound of 'Small coal!' being shouted down the street, and suddenly things had seemed brighter. She had even been able to laugh at her morbid fears of the night and had soon forgotten them in arranging her furniture and learning housekeeping from Bella. Amaryllis admitted to herself that she could not have managed without Bella. Her only drawback was the tiresome way she insisted on accompanying Amaryllis everywhere, deaf to her protests. Worse still, at dusk she stalked round the house like a gaoler, lowering the blinds, putting the chain on the door and vetoing any suggestion that they might go out after dark.

Bella's heavy tread descended the stairs from the kitchen on the upper floor.

'I'm going out to buy the watercress for tea,' she announced, putting her head round the door. 'Want to come too and get a breath of air?'

Amaryllis nodded eagerly, ran to put on her bonnet and then followed Bella out onto the pavement. The cress seller Bella favoured stood in Trafalgar Square, a couple of streets away, and Amaryllis set off at a brisk pace, enjoying the afternoon sunshine. Intent on finding her way, she failed to notice that Bella was lingering by a draper's window, and she had walked on for a hundred yards and turned a corner before she realized that she was alone.

By then it was too late. Her appearance had already attracted loud comment from a couple of grooms lounging outside a public house and a clerk murmured an obscenity as he passed her. She was about to retrace her steps with tight lips when a well-dressed man lurched up to her, grabbed her by the elbow and asked thickly, 'How much, darling?'

Amaryllis pulled herself away and looked frowningly at him, not sure if she had heard him properly.

'How much?' he repeated insistently.

'I don't know what you mean.' said Amaryllis contemptuously, trying to turn away.

His hand reached out and grabbed her skirt. 'None of that funny business with *me*! I know what's what. You're a

Pembroke Street whore. I saw you come out of one of those houses.'

Amaryllis looked despairingly round for help. The grooms stared stupidly at her and one of them sniggered. She swallowed hard and said firmly, 'You're quite mistaken. Let me go at once!'

His other hand grasped her arm and his alcoholic breath stank in her face. 'In search of richer game are you?' he asked jeeringly. 'Well, that's just too bad, isn't it?'

'Hands off cocky!' said a woman's voice suddenly, 'You've got the wrong one. *She* isn't one of us.'

Amaryllis wrenched round and found herself face to face with one of the girls she had seen leaving Number Eleven on her first day in London.

The man swore at her. 'Get out of it! Pembroke Street, isn't she? Not one of you, my arse!'

'She's respectable, you fool,' said the girl anxiously. 'Lay a hand on her and you're in dead trouble.'

Amaryllis tried to pull herself free of the man's hold but he only twisted her wrist until she cried out with the pain.

'Don't struggle, for God's sake,' muttered the girl in her ear. 'He'll break your arm.'

'Will you get out of it!' the man growled menacingly.

Amaryllis was about to give herself up for lost when she saw Bella appear over the man's shoulder. Bella's big hand grasped his collar. The man spun round to see his assailant, and was sent crashing to the ground by a single blow from her fist. He lay unmoving on the pavement, blood trickling down onto his shirt.

'My God!' whispered the girl, looking in awe at Bella, who stood blowing on her bruised knuckles.

'Scum,' said Bella.

'Too right,' the girl agreed, spitting accurately at the man's fancy waistcoat. She jerked her head at Amaryllis. 'You shouldn't let her wander about on her own.'

'I don't, as a rule,' said Bella. She looked at the girl with approval. 'Lucy Fletcher – that's your name, isn't it? You did very well, I must say. If you hadn't kept him talking, I might have been too late. We won't forget it.'

Back in Pembroke Street, Amaryllis sat down at the kitchen table, shivering slightly.

'Lucky it's no worse,' said Bella, putting a kettle on the fire. 'You'll feel better after a cup of tea. Remind me to teach you a few tricks when I get round to it. You may need to defend yourself sometime when I'm not by. Can't act as nursemaid *all* the time.'

'It was a splendid blow you gave him!' said Amaryllis admiringly. 'I'd love to be able to do that!'

Bella looked her up and down and then shook her head. 'Too puny by half. That sort of punch takes strength. *You* need a dodge or two that depends on skill.'

The kettle boiled and she turned back to the fireplace to make the tea. Then she began to prepare for Mr Yardley's visit by cutting the bread with a knife she had sharpened on the front door step.

'*Why* did that man take me for a prostitute?' asked Amaryllis. 'I wasn't looking at him or anything. Just walking along, minding my own business. And he said I lived in Pembroke Street – as if that was some sort of proof.'

Bella gave an exasperated sigh. 'Pembroke Street, as anyone but an innocent but you would have realized by now, is one big whorehouse. No use blushing like that. Why do you think Mrs Dixon was so anxious to tell you she's respectable? Because a lot of people round here aren't, that's why.'

'Who, Bella?'

'Miss Forrest, for one. A kept woman; better behaved than some, I grant you. Then there's the girls on the ground floor of Number Eleven – as you found out this afternoon. That's why Mr Yardley was so keen to get you out of there without seeing them; though he might not have bothered if he'd known the truth about you,' she added with a grin. 'Lord Vanbrugh knew what he was doing, sending you here.' She pushed a pile of bread over. 'You can butter these if you've finished your tea.'

'There's parts of London,' Bella continued, 'where a lady just doesn't go, and Pembroke Street's a sight too near them for comfort. A respectable woman daren't walk down the Haymarket after midday, nor Fleet Street, nor the Strand, nor

Portland Place, and the side streets are almost as bad. Even Regent Street isn't safe, even though it's so fashionable. So you stick close by me.'

An hour later the tea was all ready. The china had been laid out with mathematical care, the teaspoons had been rubbed until they shone, slices of ham covered one plate, triangular pieces of bread and butter formed a pleasing pattern on another, and on the third sat six circular sponge cakes from the pastrycooks in Coventry Street. When Mr Yardley appeared, prompt to his time, he looked approvingly at Amaryllis, who shook hands and then seated herself at her desk and opened her ledger. She had given Mr Yardley no cause to revise his first good impression of her. True, he was rather less certain that she was the seduced innocent he had taken her for. A seduced innocent must, he suspected, lack intelligence and common sense, and Amaryllis was not short of either. She was learning fast, and she had a down-to-earth streak he admired. She was not without faults, of course. She was hot tempered and she seemed reluctant to take advice. But on the whole he was optimistic.

'Here's the balance of the rent, Miss Vaughan, and this is my account for the month.'

Amaryllis looked down the neatly ruled columns. 'No arrears, I see.'

'None. George Jenner made a good pretence of being out, but I dodged into Mrs Clay's and caught him putting his head round the door to see if the coast was clear.'

Amaryllis looked thoughtfully at the schedule of rents open before her. 'Mr Yardley,' she said at last, 'perhaps you can explain why it is that Miss Forrest, for example, pays the same rent as Mrs Dixon for half the space and why the young women on the ground floor of Number Eleven are paying twice as much as Mr Maybird for very similar rooms.' She lifted her eyes from the page and looked hard at Mr Yardley. He gave an embarrassed cough and began to smooth his tight brown curls.

'I suppose,' said Amaryllis, since he seemed unwilling to

provide her with an answer. 'It's because they're all fallen women.'

He nodded.

'It's no good, Mr Yardley, we're going to have to be frank with one another. I can't be forever skirting round the subject and neither can you. Life's too short for it. Let's be quite open about it in future – as if we were two men.'

Mr Yardley looked doubtful for a moment. Then he said, 'I appreciate your honesty, Miss Vaughan, but I've been telling all your tenants that you purchased the property. Some of them would be most upset if they knew you were Lord Vanbrugh's mistress. Mrs Dixon, for instance, and Dr Dangerfield and certainly the Salisburys . . .' He numbered them off on his brown fingers and so failed to notice Amaryllis's startled expression.

'Yes, yes, I'm sure you're right,' she said weakly when he had finished. 'Perhaps it would be better not to tell them. And I can assure you that my liaison with Lord Vanbrugh was a – a regrettable necessity which I don't intend to repeat. I trust I shall never see or hear from him again.'

Mr Yardley looked at her rather sorrowfully. He drew a letter from the pocket of his coat. 'Mr Bentley asked me to deliver this.'

Amaryllis coloured to the roots of her hair, ripped the letter open and read the following:

> Let Bentley know when it gets too much for you and I'll come and rescue you.
>
> Vanbrugh.

She gave a gasp of indignation and held the letter out to Mr Yardley.

'Read it!' Seizing a pen, she wrote hurriedly. 'And then my reply.' She passed him the note she had written.

> Miss Vaughan has no wish to enter into correspondence with Lord Vanbrugh, now or at any other time.

'Perhaps you would give it to Mr Bentley when you next see him. Any time will do.' She retrieved Lord Vanbrugh's letter from the arm of Mr Yardley's chair, screwed it up into a ball and hurled it into the back of the fireplace. 'There, that's the last of Lord Vanbrugh! Now, let's finish our business before Bella brings in the tea. Have the tenants any complaints?'

Mr Yardley consulted a small notebook. 'Well, apart from the usual ones about damp and drains, they're mostly objecting to that tripe boiler who's set up at Number Five. Mrs Dixon tells me the smell's terrible when the wind's in the wrong quarter.'

'Yes, it's disgusting. I've noticed it myself. Can we put a stop to it?'

'Oh, I should think so. The tripe boiling must be in breach of covenant. Leases usually include restrictions on offensive trades.'

'Good. So we warn the man to stop boiling tripe and if he pays no attention to us we complain to his ground landlord and see if he'll prevent him.' Amaryllis was proud of her recently acquired knowledge of the law. 'And if that's no good we sue I suppose . . . By the way, who *is* the ground landlord?'

Mr Yardley looked at her with the air of one who breaks bad news. 'Lord Vanbrugh. He owns all Pembroke Street, except what's yours.'

Twelve

Bella's kitchen was simply furnished with a deal table and a couple of chairs. A clear fire glowed in the grate and a cat lay purring in front of the fender. When Mr Yardley had gone, Amaryllis brought the tea things upstairs to the kitchen and stayed to talk to Bella while she did the washing up. Bella had just added hot water to the soda in her bowl, when there was a loud knocking on the front door.

'Drat,' said Bella, putting down the cup she had been about to wash. 'Who's that at this hour?'

She dried her hands and went downstairs, leaving the door ajar behind her so that Amaryllis was able to hear Mrs Canning's voice when Bella opened the bottom door.

'I came at once! The minute I heard! He knows you're back, Bella. Cutler knows you're back!'

'*What* did you say?' hissed Bella.

'He came up to Meggy in the street. "Remember me to Bella," he said, and sent her home crying into her pinafore. . . .'

'He's in Newgate, they swore he was in Newgate.'

'So he was, but he's out now, the thieving devil! It was Cutler all right; you've *got* to believe me. Meggy would know him anywhere. She's had nightmares about him often enough.'

There was a long pause. Then Amaryllis heard Bella say wearily, 'Oh, I believe you. I knew this would happen. Fated, that's what I am. Well, I've made my plans. I'm grateful for the warning.'

'You do look white, Bella,' said Mrs Canning anxiously.

'I'm well enough. You be off home to your family.'

Amaryllis heard the door being shut and bolted.

Bella came back into the kitchen, stalked straight over to her bowl and began to wash up with a ferocity that threatened to smash the china. After several minutes of this, Amaryllis could bear it no longer. 'What *was* all that about, Bella? Who is Cutler?'

'None of your business!' snapped Bella.

'But I've a right to know.'

'If you say another word about it,' said Bella fiercely, 'I'll walk straight out of this house and never come back!' With this Amaryllis was forced to be content, mentally adding Cutler to the many mysteries already surrounding Bella.

The most recent of these was her refusal to take any wages. Amaryllis had offered to double her Shropshire salary with more to come as soon as she had paid for the furniture, but Bella had refused to touch a farthing. Deciding that in her present mood she was better left alone, Amaryllis got up and went uneasily downstairs.

She had just got out her ledgers when she heard a knock on the street door, followed by Bella's heavy tread going to answer it. There was a murmur of surprised voices and then Bella's face appeared round the door and announced gloomily, 'Mr Henry Chesil to see you.'

Henry Chesil stood in the doorway staring at Amaryllis. All the way up from Shropshire, he'd been imagining this scene. His father's dire descriptions of the fate of fallen women had prepared him to find Amaryllis weeping and humbled, beseeching him to rescue her, her bruises imperfectly concealed by her dishevelled hair.

But instead she was standing there with her self-respect apparently unimpaired. Her hair was neatly arranged and her clothes were neither dishevelled nor revealing, consisting as they did of a modest blue dress with a white collar and a knot of pink ribbon at the throat. She showed no signs of falling at his feet to beg forgiveness either, her eyes were dry, and her expression, though surprised, was self-possessed. Altogether she was as desirable and unapproachable as ever.

Henry gave her another confused glance and then looked

round the room. That too was disconcerting. He had expected either luxury or squalor. Instead he saw a simple sitting-room which contained nothing more exotic than a basket of sewing and a few flowers. Henry shut the door and was about to stumble to a chair, when his eyes fell on the ledger Amaryllis had left open on the desk. Its sinister masculine implications were not slow to impress themselves upon him. He turned to Amaryllis. 'Are you alone here?'

'No, of course not. Bella is with me. You'd better sit down, Henry,' she added ungraciously.

Henry subsided into a chair and studied his boots.

'Who sent you here?' asked Amaryllis.

'No one,' he mumbled, 'they don't know I'm here.'

Amaryllis looked relieved. There was an awkward pause and then she said, 'I hope my mother and Mr Chesil are well?'

'Pretty well,' muttered Henry, 'They don't talk about you any more.'

'How did you know where to find me?'

'I asked Lord Vanbrugh.'

'You asked *Lord Vanbrugh*?' Amaryllis repeated incredulously. 'How did you find out it was him? What did he say to you?'

'One of the grooms told me you'd been seen at Vanbrugh. I rode over there but they said Lord Vanbrugh was away. He must have been expecting me though. He'd left me his card with your address on it . . . So I came to London to find you,' said Henry lamely, recalling how he had ridden over to Vanbrugh, determined to choke the life out of Amaryllis's seducer, only to find him gone. 'Did you . . . love him very much?'

'Love Lord Vanbrugh? No, not at all.'

Henry's vision of a tragic infatuation evaporated at once. 'But . . . then why on earth did you do it!'

'I needed money of course. I've got four houses now and an income of my own.'

Henry looked as if he was not taking any of this in. Amaryllis felt a familiar irritation with him.

'Why did you come here, Henry?' she asked sharply. 'Nothing you can do will change anything, you know.'

Henry swallowed, looked up at her unfriendly face and then said simply, 'I want you to marry me, Amaryllis.'

Amaryllis crossed the room and shook him vigorously by the shoulder. 'Henry! Did you perfectly understand? I *lived* with Lord Vanbrugh! I was his mistress!'

Henry winced. 'I know. I want to marry you all the same.'

Amaryllis stared at him.

'You can't possibly stay here,' said Henry, taking heart. 'You *must* come home with me. I'll look after you. We'll forget the past. Lord Vanbrugh was a villain. You didn't know what you were doing . . .'

'Yes I did!' said Amaryllis indignantly. 'It was all my idea from the first.'

'Amaryllis!' he cried desperately, trying to shut out the sound of her words. 'I'm offering you marriage and a good home . . .'

'I know you are, and I'm sorry, Henry, but I'm refusing them.'

Henry took a deep breath and tried to steady himself.

Amaryllis started to feel a little sorry for him. 'It's no use,' she said more gently.

'I can't believe that.' The dread of losing her made him try one last argument. 'Amaryllis, you *must* listen to me. I'm your one hope. You're ruined: no other man will even look at you. I know you never really liked me before . . . but now everything's changed. You *must* marry me.' He saw refusal in her face and made a forlorn attempt to embrace her, which she easily avoided.

'You must put me out of your mind,' said Amaryllis firmly. 'I'm sure all you say is true but you know we'd never suit. I'm much too quick-tempered and impatient. Besides, I'm a woman of independent means, now. I don't have to marry anyone. Go home, Henry. Your father would never have allowed you to marry me, not after what I've done. You know that.'

'I shouldn't have cared,' said Henry bitterly. He went to the door. 'Goodbye,' he said, adding lamely, 'I'll see myself out.'

A few minutes later, Bella came downstairs, carrying the supper tray.

'Gone, has he?' she inquired. She sat down, and took a piece of toast. 'Well, what did Mr Chesil have to say for himself? Offered you his hand and heart, I suppose?'

'He wanted to marry me, but I refused,' said Amaryllis, her mouth full of toast.

'I'm glad to hear it. You can do better for yourself than that streak of nothing. Much, much better.'

Amaryllis thought she had almost forgotten her time with Lord Vanbrugh. Though it was only a few weeks since she had left him, it seemed an unreal episode, completely cut off from the rest of her life. Lord Vanbrugh's name on the title deeds she pored over every day, his crest on the old leather trunk in her room, were the only reminders of the month she had spent in his company. But that night, after Henry's proposal, she dreamt she was lying in Lord Vanbrugh's bed beneath the dusty canopy, feeling his arms holding her tighter and tighter, until they half-strangled her and she woke up, drenched with sweat.

To go to sleep again was impossible. Amaryllis lay in bed watching the room grow light until six o'clock struck from St Martin's. Then she leaned out of the window, craning her neck to look at Number Eleven and wishing she had the money to repair it. It was more dilapidated than ever after a violent summer storm which had ripped off an alarming number of slates and reduced a rotting window frame to matchwood. But Number Eleven was not Amaryllis's only problem. Gazing out at the empty street, she knew that she was growing restless. She was tired of simply receiving rents and she had no wish to stay in Pembroke Street for ever.

Later that morning, she told Bella that she was going to visit Lucy Fletcher. Bella looked at the new clock on the mantelpiece.

'Half past eleven. Yes, she should be fit to be seen by now. I won't come with you. You should be safe between one front door and the next.'

When Amaryllis entered the dirty hallway and knocked on Miss Fletcher's door, she opened it almost at once. She was wearing an apron over her brightly patterned dress and her black hair was done up in curl papers, hidden under a ribboned cap. She looked surprised to see Amaryllis, but she invited her in and showed her to a chair by the fire.

Looking about her, Amaryllis could see that she had interrupted the housework. The window had been opened as if to get rid of the scent of cigars which still lingered in the air. The bed had just been made with fresh sheets and the dirty ones were bundled together in a chair. Near the bed, on the dressing-table among the pots of rouge and pearl powder, stood a pile of sovereigns. Seeing the direction of Amaryllis's gaze, Miss Fletcher gave a smothered giggle and swept the sovereigns into her apron pocket. Anxious not to embarrass her hostess, Amaryllis looked away.

Miss Fletcher pushed the dirty sheets out of sight under the bed valance, stripped off her apron, closed the window and sat down opposite Amaryllis, putting her feet on the fender.

'What can I do for you?'

'I've come here to thank you,' said Amaryllis simply.

'You needn't,' said Miss Fletcher, looking pleased none the less. 'Us girls stick together round here. We have to. No one else is going to look out for us. Besides,' she added with a quick laugh, 'if those brutes are going to start accosting decent women, where's our trade?'

This argument made sense to Amaryllis. This was a fellow businesswoman. 'Do you make much money at it?' she asked.

Miss Fletcher shrugged. 'I get by.' Then she grinned and added, 'To tell the truth, I've never had so much money in my life before! I was spending it like there was no tomorrow at first, but now I've learnt sense; I'm putting by.'

'And how did you take up your line of business?'

To Amaryllis's surprise, Miss Fletcher gave her a suspicious look. 'Why do you want to know? Worried about my morals?'

'No, no,' said Amaryllis, knowing that she was in no position to criticize even had she wished to.

'Well, so long as that's clear, I don't mind telling you.' She leaned forward to stir the coals. 'I had no choice really. Oh, I know they all say that, but that's because it's true. I started as a servant but the master got ideas. I wouldn't look at him – the great lump of blubber – so he made his wife throw me out; no reference either! After that I tried sewing, for a milliner's over in Regent Street, but my health couldn't stand it. They work you fourteen hours a day and don't feed you enough to keep a mouse alive. So here I am. It's risky of course, but better than slow starvation. You've got your freedom and you can do quite well if you keep your wits about you. It's wrong to live this way; I know that. But it's wrong to let people trample on you too – you've got to put up a bit of a fight.'

Afraid she might give herself away by agreeing with Miss Fletcher, Amaryllis searched for a change of subject. 'You've furnished your room very comfortably,' she said at last.

'Well – I make it as nice as I can. The better the room, the more they pay, you see. My price went up a whole guinea when I bought those velvet curtains – second-hand, of course.'

Amaryllis reddened, remembering her own preposterous demand for £2000.

She looked at Miss Fletcher consideringly. 'If you had somewhere better to live, could your earnings increase?'

'Oh yes. But decent rooms are scarce round here. Especially for girls like me.'

'So if I cleaned up my properties in Pembroke Street – put in water and gas and everything – you and your friends would take them? Even though the rents went up?'

'Well, they'd be bound to do *that*, wouldn't they?' said Miss Fletcher. 'Yes, we'd take them. I don't live in this smelly hole out of choice.' She glanced curiously at Amaryllis. 'Why are you so keen to let to street girls then?'

'Because I can charge you higher rents than most.'

Miss Fletcher grinned. 'I didn't think you were doing it out of the kindness of your heart. Mind you, that's the way it goes. I daresay I'd do the same in your position. You'll upset your respectable tenants, of course. Dr Dangerfield for one.' She giggled. 'He'd have to leave. He couldn't stand the temptation.'

'Dr Dangerfield? The man in Number Twelve?'

'That's right. Don't you *know* him? All the girls do – not to talk to, of course. He wouldn't speak to *us*.'

'No, I haven't met him, he was out when Mr Yardley

introduced me to my tenants.'

'But you must have seen him! Lovely brown hair and blue eyes and a figure . . . Well!' said Miss Fletcher, abandoning restraint, 'I'd walk barefoot to Jerusalem for a night with him!'

Thirteen

When Henry Chesil returned to Shropshire, he found matters very much as he had left them. His father, apart from the occasional explosion of wrath when something called Amaryllis to mind, avoided all reference to her. Mrs Chesil had taken to her bed with hysterics for a week when she first heard of her daughter's disappearance, but now she seemed glad to be rid of her and happily busied herself with her husband's concerns as if her life at Monksedge had never been.

They had sent out no search parties. Amaryllis's letter to her mother had made sure of that; fallen daughters were better not found. Mr Chesil had told his neighbours that a sick relative had needed Amaryllis urgently in a remote county and, perhaps fearful that their own daughters might follow Amaryllis's example, they had pretended to believe him. After all, no one was certain that the young woman at Vanbrugh had been Amaryllis Vaughan. Vanbrugh was a full thirty miles away and in a country district thirty miles might as well have been a hundred. The news of Lord Vanbrugh's latest mistress had taken several weeks to reach the Chesils' village and by that time Amaryllis had left for London and verification was impossible. Only Henry Chesil, who had watched her at the archery contest, had been certain of the truth.

Henry kept the secret of his visit to Pembroke Street as he had kept the secret of his visit to Vanbrugh, but he could not hide his subsequent misery. He found it impossible to forget Amaryllis; a hundred times a day he would picture her sitting opposite him at the breakfast table or riding beside him along the lanes, telling him impatiently to go faster. William Chesil watched his son's misery with dismay. It was all the fault of that wretched girl . . . Well, he, for one, was glad to see the back of her. She'd never fitted in at Chesil House. They were a lot better off without her. But it was a pity Henry was taking it so hard.

'Henry, my boy,' he said to him one morning when they were alone in the breakfast room, 'let's have a little talk, before your mother comes down. I've been thinking – it's high time you were married.'

A look of acute misery crossed Henry's uninteresting features.

'I know, my boy, I know. Still thinking of Amaryllis, I daresay. No future in it of course, none at all. She was a pretty little thing I will admit – but some women just go to the bad and there's an end of the matter. Best to put it out of your head.'

'She'd never have had me anyway.'

'Nonsense! A handsome young fellow like you with a good head on his shoulders and a snug estate coming to him? She'd have jumped at it! But that's enough of that. I want you to start thinking about your cousin, little Maria Harris. She's a good-natured, reliable girl, and pretty too. Make you an excellent wife. She knows her mother's still-room inside out, so Thyrza tells me. You think about it, Henry, and try to cheer up, there's a good lad.'

As a result of this conversation, Henry told himself that his father was very kind and sympathetic and he owed it to him to try and pull himself together. He'd go to Monksedge one last time and then he would try and forget Amaryllis forever. He rode away from Chesil House along the valley, and out across the bare hillside to Monksedge. The house lay in a sheltered hollow, its black and white timbers half hidden by the trees. Henry dismounted at the gate and walked up the path through the garden, thinking that it had a settled look compared to the raw, new flowerbeds at Chesil House.

He unlocked the front door and walked across the cool hall and up the stairs to Amaryllis's room. But there was little comfort to be had there: the closets were bare, the bed stripped and the looking-glass reflected only Henry's own face.

* * *

Thirty miles away from Chesil House, Lord Vanbrugh was sleeping badly. Night after night he stirred restlessly under the dusty canopy, furious with himself but quite unable to do anything about it. At his age to be hot as hell for a country whore – it was ludicrous! He thumped his pillows into a more comfortable shape and tried to sleep. Seductive visions of almond eyelids and gleaming hair floated before him. He sat up in bed and swore.

What the hell was she doing in London? He'd written to Bentley but the fellow was so damned disapproving, he'd got precious little out of him. Amaryllis had probably found a new protector by now; one with a fat bank balance. He began to wonder whether he could afford to return to London. He was bored to death in the country and London was safe again, now he'd paid off his most pressing creditors with the money from the sale of St James's Square. Yes, he'd take some rooms somewhere and Georgiana could go to her godmother in South Street. It would mean closing Vanbrugh, of course. He couldn't afford to keep two establishments any longer; those days were over. But Vanbrugh was finished anyway. There was no point in prolonging the misery. Better to end it cleanly. He'd shut up the house, get a caretaker to shuffle round putting buckets under the leaks for a few shillings a year and the garden could go back to the wild.

Lord Vanbrugh pulled back the bed curtains and stared desolately out at a patch of moonlight on the floor. The house was an incubus. It had preyed on his family for generations, draining their wealth and destroying their peace of mind. With luck he could sell it to some ambitious railway magnate, and then the house could ruin *him*.

He got up and wandered across to the window. As he gazed out at the temple glimmering in the distance, he changed his mind. He wouldn't sell Vanbrugh, he'd allow it to die in peace. In time, the broken columns and mouldering stonework would take on the melancholy beauty of a ruin. Nothing lasted; houses died just as their owners did, it merely took a little longer. In the dark woods behind the temple, there was said to be the ruins of a Roman villa, covered in brambles. As a boy, he had spent the best part of a summer searching for it. Some day Vanbrugh would have vanished as completely: ivy masking the crumbling walls, may trees flowering in the ballroom, a vixen's litter in the hall – and the poachers would avoid it after dark just as they did the villa, for fear of hearing music from the ballroom or the sweep of Lady Roxana's skirts along the terrace.

On a sudden impulse, he dressed and went noiselessly down the great staircase, across the shadowed vastness of the hall and out onto the moonlit lawn, haunting the woods and the lakeside like the departing genius of the place, until night shaded into dawn.

He wrote to his sister Georgiana on the following morning and she returned from Gloucester three days later. Lord Vanbrugh was out when she arrived, but he was standing by the fire when she entered the saloon before dinner. She moved towards a high-backed chair by the fire and seated herself without a word of greeting.

'Well, Anthony, I'll admit I'm glad to be here. I was beginning to wonder if you'd ever send for me. Mayo has been writing to me asking for a wedding date. I hope this summons means the delays are over at last?'

Lord Vanbrugh poured himself out a glass of wine and sat down in the chair facing her.

'This summons means, Georgiana, that I'm closing Vanbrugh. It's a luxury I can no longer afford.'

There was silence for a moment. Then she said constrictedly, 'Its death struggles have been so protracted, I half thought they would last for ever.' She stared at the fire for a while and then said abruptly, 'But where shall we live?'

'We'll go back to London, of course. 'I'll take rooms somewhere and you will presumably stay with your godmother.'

'You've found a buyer for Vanbrugh, I suppose?'

Lord Vanbrugh shook his head. 'Not yet.'

'I daresay Saville will take it, if you ask him,' she said, rather bitterly. 'He has the town house, after all. Vanbrugh would round it off nicely.'

'Perhaps. I may have a word with him about it.'

'It's a pity you didn't think of it before. You could have offered him the pair at a knock-down price.'

Lord Vanbrugh sipped his wine and made no answer.

'Perhaps it's all for the best, though,' said Georgiana. 'Mayo Park borders Vanbrugh, after all, and I shouldn't enjoy having Mr Saville for a neighbour.'

'You can set your mind at rest on that score.'

'You mean – you won't sell to Saville?'

'No, I mean you won't be living at Mayo Park.'

'Explain yourself.'

'You've no dowry, Georgiana. I've been obliged to put it to other uses. For all marriageable purposes, you're penniless.'

'*What!*' Georgiana rose swiftly to her feet. 'My God, Anthony, you've ruined me!'

He shrugged his shoulders. 'Oh, it's not as bad as that. You've still enough to dress on. But I doubt if Mayo will consider it sufficient.'

'Of course he won't, *damn* you! Nor will anyone else! And *I'll* have to be the one to cry off – to spare myself the humiliation of watching Mayo do it! You've ruined me, I tell you, ruined me out of sheer malicious spite!'

'Spite! And what about you? Choosing Mayo of all men in London. Mere accident was it?'

'You're contemptible! So obsessed with your pitiful marriage, you think no one else can forget it either! As if half London isn't busy cuckolding the other half and always has been! You don't suppose Caroline stopped at Mayo, do you? I'd be hard put to it to find a man she *hadn't* slept with!'

'You're lying, Georgiana! You chose Mayo because you knew damn well it would infuriate me!'

'Very well then! It *was* deliberate! I chose Mayo because it was the only way I could be revenged on *you* – looking on, powerless to interfere while you spent a fortune on your whores and your paintings; letting Vanbrugh fall into ruin . . . '

'Damn you! Vanbrugh was ruined before ever I got to it!'

'You could have saved it! *I* would have in your place! But I was a daughter; I owned nothing. All *I* could do was look on while you destroyed it. Well, you may have Vanbrugh now, but I swear to you, Anthony, before I'm done, I'll take it from you!'

She broke off and stared suspiciously at her brother. 'My dowry – I saw the deeds before I left London. What's happened so suddenly? What pressing demands *can* there have been? You've got the money from St James's Square . . . *My God!* You've spent it on that whore of yours!'

For an instant, it seemed as if she would strike him, but she mastered herself and stood, breathless with fury, until she could control her voice. Then she said, 'That was quite unforgiveable,' and turning on her heel, walked swiftly out of the room.

Fourteen

On the morning after her talk with Lucy Fletcher, Amaryllis had an early breakfast with Bella at a coffee house in the Strand. They were almost the first customers, apart from a few morose law clerks who had been up all night, and the waiter yawned continually as he served them. Afterwards they continued down the Strand as far as St Mary's church and then stopped to ask the way of a pot boy who was taking down the shutters outside a gin-shop. He directed them down a side turning and they soon reached a two-storey building with the words 'John Yardley: Builder' painted across the front in green and gold lettering.

At one end of the façade, a brass door knocker at street level and a pot of herbs in a first-floor window suggested Mr Yardley's living quarters; at the other end, a narrow alley led through an archway into an enclosed yard at the back of the premises. In the street outside, men in white caps and trousers splashed with lime were hanging about, as if waiting for work but without much hope of getting any. A wagon got stuck trying to turn out of the alley and they elbowed each other out of the way in their anxiety to help, especially when a short, dark, bull-necked man came out of the building to take charge.

When the wagon had been freed, Amaryllis approached the bull-necked man and said briskly, 'My name is Vaughan. I'd like to see Mr Yardley. Is he available?'

The man touched his cap with fingers stained a curious blue-grey colour that looked as if it would not wash off. 'Oh yes, Miss Vaughan, Pembroke Street, isn't it? I'm Silas Jones, Mr Yardley's foreman. If you'll just wait in here, I'll go and get him.'

Bella went away to do her shopping and the foreman led Amaryllis into a cluttered office. Through the window she could see Mr Yardley standing in his shirtsleeves, directing the stacking of the roofing slates which had been unloaded from the wagon. He looked much occupied, but when the foreman spoke to him he nodded, shrugged his broad shoulders into his jacket and came across to the office at once.

'Good morning, Miss Vaughan,' he said in answer to her greeting. 'I delivered your letter to Lord Vanbrugh yesterday. Mr Bentley will have forwarded it to Shropshire by now.'

Amaryllis blushed. 'Thank you, but it wasn't important. I came to see you on quite another matter. I'm sorry to disturb you so early, but I thought I had a better chance of finding you here at this hour. You see, I think I've found a way to pay for the repairs to Number Eleven.'

Mr Yardley looked interested.

'We do the job *properly*. Thorough repairs, decoration to a high standard, water, gas all laid on . . . Then we turn the house into five or six good quality apartments and let them at high rents to cover the costs.'

She paused for breath and Mr Yardley said doubtfully, 'But who will take them? Pembroke Street's not respectable enough to attract people with that sort of money.'

'I know. That's why we'll let to prostitutes.'

Mr Yardley looked startled.

'They'll not only pay the higher rents, they'll pay extra on top. Enough to recover the cost of repairs *and* increase the rental.'

'True,' said Mr Yardley. He sat in silence for a few moments, toying with a pencil as he thought it over. Then he looked up and said, 'There's a reason why they pay extra, you know.'

'I'm in no position to complain about their morals, if that's what you mean!'

'Everyone needs a roof over their head and we're both in the business of providing it. But your other tenants won't like it at all.'

'So much the better. If they move I can let their rooms to prostitutes too.'

Mr Yardley looked steadily at her. 'There can be other problems. Noise, fights, drunkenness – the police start taking an interest in the street.'

'Yes, but we've got all that already. We'll just have to put up with it. You can't expect something for nothing, can you?'

Mr Yardley's face relaxed. 'In that case there's a lot to be said for the scheme. We'll have to give the tenants time to find other accommodation of course . . . I'll go over to Number Eleven right away and take a look at what needs to be done.'

'There *is* just one other thing.' Amaryllis looked Mr Yardley straight in the eye. 'Would you do the work on credit for a couple of months? At a reasonable rate of interest, naturally. I suggest it because the scheme will work to your long-term advantage. Your commission on the rents will be worth a good deal more when the repairs are done.'

There was silence for a moment while Mr Yardley thought it over. Then he smiled. 'Miss Vaughan, it's a pleasure to work with you. When I think you've only been in the business a month . . . It's a fine scheme, Miss Vaughan, a fine scheme!'

'So you'll give me credit?'

'Yes. As you say, I won't lose by it. I've not much capital myself but I've enough to tide you over. Shake hands on the deal. We can work out the details later.'

Amaryllis stripped off her glove and gave Mr Yardley's hand a hearty shake.

'I'll come over to Pembroke Street with you now,' he went on. 'I'd like to give you an estimate of the work as soon as possible. Then we can get down to business.' He laughed. 'You know, I was wondering all along where you were going to get the money to pay for it. This way. We can go out through the back.'

He opened a door and led the way across the yard to an archway on the far side, finding a path between the towering piles of slate stacked on the cobbles.

'Some of these'll do for Number Eleven. I keep a lot in stock. The old houses I work on are always losing a slate or two. I've no slater among my own men but Silas can fix on the odd one if needed.' He rubbed a finger over the matt grey surface of a slate. 'Lovely, aren't they? Penrhyn – good for a hundred years. I don't use anything bigger than duchesses myself – those ones over there – but a really big job would take queens and empresses.'

'You employ your own men, do you?' asked Amaryllis as they left the yard and went down an alley to the street.

Mr Yardley nodded. 'It's not usual. Mostly building work's subcontracted to small craftsmen, but that's too risky for me. The work's skimped, or one man goes too slowly and holds up the rest. If you want good, sound work, employ your men directly and treat them well. Mr Cubitt – you'll have heard of Mr Cubitt?' he asked eagerly as they turned into the Strand. Amaryllis shook her head. 'He's a builder. The greatest of them all. Pimlico, Bloomsbury, Clapham, they're all Cubitt's. And as for Belgravia – have you seen it, Miss Vaughan? He's building palaces! Street after street of them. He's used nothing but the best materials; it'll last as long as London!'

Amaryllis was no craftsman. She went straight to the point. 'And he's made a lot of money?'

'A fortune! And he started with nothing but a small workshop, just like mine. I copy him whenever I can. That's where I got the idea of employing my own men. I try and guarantee continuous work like he does. I can't always manage it – it's all slumps and booms in this business – but I do my best. That's where the rent collecting comes in.'

'Yes, I'd wondered about that. It's not usual, is it, for a builder?'

'No, but the idea is that I collect the rents for you, and for the Vanbrugh and Linklater estates as well, and when repairs are needed I'm the first to hear about it and can put in my tender before my rivals get a look in. My work's sound – I make sure of that – so nine times out of ten I get the job. It secures a steady flow of work *and* I get my ten per cent.'

'Two benefits for the price of one,' said Amaryllis.

As they walked along the Strand, she thought that she liked Mr Yardley's business methods. He had ambitions too; he wasn't content with his builder's yard any more than she was content to stay in Pembroke Street. She'd made the right decision when she'd asked him to collect her rents . . . Amaryllis suddenly realized that Mr Yardley was walking on her inside instead of on the street side as etiquette demanded. She thought of the other men she knew. Henry Chesil would have made an anxious parade of walking on the street side, Lord Vanbrugh would have walked on the inside as a deliberate insult. Mr Yardley did it quite unconsciously, as if she had been a man he was working with. Amaryllis smiled to herself as they crossed Trafalgar Square and walked up past the new Gallery to Pembroke Street.

Mr Yardley left her at the front door and went off to make his estimates. Amaryllis tried the handle and found it locked. Realizing that Bella must still be out shopping, she let herself into the house with her key and went upstairs. She had reached the first-floor landing, when she saw that there was a man sitting on the stair. His shoulders were broad and his arms muscular but they terminated in little restless hands with pointed nails. He was dressed in rough, dark clothes and his black hair was cropped short; so short that it looked almost as closely shaven as his heavy jaw.

'Who are you? What are you doing here?' asked Amaryllis.

The man got to his feet. 'My name is Cutler.'

Amaryllis wished with all her heart that she was not alone in the house.

'We'd better go upstairs,' said Cutler.

'No, we'll stay here.'

He looked at her, as if surprised that she should dare to contradict him. 'A nice house you have here,' he said consideringly. 'Not your only one, is it?' He nodded at someone over Amaryllis's shoulder. She spun round to see Bella staring white-faced up the stairs.

'Hello,' he said calmly. 'Nice to see you after all these years.'

'Get out!' gasped Bella. 'Get out – before I beat you to a pulp!'

Cutler seemed to look straight through her. He walked heavily down the stairs, and passed the two women without another word.

As the front door closed behind him, Bella stood dull-eyed and silent.

'Come on, Bella,' said Amaryllis anxiously. 'Come on up to the kitchen. I'll make you a cup of tea. *Please* Bella.'

Bella seemed to pull herself together and began to plod up the stairs, clinging to the banisters for support. Amaryllis helped her up to the kitchen, took off her bonnet and made her sit down.

'Who was he, Bella?'

Bella made no reply for a moment. Then she shrugged. 'It can do no harm now I suppose . . . That was Cutler. My husband.'

Amaryllis stared dazedly at Bella.

'Yes, Cutler's my husband – and don't I know it! You'd have found out soon enough if I hadn't told you. He won't leave me alone now he knows where I am – nor you either. You wondered why I never took any wages from you? Well, *he's* the reason.' She laughed harshly. 'I was in a good line of business when I first met Cutler. It was paying very well; I was on my way to becoming a rich woman. But like a blind fool I believed his lies: I married him. He took it all, you see. Every penny I'd earned, all my savings, everything, and spent it on his friends and his gambling. Hand it over, Bella, he'd say, the minute I got home with my wages. Hand it over. I'm your husband you know. None of it's yours. It all belongs to me.

'At first, I gave him the money. Then I fought him, when I realized there was never anything left for me. So he went direct to my employers and they'd pay him for my work and I'd never see a penny of it. I put a stop to that. I used my own name again and told my employers I wouldn't work for them if they gave my wages to him. I moved to different lodgings and never went near the old ones. But Cutler soon found me out. One day I came back to find he'd stolen everything, money, clothes, furniture – all gone. Only it wasn't theft. He was my husband – everything belonged to him.

'I was in a black rage by the time I got to his lodgings. I found my things and piled them onto a handcart and took them away. The next night he was waiting for me with a cudgel. He got my money in the end, but not before I'd marked him first.'

Amaryllis was horrified. 'But couldn't you take him before the magistrates? *They* would have punished him, even if you couldn't.'

Bella shook her head. 'Cutler was within his rights, damn him! He's my husband, remember. Husbands are allowed to beat their wives. I was lucky he didn't kill me – it happens often enough. But the husband *is* fined a few shillings. Maybe that stopped Cutler from going the whole way. He always was a mean devil.

'But he wouldn't kill you, surely?' protested Amaryllis.

'Oh, wouldn't he! He's vicious, is Cutler. He knows every villain in London; spends most of his time in the gin shops. Loungers, footpads, pickpockets, he's friends with them all. Decent people wouldn't touch him; wouldn't walk down the street with him.'

'And did no one try to help you?'

'Oh, I had friends who tried to get him to leave me alone. But not too hard. They knew he was a dangerous man to cross. Besides, I was a little gold mine to Cutler; he wasn't going to let me go that easily. So in the end I decided to vanish. That meant leaving London, but I couldn't take the coach because Cutler had friends at every inn and turnpike for fifty miles round. I took the drovers' road – sneaking out of London like a criminal under cover of the dark.'

The kettle boiled and Amaryllis made the tea, strong and dark as Bella liked it.

'We should never have shown ourselves at the Bull and Mouth,' said Bella. 'I'd heard Cutler was in prison, so I thought it was safe. He'll be after me now, bleeding me for every penny . . . Well, I'm ready for him. I've taken no wages from you and the money I saved in Shropshire is well hid.'

'But there must be *something* we can do . . . .'

'What?'

On the spur of the moment, Amaryllis was unable to think of anything.

'Cutler's dangerous,' Bella warned her. 'It takes a lot to frighten me but he's managed it.'

'I don't care,' said Amaryllis defiantly. 'I'll stand by you. *I'm* not his wife. There's nothing he can do to me.'

Fifteen

Amaryllis was watering her window box the next Sunday morning, full of self-satisfaction. Her new business venture was a very smart piece of work. The notices to quit had been distributed to the tenants of Number Eleven on the previous day and matters were well under way. There had, it was true, been some slight difficulty. The sample letter Mr Yardley provided had allowed the tenants four weeks' notice instead of only one. But Amaryllis had soon put a stop to that. She had explained to Mr Yardley that there was no need for any delay. In fact, the sooner the repairs were finished the better – the house was falling down round everyone's ears. But Mr Yardley had not been convinced and had departed frowning.

Amaryllis put down her watering-can and looked out of the window. Pembroke Street was deserted except for Meggy Canning who was playing a game of marbles in the gutter. A smell of roast beef wafted from Mrs Dixon's house and Mr Fry came out of Number Eleven and set off for the chapel in Orange Street with a violin tucked under his arm.

Yesterday Amaryllis had bought her dining-room furniture at an auction room in Adam Street. Most of the other bidders had been landladies and they had not been interested in a rosewood table and chairs too fragile for lodging-house life. There was also a sideboard to go with them which Amaryllis thought of with particular complacency. She was wondering how soon she could afford a porcelain dinner service when she heard Bella's footsteps going down to answer the front door.

'Is Miss Vaughan at home?' asked a man's voice. At the sound of it Amaryllis patted her collar into place and settled herself elegantly on the sofa. The sitting-room door opened.

'Dr Dangerfield,' announced Bella.

Dr Dangerfield came swiftly into the room, hand outstretched, his thick, well-disciplined hair gleaming like a bronze helmet. Lucy Fletcher had been right; Dr Dangerfield was exceedingly handsome. Amaryllis smiled charmingly at him as she gave him her hand and then asked him to sit down. He chose the seat nearest to her and she was conscious of his closeness. She could hear the soft rustle of his shirt as he moved and could just catch the faint sound of his indrawn breath.

'First let me introduce myself. Francis Dangerfield, a tenant of yours from Number Twelve. I have rooms on the ground floor.'

'Of course,' said Amaryllis graciously. 'You were out when I called with Mr Yardley.'

'Yes, I'm afraid I've been working hard at the hospital for most of the past month or so or I would have visited you before.' He looked down at his well-kept hands for a moment. 'There is another reason for my visit. I have been sent here on a rather delicate mission – one which I hardly know how to begin. I have been asked to speak to you by some of your tenants – perhaps they imagined that as a professional man I might be able to phrase it better than they could . . .' He smiled self-deprecatingly.

'What can you mean, Dr Dangerfield?' Amaryllis wondered, with a guilty blush, if her tenants had found out about Lord Vanbrugh. Her palms were damp with anxiety and when Dr Dangerfield said, 'It's these notices to quit, I'm afraid,' she felt immensely relieved.

'They're causing great distress,' he continued. 'The tenants have all begged me to ask you to reconsider your decision to evict, or at least give them a little more time to find somewhere else to live. Coming from the country, Miss Vaughan, you could hardly be expected to know it, but lodgings are very hard to come by in London, especially on a limited income. And as for Miss Salisbury, as a medical man I have to admit that to move her at all might prove fatal. Her condition is very serious indeed.'

Amaryllis had been feeling quite cross with her tenants –

spoiling her first meeting with this handsome young man with their wretched complaints. But this last piece of information put a different complexion on the matter. Not only did it show her in a very bad light to Dr Dangerfield, but even Amaryllis's own underworked conscience was starting to reproach her.

'I hadn't realized Miss Salisbury was unwell. I haven't yet had time to make the acquaintance of my tenants. What is the nature of her illness?'

'Consumption,' said Dr Dangerfield with a sigh. 'I am not in attendance of course, my work is at the hospital, but it's clearly a severe case. I doubt if she'll last the winter, even if she stays in Pembroke Street.'

'I'm very sorry to hear it. I'll certainly talk to Mr Yardley about it and see if something can be done for her.'

'That would be very good of you,' said Dr Dangerfield warmly. His blue eyes were fixed on Amaryllis's face in an approving gaze she found far from displeasing. She must make sure of his sympathy and admiration; it would never do to alienate him before a flirtation had even begun. She shook her head, prettily sorrowful.

'As for the other tenants, I'm afraid I can't revoke their notices to quit. Number Eleven is in a dreadful condition. I was horrified when I first saw it – to think my tenants lived somewhere like that. It's not fit for animals, let alone human beings.' She looked pleadingly at Dr Dangerfield. 'It *must* be properly repaired, but Mr Yardley tells me it will cost a very great deal and I'm quite unable to find the money out of the present rents. If I *could* pay for the repairs out of my own pocket, I would do so but I'm not a rich woman, Dr Dangerfield.'

With a sure dramatic instinct, Amaryllis rose to her feet and flung open the dining-room door. 'This room is empty because I can't afford to furnish it. You *do* understand my predicament, don't you?'

'Miss Vaughan, I understand entirely. Please don't think I came to you in any critical or unfriendly spirit. Anyone acquainted with Number Eleven must agree that repairs are long overdue. All I ask is that you allow your tenants a little longer to find other accommodation.' He leant forward as he spoke and his fingers just brushed Amaryllis's arm.

'Well . . . it won't be easy to arrange.' She gave Dr Dangerfield a demure glance. 'But perhaps we could allow them a few days longer. I might be able to make it a fortnight – though of course it's not entirely up to me.'

'That's wonderful!' said Dr Dangerfield. 'They'll be so grateful. After Lord Vanbrugh, it's good to know we have a landlord who takes a real interest. And now I mustn't take up any more of your time, Miss Vaughan, but I hope we'll meet again very soon.'

No sooner had he left than Bella appeared in the doorway in her black bonnet and shawl.

'I went out to the dairy while you were taken up with that doctor fellow,' she said sternly, 'and I met Meggy on the way there. She told me they'd been given notice, which surprised me *very* much since I'd heard nothing about it. Afraid to tell me, were you?'

Amaryllis coloured, knowing that this was true.

'I went up to see Mary,' Bella continued, 'and found her in a great state. That didn't surprise me because, being a midwife, she has to stay in one place or she loses custom.'

'Yes, Bella, I know . . . '

'I don't take wages,' said Bella, ignoring her, 'but I *do* expect the occasional favour.'

'Yes, Bella, of course, but . . . '

'The Cannings to stay.'

'Oh, very well. Maybe not in Number Eleven . . . '

'The *same* address.' Bella folded her arms. 'You're a fine one, I must say. You should know better! Didn't much like having to leave Monksedge, did you? And now you start throwing people out into the street. I'm ashamed of you! Who do you think you are – God Almighty? You don't know it all quite yet, young woman. It's time you learnt to take advice for once. I can't think what Mr Yardley was doing – letting you get away with it!'

'He's my employee! He *has* to do what I say!'

'Oh yes? Like I have to, I suppose! Mr Yardley's got more knowledge of the building trade in his little finger than you have in your whole spoilt body.'

Amaryllis was silent for a moment as she swallowed this

advice. Then she said reluctantly, 'I suppose he did try and warn me. And Dr Dangerfield's just told me about Miss Salisbury being so ill. I didn't know she'd got consumption.'

'It's written all over her, poor soul. Only a creature as callous as you could have failed to notice it!'

'Well, I'm sorry, Bella,' said Amaryllis, more upset than she was prepared to show. 'I'm putting it right as fast as I can. I'll give them all a month's notice. And I'll find other rooms for the Cannings and Miss Salisbury. Someone else will have to go, that's all.'

Bella shook her head. 'I hope you've learnt your lesson. You always were a self-centred little thing. Can be a help in some ways of course – you'll never let anyone wipe their feet on *you* – but bad landlords end up with bad tenants. You'll find yourself in Queer Street one of these days, unless you mend your ways. You've no more sense than your mother sometimes . . . Well? Don't just sit there. Be off with you!'

Amaryllis stared at her. 'Be off where?'

'To Number Eleven of course. Put those poor souls out of their misery. Let's see you acting like a real landlord for once.'

Sixteen

On the following Monday, Amaryllis walked along Warwick Street, rehearsing some tough remarks about the tripe boiler who had paid no attention to Mr Yardley's warnings. Followed by Bella, she turned in at the door of the Vanbrugh estate office and rapped smartly on the panels. It was opened by a youth in ink-stained cuffs who said that Mr Bentley was engaged.

'Very well then,' said Amaryllis. 'I'll wait for him.'

The youth nodded without enthusiasm and showed her into the outer office. It looked drabber and dustier than ever. Amaryllis took a seat and the youth disappeared into an inner room.

After a few minutes he reappeared and held the door open for her saying, 'Mr Bentley will see you now, Miss.' Amaryllis swept into the inner office, leaving Bella behind her. Mr Bentley rose to welcome her, but his reluctant politeness met with no response. Amaryllis was giving all her attention to the other occupant of the room.

'Come to take up my offer of rescue, Amaryllis?' said Lord Vanbrugh, surveying her with an air of amused superiority.

Amaryllis turned to Mr Bentley. 'I came here with a complaint about one of your tenants in Pembroke Street, but since you're occupied, I'll discuss it at some other time.'

'Good God, how businesslike she sounds!' commented Lord Vanbrugh. 'All right, Bentley, I'll handle this.' The agent gave him a disapproving glance and left the room.

Lord Vanbrugh inspected Amaryllis more closely. 'Good God. What have you been doing to yourself? You look like a damned Quakeress!'

'These are my business clothes.'

'Well, they're horrible.'

Amaryllis turned her back on him and gazed angrily at the framed certificates hanging on the walls.

'What do you want to see Bentley about?' asked Lord Vanbrugh.

'One of your tenants has been boiling tripe.'

He burst into a jeering laugh. 'What a come-down! Miss Amaryllis Vaughan of Monksedge complaining about a tripe boiler!'

Amaryllis tried to leave the room.

'No you don't,' he said, reaching out to detain her. 'Leave now and you certainly won't get what you want. Sit down and tell me more about this tripe boiler.'

'I'd rather discuss him with Mr Bentley.'

'No doubt. But you'll have to make do with me. Tell me all about it; I want to hear every fascinating detail.'

'If you *must* know, one of your vile tenants in Pembroke Street is boiling his disgusting tripe in his doubtless filthy garrett and the stench is making my tenants ill – and yours too, I should think. It certainly makes *me* sick!'

'Oh yes,' said Lord Vanbrugh, greatly amused. 'You're living in Pembroke Street now, aren't you? I was sure you'd feel at home there.'

'I've taken rooms fairly near you as it happens,' Lord Vanbrugh went on casually. 'Number Nine, Jermyn Street. I've had to close Vanbrugh. Very sad after all these years, but my expenses have been so heavy of late . . . '

'No doubt,' said Amaryllis, 'but I didn't come here to discuss your affairs. What do you propose to do about that tripe boiler?'

'Very little. In fact – I cherish him. I understand from Bentley that you're proposing to renovate Number Eleven and fill it with the most undesirable tenants. At extortionate rents no doubt, knowing your business methods, but women of that type, however wealthy, always lower the tone of a neighbourhood, don't they? So I rely on my tripe boiler to keep them away and preserve the respectability of the street.'

'You never worried much about the tone of the neighbourhood in the past!'

Lord Vanbrugh laughed. 'You'll never persuade me to evict the tripe boiler by scowling at me. Why don't you try a more amorous method?'

'Our relations in future will be strictly commercial,' said Amaryllis coldly.

'They always were.'

'Are you going to evict that man or aren't you?' demanded Amaryllis, exasperated.

'I'm thinking about it . . . Has Henry Chesil been to see you yet? He turned up at Vanbrugh just before I left.'

'Oh, *before* you left, was it?' said Amaryllis scornfully.

He shrugged. 'There was no point in enduring a scene. After all, you seduced *me*. Perhaps I should send Georgiana round to you with a horsewhip . . . '

'I'm not wasting my time here any longer!' Amaryllis interrupted him, walking out of the room and slamming the door behind her.

Lord Vanbrugh made no attempt to stop her. He stayed where he was and gazed reflectively at his family tree, hanging above Mr Bentley's desk. He was not at all happy with the situation. He had expected Amaryllis to find Pembroke Street too much for her, but she actually seemed to be enjoying it. She was too independent for his liking – and he wanted her just as badly, damn her!

Back in Pembroke Street, Amaryllis parted from Bella at the street door and mounted the stairs alone. She went into the parlour to take off her bonnet before the glass, but no sooner had she untied the strings than she saw the door of her bedroom open slowly and Cutler emerge into the room behind her. She whipped round to face him.

'Bella not here?' said Cutler. 'Good. We've business to discuss, Miss Vaughan.'

'What are you doing here? How did you get into my house?' asked Amaryllis, her heart thumping unpleasantly. A faint, disagreeable smile crossed Cutler's face. He took out a bunch of tangled steel hooks and dangled them to and fro for a moment. Amaryllis had never seen picklocks before but it was not hard to guess their purpose.

'If you dare to break into my house again I'll have you up before the magistrate! Now, leave this instant!'

Cutler put the picklocks back in his pocket and spread his little hands fanwise in front of him, surveying his pointed nails.

'I'm going just as soon as I have my wife's wages.'

'You'll not get a penny from me! I give her no wages. She has board and lodging instead.'

Cutler shook his head. 'Poor Bella. No business sense at all. But you and I, Miss Vaughan, can come to a better arrangement.' He shot her a menacing glance. 'A little less board and rather more wages? Paid to me, of course, as her lawful husband.'

Amaryllis laughed contemptuously, though her mouth was dry. Cutler took a silk handkerchief out of his pocket and wound it about his fingers with little, jerking movements.

'I'll give you time,' he said, 'but you'll pay me in the end. At least, I hope you do. Because if you don't . . . ' He left the alternative blank but illustrated his meaning by tying his handkerchief into a noose, suspending it from his thumb, and hanging a finger in it.

'I'll never pay you! I don't want to see or hear from you again! And keep away from Bella too!'

'Sheltering her, are you? That's not lawful either. I could bring an action for enticement.'

'Get out of here and don't you dare to come threatening me again!'

Cutler seemed not to have heard her. He unwound the handkerchief, smoothed it out, folded it with extreme care so that the edges of the silk matched exactly, and slid it back into his pocket. Then he turned and shouldered his way out of the room and down the stairs.

Amaryllis, weak with relief, sank down on the nearest chair. A few minutes later Bella came into the room, her gold earrings bounding about on either side of her pallid face.

'I've seen Cutler! Oh, I'm quite winded! I ran all the way back . . . He was skulking along Coventry Street. He hasn't been here, has he?'

'Yes, he has, the brute!'

Bella gave a moan. 'You never let him in!'

'No, I certainly didn't! I found him here when I came upstairs. He'd picked the lock!'

'That sounds like Cutler,' said Bella bitterly. 'He wanted money, I suppose? He always did.'

'He asked for your wages. But he'll not get a penny from me! I told him so and threw him out. How could you have married him, Bella? He's quite horrible!'

Bella gave a harsh laugh. 'I was a plain woman. Most men weren't interested. Cutler came out of nowhere and said he loved me. I didn't know the truth about him then. I'd have been happy enough living with him; not many bother with marriage in my walk of life. But Cutler said marriage it had to be. I was flattered he should want me; I never thought to ask why . . .' She broke off and looked at Amaryllis. 'Ah, *you* don't understand,' she said, without rancour. 'You're too good looking and too self-centred. You'll always wonder how I could have been so blind.'

Amaryllis coloured uncomfortably and wished she'd held her tongue.

'Did he make any threats?' asked Bella.

'Yes, he did. Nothing definite though – perhaps he didn't mean it.'

Bella shivered. 'He meant it all right. We'll find out what's coming to us soon enough.'

Seventeen

Amaryllis had been more alarmed by Cutler's threats than she had liked to show to Bella, but it was not long before more exciting matters ousted him completely from her mind. That evening, a letter arrived from Dr Dangerfield, inviting Amaryllis to go with him for a drive on the following Sunday. Mr Rugby, the young solicitor from Number Twelve, would also be making one of the party. The letter added that there would, of course, be room for Amaryllis's maid in the carriage.

Bella, when shown the letter, gave a ribald laugh. 'He *must* think you're an innocent little flower! He's in for a nasty shock, poor soul.'

'Why?' demanded Amaryllis. '*I* shan't tell him. He doesn't really expect you to come, does he, Bella? He just put that in to show respect.'

'Hmm. Well, I suppose not even *you* need chaperoning in an open carriage on a Sunday afternoon.'

'Good,' said Amaryllis, with great satisfaction. 'I think I'll wear the white muslin.'

'That dress again! You watch your step. I've not forgotten what happened the last time you wore it.'

'Be quiet, Bella! I just want to dress up for once, that's all.'

'Suit yourself. Those double flounces will take a deal of ironing though. And I suppose you want ringlets too. Flighty as ever!'

'I'm *not* flighty,' said Amaryllis indignantly. 'I know *exactly* what I'm doing. I always have. I got four houses out of Lord Vanbrugh, didn't I? He was besotted with me.'

'Well, that didn't last very long,' said Bella. 'Didn't seem very besotted the next time you met, did he?'

'Oh, who cares about him, now that Dr Dangerfield's going to fall in love with me!'

'Fall in love with you! Not him! He's too much in love with himself to have any to spare. Mind you, for your property, I daresay he *has* an affection. He looks like a sensible man and he's got his way to make in the world . . . ' But Amaryllis had stalked out of the room and Bella's words fell on empty air.

Dr Dangerfield presented himself promptly at two o'clock on the Sunday afternoon. Delightfully conscious of the fact that he could hardly take his eyes off her, Amaryllis disposed her skirts becomingly about her when she had been handed up into the carriage and sat back with care so as not to crush her blue satin sash. Returning Dr Dangerfield's gaze demurely from under her bonnet brim, Amaryllis thought that he was infinitely preferable to Lord Vanbrugh. Dr Dangerfield's high forehead, noble profile and strong chin were in the most fashionable style and would have done credit to any London drawing-room. Lord Vanbrugh's black locks scarcely benefited by comparison with the thick glossy hair waving back from the doctor's forehead, and his sensual mouth contrasted very unfavourably with the younger man's firm thin lips.

Amaryllis had been looking forward to the drive with eagerness – it was so long since she had had anyone to flirt with. In Shropshire, several young men had shown an interest in her and though she had thought them dull, some of them had been handsome enough. They had even exchanged hot shamefaced kisses in a secluded corner of the garden, though they knew it was strictly against the rules. Amaryllis cast a sidelong glance at Dr Dangerfield's firm mouth and wished an open carriage was not quite such a public place.

Mr Rugby had been relegated to the driver's seat. He shook the reins and the carriage moved off down the street, attracting envious glances from two of Mrs Dixon's lodgers who were out for a walk before dinner. As the carriage turned the corner into Coventry Street, Amaryllis saw Lucy Fletcher coming towards them, her black curls cascading down her back. Amaryllis turned and gave her a smile, but Lucy gave no sign of having seen her. Amaryllis sat back, hurt and surprised.

'You have a house in the country, I think Mr Yardley told me. Is that right, Miss Vaughan?' asked Dr Dangerfield.

'Yes – a house and some land. Do you come from the country?'

'No – from Winchester. My father was a banker there but the bank failed shortly before his death. So now I'm walking the wards at St Bartholomew's. No chance of a practice of my own unless I can lay my hands on some money! Rugby's in the same position. But he's better off than I am. There's an uncle who'll take him into partnership before he's much older . . . but at present we're both waiting for better things, which is why, if you'll forgive me, Miss Vaughan, we're living humbly in Pembroke Street instead of setting up our brass plates in Bloomsbury in proper professional style.'

He turned for a moment to give Mr Rugby some directions.

'I thought we might drive to the park to start with and then go on wherever else you'd like. We should just catch the end of Church Parade.' Seeing Amaryllis's puzzled look he smiled. 'That's just a nickname, of course. When fashionable people come out from morning service they make a circuit of the park in their carriages to show off their clothes. It's one of the sights of London, Miss Vaughan – you mustn't miss it.'

'Yes, I'd like to see it,' said Amaryllis politely. Privately, she thought that it sounded rather dull but she was on her best behaviour – and besides, Dr Dangerfield's nearness was enough to make anything interesting. She wished she dared inspect him openly, but one did not stare at a man one wanted to impress.

They entered the park by the Stanhope Gate and drew up to watch the procession of carriages. Each gleaming vehicle was driven by a coachman in a cockaded hat and gilded livery and the grandest were also equipped with a pair of footmen hanging on behind, matched for size like the horses and almost as well fed and groomed.

The occupants equalled their carriages in opulence, the gentlemen in splendid waistcoats, the ladies in silks and plumed bonnets. The younger women were dressed with deceptive simplicity, many of them in white like Amaryllis, but their muslins were of the finest, most aerial quality and were frosted at the neck with French lace. Amaryllis, painfully conscious of her hired carriage and countrified clothes, comforted herself with the thought that none of them had her silver gilt hair and none of them, no, *none* of them, had an escort as handsome as Dr Dangerfield. He was attracting quite as many glances as she was and more than one elegant lady had abandoned her languid pose for a moment in order to secure a better view of his profile.

The procession's progress round the park was very leisurely since the fashionable ladies sometimes beckoned to acquaintances on the pavement, who approached their carriages and exchanged a few words while the rest of the traffic waited. The procession had just come to a halt due to a lady in a landau who was discussing the weather with two military men, when, to her dismay, Amaryllis caught sight of Lord Vanbrugh, sitting in a dark green barouche, only four carriages away from her.

He was accompanied by an elderly lady in black and a tall young woman with mouse-coloured hair under a bonnet trimmed with grey ostrich plumes. Lord Vanbrugh seemed impatient at the delay and was looking about him, as if he thought the whole business was a great waste of time, when he suddenly saw Amaryllis. For a moment, his gaze was riveted to her face; then it dropped to her muslin dress. He gave this a reminiscent smile and turned to subject her companions to a hard stare. Lord Vanbrugh did not seem to like what he saw. He climbed down from his seat and walked straight over to Amaryllis's side.

'Good afternoon, Miss Vaughan,' he said coldly.

Amaryllis, dismayed at meeting him in Dr Dangerfield's company, reluctantly returned his greeting.

She was about to introduce him to her companions when he prevented her. 'No, *don't* introduce me. I've no wish to meet them. Who the devil are they?'

'Some of my tenants,' whispered Amaryllis, in a fever of anxiety lest they should overhear the conversation. 'Do please go away. I can't talk to you now.'

'Some of your tenants!' he repeated in a voice which, though fortunately inaudible to the other occupants of the carriage, made his disgust quite evident to Amaryllis. 'Inhabitants of *Pembroke* Street . . . Do you normally associate with such people?'

'They're friends of mine!'

'I'm sorry to hear it. They look appallingly respectable. Shall I tell them you're a whore?'

'If you don't go away at once, I *will* introduce you!'

'Oh my God – rather than suffer that fate . . . ' He broke off abruptly and walked away.

When Lord Vanbrugh returned to his own carriage, the tall young woman asked him some question and then gave Amaryllis a cool, measuring look, which lasted until the procession of carriages moved off again. Dr Dangerfield leant forward in his seat to watch the green barouche as it drew ahead of them.

'A fine turnout. Have you known Lord Vanbrugh long, Miss Vaughan?'

Amaryllis, who had been dreading this question, said uncomfortably, 'Yes . . . at least . . . I met him in Shropshire. You know how it is in the country; people one wouldn't normally have much to do with one can't help meeting now and then . . . ' Realizing she was making too much of her answer, she stumbled lamely to a halt.

'And you must have had dealings with him in connection with Pembroke Street, I suppose?'

'No, none at all,' said Amaryllis emphatically. 'I dealt solely with his agent.'

'Oh, of course. How stupid of me. He's never shown much concern for Pembroke Street in the past, so it's hardly surprising . . . ' He broke off with an apologetic look. 'Oh, I'm sorry. I forgot he was a friend of yours.'

'No, he's not,' said Amaryllis vehemently. 'A mere business acquaintance – I don't know him socially at *all*.'

Dr Dangerfield seemed a little disappointed but he said, 'It's probably just as well. He's got an unpleasant reputation and he's allowed his properties to fall into a shocking state of disrepair. Vanbrugh's gone to rack and ruin, so they tell me, and I can well believe it, if Pembroke Street's anything to go by. That must have been his sister Georgiana with him in the carriage. Did you ever meet her in Shropshire?'

'No, never,' said Amaryllis, wishing he would drop the subject. 'I've seen her from a distance once or twice but the Vanbrughs didn't visit locally.'

'They'll come to it soon enough, you mark my words. The family's been going downhill rapidly. Lord Vanbrugh will be lucky not to end up in debtor's prison the way things are going. He's no children, of course, so I suppose it doesn't matter to him that there's nothing left to inherit . . .'

'He was married though, wasn't he?' Amaryllis was interested in spite of herself.

'Yes, but it wasn't a success. Lady Caroline was notorious, even by their lax standards, and they lived virtually apart almost from the outset – and now Georgiana Vanbrugh seems to have jilted someone . . . or so the latest rumour has it.'

'You seem to know a great deal about the Vanbrughs.'

'Well, I read the Court page and the fashionable intelligences. I've done so for years. It's foolish I know, but I can't help taking an interest in it all.' He laughed. 'Every doctor secretly hopes to become a fashionable physician one day.'

By this time, the number of carriages was dwindling and Dr Dangerfield asked Amaryllis where she would like to go next. She did not know what to suggest, until she remembered Mr Yardley's enthusiastic description of Belgravia.

'Oh, I *should* like to see Mr Cubitt's development at Belgravia,' she said eagerly.

'Belgravia?'

Her face fell. 'Oh, is it very far away?'

'No, no. It's just on the edge of the park over there. But . . . wouldn't you like to go somewhere more rural? There's some very pretty countryside at Kensington.'

But Amaryllis was not to be put off. 'No, I really would like to see Belgravia. I'm interested in it from a business point of view. If it's not too much trouble.'

'Oh, no trouble at all,' he answered with his ready smile. 'I'd be happy to go there.'

She leant forward in her seat, determined to miss nothing, as the carriage turned out of the park past Apsley House. They soon reached a desolate region covered with mounds of earth and jagged heaps of brick and stone. This gave way to a more ordered territory, where the ground had been levelled and cleared and building plots of impressive dimensions had been staked out with a labyrinth of string and a small forest of wooden markers. They drove past embryo buildings in various stages of development, some a mere skeleton of timber scaffolding, others fleshed out with brick and stone and then, at last, they turned a corner and came upon a great avenue of completed houses, stretching away into the distance.

Amaryllis gave a gasp of delight as she saw the shining terraces, six, eight, ten stories high, their cream-painted stucco gleaming in the sunlight against a bright blue autumn sky. Not all Mr Yardley's enthusiastic descriptions had prepared her for the size and splendour of the reality. The contrast with the shabby brick tenements of Pembroke Street was so sharp that it was hard to believe they were part of the same city.

The carriage came to a halt before a barrier and the barkeeper subjected them to a severe scrutiny before he waved them on. Amaryllis looked about her in awed admiration as they drove down the avenue, their wheels making little noise on the smooth macadamized surface of the road. There was a hushed silence about the great terraces which spoke of extreme luxury. No hawkers or street entertainers were allowed to disturb their dignified repose and no shops or public houses disfigured their immaculate cream façades, although here and there a touch of colour was provided by window boxes spilling over with exotic flowers or awnings of dark green or rose colour protecting costly furnishings from the sun.

The carriage turned out of the avenue and made the circuit of a majestic square, its gardens full of mature trees and shrubs. Amaryllis looked at them in surprise and asked Dr Dangerfield when the square had been built.

'About two years ago, I think – ah,' he smiled, 'you're looking at the trees. All imported, ready grown, from Cubitt's own nurseries. Incredible, isn't it?'

'I think it's wonderful.' Amaryllis fell silent again. The great Italianate façades looked in the sunlight like some splendid Renaissance city, except that no Renaissance city was as calm and clean as this one. Poverty and squalor had been banished; the air was fresh; even the pavements were spotless.

Amaryllis returned to Pembroke Street and spent the evening dreaming of new cities, each more wonderful than the last. Her head full of magnificent Belgravian terraces, she covered sheet after sheet of paper with a series of very inadequate sketch plans for wholly unpractical developments, consisting largely of grand avenues and showing no grasp of drainage.

In the first flush of excitement over Belgravia, Dr Dangerfield had been pushed to the back of Amaryllis's mind, but as she lay in bed that night his handsome features began to outline themselves in the darkness and Amaryllis smiled as she remembered the pressure of his hand as he helped her out of the carriage.

Eighteen

Lord Vanbrugh's drive in the park had given him a good deal to think about when he returned to his rooms in Jermyn Street. His sister Georgiana, cold and furious, had avoided him since his disclosures about her dowry, but when it became generally known that they were both in London, she had suggested a drive in the park for appearance's sake. Lord Vanbrugh, whose conscience was not entirely easy about her, had agreed to this proposal and accepted a seat in her godmother's carriage. He had had his reward. Lord Mayo, coming across them in Rotten Row, had cut them dead, his blond moustaches bristling with resentment.

'What a fool that man is,' Lord Vanbrugh had commented to his sister. 'He should have come up and complimented you on your hat. That would have scotched the rumours.'

'It would take more than a few compliments to do that,' Georgiana had answered. Several of her acquaintances had already given her disapproving glances and she had taken care to pass them on, with interest, to her brother.

But Georgiana was not Lord Vanbrugh's only problem. He had been startled to see Amaryllis in the park and very disturbed by the presence of a handsome young man in her carriage. He had known, of course, that it would not be long before other men appeared on the scene, but rivals of Henry Chesil's calibre he could dismiss from his calculations. This man was different. Extremely good looking, he represented a threat. He was probably not rich enough to induce Amaryllis to become his mistress, but he might offer her marriage, in Lord Vanbrugh's eyes a much more irreparable disaster.

As he dwelt on the memory of Amaryllis's flushed face gazing down at him from her carriage, the determination to possess her overwhelmed him once more. Impossible she might be – naive, selfish, spoilt and greedy – there were a thousand whores in London more accomplished than she, but none at this moment more desirable. Her resentful independence, while it enraged him, also tantalized him. He was determined to subdue her so that he could settle back into his accustomed ways and despise his women in comfort.

Amaryllis, meanwhile, spent much of the next day closeted with Mr Yardley, going over his estimates for Number Eleven. He left shortly after tea and she decided to spend the rest of the afternoon visiting Lucy Fletcher to find out why she had behaved so strangely when she had seen her with Dr Dangerfield.

Lucy answered the door in a yellow silk dress, her hair loose down her back and a hairbrush in her hand.

'Oh it's you, is it? Come in and take a seat. I'm just dressing to go out. You were lucky – catching me in at this hour.'

'It won't take long,' said Amaryllis. 'I just wanted to ask you – why did you walk straight past me when I was out with Dr Dangerfield yesterday? Didn't you see me?'

Lucy went back to pinning and smoothing her black curls. 'I saw you all right,' she said, through a mouthful of hairpins, 'but if I *had* smiled back at you, Dr Dangerfield would have noticed.'

'Well, what of it?'

Lucy spat the hairpins out into her hand. 'He'd have fainted – dead away – to think you knew a street woman!'

'But he wouldn't mind – would he?'

'Mind? Of course he would! But don't let that worry you, most of them do. He's not special.' She peered into the mirror as she dabbed pearl powder on her cheeks, 'If *I* had a man like that, I'd let him think what he pleased. Did he kiss you?'

'No,' Amaryllis admitted regretfully.

'No, I suppose he wouldn't, would he. Not the first time. Or even the second, I daresay.' Lucy picked up her hat and fixed it on her head with a glittering pin. 'I must be off. Now what have I done with my gloves . . . ? ' She began to hunt through a pile of stockings heaped on a chair.

'You caused a fine old to do with your notices to quit,' she remarked suddenly. 'Tears, shrieks, we had the lot! Well, it was a bit hard, I must say. One week! What made you change your mind – the handsome doctor was it?'

Amaryllis blushed. 'Not entirely . . . What do the other tenants think about it all?'

'Oh, they don't blame you really. They think you're just a girl. It's Yardley who's getting most of the black looks.'

'But that's not fair! I'm the landlord. It was *my* decision and I take full responsibility for it. Mr Yardley wanted four weeks' notice from the first.'

'Did he indeed? I had wondered. He always played fair in the past and I'd a feeling you'd a mind of your own. Oh well – it's all water under the bridge now.'

The next morning, a hackney cab drew up in Pembroke Street and a magnificent footman with white silk stockings alighted from it.

He advanced towards Number Ten, poked a letter gingerly beneath the door and then retreated into the cab again, which drove off at once in a westerly direction.

The letter, when Bella brought it upstairs, proved to be written on the best gilt-edged paper. It conveyed the information that Miss Vanbrugh would be happy to receive Miss Vaughan at Number Eight, South Street, to discuss a matter of some urgency. A carriage would collect Miss Vaughan from Pembroke Street at eleven o'clock on the following morning. Miss Vanbrugh trusted that Miss Vaughan would find it convenient to call at that hour. If not, another time could be arranged.

Resentful at this high-handed invitation, Amaryllis entered the carriage in an aggressive mood the next morning. The coachman had not been impressed by Pembroke Street and he took several wrong turnings, as if to emphasize the fact. At last, however, he drew up before a tall, dignified house and a footman helped Amaryllis out of the carriage and into the hall.

She was received there by the butler, who eyed her rather as if she had been an unpromising scullery maid, and led her upstairs to a drawing-room on the first floor.

Amaryllis chose the most comfortable chair, settled herself into it and then gazed enviously about her. The room was furnished with great richness: velvet curtains swathed the windows, and the gilded furniture was heavily stuffed and padded. Amaryllis's admiring gaze wandered from bloated sofas to obese armchairs and rested on a tasselled footstool so plump it seemed about to burst open in the heat of the fire like an overripe fig.

She was still looking at her surroundings when the butler opened the door and her hostess entered the room.

Georgiana Vanbrugh was dressed in a morning gown of olive silk with a falling collar fastened by a brooch in the shape of a crescent moon. She bowed distantly to her guest and moved towards an armchair near the window, gesturing Amaryllis to a seat opposite hers.

'It is advisable to sit near the window when discussing private matters,' she observed. 'One never knows when servants are listening at the door.'

She waited until Amaryllis had seated herself and then said coolly, 'No doubt you are wondering why I have asked you to visit me, Miss Vaughan. Of course, we have never met, but I saw you in the park on Sunday.' She paused for a moment, looking closely at Amaryllis, who wisely remained silent.

'Before I explain the reason for my invitation to you,' Georgiana went on, 'I should like to make two things clear. First of all, Miss Vaughan, I am well aware of the nature of your profession. I am still a young woman but I have not led a sheltered life and I don't propose to waste my time and yours with any false modesty on the subject. Secondly, I know of your relationship with my brother, in payment for which he gave you his properties in Pembroke Street.'

'Only Numbers Nine to Twelve,' Amaryllis demurred. 'He still owns the rest of the street.'

'I am sorry, I should have said his unencumbered properties – all the others are so heavily mortgaged they bring in no income to speak of. But even Numbers Nine to Twelve were encumbered in a sense, Miss Vaughan. When my father died, the estate was so burdened with debt that he was obliged to leave provision for me to my brother's discretion and Anthony promised me those properties in Pembroke Street for my dowry. My engagement to Lord Mayo was to have been announced last month, but when I discovered that my dowry had been given to you I was obliged to draw back from the contract, knowing that my prospective husband would not be able to marry a portionless woman. I am left,' she continued levelly, 'with nothing but a few fields to my name and I am obliged to live here, in my godmother's house, on an income barely sufficient to cover the cost of my dresses, and with no prospect of ever marrying.'

'I'm sorry,' said Amaryllis, cautiously, since she was wondering why Georgiana was telling her all this. But one thing was certain; Lord Vanbrugh had behaved disgracefully as usual. Looking at Georgiana, she felt a flicker of fellow feeling.

'I shall come to the point now, Miss Vaughan. I am appealing to you. Give me back my dowry and enable me to marry. Lord Mayo is an influential man and you may be sure I won't forget my obligations to you.'

Amaryllis thought that Georgiana might as well have been reciting the multiplication table for all the emotion she showed.

'I am not suggesting that you beggar yourself, of course,' Georgiana continued. 'I know my brother already regrets ending your relationship. He made that clear by his attentions to you on Sunday. He'd take you back tomorrow if I smoothed the way a little, and to be the mistress of Lord Vanbrugh is no mean thing, I imagine? Better than life in Pembroke Street at all events.'

'I'm sorry for you, Miss Vanbrugh. Your brother has treated you very badly, that's plain enough. But I can't give you back your dowry. You say that without it you can't marry. Well, I can't marry either, now I've lived with your brother, and those properties are my only means of support.'

'You've your profession as well, I imagine,' said Georgiana coldly.

'I gave your brother a fair bargain,' said Amaryllis angrily. 'Ask Lord Vanbrugh for your dowry. He's the one who's stolen it from you!'

'My brother is the most selfish man alive where his relatives are concerned,' stated Georgiana calmly. 'I'll get nothing from him, you may make up your mind to that! But to his mistresses he is generosity itself–as you've reason to know. Four London houses in return for one virginity – a little excessive, isn't it?'

'I don't find it so!'

'No doubt. I am not a fool, Miss Vaughan. You appear to be to be fully in control of your wits and of well above average intelligence. I don't for one moment imagine that you are an injured innocent, any more than I suppose my brother was your unwilling victim. I am well aware that the major part of the blame lies with Anthony, but you too were responsible for the loss of my dowry. Your demands from him were extortionate.'

'Lord Vanbrugh knew quite well what he was doing. Why should I be blamed? I didn't even know it was your dowry he was spending!'

Her protests left Georgiana unmoved. 'I hold you to blame, Miss Vaughan.'

Looking at the bitter expression in Georgiana's grey eyes, Amaryllis did not doubt it.

That evening Amaryllis was sitting, listless and gloomy, in the last of the daylight, when the lamplighter came down the darkening street. As he attended to the lamp opposite Number Ten, the parlour filled with a faint soft glow, reminding Amaryllis that it was time to light the oil lamp. Then she went into the bedroom and lowered the blind. She was just turning away again, when she heard a faint tapping on the window. Thinking that perhaps it was a bird, she drew up the blind again, raised the sash and looked out. She could see very little in the twilight and was about to draw in her head again when she heard a flat voice speak her name.

Amaryllis conquered the impulse to slam down the window and retreat into the parlour.

'Where are you?' she said, not quite as calmly as she would have liked.

'In the next house,' said Cutler, out of the shadows. 'The workmen left a ladder. I'm at the window next to yours, Miss Vaughan. I want my money. My Bella's wages, the poor hardworking soul. I was sure you'd have them ready.'

'I've told you – you'll get nothing from me!' Amaryllis very much wished she could see him, but though she craned her neck towards Number Eleven she could make out nothing in the darkness.

'These houses!' said Cutler, 'Lord Vanbrugh's, weren't they?'

'Until I bought them.'

'Bought them! He was the one who did the buying . . . I could make trouble for you over that. But you give me my due and I'll keep silent.'

'I bought the houses!' said Amaryllis desperately.

Cutler laughed. 'Bella knows what will happen if you don't pay me. You ask her. She'll tell you. I'll give you time to think about it. Just a little time. But if I don't hear from you soon, I shall have to take steps and then you'll wish you'd paid me the first time I asked.'

Nineteen

At last, after what seemed to Amaryllis an endless four weeks, the tenants moved out of Number Eleven and the workmen moved in. They ripped great holes in the roof, tore down rotting joists and beams and destroyed a good deal of plaster in the process. To Amaryllis the confusion seemed hopeless, but Mr Yardley assured her that it was quite usual and things would soon sort themselves out.

Events proved him right. By the middle of the third week, two of the apartments had already been completed and were ready for occupation. Amaryllis was delighted with them and spent a whole morning sniffing up the satisfying fragrances of wood shavings, varnish and fresh paint, and asking the long-suffering Mr Yardley innumerable questions.

'Has anyone asked to see the rooms yet?' she said.

Mr Yardley shook his head. 'No, but I had a word with Miss Forrest and she's recommended a friend of hers who she says is very quiet and well spoken.'

'Good. We don't want anyone bringing back a stream of drunken clients like that slut at Number Thirty.'

'I understand,' said Mr Yardley, choosing his words carefully, 'that the lady has a private connection. There's no shortage of money. She'll take the best apartment.' He broke off and listened for a moment. 'I think I hear someone coming up the stairs.'

Amaryllis darted out onto the landing. 'It's not a tenant,' she called back to him. 'It's Dr Dangerfield . . . Good morning, Doctor.' She leaned over the banister to smile at him. 'Have you come to inspect the new apartments? I warn you, they're very expensive.'

'Well, I thought I'd take a look – out of curiosity, if nothing else. How are you, Miss Vaughan? It's so long since I last saw you – ' He broke off in barely disguised vexation as Mr Yardley appeared in the doorway and gave him a friendly greeting.

'Dr Dangerfield has come to inspect our alterations,' said Amaryllis hurriedly. 'I'll show him round, shall I? You must be busy.'

'Well, I should like to have a word with Silas about that roof,' Mr Yardley admitted.

'Yes, of course. We'll start with the first floor so as not to get in your way.'

She led Dr Dangerfield downstairs to a high-ceilinged room, freshly papered in the latest style. It was provided with gas lighting and a modern fireplace which, if not quite marble, was a passable imitation.

'This used to be the Salisburys' apartment,' Amaryllis explained. 'It's quite transformed, isn't it?'

'Yes indeed,' said Dr Dangerfield. 'I wouldn't have known it for the same room. What's happened to that enormous old carved fireplace they used to have?'

'Boarded up.' Amaryllis tapped the wall around the new fireplace, which gave off a faint hollow sound. 'You'd never guess it, would you? It looks completely modern. But it's there all right, underneath.'

'You couldn't demolish it altogether?'

'Not without bringing the house down.'

'A pity. Those old fireplaces are very inconvenient. I remember Miss Salisbury telling me what trouble she had with it. I'm sure she's more comfortable in Number Ten. It was good of you to arrange it for her, Miss Vaughan.'

Amaryllis smiled sweetly at the compliment, her lashes modestly lowered. She meant to make the most of this chance of being alone with Dr Dangerfield. Since their drive to Belgravia, they had had several chance encounters in the street, but their meetings were always in public since Amaryllis dared not invite him up to her rooms alone for fear of shocking him. She moved to allow a patch of sunlight to gild her hair. 'I do hope the move hasn't damaged Miss Salisbury's health?'

Dr Dangerfield was about to reassure her, when they heard the front door open. A woman's voice called out, 'Is anyone there?'

A tapping of heels and a swish of silken skirts announced that the owner of the voice was mounting the stairs. Amaryllis reluctantly went out onto the landing just as a good-looking woman with an ample figure reached the last stair and came to a halt, panting slightly.

'Can I help you?' inquired Amaryllis, rather coldly.

'I've come to view,' the lady explained. 'I saw the notice in passing and I thought it just *might* be what I'm looking for. The door was open, so I ventured in . . .'

'Yes, of course,' said Amaryllis, much more cordially. 'I should be happy to show you round. We have several apartments available, all freshly decorated to a very high standard. My name is Vaughan, by the way. I'm the owner of this property. And this is my builder, Mr Yardley,' she added as he came down the stairs towards them. After a cursory glance the lady paid him no further attention, but her reaction was quite different when Dr Dangerfield joined the group on the landing. She gave him an admiring stare and followed it up with an inviting smile. Receiving no response, she returned to Amaryllis.

'Mrs or Miss Vaughan?'

'Miss Vaughan.' Amaryllis looked inquiringly at the lady who said readily, 'My name is Parsons, Mrs Parsons. A widow.'

Amaryllis, looking at Mrs Parson's bright silks, thought that she did not look at all like a widow. Mr Yardley's face was unreadable, but from Dr Dangerfield's supercilious look she guessed that he shared her opinion. 'I'm so sorry to hear it,' she murmured.

Mrs Parsons extracted a lace-trimmed handkerchief from her pocket and applied it to her eyes, casting Dr Dangerfield a coquettish look as she did so. He looked away, a frown gathering. Mrs Parsons gave a mock pout and then addressed Amaryllis again. 'My friend Mrs Wilson, in Number Thirty-one happened to mention there were rooms to let and thought they might suit me. But knowing I'm very *particular* in my tastes, she told me I couldn't do better than see for myself. I must say,' she looked Dr Dangerfield up and down, 'they do seem *very* nice, very nice indeed . . . ' and she flicked imaginary dust from the bosom of her gown.

Amaryllis stifled a giggle at the sight of the doctor's red face and said hastily, 'I'm glad you like them. Come this way and I'll show you our ground-floor apartments.'

'All right . . . ' said Mrs Parsons, clearly reluctant to leave Dr Dangerfield. 'Unless one of the gentlemen would care to escort us . . . ? ' But neither of the gentlemen showing the least desire to do so, she was obliged to follow Amaryllis unattended.

Dr Dangerfield, meanwhile, accompanied Mr Yardley upstairs to the third floor with a thunderous expression on his face. 'That woman's a prostitute!'

'Yes, almost certainly, I should think.'

'Then what the devil do you mean by allowing her to associate with Miss Vaughan!'

'Miss Vaughan is my employer,' said Mr Yardley stolidly. 'It's not for me to control her actions.'

'She's an innocent girl and you know it! You've a duty to protect her from such women!' Mr Yardley making no attempt to defend himself, Dr Dangerfield's anger grew. 'I see your game of course! Trading on Miss Vaughan's innocence to secure higher paying tenants and a fatter commission!'

Mr Yardley gave him a very stern look but all he said was, 'Miss Vaughan needs the income.'

'Then you should shield her from her tenants! Housing them at all is bad enough, but allowing Miss Vaughan to show them round, speak to them, go anywhere near them . . . by God, it's scandalous!'

'It's not for me to interfere.'

'You're contemptible!' shouted Dr Dangerfield. 'She's an inexperienced girl! She looks to you for advice and this is the treatment she gets! Well, not for much longer, if I have anything to say in the matter!' And he flung out of the room.

Mr Yardley was still where the doctor had left him, when Amaryllis came upstairs alone a few minutes later. She was very apologetic about Dr Dangerfield's outburst.

'We could hear him all the way downstairs, and I'm afraid

he was dreadfully rude to you – and to Mrs Parsons, of course. She was furious at first but I think that she'll take the rooms just the same. I'm sorry Dr Dangerfield was so ridiculous. You should have told him it was my idea to let to prostitutes in the first place.'

'I don't think Dr Dangerfield would be at all happy to hear that the scheme was yours,' said Mr Yardley quietly.

A few days later Amaryllis and Bella had just finished supper when there was a frantic knocking on the door and Mr Salisbury came in.

'It's my sister, Miss Vaughan – she's having a dreadful attack! Could your servant go for a doctor? Here's the address . . . I wouldn't ask you, but it's urgent. I daren't leave her!'

Bella took the address and swiftly departed.

'Come down and see her,' Mr Salisbury begged Amaryllis. 'I'm so helpless in these situations but another lady . . . I *know* she will feel more comfortable if you're there. The first attack is over but the main one always follows. *Please* come, Miss Vaughan.'

'Very well,' she said reluctantly, 'I'll do what I can.'

Mr Salisbury led the way downstairs and Amaryllis followed him, feeling singularly helpless. She entered the sickroom half afraid of what she might find there. Having no experience of invalids, at first she thought the figure propped up in an armchair by the fire must be dying, she looked so pale and wan. Her exhausted face seemed half-drowning in her hair and her breath came in gasps. Guiltily, Amaryllis remembered that this was the woman she had been proposing to evict.

'It's Miss Vaughan, Eliza,' whispered Mr Salisbury. 'Come to stay with you till you're better. I've sent for the doctor. He'll be here soon, I'm sure.'

Amaryllis withdrew to a seat near the door and silence fell in the shabby little room, broken only by Mr Salisbury stirring the fire. He glanced incessantly at the door and once or twice started up at an imaginary knock. Amaryllis found herself praying that the doctor would come soon. Bella had been gone a full fifteen minutes though the doctor only lived in Wardour Street. There must be some reason for this awful delay. What ever should she do if Miss Salisbury had another attack before the doctor arrived?

After a further interminable five minutes, there was a soft knock on the door and Bella entered at last, followed not by the Salisburys' physician but by Dr Dangerfield, wearing his black frock-coat and carrying a leather drugs case in one hand.

'Your man was out on a deathbed case,' she told Mr Salisbury, 'so I brought Dr Dangerfield instead.'

The doctor shook hands with Mr Salisbury in a reassuring fashion, and gave Amaryllis a smile of recognition before he went over to his patient and took her pulse. But no sooner had he done so than Miss Salisbury was racked by another paroxysm, her body arching forward, shuddering and choking. Bella leapt to her side and helped the doctor support her as she coughed up bright red blood. Her brother hovered about her, ineffectual and despairing, and Amaryllis watched them all with frightened eyes.

The attack seemed endess. There was no conversation in the room; only the sound of Miss Salisbury's gasping breath, while Bella and Dr Dangerfield supported her wordlessly and tirelessly and her brother chafed her hands in a frenzy of anxiety. At last, after two in the morning by St Martin's clock, Miss Salisbury had fallen asleep and the attack was over. Amaryllis got to her feet and cautiously turned up the lamp a little. She looked up and saw Dr Dangerfield's weary eyes upon her.

'Come upstairs and I'll give you some coffee,' she said softly. 'You must be tired to death. Bella – you stay down here and help Mr Salisbury.'

Dr Dangerfield followed her upstairs to the kitchen where the fire sent ruddy lights flickering over the whitewashed walls and the cat lay drowsing by the hearth. With a sigh of relief he collapsed into a chair and flexed his tired shoulders.

'Should I send Bella for the Salisburys' own doctor again?' Amaryllis asked when the coffee was made and she had brought it to the table.

He shrugged wearily. 'He should be told, of course, but

tomorrow morning will do for that. There's nothing he or anyone can do to help her. There's no cure for consumption.'

'But surely there's *something* you can do.'

'Oh, of course there is,' he said, with a bitterness that surprised her. 'I can take her pulse and support her through an attack and mix a few useless inhalations. I can inspire confidence in her relations and allow them to believe for a few days longer that there's some hope left . . . Our profession is three-quarters fraud. We're someone to turn to in a crisis, that's all. Nine times out of ten we can't *do* anything . . . '

He broke off and stared at Amaryllis, who had quite forgotten to be demure and was pouring out the coffee in her crumpled dress without sweet smiles or lowered eyelids. Normally, Dr Dangerfield would have found this change disturbing, but after his hopeless struggle with a disease he could not alleviate, he was briefly freed from his conventional self. Amaryllis, in her turn, as she watched the firelight flicker on the walls, was conscious of a tension and expectancy which filled the shadowy room, enveloping them both. With Dr Dangerfield she felt none of the aggression Lord Vanbrugh had aroused, only the exciting conviction that soon her arms would be around him and his lips would meet hers.

Dr Dangerfield was never quite certain of what happened next. The fire spluttered and a glowing coal fell on the hearth. He and Amaryllis both leapt up to attend to it but he got there first and kicked it back into the fire. Then he turned, and either Amaryllis moved towards him or he seized her – he hardly knew and once she was in his arms he didn't care. All that mattered was kissing her eager lips and gripping her body against his . . . Bella's heavy footsteps sounded on the stairs; he gave a groan as he felt Amaryllis pull herself away. With an immense effort he regained his self-control, stammered that he must go, and turned and ran out of the room. Amaryllis, trembling a little, stared angrily at Bella, who sat down and poured herself a cup of coffee.

'Well!' she said, grinning a little. 'Where's he off to in such a hurry?'

'You might have had the sense to stay downstairs till you're called for!'

'Interrupt something, did I? Dear, oh dear. Your hair's in a shocking mess.'

Amaryllis pulled out the remaining pins and shook her hair down over her shoulders.

'You came up here deliberately!'

'Well I don't take to that young man.'

'It's none of your business!'

'I wanted some coffee,' said Bella. She sipped her coffee consideringly. 'Of the two, I prefer Lord Vanbrugh. He's got more meat to him somehow.'

'Lord Vanbrugh's got nothing to do with it! That was a business matter. This isn't.'

'You never said a truer word. Your doctor hasn't a penny to his name.'

'He doesn't need it. *He's* quite attractive enough without it!'

'Is he indeed? I knew how it would be, of course. It's always the same with your sort. One man after another. Lord Vanbrugh, Henry Chesil, Dr Dangerfield; three of them in as many months – shameless!'

'I'm not shameless! It's not my fault all those others kept pestering me. *I* didn't want them to. But Dr Dangerfield's different; he's so handsome and charming . . . '

'Sounds too good to be true. I like a man who shows you his worst side straight off. That way you know where you are.'

'Some men haven't *got* a worse side!'

'Everyone's got a worse side,' said Bella.

Twenty

Amaryllis was in high spirits at breakfast the next morning.

'I've been thinking,' she said as she bit into a large slice of bread and butter, 'I ought to have a dinner-party. After spending all that money on furnishing the dining-room it seems silly not to use it.'

'There's something in that,' said Bella. 'Though *I* can't cook for it – not unless you buy a kitchen range as well.'

'No, we'll order the food in from somewhere. The Royal George has a good reputation; we'll try them.'

'And who are you going to ask?'

'Well, that is a bit difficult,' said Amaryllis, teasing the cat with a crust of her bread. 'I know so few people in London. And no women – at least not the sort I could invite to dinner . . . There's Mr Yardley of course, I'll *certainly* ask him. And perhaps Mr Rugby; lawyers always come in useful some time or other. But I don't want to make it *too* businesslike . . . ' Amaryllis avoided Bella's eye, 'so I thought I'd ask Dr Dangerfield as well.'

'Yes,' said Bella, 'I wondered when we were going to get round to him.'

Later that morning, Dr Dangerfield called. Amaryllis was writing a letter when he was announced and she threw down her pen and jumped up delightedly. But Dr Dangerfield was not looking at her. He stood just inside the door, his face pale and his lips tightly set together. Amaryllis stopped dead; her smile faded.

'Miss Vaughan,' said Dr Dangerfield, in a low anxious voice, 'I've come to offer you my deepest apologies for what took place last night.'

Amaryllis stared at him in astonishment.

'I took advantage of your hospitality, forced myself on you – it was wholly contemptible!' His hand reached behind him for the door knob, as if he expected instant dismissal.

'But I didn't mind . . . ' Amaryllis began.

He wasn't listening to her. 'I can only beg you to forgive me!'

Amaryllis was hardly able to believe her ears. He'd been quite as much kissed against as kissing.

'Of course I forgive you – but there's nothing to forgive!'

'It's like your generosity to say so. But you must let me be the judge.'

Amaryllis looked at Dr Dangerfield's averted face in perplexity. Had she done wrong? It was very hard. She'd have loved to have kissed him again. She'd been thinking of little else all morning.

'Miss Vaughan,' he said hesitantly, 'would you permit me to visit you still, in spite of last night?'

'Yes, of course, I should be happy to see you.'

Dr Dangerfield's hand left the door knob. He moved forward a little way into the room. 'I wish you were not so alone and unprotected in London! You have no family to take care of you?'

'No, none,' said Amaryllis, lying firmly.

Dr Dangerfield looked at her keenly for a moment. Amaryllis quivered in anticipation.

'I wish I could introduce you to my mother,' said Dr Dangerfield earnestly.

Amaryllis swallowed her disappointment as best she could. 'That would be very nice.'

'She's visiting relations at the moment. But I know she'll want to meet you when she returns next month.'

There was rather a heavy pause. Then Amaryllis said with forced brightness, 'I'm giving a dinner-party on Friday. I should be so glad if you could come.'

'I should be delighted,' he said. His very blue eyes rested

lingeringly on her face. Amaryllis waited hopefully.

'I must go,' he said suddenly. 'We'll meet again on Friday, Miss Vaughan, and I promise you that what took place last night won't occur again.'

Amaryllis managed a smile and Dr Dangerfield turned to go. Then, seeing her hand outstretched to say goodbye, he suddenly turned back, seized it, pressed it to his mouth in a hard kiss and was gone, leaving Amaryllis staring at her hand, as if she half expected his lips to have left a mark.

She sat down at her desk and had taken up her pen again when Bella stumped in.

'Here's another one!' she announced. 'It's Lord Vanbrugh this time.'

'Oh *Bella*!' said Amaryllis angrily, 'why didn't you say I was out?'

'Possibly because you weren't,' said Lord Vanbrugh, striding into the room and shutting the door behind Bella.

'What do *you* want?'

'I'm calling on you,' Lord Vanbrugh pitched his greatcoat into a chair and perched himself on the edge of the desk, 'as a fellow landlord.'

Amaryllis moved her chair away from him.

'Bentley tells me the whole street's in an uproar over Number Eleven.'

'Oh no, it isn't,' said Amaryllis crossly. 'Pembroke Street's always been notorious. That's why you sent me here. Remember?'

'Oh, I'm not talking about the morality of the enterprise,' said Lord Vanbrugh promptly. 'It's the rents you're charging, Amaryllis. Outrageously high, by all accounts.'

'Number Eleven has been repaired and redecorated throughout . . . '

'*Still* outrageous.'

'You know very well prostitutes pay more! They always have. They certainly did when *you* owned Number Eleven!'

'True. But I'm not one of the sisterhood. I'm entitled to my full share of moral indignation. But there's a certain irony in the situation where *you're* concerned.'

'You may not *be* a whore, but you certainly use them. What's the difference?'

'I'm a man,' said Lord Vanbrugh. 'Purity is the woman's province.'

After Dr Dangerfield's visit, Amaryllis was in no mood for this sort of remark. She lost her temper.

'Why don't you go away and stop *pestering* me? I've got work to do!'

'I shouldn't throw me out just yet. I had another reason for calling. No, Amaryllis, *listen* to me. This is important. And take that nasty look off your face!'

Amaryllis's expression relaxed a little. 'Oh very well, I suppose you won't go away till you've told me. Go on – I'm listening.'

He took her hand. She pulled it away and he made no attempt to recapture it.

'I want you to come back to me.'

'Oh, you do, do you?'

'Don't you want to know why?'

'I can guess.'

'Well, why?'

'You probably want Pembroke Street back.'

He laughed. 'No, I don't hope for the impossible. It's you I want back, not Pembroke Street.' Amaryllis gave him a sceptical glance. 'You don't believe me?' he asked.

She shrugged. 'You told me at Vanbrugh, you didn't want *me* particularly. Any woman would have done, you said.'

'Forget all that. I want you all right. Why else should I bother with you?'

'Well, I don't want you!' said Amaryllis. 'I've more important things to occupy my mind.'

At this, Lord Vanbrugh's jealousy got the better of his self-control. 'Ah yes, so you have. Bentley told me that doctor of yours had been to see him. Casually, of course. Just to chat about whether you owned the freehold of Pembroke Street . . . I'm surprised at you, Amaryllis. You, of all people, to fall into the hands of a fortune-hunter! Not much of a fortune, of course, but more than that snivelling little doctor could lay his hands on by his own efforts!'

'I shouldn't sneer at him, if I were you! Money's got *you* what you wanted before now!'

Lord Vanbrugh gave her a look of hatred. 'Hot for him, are you?' he asked viciously.'

'He's extremely handsome,' said Amaryllis. Her reminiscent smile proved too much for Lord Vanbrugh.

'You *devil*!' he shouted.

Before Amaryllis had time to struggle or protest, he had seized the paperknife from her desk, thrust her onto the sofa, pushed her skirts out of the way and with unhesitating savagery slashed five shallow cuts on her thigh: his initials in bright red blood.

'There!' he panted, his voice shaking with fury. 'Marked as mine! When that damned doctor beds you, he'll see I was there before him!'

'You filthy brute!' shrieked Amaryllis. She was so beside herself with anger that the words choked in her throat. She made a sudden effort to gain possession of the knife which he still held cold against her skin. But he hurled it away, so that it inscribed a shining arc in the air and struck, quivering upright, in the carpet.

'You won't murder me this time,' he said jeeringly.

'I can wait!' snarled Amaryllis. 'Let me go!'

Lord Vanbrugh took his hands away, surprised to find them trembling. Amaryllis would not even look at him. Numb with rage, she found a handkerchief and began mechanically to soak up the threads of blood. Then she started to laugh. She looked across at Lord Vanbrugh, her eyes bright with contempt.

'Those initials of yours, that were supposed to frighten off my lovers – they're my initials too!'

Lord Vanbrugh did not stay to be laughed at. He leapt to his feet and left the room without another word, slamming the door behind him with a ferocity that shook the house.

Twenty-one

Dusk was falling, when Bella came into the parlour where Amaryllis was sitting brooding by the fire.

'Dr Dangerfield . . . ' she began.

'Oh, is he here?' asked Amaryllis eagerly.

' . . . has left this for you,' finished Bella, handing her a letter before going away again, with a disapproving shake of the head.

Amaryllis opened the letter, a little sulky that he had not called instead of writing. She read it with dawning delight. It contained a proposal of marriage.

Amaryllis hugged herself gleefully. Dr Dangerfield was within her grasp at last! All she had to do was write a letter of acceptance. And once respectably engaged, surely he'd forget the proprieties. She'd be able to kiss him until her lips were sore. And once they were married . . . Amaryllis felt a sudden qualm. Well, never mind. He need never know. Bella would show her what to do . . . And as for Lord Vanbrugh – maybe this would show him she wasn't his property any longer. Even he would stop plaguing her if he knew she was married to another man. Though perhaps it wouldn't do to tell him just yet. He had it in his power to make things very difficult for her. If Dr Dangerfield found out the truth about her relations with Lord Vanbrugh, would he still want to marry her? Thinking over his past behaviour, Amaryllis was very much afraid he would not. As she wrote her letter of acceptance, Amaryllis modestly suggested to her betrothed that it might be as well to keep their engagement a secret, until his mother returned to give them her blessing.

Amaryllis had assumed that Dr Dangerfield would answer her acceptance in person, and was very disappointed when Bella brought up another letter. 'My dearest,' Dr Dangerfield had written,

> Your answer has made me the happiest of men. Only the fear of compromising your reputation prevents me from coming to pour out my heart to you in person. If only my mother were here to chaperone you! But we shall meet at your dinner-party, my darling, and I shall have the joy of knowing that you are entirely mine! Of course I understand the motives which prompt you to keep our engagement secret, but we must be married very soon. I once thought that to know you loved me would be bliss enough. Now I find it is torment, waiting until I can call you my wife . . .

Amaryllis flung down the letter in disgust.

Friday seemed an eternity away, but it came at last. Shortly before eight o'clock, Amaryllis stood before the fire, waiting for her guests' arrival, wearing one of the evening gowns Mr Chesil had provided. The dress was of rose-coloured satin, very full in the skirt, its low-cut bodice edged with a deep fall of lace.

The dining-room was full of candlelight, gleaming on the polished table. Amaryllis stayed there for a moment, drawing comfort from her new white and gold dinner service. But she was too restless to remain long. She straightened a couple of forks and returned to the parlour again. Here, the candles had not yet been lighted and there was only the red glow of the fire. Amaryllis lingered by the window, pulling up the blind and looking idly out on the gaslit street. After a while, Lucy Fletcher came in sight, hanging on the arm of a stout, middle-aged man. She was laughing too much and talking too loudly. Across the street, a lady gave her one disgusted glance and quickened her step. The man accompanying her took care not to look in Lucy's direction.

Amaryllis pulled down the blind with a snap, turned away from the window and lit all the candles. Dr Dangerfield would get her out of this. *He'd* make her respectable once more: a respectable married woman. If only Lord Vanbrugh kept his mouth shut . . .

Her anguished thoughts were cut short by the arrival of her first guest, Mr Rugby the solicitor, a serious young man with a slight stoop. He seemed alarmed at being the first, but managed to utter a few disjointed remarks until Mr Yardley appeared, when he took courage and mentioned that Dr Dangerfield might be a little late.

'He had a man with him, when I looked round his door just now, a rather unsavoury character by the looks of him. Probably one of the Dispensary patients – I hope he won't keep him long.'

The words were hardly out of his mouth, when Bella came in, holding a letter.

'It's from Dr Dangerfield,' said Amaryllis, looking at the handwriting. 'Who delivered it, Bella?'

'No one,' said Bella. 'At least, he didn't wait to introduce himself. There was a knock on the door and I found this on the mat.'

'Oh,' said Amaryllis blankly. 'Well, I'd better read it, I suppose. Excuse me, gentlemen.' With a smile at her guests, she withdrew to the landing.

'Bella!' she said, turning the letter over, 'It's already been opened. Look! The seal's broken.'

'So it is. Nothing to do with me.'

Amaryllis was already spreading out the single sheet of paper.

> I have just been told of your connection with Lord Vanbrugh. My informant has given me irrefutable proofs – there can be no doubt in the matter. I am unspeakably shocked and distressed. I can never see you again and shall leave Pembroke Street tomorrow.
>
> Francis Dangerfield.

For a long moment, Amaryllis stood as if turned to stone. Then she thrust the letter at Bella.

'Lord Vanbrugh!' she hissed. 'This is all *his* doing!' Her desolation turned to rage.

'My cloak, quick!' she ordered.

'You can't go out at this time of night! And what about your guests?' protested Bella.

Amaryllis stamped her foot. 'Do as I say!'

The streets were full of people but Amaryllis was conscious of nothing but her furious purpose. She saw only a confusion of lights and carriages and paid no heed to the lecherous advances of gentlemen in opera cloaks or the obscene comments of the drunkards in the gutter. She reached her destination and hammered on the door until it was opened by a manservant. He led her upstairs to a room lined with pictures and after a moment Lord Vanbrugh came in with a look of surprise on his face.

'Well, well, Amaryllis. To what do I owe the honour of this visit?'

Amaryllis thrust the letter at him, her hood falling back to reveal her bright ringlets and her angry eyes.

'You know very well! There are *no* depths you wouldn't sink to! I thought you'd done your worst the last time I saw you – but it seems I was wrong! You make me want to vomit!'

Lord Vanbrugh started to answer in kind, but changed his mind and read the letter instead. His scowl turned to a pleased smile. He handed it back to Amaryllis.

'Excellent,' he said. 'But *I* had nothing to do with it.'

Amaryllis's gaze dropped to the letter clutched in her hand. Scrawled on the back in illiterate capitals was a message she hadn't noticed before: 'I WARNED YOU TO GIVE ME MY DUE.'

Amaryllis stared at it: Cutler. In her rage at Lord Vanbrugh she had forgotten him. She suddenly felt very much afraid. Well, she'd show Cutler he hadn't hurt her. *And* show Dr Dangerfield she didn't care what he thought of her. She shot a quick look at Lord Vanbrugh, her hatred of him lessening. Amaryllis took a desperate decision.

'You *must* dine with me this evening!'

Lord Vanbrugh looked surprised. 'Do you always deliver dinner invitations in such commanding tones?'

'You *must* come!'

'I must, must I? But I'm not at all sure that I want to. This is very sudden. You will have to explain yourself. Let me take your cloak.'

'There's no time! My guests are waiting and the dinner will spoil.'

Lord Vanbrugh paid no attention to this. He removed her cloak and looked approvingly at her dress. 'I'm so glad you're dressing like a civilized human being again.'

'Never mind my clothes! Do hurry!'

He gave a resigned sigh and called to his servant to bring him his cloak. With unusual deliberation, Lord Vanbrugh put it on, making several turns in front of the mirror to assure himself that it sat correctly on the shoulders. Amaryllis watched the proceedings with impatience and was about to lead the way downstairs again when Lord Vanbrugh stopped her.

'No, no, Amaryllis, we're not going yet.' He nodded to his servant, who left the room and came back carrying a hat. Lord Vanbrugh put it on.

'Yes, I think that will do . . . Where are you going, Amaryllis? I'm not *nearly* ready. My gloves,' he said to the servant, 'and my cane. The ebony cane, or would I prefer malacca? No, the ebony will do.'

Amaryllis waited with tapping foot until he had smoothed on his gloves and then she said, '*Now* are you ready?'

'Ready for what?' asked Lord Vanbrugh maddeningly.

'To go to Pembroke Street, to my *dinner-party*.'

'But my dear Amaryllis, I can't possibly come with you till I know the reason for this sudden invitation. I thought I'd made that perfectly plain.'

Amaryllis gave a furious sigh. 'Oh very well then! If you *must* know, one of my guests sent his regrets at the very last minute.' And again she tried to leave the room. He put out a hand to detain her.

'You're explaining things very badly, Amaryllis. *Which* guest and why does his absence matter so much?'

'You read the letter – it was Dr Dangerfield,' muttered Amaryllis, refusing to look at him. 'He's found out about you and now he's leaving Pembroke Street and I'll never see him again!' To her chagrin she ended on an angry sob.

'And you think inviting me to dinner will heal the breach, do you?'

'No, of course I don't!'

'Then why involve me at all . . . ? Ah! An act of defiance! Flaunting your lover in the eyes of a disapproving world!'

'You're not my lover!'

'No? But everyone will think so if I appear at your dinner table. I look forward to an amusing evening.'

Once out in the street, Lord Vanbrugh hailed a cab and they soon arrived in Pembroke Street. The door was opened immediately by Bella, who'd been waiting in growing anxiety for Amaryllis's return.

'Where have you been!' she said roughly as she took Amaryllis's cloak. 'Is that Dr Dangerfield with you?'

'Dr Dangerfield? Of course not! I wouldn't go grovelling to him! I've invited Lord Vanbrugh to dinner!' Ignoring Bella's startled gasp, Amaryllis swept past her up the stairs.

'Ah, Miss Vaughan, have you brought Dr Dangerfield back with you at last?' asked Mr Yardley, as she entered the parlour.

'No,' said Amaryllis with her sweetest smile. 'I'm afraid Dr Dangerfield won't be joining us tonight. He is unavoidably detained. But Lord Vanbrugh has kindly agreed to take his place.'

Amaryllis stood to one side and Lord Vanbrugh came into the room, looking very amused at the stunned silence his entrance created.

Twenty-two

The party sat down to dinner almost immediately. Amaryllis was keeping an eye on the waiter, Lord Vanbrugh was keeping an eye on Amaryllis, and Mr Rugby and Mr Yardley were both too embarrassed to attempt any conversation. From the moment Lord Vanbrugh walked into the room, they had known something was badly wrong. They drank their soup in silence, resolved to leave as soon as was decently possible.

But by the time the fish course appeared, things had improved. Amaryllis, remembering her duties as a hostess, managed to draw her guests into a discussion of the latest government scandal and they were soon talking naturally together. Even Lord Vanbrugh joined in the argument, and since his politics were diametrically opposed to everyone else's, all restraint had gone by the time they had finished the baked carp and the salmon in aspic.

Watching Amaryllis, sitting opposite him at the head of the table, Lord Vanbrugh was impressed by her self-control. That young fool of a doctor had clearly left her before their affair had come to anything. It was very satisfactory – exactly the result he wanted and he hadn't had to dirty his hands in the matter . . . But God, what a rage Amaryllis had been in!

Their plates were changed and a brace of roast pheasant appeared on the table, together with a crab, some Maintenon cutlets and a mould of vegetables. Lord Vanbrugh compared the meal in front of him with the dinner he had attended on the previous evening. On that splendid occasion, a blaze of light had revealed every corner of the dining-room, glinting on the rows of silver and glass at each place. The guests had sat rigidly upright, separated from each other by acres of damask across which they exchanged a few formal remarks, and course had succeeded course with the utmost smoothness and efficiency. At Amaryllis's dinner party, by way of contrast, the guests were restricted to one glass and knife and fork at a time, still warm from contact with hot water. There was no formality either. Her guests interrupted one another and put their elbows on the table, talking quickly and earnestly as if genuinely interested in the subjects under discussion.

The conversation soon turned to property and Lord Vanbrugh was taken aback to discover how much Amaryllis knew and alarmed to find that the other men respected her opinions. With that doctor out of the way, he'd hoped to have a clear field, but it looked as though a new rival had appeared: one much harder to dislodge. Amaryllis seemed to be fascinated by property and everything connected with it. When the subject of Belgravia came up, her response left no room for doubt on the matter.

'What I'd really like to know,' she said eagerly, 'is where Cubitt gets his capital from?'

'Well, Belgravia's special, of course,' answered Mr Yardley. 'It's being financed by a syndicate: City men chiefly. Earlier on in his career, he'd have borrowed money on mortgages, I suppose. That's how it's usually done.'

Mr Rugby nodded. 'A lot of my clients have money invested in building projects. Widows and retired officers and so on. It's a very safe investment if the builder's reliable and has property to secure the loan. I wouldn't take a risk on a new man, of course.'

'So if one has mortgageable properties . . . ' began Amaryllis excitedly.

'One can borrow money,' Lord Vanbrugh finished dryly. He knew, none better, the ease with which it could be done. Was Amaryllis in debt, he wondered? If so, she should be receptive to his offers of relief . . .

Amaryllis's next words dashed these hopes. 'And the land,' she demanded. 'How did Cubitt get the land? Did he buy it?'

Mr Yardley smiled. 'In the middle of London? No – that *would* be prohibitive. The land's leased to him – a building lease, it's called. He pays ground rent to the landlord, builds houses on the land and then lets them to his own tenants – at a much higher rent, of course.'

'But how does the ground landlord benefit from that?' asked Amaryllis.

'In the short term, the ground rent on a building lease is a good bit higher than it would be on an agricultural tenancy. In the long term, after ninety-nine years when the building lease runs out, the landlord gets his land back with houses built on it, all for free. That's where his real profit lies. He can't lose – the builder takes all the risk.'

'Oh, come now,' said Lord Vanbrugh, stirred to defend his fellow landowners. 'It's not all plain sailing for the ground landlords. They have to put up with a reduced ground rent at the start of the lease, remember. In some cases, no rent at all. And their short-term profits are negligible, compared to those of the builders.'

'Yes, but the builder takes all the risk,' said Mr Yardley. 'In a slump, hardly a week goes by without some builder going bankrupt. Besides, look at the landlord's long-term profits. Cubitt may be making a fortune out of Belgravia *now*, but it's a drop in the ocean compared to the wealth accruing to the Grosvenor estate when Cubitt's leases run out. You know what they say – "Bricks and mortar are the finest crop of all." '

'True, but the original landlord won't benefit,' Lord Vanbrugh pointed out. 'He'll be dead and gone by the time a ninety-nine-year lease runs out. All the profit goes to his grandchildren.'

'Well, I'll admit that,' said Mr Yardley, 'but that's led to problems too. Landlords want high-quality houses that'll last till the leases expire. Understandable, but what's the result? The top end of the market's badly over-stocked. They're all fighting for the carriage trade.'

Lord Vanbrugh had been watching Amaryllis during this interchange. She had been listening closely. If he wasn't careful, thought Lord Vanbrugh uneasily, she might become a developer herself. She might even make money out of it and then what were his chances of persuading her to come back to him? Cursing himself for a fool, he hastily changed sides.

'Well, Mr Yardley, perhaps you're right. Builders do have a hard time. It's a very speculative business – I shouldn't like to risk any of my money on a development. There was that poor devil who built an estate near Regent's Park; for the Fitzroys, I think it was. He made a good job of it too, but that didn't save him. He went bankrupt and shot himself.'

'But the ground landlord was safe enough, I take it?' said Mr Yardley acidly.

'Oh yes, he was all right,' agreed Lord Vanbrugh. 'I knew him as a matter of fact, which is how I got to hear of the business. He was sorry for the builder, of course, but as you say, the risk was his and he lost everything.'

'Oh, but it's not always as bad as that,' said Mr Rugby, much to Lord Vanbrugh's irritation. 'Providing you judge your market carefully, there's a good bit of money to be made. Cubitt's not the only one to have done well by any means. But you do need common sense, and flair too – something extra to make your development stand out from the rest.' Lord Vanbrugh, seeing Amaryllis nod approvingly, realized that she had paid no heed to his warnings and was so engrossed in the discussion that she had quite forgotten Dr Dangerfield.

But if Amaryllis had forgotten Dr Dangerfield over dinner, it was only temporary and her misery returned with redoubled force when her guests had left. She retired to bed in floods of tears and spent a dismal night wishing she had never been born. The morning dawned grey and cold. For a long time Amaryllis lay in bed, drearily wakeful but too depressed to get up. At last, restlessness got the better of her. She left her bed and went upstairs to the kitchen looking pale and heavy-eyed. Her hair, which she had not had the strength of mind to brush, straggled over her nightdress and her shoulders drooped forlornly.

'You look like a wet washday,' said Bella.

'I've got reason, haven't I?' Amaryllis threw herself into a chair by the fire and burst into tears of self-pity. Bella shook her head, poured out a cup of tea, placed it at Amaryllis's elbow and waited for her sobs to subside.

At last Amaryllis blew her nose, dragged a hand across her reddened eyes and demanded fiercely, '*Why* did he leave me like that, Bella?'

'Because Lord Vanbrugh bought your virginity, of course.'

'But Mr Yardley didn't mind, so why should *he* care? You saw the letter. You read what he said . . .' Amaryllis started to cry again.

'Pull yourself together. You'll put the fire out if you cry over it much more. Mr Yardley hasn't got his eye on you – that's the difference. Besides, that doctor of yours is a cut above Mr Yardley. Socially I mean, not in any other way. The higher you go, the more fuss people make about such things, until you get to the top, and then they don't mind *what* they do. Worse than drabs in the gutter, some of them. But Dr Dangerfield's got your mother's way of looking at things.'

'He's not a bit like my mother!'

'All right then, he's got to get *on* with people like your mother! He's a doctor; he can't shock his patients' ideas of what's right and proper. You can't blame him. He's got his way to make in the world. A doctor can't take up with fallen women, whether he wants to or not. No use crying, my girl. He had to drop you.' Realizing she would have done much the same in Dr Dangerfield's position, Amaryllis was a little comforted. But her rage at losing him still had to find some outlet. She turned on Bella as the most convenient scapegoat.

'Why didn't you warn me!'

'Well, how was I to know? *I* didn't think he'd rush off like this. I thought he'd ask for a secret affair, like any normal man. Perhaps he's afraid of blackmail. If so, he's not the fool I took him for.'

'Don't be so revolting, Bella!'

Bella sniffed.

'And what about *me*!' demanded Amaryllis tearfully. 'What am I to do if no man will even come near me! Why didn't you tell me it would be like this?'

'I did,' said Bella. 'Not that I suppose you were listening. And if you had, you'd have acted differently, would you? Stayed meekly put at Chesil House and married Henry? You can't have your cake and eat it.'

'But I'm an outcast, Bella! And I could have married Dr Dangerfield . . .'

'Don't you bleat "Dr Dangerfield" at me once more, my girl! If you'd married him, I'd have washed my hands of you. Don't you *ever* use your brains? Suppose you had married that doctor – what do you think would have happened? He'd have sold your property, of course, the minute his ring was on your finger. He'd have bought himself a nice plump little practice with the proceeds and left you with nothing to do but rear his children and be grateful for a new bonnet once in a while. You might as well have stayed in Shropshire!'

Amaryllis tried to protest but her words lacked conviction.

'I'm not working for you for the good of my health,' Bella continued remorselessly. 'While Cutler is alive and kicking my one chance of bettering myself is working for a rich mistress, and rich you'll be one day, if you keep the reins in your own hands. You've got the knack of it. I can tell.'

'But what's the good of being rich,' wailed Amaryllis, 'if I've got to live like a nun?'

'Who says you have to? You can have hundreds of men if you like. Just don't marry any of them. And if you *must* fall for the respectable sort, tell them the truth from the start. It's only fair. But if I were you I'd stick to the gentry. *They* know how these little games are played.'

Twenty-three

Amaryllis was just blowing her nose for the tenth time since breakfast and wondering whether she would ever see Dr Dangerfield again, when there was a slight commotion at the front door and a pair of masculine boots began to mount the stairs. Filled with the delightful conviction that this was Dr Dangerfield come to apologize, Amaryllis jumped up and tried to wipe her eyes, smooth her hair and settle her collar at one and the same time. She ran over to the door and pulled it open, only to discover not Dr Dangerfield but Lord Vanbrugh mounting the stairs. Amaryllis's disappointment was so intense that she retreated to the sofa, forcing back her tears.

'I called to thank you for your dinner-party,' said Lord Vanbrugh untruthfully. He looked at Amaryllis's face and was dimly conscious of feeling sorry for her. It was not a familiar emotion and it made him ill at ease. 'You don't look well,' he said awkwardly.

His voice was kind and Amaryllis, taken off guard, mumbled something inaudible and burst into tears.

Lord Vanbrugh viewed this development with dismay. He had visited Amaryllis wth seduction in mind, hoping to catch her on the rebound from Dr Dangerfield, but it was really very difficult to seduce someone who sat sobbing into a handkerchief.

'Don't cry,' he said, patting her uncertainly on the shoulder.

'I'm *not* crying,' sobbed Amaryllis.

He took heart at this familiar aggressiveness. 'Oh yes, you are, Amaryllis. Don't look so dismal. It's not like you.' To his own surprise, he put an arm round her and gave her a quick brotherly hug. 'Cheer up, for God's sake. The weather's bad enough without you making it worse.' With an effort, Amaryllis managed to control her sobs. She wiped her eyes and looked at Lord Vanbrugh with what dignity she could.

He smiled at her encouragingly. Then he took her unresisting hand in his and said, 'Look, Amaryllis, don't pretend any longer. You know you can't cope with it all. Pembroke Street's much too much for you – I ought never to have let you take it on. You're young and beautiful; you should be enjoying yourself, not worrying over tenants and leases . . . ' His arm crept about her shoulders and rested there. 'Come back to me. I'll take care of you. You'll never have to worry again. You won't find me ungenerous, you know that. Forget the past. You say this young fool left you – that was bound to happen! People like him don't understand these things. But you and I, Amaryllis, we understand each other . . . ' With his free hand, he turned her face towards him and saw, with dawning hope, that her eyes had filled with tears.

Amaryllis, listening to Lord Vanbrugh's gentle words, for a moment almost believed him. Weary and miserable as she was, it was only too easy to convince herself that she was burdened with responsibilities far too heavy for her. Looking back on it, with the tears rolling slowly down her face, her time at Pembroke Street seemed liked a series of disasters. How simple, how tempting it would be to shift her problems onto someone else's shoulders . . . and how boring, said Amaryllis's normal self, resurfacing. Besides, she would have to become Lord Vanbrugh's mistress again, and he was lying anyway – of course he was. Pembroke Street hadn't been too much for her. She'd managed perfectly well, far better than he had at any rate, and she had account books to prove it. Amaryllis removed Lord Vanbrugh's arm from about her shoulders and looked at him with deep suspicion.

'I'd have to sleep with you again though, wouldn't I?' she said.

Lord Vanbrugh controlled his temper with an effort, 'You can't do without men for ever, Amaryllis. All I ask is that you think carefully about what I've been saying to you. You have only to lift a finger and I'll take you away from all this and install you in luxury.' How this luxury was to be paid for was something he didn't explain.

'I'm quite happy here,' muttered Amaryllis.

'You don't look it.' As he turned to leave, his humanity again got the better of him. He reached out in passing and gently stroked her hair. 'Don't look so upset, Amaryllis; he wasn't worth it.' Then he left the room before her sad face could provoke him to commit any further acts of kindness.

Amaryllis, also regretting her display of human weakness, went to her desk and took out her account book, hoping to restore her self-confidence by the perusal of its neat columns. Their totals and subtotals were neatly ruled off, but somehow they failed to soothe her bruised spirit. She was growing more and more disheartened when Mr Yardley was shown into the room. He gave Amaryllis his usual quiet greeting and explained that he had come to see her on business.

'To begin with,' he said, avoiding her face and fixing his gaze on the carpet, 'Dr Dangerfield has just been to see me. He'll be leaving today. We ought to start looking for a replacement, but there's no urgency as he's paid till the end of the month.'

Amaryllis nodded, her cheeks hot with embarrassment.

'But there's another more important matter I'd like to discuss with you.' Mr Yardley spoke more easily now that he had got Dr Dangerfield off his chest. 'It's something I've been thinking about for quite a time now. I wondered, Miss Vaughan, if you would consider going into partnership with me.'

He paused for a moment, to gauge her reaction. 'It seems to me that with your capital and my experience we might be able to start out as developers ourselves. Nothing grand at first, of course, but with care it could prove to be a profitable venture. What do you say, Miss Vaughan? Our talk last night made me hope you might consider it.'

Amaryllis's face had brightened as he spoke; she nodded eagerly.

'I have some savings of my own, of course,' Mr Yardley continued. 'And there's always the workshop to mortgage, but

I've not enough capital to finance a full-scale development. But if you came into partnership and mortgaged your Pembroke Street properties, *then* the thing becomes a possibility!'

'Well,' Amaryllis tried her hardest to sound businesslike, 'I'll have to consider it carefully, of course, but it seems very interesting. I've been looking for a way to expand my business for some time now and I know I can't do much more with Pembroke Street.' She smiled. 'To tell you the truth, I've wanted my own development ever since seeing Belgravia . . . Have you any particular site in mind?'

'Yes,' he said eagerly. 'I've had my eye on one for some time, on the edge of the Linklater estate, east of Drury Lane. You remember, I collect some of Mr Linklater's rents so I know the area pretty well. It's respectable but not at all fashionable. The site's a mews at present, Crewe Mews, running from Saracen Street at one end to Selby Street at the other. It was built to service the big houses in Crewe Street eighty years ago, but the houses have gone down in the world and the mews has fallen into disrepair. It's been taken over by slum dwellers.'

'And how do you propose to develop it?'

'I want to knock down the mews and build a good street of decent residential properties in its place. They wouldn't be grand houses, of course, it's not that sort of area, but they'd be substantial enough to fetch a good price. It's a wide mews, there's plenty of room to turn a carriage. We could fit in a double row of houses without too much skimping.'

'Yes,' said Amaryllis thoughtfully. 'It sounds worth looking into. But what do you think of our chances with Mr Linklater? Will he lease it to us, do you think?'

'I've been wondering about that. Probably he will, if it's put to him in the right way. He can't lose by it, after all. But he's a hard man and he hasn't granted any building leases that I've ever heard of. We may have our work cut out to persuade him.'

'Could we go and take a look at the site now?' Amaryllis asked eagerly.

'Of course. If you'll wait here, I'll go and fetch a cab.'

Their journey to Crewe Mews took them past Charing Cross and along the Strand, the driver avoiding the more direct but infinitely less pleasant route through the slums of St

Giles. The cab turned north along Drury Lane and soon reached the lower end of Saracen Street. This proved to be respectable enough. Although no longer elegant, the houses were well cared for and the only commercial premises were clustered at the extreme southern end of the street. Since these consisted of nothing worse than a draper's, a grocer's and an empty flower stall, Amaryllis felt that their contaminating influence could be safely disregarded.

'What do you think of it?' asked Mr Yardley, as the cab proceeded at a snail's pace up the street behind an ancient butcher's cart.

'It's not too bad,' said Amaryllis. 'It's a pity about the shops, but luckily they're out of sight of most of the street. I'm surprised the estate allowed them though.'

'Oh, the shops aren't on the Linklater estate,' Mr Yardley explained. 'Saracen Street's a boundary. This side of the road, free of shops as you can see, belongs to Mr Linklater. That side is Vanbrugh land.'

Amaryllis sighed heavily. 'I might have known it. Lord Vanbrugh must be a byword for bad management. And really,' she added in an injured voice, 'you'd think it covered half London, the way his estate seems to follow me about.'

Mr Yardley smiled. 'It's not that large, but it's rather scattered about in pockets here and there. The Vanbrughs were new rich a hundred years ago. They came to the London land market a bit late in the day and had to pick up what they could in odd fields here and there. Most of their larger pieces of land were won at the gaming table, Mr Bentley tells me.'

'So who owns most of London?' asked Amaryllis.

'Various great families; not so very many of them either. Whoever owned the land when it was farms, I suppose. The Church and the Crown have a good bit of it too. The City's another matter of course.' He looked out of the window. 'Ah, there's Crewe Street, Miss Vaughan!' He pointed to a row of stuccoed Georgian façades with pillared doorways. 'And here's Crewe Mews, behind this archway. Stop here, driver! This is the place we want.'

The driver gave them a surprised look but pulled up none the less and agreed to wait.

Mr Yardley handed Amaryllis out of the carriage and she went through the archway into Crewe Mews. Her emotions were very different from those she had experienced on first seeing Pembroke Street. This time, she had a good idea of what to expect and Crewe Mews did not disappoint her. It was not quite a slum, though it came near it in places, but no one would have described it as well cared for. The buildings were dirty and dilapidated and the tattered washing hanging on poles out of upper windows testified to the poverty of their inhabitants. The former stables were occupied by a variety of humble commercial concerns which did nothing to improve the standing of the neighbourhood. Despite the bleak November weather, several businesses were being carried on in the open air and the cobbles were littered with the belongings of chair caners, walnut shellers, barrel pitchers and sign painters. A few cats slunk round in malodorous corners and in the centre of the mews women in dirty aprons were clustered round a water seller, discussing some local crime as he filled their buckets.

Mentally, Amaryllis tore down the stables, evicted the tenants and substituted two rows of neat terraced residences with City clerks taking the air on their front doorsteps. The vision pleased her. She turned to Mr Yardley and said, 'Yes, I think it will do.'

Their return to Pembroke Street coincided with Dr Dangerfield's departure. As Amaryllis got down from the cab she could not fail to notice him outside Number Twelve, loading portmanteaux and boxes into a hackney. But if he saw her, he gave no sign of it and Amaryllis hurried into Number Ten, miserable but glad to avoid an embarrassing confrontation.

Twenty-four

A week later, much to Amaryllis's surprise, Henry Chesil reappeared in Pembroke Street, poking his head round the door as if he was unsure of his welcome. He was followed by a sturdy boy with a hamper, which he dumped unceremoniously on the carpet before pocketing a sixpence and retiring. Amaryllis looked from the hamper to Henry and back again. She made no move to open it but said distrustfully, 'I warn you, Henry, if you've come here to take me back to Chesil House, you're wasting your time.'

'No, no,' said Henry, reddening as he spoke. 'Nothing like that I assure you! Far from it – I've no wish to interfere in any way. In fact . . . ' He seemed about to tell her something but, losing the courage, said feebly, 'Why not open the hamper? I brought it from home.'

Amaryllis knelt down on the rug and lifted the lid to reveal a goose, a home-cured ham, a jar of peaches preserved in brandy, a basket of apples and a dozen eggs, each wrapped in a wisp of hay. Her evident pleasure at the sight gave Henry the courage to speak again.

'The thing is, Amaryllis,' he said in a rush, 'I'm engaged to Maria Harris!'

'You are?' cried Amaryllis. 'Oh Henry, I'm so glad! When's the wedding?'

'Not till next year. We'll have to wait till our house is ready. My father's building it for us in the village. I hoped,' he mumbled, blushing brightly, 'that you'd forget I ever wanted . . . '

'Oh, of course I will,' said Amaryllis, taking the eggs out of the hamper and laying them carefully on the table, each in its nest of hay.

Henry was rather disappointed to find Amaryllis so cheerful at the news of his engagement. 'I would have written, but I thought I'd come and see you instead. Maria's cousin Hetty's to be married at Christmas and I've brought Maria up to London for the wedding.'

'And how long will you be staying here?' asked Amaryllis, counting eggs.

'I'm not sure – at least a month. I'd like – if you wouldn't mind that is – I'd very much like to bring Maria to visit you.'

Amaryllis looked at him, her eggs forgotten for the moment. 'You would?' she asked disbelievingly. 'Henry, are you sure?'

'Yes. Quite sure. Maria doesn't know about what's happened – no one does outside the family, or if they do they don't admit it. And anyway, I think it's right that she should visit you. After all, we are brother and sister – in a manner of speaking.'

'It's nice of you to say so, Henry, but do you really think it's wise to bring Maria here, under the circumstances?'

'Yes, I do,' said Henry. 'I know most people wouldn't agree with me but I can't help the way I feel. After all, it's not as though you'd stolen something or killed anyone. I know I'm just an ordinary sort of fellow. But – well, it seems downright wrong to me, ignoring your existence, and so I've told our parents.'

'It's very good of you,' said Amaryllis hastily, 'but I don't want to cause a breach between you and your father. I know how fond you are of each other. I don't *mind* being ignored, really I don't . . . ' She broke off and looked hard at Henry. 'Tell me,' she demanded, '*why* are you so anxious I should meet Maria? Is something wrong at home? Tell me, Henry!'

Henry looked acutely uncomfortable.

'What is it?' Amaryllis insisted.

'My father . . . ' Henry stopped and thrust his fingers through his hair. 'It's not like him. In the ordinary way he wouldn't dream of . . . but I *cannot* think it right, whatever you may have done. And he's a churchwarden, which makes it worse, and a justice of the peace . . . '

'Henry, what *are* you talking about?'

He muttered an apology and tried to pull himself together. 'I'm sorry, Amaryllis, it's Monksedge . . . '

'What about Monksedge?' said Amaryllis sharply.

Henry's brow puckered. 'He's letting it go to rack and ruin. I do what I can but it's not much use. I've told him time and again it's a breach of trust under your father's will, not to look after your property for you . . . '

'And my mother?'

Henry shook his head. 'You see . . . they don't want you to come back. They think if your house is a ruin you won't be able to. Whenever I go there I find windows left open and the rain coming in, tiles fallen off the roof and not replaced . . . ' Seeing Amaryllis's dismayed gaze he said vehemently, 'I've *told* them it's wrong but they don't seem to see it that way. I tried to talk to your mother but all she did was cry and say it was a judgement on you. As for my father – I'm afraid,' said Henry shamefacedly, 'he's doing it to reduce the value of the land, so that when you inherit you'll have to sell at a lower price. He'll buy Monksedge, pull down the house and add the land to ours. That way the whole valley will belong to him. It's always been a dream of his . . . I'm sorry, Amaryllis.'

'That's all right. It's not your fault.' She looked forlornly at him. 'Isn't there *anything* I can do to stop him?'

'I can't promise it'll work,' said Henry, 'but if I could tell him that you no longer have any connection with . . . anyone, that you've made a fresh start in London, it's sure to help a little.'

'Do you really think so?' asked Amaryllis dubiously.

'It must do – in the long run. You see, if you *have* made a fresh start, I can bring Maria to see you and when she goes home she'll tell everyone about you. Then my father will have to look after Monksedge or people will start asking questions. When you left there were rumours; it wasn't talked of openly but people suspected you'd gone to Vanbrugh. But if Maria visits you, then they'll all know you're respectable and you'll be able to come back to Monksedge when you inherit. You do *want* to come back, Amaryllis?'

At Henry's words she suddenly felt homesick. 'Oh yes, I

want to come back.'

'Then can you promise me it's all over, Amaryllis? Can I bring Maria to see you? I'll tell her you inherited Pembroke Street from an aunt.'

'Yes, I promise,' said Amaryllis. 'I've made a fresh start and I'll never see Lord Vanbrugh again, that's what you want isn't it? Only save Monksedge for me, Henry, do the best you can!'

When Henry had gone, much heartened by the interview, Amaryllis knelt down beside the hamper again. The scent of hay rising from its contents brought Monksedge so vividly before her that tears filled her eyes. She brushed them away and, taking up a wisp of hay, spread it out on her palm. As she separated the dried meadowsweet from the bleached grasses, she thought contritely that she had underestimated Henry.

He had promised to bring Maria to tea on the following afternoon and Amaryllis was ready a full half-hour before they were due to arrive. She was wandering nervously about the room, picking things up and then putting them down again, when she heard steps on the stair. There was a cursory knock on the door and Lord Vanbrugh walked into the room.

'Good afternoon, Amaryllis,' he said affably. 'The door was open so I showed myself up.'

Amaryllis looked at him in dismay. 'You can't stay! No, don't sit down!'

'Ah – your usual warm welcome.' Lord Vanbrugh sat down, crossing his legs in a relaxed manner. 'Expecting company?' he asked, looking at the tea table.

'Yes, but you must *go*. I can't possibly talk to you now. *Please* go.'

'You're always trying to get rid of me.' He gazed appreciatively at her ringlets and reached out a finger to touch one. Amaryllis twitched it impatiently away.

'Lord Vanbrugh, please, *please* leave at once. If he – if my guests found you here it would be disastrous!'

'He? Not that doctor back again, I hope? I thought we'd seen the last of him.'

'No, no,' said Amaryllis, cross with herself for blushing. 'It's only Henry Chesil; but he mustn't find you here. I suppose,' she said reluctantly, 'I'd better tell you the truth.'

'I should enjoy that.'

'My stepfather's at the bottom of it, of course. He's neglecting Monksedge so that he can buy it cheap when I inherit. Henry's going to stop him, but only if I promise never to see you again. He'll be here in twenty minutes and if he finds you here too, *then* what shall I do? I'm sorry if I sounded rude, but it's vital you shouldn't be seen here.'

'Strange,' mused Lord Vanbrugh, still lolling in his chair. 'Last week you told me it was vital that I *should*.'

Amaryllis had the grace to blush. 'Yes, well, things have changed.'

'Have they? Well, I wait to learn in what way.'

'I've *told* you. It's my stepfather!' said Amaryllis with an anguished glance at the clock. 'And last week – that was to show them that I didn't care! But now Henry's made me promise not to see you again, things are different . . . '

'I appreciate your problem, Amaryllis; in fact I'll leave at once,' said Lord Vanbrugh, showing, however, no signs of doing so, 'on certain conditions.'

'Yes, yes, only *hurry*!'

'I'll engage to stay away from you,' said Lord Vanbrugh, unhurriedly, 'for as long as Henry Chesil stays in London, on the strict understanding, Amaryllis, that you come to see *me* whenever I send for you.'

'But . . . but you might do that every day!'

'You needn't worry. Your company isn't *that* fascinating.'

'But I can't just drop everything whenever you want! I've my business to run . . . '

Lord Vanbrugh looked at the clock and held out his hands to the fire in a leisurely manner.

'Oh, very well!' snapped Amaryllis, as the minute hand moved on towards the hour. 'Anything you want! Only for heaven's sake go *away*!'

Lord Vanbrugh got up at last. 'Remember – I'll hold you to your promise.'

Maria Harris proved to be much as Amaryllis remembered her: an ordinary girl with a big face and plenty of bunchy brown curls.

'Is this house *really* yours?' she asked as she drank her second cup of tea.

'Yes, this and three other houses in Pembroke Street.'

'Four houses!' Maria was wide-eyed with envy. 'Did you hear that, Henry? I wish someone would leave a legacy like that to me! Did you know your aunt well?'

Amaryllis gave Henry an anguished glance.

'Of course, dear,' he said hastily. 'You forget, Amaryllis left Shropshire to nurse her aunt in her last illness.'

'Oh yes, how silly of me!' cried Maria.

'Have a muffin,' said Amaryllis.

But Maria was not to be diverted. 'And you live here all by yourself? How very strange! Don't you find it lonely? Who does your business for you? And how do you manage without your Mama?'

'I do my business for myself,' said Amaryllis, trying to sound as if it was the most natural thing in the world.

Maria stared at her. 'Do you really? Think of it, Henry! Amaryllis looks after her own business! I *never* could.'

'Why on earth not?' asked Amaryllis, irritated.

'Oh, I'm much too silly! Besides,' she bit into a sandwich, 'where do you find the time?'

'The time?' said Amaryllis blankly.

'Yes – I never have a moment, I'm so busy. What with my bead work and my netting and my pressed flowers and the missionary basket, I'm rushed off my feet from morning till night. And then I have to help Mama with the servants and practise my music and fill my album – there's never a minute to spare. Henry will tell you, some days I'm so busy I can hardly find the time for *him*!'

'Yes? Yes, I suppose you must be busy,' said Amaryllis, refilling Maria's cup of tea.

'Do have a muffin, Henry, you've hardly eaten a thing!' urged Maria, putting one onto his plate. Henry accepted it with a fond look and patted her hand discreetly under the table. Maria smiled proudly at him.

'Don't you find it dull here,' she asked Amaryllis, 'without any beaux?'

Henry looked as if he wished the floor would open and swallow him up.

'I don't mind it,' said Amaryllis briefly, passing Maria a large wedge of plum cake in the hope that it would silence her for a moment.

'I should hate it,' said Maria. 'But I'm lucky of course,' she added, with a tender glance at Henry's red face.

'We mean to be very busy in London,' Maria went on. 'There's my bridesclothes to get, and furniture and china, and we're going to help my cousin Hetty choose her new house . . .'

'What sort of house?' Amaryllis interrupted.

Maria would rather have talked about her bridesclothes but she answered readily enough, 'Well – not *too* large, since it's their first. Hetty says they're lucky to have a house at all, they're so dear in London. Most of her married friends had to start in lodgings. And George says it must be near the City. Hetty wanted somewhere farther west because the City's not fashionable, but George said the rents are dreadfully high near the park and she'd just have to make do. And Hetty said she supposed so, but she wouldn't live near any shops or live in a street either, because it's common. Nothing but a place or a square will do.'

George and Hetty sounded like the sort of buyers Amaryllis had in mind for Crewe Mews. She asked what size of house they were looking for.

'Let me see: a basement for the servants, and a dining-room and parlour on the ground floor,' Maria checked the list off on her fingers. 'And a drawing-room and best bedroom on the first floor, and two spare bedrooms on the next floor – well, you never know, do you? – and maybe an attic where the servants can sleep. It sounds nice, doesn't it, Henry? I wish we didn't have to wait so long for *our* house to be ready.'

Looking at Maria, Amaryllis suddenly had an idea. She considered it for a moment, with growing enthusiasm. Then she said decisively, 'Maria! Henry! You needn't wait any longer. Why not live at Monksedge till I inherit? I can't let the house and I don't like leaving it empty. You can look after it for me and live there till your new house is ready. What do you say?'

Their delighted faces left her in no doubt of their acceptance.

'Why, that would be wonderful, Amaryllis!' cried Maria. 'How can we ever thank you! Oh Henry, we can be married in the spring! At least,' she added, recollecting herself, 'if *you* think so, Henry, and if your Papa doesn't object.'

'I'm sure my father would agree to the plan if *you* asked him, dear,' Henry answered, giving Amaryllis a significant glance as he spoke. 'Why not write to him tonight to tell him of Amaryllis's kind offer?'

Maria was only too happy to agree to this suggestion and when she and Henry took their leave, Amaryllis was able to wave them goodbye, secure in the knowledge that she had spiked William Chesil's guns.

Twenty-five

Later that evening, Mr Yardley appeared with a roll of drawings under one arm.

'I've just finished my sketch plans for Crewe Mews,' he said. 'They took longer than I'd hoped so I thought I'd let you see them right away.'

Amaryllis helped him to move the furniture back against the walls, and then they spread the plans out over the floor and weighted them down with teacups from the china cupboard.

'This is the plan of the street we'll build.' Mr Yardley pointed it out with his ruler as he and Amaryllis knelt on the carpet. 'You see I've managed to fit in twenty houses. And *this* is the plan of an individual house, four floors with two rooms on each floor.'

'But no basement? We must have basements, Mr Yardley. If the kitchen's on the ground floor, the reception rooms will smell of cooking.'

'It can't be helped. The cost of excavating basements would be much too great. We simply can't afford it.'

'But all the new estates have basements.'

'New *estates*, yes. They do it by building the basements at ground level.'

'I beg your pardon?' said Amaryllis, temporarily at a loss.

'The basements are built at ground level,' Mr Yardley repeated, 'and the ground floor and the road surfaces are built on top.'

'So the street is really eight feet above the ground – I see.'

'That's right. But we can't do that sort of thing for one

isolated street. They didn't build basements on the Linklater estate.'

Amaryllis accepted this but she still looked worried. 'It's a great pity. People want basements for their servants. No area steps either – they'll have to receive tradesmen and delivery boys at the front door. I can see *you* don't think it matters, Mr Yardley, but to our buyers it will matter very much indeed.' She sighed. 'Oh well, I suppose it can't be helped. If you say basements are out of the question, we'll just have to offer them some other inducement.'

Amaryllis studied the plans again, frowning slightly.

'Couldn't we . . . ? ' she began. 'Yes, I have it. Not a street, Mr Yardley, a place. Crewe Place. See here – ' she took the ruler out of his hand and pointed with it ' – cut off access to Selby Street at *this* end of the mews, add another house to fill the gap and we've increased our profits and improved the class of the development. No through traffic and all the prestige of a place as opposed to a mere street.'

Mr Yardley rubbed his chin thoughtfully for a few moments. Then he said with a tinge of admiration in his voice, 'Yes, Miss Vaughan, yes, I can see there's something to be said for that idea. Always providing there's no problem about rights of way, of course.' He retrieved the ruler and made various calculations in pencil on the edge of one of his plans.

Amaryllis squinted down at his sketch of the street. 'We'll call the extra house something grand, shall we?' she suggested. ' "Crewe House" will do. It'll be a bit bigger than the others by the looks of it.'

'It'll be harder to let, though.'

'But it'll make letting the others easier. We want our development to seem special. Can we fit a garden in the middle, do you think?'

'No,' said Mr Yardley firmly. 'The houses will be cramped enough as it is. I've had to give them a double frontage; there's no space for one room to go behind another – and no light either.'

'Well . . . a line of trees then and a patch of grass,' said Amaryllis coaxingly. 'Just a bit of green. It'd make all the difference – really it would.'

Mr Yardley admitted that something of the kind might be possible. 'But it'll be a pretty gimcrack affair.'

'It'll be charming, you'll see. Now, how are we going to finance it all and when are we going to talk to Mr Linklater?'

Mr Yardley, it turned out, had already arranged for them to visit Mr Linklater on the following Thursday. When the time came, he called for Amaryllis at Pembroke Street and together they went to Mr Linklater's house in Grosvenor Square. It was crowded with the heavy bronzes its owner collected and its sombre atmosphere added to Amaryllis's nervousness. Mr Linklater received them in his library, a room so large and dark that at first Amaryllis could hardly see him. Then she discovered him, sitting at an immense kneehole desk surrounded by a fortification of little drawers and pigeonholes. He had a thin face with a scrub of grey hair, and his bony hands lay on his blotter, as if waiting to grasp the next piece of property that came within their reach.

After the briefest of introductions and a grudging request that they be seated, Mr Linklater got down to business. 'Before we discuss Crewe Mews, Miss Vaughan,' he said with a sharp, calculating look, 'I must tell you that I propose to treat you precisely as I would treat a man in similar circumstances. My mother was a woman of business. She ran this estate throughout my minority, making no allowances and asking for none. So I'm under no illusions with regard to your capacities. If you succeed, you succeed. If you fail, you fail. But in neither case will you receive any special treatment from me. And now, kindly state your business.'

When Amaryllis had done so, as well as she could with Mr Linklater's eye upon her, he leaned forward and said brusquely, 'I'm not convinced, Madam. Houses of that nature are a poor investment for the ground landlord. Shoddily built, most of them. Besides, others are building for the middle classes – anyone, indeed, with insufficient capital to do better. Tell me, how do your propose to finance this venture?'

'I hope to borrow money on mortgages,' Amaryllis explained. 'I have four houses in Pembroke Street, near

Leicester Square, of which I own the freehold. Mr Yardley will be mortgaging his workshop and he has a certain amount of ready cash as well. We have a solicitor interested in our venture – Mr Charles Rugby, junior partner in Rugby and Weatherall of Bedford Row. But in addition,' said Amaryllis, wishing Mr Linklater did not look quite so implacable, 'we were hoping that you would consider making a contribution to the funding of the development – in return for a share of the improved ground rents or interest at five per cent, whichever you prefer.'

'I'll lend you nothing without security,' said Mr Linklater emphatically.

'Surely, sir, the development will be your security,' put in Mr Yardley.

Mr Linklater gave a cackle of contempt. 'Fine security! Suppose you fail within six months? I've known it happen often enough. And then all I'm left with is a few useless brick carcases. Not even the rents from the mews coming in!'

'Your share in the profits could be adjusted to allow for the risk . . . ' began Amaryllis reluctantly.

'No, no, Miss Vaughan, I've no mind to speculate at my time of life. I leave that to you and Yardley here. I must have security,' and he shut his mouth like a trap and laid his hands flat on the desk before him.

Looking at him, Amaryllis could see that he meant what he said. She took a desperate decision. 'I can give you *some* security.'

'Can you indeed?'

'Yes. I have property in Shropshire. A house and some land. More than enough to secure a small loan.'

'Do you think we made any impression?' asked Amaryllis gloomily, as she and Mr Yardley stood outside Mr Linklater's house waiting for a cab.

'Oh yes. He's always disagreeable – it means nothing. He'll talk it over with his agent and let us know his decision soon enough . . . Miss Vaughan, do you think it was wise to risk everything on this venture? There's still time to change your mind about Monksedge and I think you should. If it goes against us, Linklater's sure to foreclose. He wouldn't cheat us but he'd show us no mercy either.'

'I know. But he gave me no choice. If I hadn't pledged Monksedge, he would never have lent us the money. Besides – you've risked everything.'

'Not everything. I've still got my trade to fall back on.'

And if the worst comes to the worst, so have I, thought Amaryllis.

When Bella heard about the interview with Mr Linklater she asked if Amaryllis was going to tell Henry Chesil that she was pledging Monksedge.

'No, why should I? It's none of his business.'

'It will be – if he's living in the house when Mr Linklater forecloses,' said Bella, with her usual pessimism.

'He'll only do that if the development fails – and it's not going to.'

'All the same, it's a pity you had to pledge Monksedge.'

'I had to, Bella. Nothing venture, nothing gain . . . We haven't heard from Lord Vanbrugh for weeks, have we? And Georgiana seems to have forgotten us too. I'm sick of living on a tightrope, but I must keep on the right side of Henry or Monksedge won't be *worth* pledging.'

Two days later, a porter brought round the letter Amaryllis had hoped would never arrive.

> I have kept my part of the bargain. The time has come for you to keep yours. Jermyn Street, tonight at nine.

The night was dark and cold and the streets were almost empty. Clutching their cloaks about them against the wind, Amaryllis and Bella were half glad to reach the shelter of Lord Vanbrugh's lodgings. They were taken upstairs by a manservant and shown into the picture-lined room Amaryllis had seen on her previous visit.

'You're prompt to your time, I'll say that for you.' said Lord

Vanbrugh, as she entered. He put aside the drawing he had been studying. 'Oh God, not her as well!' he said disgustedly, as he caught sight of Bella. 'This passion for bringing your maid along on all the most unsuitable occasions . . . she'd better go down to the kitchen.' He looked hard at Bella, who stood unmoving. 'Did you hear me, woman?' he asked menacingly. Amaryllis gave Bella a significant look and she left the room. There was no sound of footsteps on the stairs. Lord Vanbrugh strode over to the door and flung it open.

'Downstairs, I said!' Bella muttered something and her heavy tread descended kitchenwards.

'I hope,' said Lord Vanbrugh, 'that you're not going to be troublesome too. A glass of wine?' He crossed to the decanter, poured two glasses of burgundy and held one out to Amaryllis.

'It's not poisoned. Here – take it! Now, come and sit down. No, not there! Here, beside me on the sofa. Come on – I won't bite you! That's better . . . Now, Amaryllis, I've asked you here because, as I've told you before, I want you back.'

Amaryllis shrugged and sipped her wine.

Lord Vanbrugh set his teeth. 'You needn't think I'm enjoying this situation! You're giving me a damn sight more trouble than you're worth . . . '

'*Good*,' said Amaryllis viciously.

Lord Vanbrugh put a warning hand on her arm. 'I wouldn't try me too far. I might withdraw my offer. Linklater tells me you're about to take a very foolish step – '

'How did you know?'

'He told me. I met him at the club yesterday and heard all about Crewe Mews. He expects it to fail, of course. He was quite frank about that.'

'Not to me, he wasn't!'

'No? Well perhaps not. He's nothing to lose after all. But you, Amaryllis, where have your wits gone begging? Risking everything on a speculation. It's madness!'

'It's a very sound proposition,' said Amaryllis indignantly. 'We're certain of success.'

'Nothing's certain in the building trade. I'm warning you, Amaryllis, get out before it's too late.'

'I don't trust you,' said Amaryllis bluntly.

He gave an exasperated sigh. 'I wish you would. I know what I'm talking about.'

'No you don't. You know next to nothing about property! I've done better in Pembroke Street in five months than you did in ten years!'

Lord Vanbrugh thought it best to change the subject. 'Come back to me, Amaryllis. It'll be different this time, I swear it. I'll treat you well. I'll show you how to enjoy yourself. And I'll make you much richer than any mad building project could . . . '

'You know that's not true! You've no money at all – even Pembroke Street was your sister's dowry! You're not rich enough to tempt me,' she said cuttingly. 'Not nearly rich enough!'

'You mercenary little wretch! You've cheated me, exploited me, and now, *now* you try and get rid of me because I'm not rich enough for you. Not rich enough, by God! And *you* were a penniless little provincial nobody when I first saw you! If you've made money now you've done it by thieving from me! You sit there, you hell-cat, and tell me I'm not rich enough to tempt you . . . '

Before Amaryllis had time to defend herself, he had swooped on her and caught her in an embrace so murderously tight she could scarcely breathe. For a moment he held her powerless, looking down at her in triumph at her humiliation, and then his face forced itself on hers. It was his undoing. Seizing her chance, Amaryllis gave him a vicious bite on the cheek. The shock made him loosen his hold for a moment, swearing violently at the pain, and she managed to wrench herself free.

'You little *devil*,' he gasped, one hand held to his bleeding cheek. Amaryllis ran for the door, but her skirts impeded her and he grabbed her by the arm and threw her roughly down onto the sofa.

'I'll teach you to bite me!' he roared.

'You asked for it!'

Lord Vanbrugh stood, gasping for breath, his cheek bleeding freely. He stared down at Amaryllis, who was lying where he'd pushed her, her face flushed and her eyes narrowed with fury. He felt suddenly disgusted, both with himself and her. All his anger vanished and he felt very tired.

'I'm not going to touch you,' he said wearily. He handed Amaryllis her cloak. 'Put it on and get out of my sight – I'm sick of the whole miserable business!' he added savagely as the door slammed and Amaryllis's running footsteps echoed up the stair.

Lord Vanbrugh leant one arm across the mantelpiece and stared at the wall, wondering what could have possessed him to lose control like that. Realizing he was bleeding, he wiped his cheek impatiently and rang the bell.

'I'm going out,' he said when his manservant appeared. 'God knows when I'll be back.'

Out in the street, he walked rapidly, caring nothing for his direction. He passed through the Haymarket and the Strand, oblivious to the lights and the noise, thrusting the street women aside when they accosted him. Then he wandered into Covent Garden, where a faint scent of flowers still lingered in the cold air. Above him, the great church loomed up into the darkness, and the ragged creatures crouched about its base held out their dirty palms as he passed. He tossed them a few pence and walked on across the sleeping city, reaching streets where the only light came from the moon shining wanly through the smoke haze. He passed drowsy watchmen huddled over braziers and children curled up asleep in packing cases or sheltering in doorways from the wind. He came upon factories where the lights still burned and the relentless thud of a steam hammer echoed out into the night, and saw gin-shops where the prostitutes lingered, silent and watchful, by the fireside. And all the while Lord Vanbrugh thought of Amaryllis.

The weather worsened but he paid no heed to it beyond retracing his steps westwards, out of the teeth of the wind. He walked back across the silent city as heedlessly as he had come, turning his problem over and over in his mind. Money – that was the key to it. If only he had money. Ten years ago, perhaps, he could have borrowed some, but now he had held off his creditors for so long they would lend to him no longer. A wealthy marriage? Possible once, but who would look at him now? A penniless widower, past his first youth. Besides, one couldn't marry to pay for one's whoring.

He could hope for nothing from Vanbrugh; he'd sucked it dry long ago. His town house had gone, the London estates were all mortgaged and worthless. Gaming? No, he always lost at cards and he found games of chance so tedious he could hardly keep his mind on the business. His horses he'd already sold and most of the paintings had gone the same way . . . Lord Vanbrugh stopped dead in his tracks as the solution occurred to him. Paintings! Fool that he was, not to have thought of it before! His one stroke of luck this year had been that disputed Reni. Landsdown had paid him a fortune for it. Well, why not? Why shouldn't he deal in paintings for a living? If he could just tear himself away from that wretched little whore in Pembroke Street for a few months, he'd go south for the winter and see what he could find. There were still some good things to be picked up if you knew where to look. Not just the Italians either; the Dutch were cheap in Europe, but they fetched high prices on the London market. It was trade of course; his father would turn in his grave. But he'd no wish to starve to death in a debtor's prison. He'd go to Italy till the spring and by then Amaryllis, curse her, would have had time to discover that her little venture with Linklater wasn't going to be as profitable as she'd thought. He'd show her his fat bank balance and she'd come running to him. Oh yes, he'd be sure of her then.

Twenty-six

Regent Street was one of London's most fashionable thoroughfares and its shops were famous throughout Europe. They could be relied on to supply any luxury you cared to mention, from marble statuary to gilded sword knots. Even the street traders on the pavement catered for the wants of the wealthy. The flower girls sold exotic blooms for gentlemen's buttonholes and the dog fanciers displayed little spaniels washed in scented soap. Regent Street was always crowded, and never more so than at eleven o'clock in the morning. At that hour, the carriages of the rich monopolized the roadway and middle-class pedestrians filled the pavements, relegating the poor to the gutters where they opened carriage doors and held horses' heads for a penny a time.

This particular morning was no exception. Despite the chill November weather, the street was full of activity and the shops were doing a brisk trade in preparation for Christmas. Several carriages were drawn up at the kerbside while their occupants looked over the goods brought out for their inspection from nearby shops, keeping the proprietors standing shivering on the pavement until they had made their choice. Miss Georgiana Vanbrugh was among the most exacting of these customers, and her requirements sent the shopkeepers' assistants running to and fro until their faces were red with exertion. Seated in a carriage drawn by a pair of black horses, she appeared to be impervious to the cold and looked loftily down at the shopman unrolling a bolt of vermilion silk for her inspection. It flared out against the grey of the wintry street and caught the eye of Lord Vanbrugh who was strolling along the opposite pavement.

Seeing his sister's carriage, he crossed the street and approached her.

'A word with you, Georgiana.'

She raised her brows at his tone but none the less nodded dismissal to the shopkeeper and turned to her maid. 'You may take a pattern of the silk,' she said. 'I shall collect you at the Quadrant in twenty minutes.'

She waited until the maid had disappeared into the shop and then made a place beside her and beckoned Lord Vanbrugh into the carriage. 'You had better sit down, Anthony. I have something of great importance to say to you, and you apparently wish to speak to me also?'

Lord Vanbrugh swung himself up into the carriage and sat down. 'Only to take my leave of you,' he answered. 'I'm visiting Italy for several months. I'm off next week and shan't return until the spring.'

'Italy? That's extremely inconvenient just at present.'

'Unfortunately, it's a necessity. You had better prepare yourself for a shock, Georgiana. I have decided to become a picture dealer. I'm going to Italy to make my first purchases.' Observing her tightening lips, he smiled scornfully. 'Dreadful, isn't it? A Vanbrugh in trade!'

'Our parents would certainly think so,' she replied, controlling her features with an effort, 'but I don't suppose you're doing it from choice. Your financial situation must be worse than I'd realized. Besides, I'm in no position to complain and you may be sure I shall not do so.'

'You startle me, Georgiana.'

'I'm about to startle you still more. I have accepted an offer of marriage.'

'What the devil! Not Mayo!'

'No, not Lord Mayo. Mr Gregory Saville.'

Lord Vanbrugh stared at his sister. 'I don't believe it. No, I don't believe it. Marry a manufacturer? Not you, Georgiana – the very *last* person to do such a thing!'

'I am very well aware of Mr Saville's deficiencies in the matter of birth – '

'I imagine you might be! His father was nothing but a weaver – clogs and all!'

'I have yet to learn that *you* are so very particular in such matters!'

'Oh, I don't give a damn for any of it. But you, my dear sister, are always so very careful whom you honour with your acquaintance; and that you should agree to marry a man with the cotton waste still under his fingertips I find very hard to believe!'

'I have no alternative. Thanks to your mismanagement of our affairs I am virtually destitute. Mr Saville is probably the only man in London who can afford to marry me. Being extremely wealthy himself, my lack of dowry is a matter of indifference to him.'

'But not your birth.'

'An alliance with the Vanbrughs is, of course, his object.'

'Well, you'd better marry the fellow, I suppose. I've no objection. I leave for Italy next week, just the same, though. You and Parrish can handle the contracts between you; you don't need my assistance in the matter.'

'True . . . I intend to marry as soon as it can reasonably be arranged. Your absence from the ceremony will be remarked on, of course, but I don't suppose you will care for that.'

'You're right, I won't.' Lord Vanbrugh frowned suddenly as an unwelcome thought occurred to him. 'So that's it! If you marry Saville you'll have St James's Square!'

Georgiana allowed herself a brief, complacent smile. Ignoring her brother's suspicious glance she said, 'Mr Saville, in a gesture you will agree is princely, has waived all claim to a dowry, though he proposes to make a settlement on me in the usual way –'

'No doubt you've seen to that!'

'Of course. I am not in the habit of leaving important arrangements to the incompetence of others. Mr Saville does, however, make one stipulation – not unreasonable under the circumstances.' She hesitated for an instant. 'He asks, Anthony, for your word of honour that you will never marry.'

For a moment there was a stunned silence. Then Lord Vanbrugh said explosively, 'What the devil?.Ah – I see what he's getting at – for fear I might beget legitimate heirs, no doubt.'

'Exactly.'

Lord Vanbrugh took a deep breath and controlled his temper with an effort.

'So *that's* your idea of a reasonable stipulation . . . Good God, you must be mad. It's quite outrageous! Saville doesn't stint himself, does he? The Vanbrugh barony for a manufacturer's brats!'

'For my children too,' Georgiana reminded him.

'Thank you – I hadn't forgotten! I've no doubt you concocted the entire scheme from first to last. And what,' he asked savagely, 'if you die childless?'

'In that case, you'll be free to marry again. But I shouldn't rely on it. I'm several years your junior; I'm not likely to predecease you. If I thought you had the least intention of marrying, I shouldn't ask this of you. But that's clearly not the case. You've been a widower ten years. In all that time you've shown no interest in women of our own class. Your reputation is not good. You no longer have a proper establishment or sufficient income to support a wife . . . '

'Really, Georgiana, you make my marriage sound so improbable, I'm surprised Saville isn't prepared to dispense with my word in the matter.'

'That would be foolhardy. We both know you're capable of marrying someone unsuitable purely to enrage me.'

'True.'

'Agree to my marriage, Anthony. You'll lose nothing by it – and at least it'll ensure that the family doesn't die out altogether. Remember, you'll be relieved of all expense on my account. My income will revert to you; the wedding will cost you nothing. Mr Saville has even agreed to pay for my trousseau – '

'Good God, that *was* generous. How could you bring yourself to suggest it, Georgiana?'

'Oh, I was quite frank about my circumstances. I'd already explained that a wealthy marriage was essential for me. He understood the position. After that, the trousseau was a minor matter.'

'And this accommodating gentleman won't take you without the title?'

'No. It's the title he wants. All his eager services to the last ministry have failed to procure him so much as a knighthood. He knows I'm his only hope. I explained the advantages of a marriage between us and he was much struck with my proposals. So much so that he made his own on the very next day.'

'After a few hasty researches in his copy of the *Peerage* . . . No pretence of affection I hope?'

'None. His good sense is commendable. He won't disgrace me – or you either. Agree to the marriage, Anthony. The loss of a wife can't matter to you, but the money most certainly does. My income could help to pay for your Italian journey. It may even make it unnecessary. What do you say?'

Lord Vanbrugh did not answer her immediately. Instead, he stared across at a glass case in an upholsterer's window, filled with an elaborate arrangement of wax flowers. He told himself that Georgiana was right; right on both counts. He needed her income badly and he certainly had no intention of marrying. His first experience of marriage had been warning enough. Why then, did he feel so uneasy?

Searching for the reason, he suddenly remembered the evening at Vanbrugh when he had told Georgiana of the loss of her dowry. He remembered too, with growing disquiet, the bitterness of her words: 'You may have Vanbrugh now, but I swear to you, Anthony, before I'm done, I'll take it from you!' Georgiana's anger was not lightly incurred or soon forgotten. His gaze returning to her motionless face, Lord Vanbrugh shivered slightly. A brilliant stroke, this marriage, if revenge *was* her object. It would give her the Vanbrugh town house and ultimately the title too; for herself if she outlived him and certainly for her children . . . how soon would it be before she began to encroach on Vanbrugh itself?

But then, he needed her income, that was all too true. He needed it desperately.

And besides, he had not behaved well to Georgiana over her dowry. It would have been enough to forbid the marriage to Lord Mayo; to spend her dowry on his mistress was an insult so gross as to be inexcusable. Despite his selfishness, his conscience had troubled him ever since . . . He owed her this marriage.

'Do you agree, Anthony?' Georgiana repeated.

'Yes,' he said curtly. 'I agree. You'd better tell Saville to come and see me at eleven tomorrow. I'll get Parrish over and he can draw up the settlements then and there. You'll be married by the time I return from Italy, Georgiana. It's not likely I'll see you before I leave, so I'll wish you joy now'

Twenty-seven

A fortnight later, December arrived and winter closed in, bringing with it biting winds and frosty weather. Despite the doubts he'd supposedly expressed to Lord Vanbrugh, Mr Linklater had accepted the development proposals and had evicted the occupants of Crewe Mews with ruthless speed. Mr Rugby had drawn up the partnership deeds and loan agreements and by the seventh of the month Mr Yardley's men were hard at work demolishing the mews. Amaryllis visited the site daily, delighting in the shattering of brick and the splintering of timber and watching the workmen with glowing eyes as they smashed through walls and ripped up flooring.

One morning, a week after the work began, Amaryllis arrived at the mews for her usual inspection. The day was cold under a soft white sky and as the cab drew up at the entrance to the mews a few flakes of snow began to fall. Amaryllis found that the arch was still standing; but behind it a whole row of stables had already been demolished, and decaying planks retrieved from the rubble were being used to feed a leaping fire. Men were hard at work, clearing the broken brickwork, watched by a few chilled sparrows.

Mr Yardley was standing at the far end of the mews, conferring with Silas over a plan held in his gloved hands. Amaryllis advanced towards him, her scarlet cloak showing up vividly against the duns and greys of the building site.

Mr Yardley looked up and hailed her. She stepped over some scattered bricks and a pothole, reached his side and returned the greeting. She looked anxiously up at the sky.

'I hope the snow won't delay you. Will it settle, do you think?'

'Oh no, it's just a light fall. It would take more than that to stop the work. Particularly after the stroke of luck we've just had.' He grinned at Amaryllis, his eyes excited. 'In a way, it's the snow we owe it to. It means the weather's warming up a bit. We couldn't break the ground at all in the frost we had last week. But this morning we were able to start digging foundations, here, where the ground's been cleared.' He led Amaryllis over to the place. 'And *this* is what we found!' Amaryllis looked down at a ragged hole, dark against the snow covered earth

'Can you see it? There's a room down there! Not just one room either, but a whole series. We've been down with a lantern and they stretch out right under the mews and beyond, almost into Crewe Street. Do you want to go down and take a look?'

'Oh yes,' said Amaryllis eagerly. 'Is there a stair?'

'Yes, but it's over at the other side, blocked up with rubble. This is the only access at the moment. There's a ladder if you can manage it.' Amaryllis thought that the ladder looked very precarious but Mr Yardley clambered down first and then reached up to help her. Clutching her skirts about her, she descended gingerly into the darkness. It smelt very damp and musty underground and she was thankful for the grey light from the hole above her and the rush of fresh cold air. A few snowflakes fluttered down from the outer world and settled on the paved floor.

'Is the roof safe?' asked Amaryllis.

'Yes, quite safe.' Mr Yardley lit the lantern and held it up so that it shone on squared stone walls and a vaulted roof.

'Beautiful work, isn't it?' he said lovingly. 'I'm sorry we had to break into it as we did. But we'll soon have it back as it was.' He shone the lantern onto the wall behind Amaryllis and revealed an arched opening.

'See, Miss Vaughan? There's another cellar through there and plenty more beyond that. All empty and as sound as if they were built yesterday. We took a good look at the walls when we did our bit of excavating and they're solid right through – not like some of these old buildings, all stone facing and rubble infill. Come with me and I'll show you the rest of it.'

Taking Mr Yardley's arm, Amaryllis ventured through the dark archway and found herself in another vaulted cellar, a replica of the first. Ahead of her she could see still more stretching away into the darkness. But the airlessness and smell of damp was unpleasant, and she shook her head and turned back to climb the ladder again and get out into the fresh air.

'Well, what do you make of it?' she asked, as Mr Yardley joined her above ground.

'I'm not sure. It's a godsend to us, of course, but I'd no idea it was there. It's old, certainly, much older than the mews. It must have been wine cellars or some such thing, belonging to a monastery perhaps, or a great house. There were several round here a few centuries ago. This would have been well outside London then.'

'But what happened to the house?'

'Maybe it was burnt down or just fell into decay, who knows?'

He was interrupted by a shout from one of the workmen who'd been excavating the cellar stairs. Mr Yardley and Amaryllis went over there and the man stood back and showed them a cavity in the wall containing a sinister little heap of dried skin and bone with a few hairs still adhering to it.

Amaryllis looked at it in disgust. 'What on earth is it? It looks . . . it almost looks like a dead child.'

Mr Yardley went down on his knees to investigate more closely. 'No, no, nothing like that.' He prodded it with a trowel. 'Yes, it's as I thought; a dead cat. Not very nice, I know, but it was the custom once to bury them in the walls of a building – for luck I suppose. My father did a lot of demolition work and he came upon such things quite often. He'd have nothing to do with them. Ungodly, he called them.'

'He was quite right.'

Mr Yardley turned to the workman. 'Get rid of it, will you? Throw it on the fire over there.'

He walked away with Amaryllis and neither of them noticed the workman drop the cat back into its cavity and mortar the covering stone into place again.

'Well,' said Mr Yardley, 'you can have your basements now and wine and coal cellars under the roadway too. It only needs a bit of clearance and a few extra partition walls.'

'We'll have to hide the fact that it's old though. We'll need false ceilings to conceal the arches and plenty of plaster on the walls. The floors can stay. They look in reasonable condition and they're much the same as a modern floor would be . . . '

Mr Yardley looked at her in dismay. 'But *why*? It's all as sound as a bell. You couldn't ask for better workmanship. It only needs a bit of clearing . . . '

Amaryllis shook her head. 'You've got to remember our buyers. They'll be very ordinary people, frightened of anything strange. They want a modern house, one that looks like everyone else's. We won't destroy anything – just cover it up a little. We've got to cater for our purchasers' tastes. If they want the second-rate, we'll have to provide it. She was still trying to convince him, when a carriage, piled high with luggage, drew up at the entrance to the mews. Lord Vanbrugh got down from it and advanced purposefully through the archway and down the mews, ignoring the stares of the workmen.

'Miss Vaughan!' he shouted.

Amaryllis jumped as if shot. Lord Vanbrugh reached her side and nodded curtly to Mr Yardley.

'Good day to you. A word with Miss Vaughan in private, if you please.'

Mr Yardley gave him a thoughtful glance. 'I suggest you go to the other end of the mews. I'll tell the men to come and take their dinners here, round the brazier.'

'I'm obliged to you,' said Lord Vanbrugh. 'Come, Miss Vaughan, this won't take long. I'm about to leave for Europe so I shan't inconvenience you any longer than I have to.'

Amaryllis followed him reluctantly to the far end of the mews.

'We'd better go in here,' said Lord Vanbrugh, leading the way into an empty stable, not yet reduced to rubble. 'At least we'll be out of the snow.'

The stable was bitterly cold and smelt of horse dung.

'Do you really enjoy this sort of thing?' he asked, looking round disapprovingly.

'Yes,' said Amaryllis. 'How did you know where I was this morning? You didn't go to Pembroke Street, did you?'

'No. Your servant told mine where to find you.'

Amaryllis looked at the faint scar her teeth had left on his cheek.

He touched it. 'It won't fade,' he said.

'Nor have your initials,' she said resentfully.

He looked uncomfortable. Then said 'I'm about to leave for Italy. I shan't get back till the spring, by which time Henry Chesil will be safely in Shropshire.'

He looked down at her face, her eyes bright with relief and her lips slightly chapped with the cold. There were snowflakes melting on her scarlet hood and her warm breath was visible in the icy air.

'You should be grateful to me,' he said. 'I could have made things very difficult for you, had I chosen. I still might, if you don't please me.'

Amaryllis made no reply. He looked at her again, carefully, as if to impress her features on his memory.

'I'm going to kiss you goodbye. It's the least you can do for me.' He bent down to kiss her, his lips warm on hers. For one exquisite moment he felt her mouth beneath his and breathed in the sweet scent of her skin, and then he strode out of the stable without another word.

Twenty-eight

May Day dawned bright and clear with a few traces of cloud high up in a sparkling blue sky. Pembroke Street's grimy housefronts basked in the spring sunshine and the red tulips in Amaryllis's window box swayed in the breeze. There was a feeling of anticipation in the air all morning, but it was not until midday that music was heard in the distance. The shout went up of 'The sweeps are coming!' and a ragged company turned the corner into Pembroke Street and began to dance along the roadway.

Instantly, maids appeared on doorsteps, errand boys ran out of side turnings and passing hackneys halted to see the show. Even the local dogs joined in the excitement, barking ferociously to warn off the alien mongrel staggering along on its hind legs with a sprig of may in its collar.

Amaryllis, watching from her window, thought that the rest of the show had little to recommend it. A trio of sweeps with blackened faces danced round a Jack in the Green, who had a few hawthorn branches inexpertly attached to his clothes and a wreath of blossom in his hat. They were accompanied by a slatternly girl, who banged a drum and held out a tin mug for halfpennies, and an old man who played the fiddle and was already the worse for drink.

It was a pale shadow of the May Day festivities Amaryllis remembered from Shropshire, but she threw the sweeps a sixpence before returning to the letter from Henry Chesil she had received that morning. Henry was a painstaking correspondent and since his return home he had sent her several careful letters detailing his marriage, his removal to Monksedge and the steps he was taking to reinstate Amaryllis in her neighbours' good opinion. He assured her that her loan of Monksedge had been of great assistance in promoting this end. At the wedding everyone had talked of it and her generosity had been commended on all sides – even by those who still discussed the probable identity of the golden-haired woman who had appeared at Vanbrugh at precisely the time Amaryllis had left Chesil House.

To his sorrow, however, Henry was unable to persuade himself that Amaryllis's mother showed any signs of forgiving her, and Mr Chesil was equally unreconciled to his stepdaughter, however much he might nod and smile when her name was mentioned in public.

Amaryllis put the letter down and gazed thoughtfully at the pattern of sunlight on the wall in front of her. It was strange to think that last May Day she'd still been living at Monksedge. So much had happened since then. She'd done very well for herself financially. But she had bought success at the cost of respectability. Many times, in the long winter evenings with only Bella to talk to, she had wished for the company of people of her own age and background, though she knew that her liaison with Lord Vanbrugh had barred her from their society for ever. She often thought longingly of Dr Dangerfield. Sometimes, she had even felt she would be grateful for a taste of Lord Vanbrugh's acerbic personality.

A sudden fusillade of knocks on the street door interrupted her thoughts. Amaryllis ran downstairs to answer it, knowing that Bella was out. She pulled the door open and found herself staring up at Lord Vanbrugh. He looked at her searchingly for a moment and then said simply, 'Good morning, Amaryllis. I'm back.'

It was five months since they had last met, surrounded by dust and rubble in the cold stable, and Amaryllis was surprised to discover that she was not altogether sorry to see him.

'You'd better come in,' she said, holding open the door.

Lord Vanbrugh followed Amaryllis upstairs to the parlour and stood in the doorway, looking around. The furniture was much as he remembered it but builders' plans were pinned up on the walls and samples of bricks were arranged along the mantelpiece. The desk was open and stuffed with papers, wholesalers' catalogues were heaped on the table and a bundle of prospectuses had been deposited in a corner of the sofa.

'Did you think I'd forgotten you?' he said.

'I didn't consider the matter.'

'I was delayed in Bologna by a genuine Caravaggio. The old devil of a priest needed a lot of persuading before he'd part with it, but he gave way in the end. I've just sold it to Landsdown at a handsome profit.'

'Does this mean your sister will be able to marry Lord Mayo after all?'

Lord Vanbrugh grinned. 'No. I've a better use for the money. Besides, Georgiana's in no need of a dowry. She's already married to Saville, the cotton magnate. The wedding, they tell me, was sumptuous beyond belief . . . You seem almost pleased to see me, Amaryllis. At least you haven't asked me to leave yet,'

'I shouldn't make too much of it, if I were you,' said Amaryllis promptly.

He sat down without being asked. 'Now I'm in trade, I'm impervious to snubs.'

'In trade?'

'Yes. Didn't you know? Ah, perhaps I didn't tell you. I was still sensitive about it in those days. I deal in paintings. That's why I went to Italy; to purchase my stock. I'm good at it too, I've been making money.'

He leaned back in his chair and gazed at her. She was just as beautiful as he'd remembered; her hair that strange shade of silver gilt, her face soft and rounded, with lips a trifle too full and eyes suggestive of pleasures far from respectable.

'How is your friend the doctor doing these days?' he asked maliciously.

Amaryllis gave him a reproachful glance. 'I've not seen him since the day of that dinner-party. Please don't mention him again.'

'So you're quite unattached, are you?'

'You've made sure of that,' said Amaryllis crossly. 'No one

will look at me now.'

'I'm looking at you, Amaryllis.'

'Oh, I don't count you! I mean respectable men.'

'Like that doctor, I suppose,' said Lord Vanbrugh. 'No, don't scowl at me. I apologize unreservedly. I came here today determined not to quarrel with you.'

'Why?'

'Because I'm grateful to you. If it hadn't been for you, I shouldn't have gone to Italy and I've quite enjoyed it on the whole. Dodging creditors gets a bit tedious after a while. I find picture dealing much more stimulating.'

'But I had nothing to do with it.'

'Oh yes, you had. Why do you think I took it up?'

'I don't know. I suppose you were in debt again.'

'I'm always in debt. No – I wanted to make money to persuade you to come back to me,' he said with careful lightness. Now that he had committed himself at last, he waited tensely for her response.

'But I'm not for sale,' said Amaryllis abruptly.

His face went rigid. 'Don't talk nonsense! What's your price? I can afford it.'

'There *is* no price!'

He refused to listen. 'How much do you want?'

'Nothing! How often do you want me to say it? I'm not for sale!'

He began to stride about the room. 'Who is he?'

'There isn't anyone. I *told* you.'

'There must be. Tell me his name and I'll buy him off!'

'Can't you understand? I don't need your money any more! I don't have to sell myself this time and believe me, you're the last man I'd go to for free!'

Lord Vanbrugh turned on her in a fury of hurt pride. 'You'd better give in! I'll never leave you alone till I've got what I want from you – *never*, do you hear me?'

'You make me *sick*!' Amaryllis shouted at him. 'You could buy hundreds of women who'd do perfectly well! You don't give a damn about me – you just can't bear to be crossed and that's the truth of it!'

For a moment Amaryllis thought he would choke with rage.

Then he said savagely, 'I'm going to ruin you! I'm going to ruin you, past hope of redemption, and then we'll see whether you refuse my offer! I'll have you grovelling in the dirt for a sixpence before I'm done!'

He flung out of the room. For a moment, Amaryllis stayed where she was, staring angrily after him. Then she went to her desk and picked up Henry's letter. She forced herself to concentrate.

'Yesterday,' Henry had written,

> we visited the site of our future home. It is a good piece of land to the right of the vicarage and commands a fine view of the church. There is space for a garden, and a field behind the house where Maria plans to keep a cow . . .

Amaryllis realized she was not absorbing a single word of it. She put down the letter and stared desolately at the wall.

Out in the street, Lord Vanbrugh strode along at such a furious pace that he failed to notice the figure in the heavy greatcoat which followed him from Pembroke Street almost to his own door.

'Friend of Miss Vaughan's?' said Cutler in a low voice, just behind him. Lord Vanbrugh paid no attention. 'Friend of Miss Vaughan's?' repeated Cutler.

Lord Vanbrugh told him to go to hell.

Cutler looked satisfied. 'Enemy of Miss Vaughan's, then, I could help you to do her a bad turn; for a fee.'

'What do you know of her?'

'A lot. Almost as much as you do, Lord Vanbrugh.'

'You know who I am, do you?'

'I also know you need my help,' said Cutler. 'I've connections with that household. I can find things out when needed.'

'I see,' Lord Vanbrugh looked at Cutler contemptuously. 'Well, I might use you – if I find you competent.'

'You will,' said Cutler with a thoughtful smile.

Twenty-nine

On the following Saturday, Amaryllis dressed with care and took a hackney round to Saracen Street, telling the driver, with some pride, to put her down at Crewe Place. Its appearance had altered considerably since December and the only trace of the former mews was a mound of broken bricks Mr Yardley was keeping to use as hardcore. In its place on one side of the site stood a terrace of white stucco, with arched front doors and window bars that interlaced at the top in the Gothic manner. On the other side a similar terrace was present only in embryo and between the two, at the far end of the site, stood Crewe House, completed right down to the door scraper.

A makeshift path of planks had been laid across the waste of mud and rubble where one day the pavements would be. Amaryllis followed it to Crewe House where a temporary site office had been established, and found Mr Yardley attired with a smartness to equal hers. He was wearing a gold watch chain which he bashfully admitted had belonged to his father.

'We've got good weather for our first letting day,' said Amaryllis cheerfully. 'Have there been any inquiries yet?'

'No, but it's early still. Pugh told me he'd recommended us to half a dozen hopefuls and the advertisements will bring in a few more, so we should have our hands full soon enough.'

But despite Mr Yardley's prophecy there were no inquiries at all, and after two hours' waiting he and Amaryllis were growing very anxious. An unusual number of cabs and four wheelers had, it was true, passed Crewe Place, and some had even shown signs of slowing down, but none had ever stopped. At last, when Amaryllis had almost given up hope, a hackney cab drew up at the entrance to the Place and a small, thin man got out. He paid the driver and then walked towards them down the plank path, clutching a notebook and looking doubtfully about him.

Amaryllis and Mr Yardley advanced to welcome him.

'My name is Snaith,' he said, holding out his hand and then changing his mind and withdrawing it again. 'I *had* come to look at a house, a family house, three floors and a basement, but I fear . . . '

'Do let me show you round,' said Amaryllis. 'I'm sure we have just what you're looking for.'

He looked nervously at her. 'Dear me. No. I fear it will not do . . . '

'The rooms are very spacious. Gas and running water on all floors, of course.'

'Thank you. Yes. I am sure they are all that you say. But you misunderstand me. The *area* will not do.'

Amaryllis looked at Mr Yardley in surprise.

'What objection do you have to the neighbourhood?' she asked.

'There are some very rough characters about,' said Mr Snaith. 'I saw them from the cab as I came along.'

'Well, I know there are some poorer quarters round Drury Lane, but that's several streets away,' said Mr Yardley.

'No, no. Not Drury Lane. Here, in Saracen Street.'

'Saracen Street?'

Mr Snaith nodded vigorously. 'Some very rough characters indeed. I was not at all happy with their looks; lounging around on street corners, as if they had no work to go to. No, it will certainly not do. I would have driven past without troubling you but I promised my wife to inspect *every* property on our list.'

When Amaryllis and Mr Yardley escorted Mr Snaith back to his cab, a disturbing sight met their eyes. A couple of ill-shaven men were squatting in the gutter throwing a dice, watched by a third in a greasy muffler. On the other side of the road a man in a moleskin waistcoat leant against a lamp post, smoking a short black pipe and surveying the street as if he owned it. Beyond him, other groups of men lounged against walls or idled at street corners and a small crowd of them watched some building operations just beginning at a house on Lord Vanbrugh's side of the street.

'There must be twenty or so of the brutes,' said Mr Yardley.

As he spoke a four-wheeler came down the street and drew up at the entrance to Crewe Place. As the door opened, the two men dicing in the gutter broke into a volley of oaths and one of them leapt on his companion, bringing him to the ground. The carriage door closed again and the four-wheeler moved off at a smart pace. As soon as it was out of sight, the men picked themselves up, brushed each other down and returned amicably to their dicing.

'They're deliberately trying to frighten off our buyers!' said Amaryllis.

'It certainly looks like it,' said Mr Yardley.

He advanced towards the man with the pipe and asked him curtly, 'What's your business here? What are you doing in this street?'

The man stared insolently back at him. 'Working,' he said, not bothering to remove the pipe from his mouth. At a jerk of his head, the men who had been dicing crossed the road and came to stand just behind Mr Yardley.

'Working at what?' Mr Yardley persisted.

'I'm street watching,' said the man, grinning unpleasantly.

'What did you say?'

'Watching the street – to see it don't run away.' There was a howl of merriment from his companions.

'And who's paying you to do it?'

The man laid a grubby finger to the side of his nose. 'Ah. That would be telling.'

'Well, we'll just have to see if you're more forthcoming to the constable,' said Mr Yardley.

The man shrugged. 'Suit yourself,' he answered, relighting his pipe.

An hour later Mr Yardley returned to the site office.

'Well? What did they say?' asked Amaryllis.

He sat down heavily on the nearest chair. 'The news isn't

good. The police are almost as worried as we are. They told me they'd already sent a couple of men down to arrest the leader for loitering . . . The trouble was, so the sergeant told me, the man said he was there on Lord Vanbrugh's orders.'

'*What?*'

'Not believing him, of course, they took him over to the estate office, where Mr Bentley reluctantly confirmed that the man was telling the truth. After that, the sergeant said, there was nothing he could do. His lordship's got a perfect right to employ men to work on his estate. So I thanked him and came away. No doubt Lord Vanbrugh's got his reasons.'

Amaryllis blushed. 'I would have told you but I never thought he meant it.' She twisted her fingers together in her lap. 'Lord Vanbrugh came to see me a few days ago. He asked me to become his mistress again. I refused him, of course, and he was very angry. He threatened to ruin me. I think he's mad.'

Mr Yardley looked stern. 'I wouldn't have believed it – even of Lord Vanbrugh.'

'I never thought he'd go to these lengths. I thought he was just trying to frighten me. I'm dreadfully sorry, Mr Yardley. Perhaps if I were to reason with him . . . '

'No, that's probably what he's hoping you'll do. I expect he's just trying to frighten you. We'll wait a day or two and see if he wearies of it. It'll be time enough then to take steps.'

But Lord Vanbrugh showed no signs of wearying. Day after day, his men took up their positions in Saracen Street and every time a carriage showed signs of drawing up outside Crewe Place, they surrounded it with hostile faces or, if the occupants looked bolder than most, let out a stream of oaths and obscenities until the order was given to drive away. After a week of this treatment, Amaryllis could bear it no longer.

'This has got to stop,' she told Mr Yardley. 'We've not had a single offer – no one has so much as looked over a house! Our first interest payments are due next month and we won't be able to meet them unless someone signs a lease soon. I'm going to see Mr Linklater. He knows Lord Vanbrugh. Perhaps he can make him see sense.'

Mr Linklater's house was as unwelcoming as ever and when Amaryllis entered the library she found Mr Linklater sitting behind his desk observing her with eyes as bleak and calculating as on the first occasion they had met.

'Well, Miss Vaughan, what can I do for you?'

His words were helpful, but his tone was not. Amaryllis managed to explain that they were in some difficulties over Crewe Place.

'I see,' said Mr Linklater, tapping his ledgers with a bony finger, 'that the first interest payments are due next month.'

'That is correct,' agreed Amaryllis nervously, 'but I will tell you frankly that if the present situation continues we will not be able to meet our obligations.'

'You do not altogether surprise me. I always thought that you and Yardley were stretched to the limit financially.'

Amaryllis had an uneasy feeling that the shadows in the corners of the room were closing in on her. 'We would normally have experienced no difficulty in paying the interest. But it has proved impossible to let any properties. We had hoped to have signed several leases by now. Fifteen of the houses are virtually completed. But due to an unforeseen interference in our affairs . . . '

'Kindly come to the point, Miss Vaughan.'

Amaryllis pulled herself together. 'Lord Vanbrugh is paying men to frighten away our purchasers.' She hoped desperately that Mr Linklater would not ask why Lord Vanbrugh was behaving so strangely. She need not have worried; Mr Linklater was quite uninterested in his fellow human beings, except when they affected his bank balance.

'Why have you come to me with this story?'

'To ask for your help, of course. If this goes on much longer we'll be ruined.'

'You've come to ask for my help,' repeated Mr Linklater. 'Well, you'll not get it, Miss Vaughan!'

Amaryllis stared at him in dismay 'But – why not? You know Lord Vanbrugh. You could talk to him . . . You can't *want* him to ruin us, surely? Unless something's done soon, we've no hope of covering our expenses.'

'I'll not help you, Miss Vaughan. I warned you at the outset to look for no favours from me. I propose to adhere to the letter of our agreement and I advise you, Madam, to do the same – if you can.'

Amaryllis suddenly realized that he did want Lord Vanbrugh to ruin her. She thought fast, reviewing the situation in this new light. Usually ground landlords helped their developers; if the venture failed, they stood to lose money. But this case was different. The developers would fail, because of Lord Vanbrugh, not because of any defect in the development. Mr Linklater would be left with a substantial claim on the assets of a potentially profitable venture and would also become the owner of Monksedge. His interests were safe. He'd be able to buy back his leases at well below the market rate and relet the houses at a fat profit. Amaryllis knew that further appeal was useless. Where his profits were concerned, Mr Linklater was as immovable as the Bank of England.

Amaryllis was too lost in gloomy reflection to look out of the window as her cab drove down Saracen Street. It stopped at the entrance to Crewe Place and she was about to open the door when it was done for her and Cutler appeared in the opening, his muddy greatcoat blocking out the light.

Behind Cutler's shoulder she could see some of Lord Vanbrugh's men, shoving each other aside to leer at her. With an oath, Cutler rounded on them and they fell away at once. He turned back to Amaryllis, his little hands resting on the door frame. She could see the contours of his cropped skull as he lowered his head to look at her.

'No buyers yet, Miss Vaughan? No one even come to view?'

Anger gave Amaryllis courage. 'So you're working for Lord Vanbrugh! I might have guessed it!'

'It was my scheme,' said Cutler. 'The men are mine too. Lord Vanbrugh pays, that's all.'

The information gave Amaryllis no comfort.

'Give me what I want,' he said, 'and I'll take the men away.'

'*No*!' said Amaryllis.

Cutler's face did not change but his nails dug into the wood of the door frame. 'I don't want to break you. It's killing the goose that lays the golden eggs, I know that. But then there's others need warning . . . Well, Miss Vaughan?'

'I'll never pay you!'

'You're finished then,' he said, and stepped back onto the pavement, pushing the carriage away from him with such ferocity that it swung on its springs and Amaryllis had to clutch at the strap to save herself from falling.

Thirty

Amaryllis found that it was easier to be brave now that Cutler was no longer close to her and by the time she found Mr Yardley in the site office she had managed to push him to the back of her mind. Mr Yardley was bent over a plan but he straightened himself when he saw Amaryllis and asked her what Mr Linklater had said.

'He *wants* us to fail – the old vulture!' said Amaryllis indignantly. 'We'll have to take steps ourselves. *Drastic* steps.'

Mr Yardley waited, in some trepidation, to discover what they might be.

'We'll ask those men to leave Saracen Street one more time. And if they refuse, we'll evict them by force. It must be done. There's nothing else for it.'

'I see,' murmured Mr Yardley.

'A concerted attack is all that's needed. We won't hurt them seriously, of course, just frighten them away.'

'We?' asked Mr Yardley gently.

'Well, of course *I* can't fight them, but the rest of you could. Our workmen are sure to be stronger than Lord Vanbrugh's men. They do nothing but smoke and drink and lounge about all day. Their muscles must be as soft as putty!'

'Street brawling is not normally part of a workman's duties.'

'No, but they won't care for that. They know their jobs are at risk. They're spoiling for a fight. We'd better do it this afternoon at about five o'clock, when the street's fairly empty.'

'It's not something I'd approve of in the usual way . . . '

'But what else can we do?'

Mr Yardley rubbed his chin unhappily. 'I suppose it is the

quickest way. We could go to law, but that would take months.'

'This afternoon then,' said Amaryllis. 'And if there *should* be any difficulties with the police, I'll come and bail you out as soon as possible.'

Mr Yardley said that he was grateful.

At half past four that afternoon, Amaryllis and Bella stood at the window of the site office watching the workmen gather outside. Mr Yardley had failed to persuade Lord Vanbrugh's men to leave and he was now reluctantly prepared to fight. After much rolling up of shirtsleeves and flexing of muscles, the men said that they were ready, and Mr Yardley led them through Crewe House and out into Selby Street with Silas bringing up the rear.

For a long five minutes Amaryllis and Bella heard nothing. Then a sudden burst of shouting in the distance told them that Mr Yardley's men were beginning the advance up Saracen Street. The sound of running feet became audible as Lord Vanbrugh's men fled down the street, hotly pursued.

Amaryllis turned excitedly to Bella. 'They're running! Can you hear them? We've beaten them!'

'They're just rallying their men to a strong point. There – what did I tell you,' said Bella as a man ran past Crewe Place towards the attackers. 'We'll have a fight yet.'

Almost as she finished speaking, there was a burst of confused yells.

'They're getting close,' said Bella. 'Can't be more than fifty yards away by now.'

There were more shouts, the trample of feet and then a struggling tangle of men came briefly into view and reeled back again out of sight.

One of Lord Vanbrugh's men, wearing a shirt stained red with blood from an opponent's nose, had shaken off his attackers and was running down Crewe Place, chased by a young carpenter. Cornered near a stack of bricks just outside Crewe House, the man turned and gave fight. Amaryllis looked away wishing she could block out the ugly sounds of punches and gasping breath.

Bella watched with keen interest, imitating the combatants' blows with her own fists against the windowsill.

'Look at that!' she exclaimed. 'The neatest left hook I ever saw! He knows a thing or two, that lad. He's winded him, I do believe. No, the other fellow's up again. He's fending him off – now they're hard at it again! Going for the kidneys too, the dirty scoundrel! That's right, my lad! You give it to him! Go for the eyes . . . He's got him – he's done for!'

Amaryllis opened her eyes to see the man in the blood-stained shirt doubled up against a wall. Then she clutched Bella's arm. 'Over there!' she said. 'More of Lord Vanbrugh's men coming to help him!'

'So there are. Three of them,' said Bella with satisfaction. 'Well, that settles it. I can't leave that poor lad to fight them all on his own, now can I?'

She rolled up her sleeves, took off her golden earrings and handed them to Amaryllis. 'You look after these,' she said. 'I'm going out there.'

Bella marched out of the house straight into the fight. She grabbed the waist of the man in the blood-stained shirt, tripping another man up with her foot as she did so. He went sprawling, and the third man gave Bella a punch in the face before her own fist landed on his chin. The man in the blood-stained shirt wrenched himself free and was turning on Bella, when a shout went up on Saracen Street. Lord Vanbrugh's men, realizing that victory had gone to their opponents, took to their heels and fled, leaving Bella more indignant at their lack of spirit than at the black eye she had received.

The next morning was particularly wet and dismal, but no amount of rain could dampen Amaryllis's spirits. She made her usual inspection of the work and then joined Mr Yardley in the site office, beaming at him as she balanced herself on a campstool.

'There's no sign of them,' she announced. 'I was looking out of the cab windows all the way up Saracen Street. We must have frightened them off for good!'

She smiled triumphantly at Mr Yardley but he did not smile back.

'Is your face hurting you?' she asked.

Mr Yardley had a swollen lip and a grazed cheek, but he hastily denied any feeling of discomfort.

'Bella has a dreadful black eye. She spent most of yesterday evening holding a piece of raw steak against it but it's worse than ever this morning. She says it was all in a good cause . . . I hadn't realized how easy it would be to get rid of them. I half expected them to be here again this morning. I can't think why we didn't throw them out before. I expect Lord Vanbrugh's heard all about it by now. I hope it's taught him a lesson!'

'I don't think Lord Vanbrugh will be particularly upset about it,' said Mr Yardley with a sigh.

'What do you mean? The men *are* all gone, aren't they?'

'Oh yes. They're all gone.'

'Well then. What *can* be the matter?'

'The building works have been completed.'

'Building works?'

'Yes. You remember the house that had hoarding in front of it last week – on Lord Vanbrugh's side of Saracen Street?'

'I suppose so . . . '

'You'd better come and see for yourself.' Regardless of the rain, Mr Yardley led Amaryllis out of Crewe Place and up Saracen Street.

'There,' he said. 'You wouldn't have seen it from the cab, coming from the other direction.'

Amaryllis followed his pointing finger through the rain to the newly completed façade. She gave a gasp of dismay. There, in disastrous proximity to Crewe Place, were plate-glass windows, ornamental ironwork, brass gas-lamps and a sign with 'The Vanbrugh Arms' written beneath it in gilded letters.

'A public house!' cried Amaryllis despairingly.

Silas came towards them with a grin on his face. He nodded scornfully at the Vanbrugh Arms. 'That's no pub. I've just been to have a look. It's nothing but a shoddy frontage and a fancy sign. There's not a drop of drink in the place.'

Amaryllis's hopes rose, but Mr Yardley said, 'It doesn't make any difference. One look at that sign and our buyers will turn and run. They won't stop to inquire whether it's a real pub or not.'

Amaryllis refused to believe Mr Yardley but experience soon proved him right. Buyers approaching from the southern end of Saracen Street looked around, expressed interest and left names and addresses, but no sooner had they driven away to the north than they saw the Vanbrugh Arms and were never heard of again. Buyers approaching from the north saw the public house before they reached Crewe Place and did not even bother to stop. One man, with a red and swollen nose, made a tentative offer for a house but he soon discovered that the Vanbrugh Arms was a pub in name only and changed his mind. A few other people said that they might consider taking a house at a lower price but felt that the present one was much too high for such an ungenteel neighbourhood. The only bit of comfort in this bleak situation was the increasing discontent of Lord Vanbrugh's own tenants in Saracen Street.

Silas and some of the bolder spirits among the workmen wanted to go over to the Vanbrugh Arms one night and tear down the façade. But Mr Yardley pointed out that if caught they risked transportation and the scheme was abandoned. Amaryllis, knowing that her involvement with Lord Vanbrugh was to blame for the crisis, was consumed with guilt, and she grew increasingly anxious as the day for the first interest payment drew near.

One morning, after a restless night, she awoke even earlier than usual. She got up and dressed, left a note for Bella and went outside, just as the sky was paling with the dawn. At this early hour the streets were safe and Amaryllis decided she would visit the market at Covent Garden. The fresh air stimulated her and brought a little colour to her cheeks and the only pedestrians she met were an occasional policeman and once a doctor's man, stumbling along half-asleep with a box of drugs.

The roadway was busier than the pavements. In Trafalgar Square a quartet of sweeping machines moved slowly along the street and in the Strand coal waggons and brewers' drays rumbled past, along with the occasional hackney cab dashing to catch an early train. As Amaryllis neared her destination, the market gardeners' carts became more frequent and heavy country waggons, piled high with vegetables, lumbered along the middle of the road, outmanoeuvred on either side by the little darting costermongers' shallows.

By the time Amaryllis reached Covent Garden, the vegetable market was in full swing. She wandered between the piles of cabbages and potatoes, watching the porters bearing their towering headdresses of high-piled baskets as lightly as if they had been paper hats. She breathed in the fresh green smells exhaled by nets of lettuces and bunches of asparagus and listened to the soft country accents of the wagonners. Surrounded by the comforting anonymity of a place where everyone was much too busy to stop and stare, Amaryllis did not trouble to avoid the coffee stall, in the no man's land between the vegetable and flower markets.

Here porters and stall holders drank coffee out of thick mugs and wolfed down breakfasts of hot roast mutton, sandwiched between hunks of bread. This morning, as usual, a few pallid gentlemen in evening dress lingered round the stall, coffee mugs in hand, trying to revive themselves sufficiently to return home after a night's drinking.

Amaryllis passed them with no more than a cursory glance, and failed to notice one of their number start violently at the sight of her and then follow her into the flower market. She had not gone far and had paused to admire a great bunch of jasmine when he caught up with her and spoke her name. Amaryllis turned sharply and found herself face to face with Lord Vanbrugh, white with alcohol and sleeplessness.

She stared at him. 'What are you doing here?'

'Isn't it obvious? Recovering from the delights of last night, of course.'

His recovery looked far from complete. His eyes were strained under his thin black brows and his pupils were enormous.

'*Why* won't you sleep with me?' he said, scowling at her.

'Oh God . . . ' said Amaryllis. '*Must* we discuss it now?'

'Why won't you sleep with me? I'm not a monster, am I?'

'Yes! And keep your voice down!' hissed Amaryllis.

He looked at her unhappily. 'You can't hate me that much. I did you no harm.'

'If you didn't then, you're making up for it now.' Her voice wavered with fatigue and tension. 'Why can't you just leave me alone? You know I don't want you . . . '

He cut her short. 'I don't care any more – I want you. I'm sick of pretences anyway. I'll take what I can get,' he ended desolately. He swayed a little and put out a hand to steady himself.

'Well, you'll never make me sleep with you!' said Amaryllis. 'If you ruin, by a mean trick, all I've worked for, all I slept with you for – '

'Yes,' he said with vicious satisfaction. 'Your precious two thousand pounds – all gone. And Monksedge disappearing into the gaping maw of Mr Linklater.'

'And after that, do you think I'd *ever* become your mistress? I'd sooner hire myself out as a kitchen maid!'

'Yes, Amaryllis, I dare say.' He dwelt on the picture lovingly. 'You as a kitchen maid. I should enjoy that. Though no doubt it wouldn't be long before you were making up to the gardener's boy – for a bunch of parsley or a basket of turnips.'

Lord Vanbrugh swayed on his feet again. 'What in God's name was I drinking last night?' he muttered, clutching his stomach.

Amaryllis looked at him in disgust. 'If you're going to be sick, please do it elsewhere. Much more of your company and I'll probably join you.' She turned on her heel and walked away from him, among the flowers.

Thirty-one

Back in Pembroke Street, Mr Yardley called on Amaryllis after breakfast. He looked as tired and anxious as she did.

'Any lettings?' asked Amaryllis, in a voice that held no hope of any.

'None. A letter from Mr Linklater though – reminding us of the date of the first interest payment.'

'Gloating.'

'I'm afraid so. I take it there's no further news of Lord Vanbrugh?'

'I can't begin to tell you how sorry I am . . . '

Mr Yardley got up and walked to the window. 'It's part of being in business, that's all. I knew how you made your money and without it we couldn't have started this venture. Lord Vanburgh is just one of the risks we both have to take. Like flood or fire or a fall in the market.'

'Well, I'm not finished yet. There's still time to think of something.'

The day wore on into a grey afternoon. Amaryllis sat alone in her parlour, listening to the rain spattering against the windows. Her prospects seemed as dismal as the weather. Twilight came and Bella entered the room to draw down the blinds and light the lamp.

'You'll have to give in to him,' she said.

'Never.'

'Why not? It's better than ruining yourself. And others.'

'He's playing dirty.'

'True,' agreed Bella. 'But he's winning.'

'Whose side are you on? His or mine?'

'Neither,' said Bella promptly. 'I'm sick to death of the pair of you; always at each other's throats. I've no patience with you! But I can't stand waste. There's good money in Crewe Place just waiting for you to pick it up. And if you've got to sleep with Lord Vanbrugh to do it, then I say sleep with him. He hasn't got two heads, has he?'

'I *can't* do it. Not like this. It was different at Vanbrugh. I needed the money and I went there of my own free will.' Seeing Bella's sceptical expression, she said with sudden vehemence, 'Why didn't you pay off Cutler? It would have saved a lot of trouble in the long run; you wouldn't have had to leave London if you'd come to some agreement with him.'

'That was different!' said Bella, but her voice lacked conviction.

'Well, I just can't let him win, not this way.' She got up. 'Get me a cab, Bella. I'll go for a drive and see if that clears my mind.'

Thinking that it might comfort her, Amaryllis told the cab driver to take her to Belgravia. He asked for an address and gave her a knowing look when she told him to drive slowly round until he heard otherwise.

The rain had stopped shortly after dusk but the night was stormy under a troubled sky. By the time the cab reached Belgravia, great clouds were racing across the moon which shed a watery, uncertain light on the pale façades. Belgravia by moonlight seemed to Amaryllis as unreal as a stage set, a grandiose sham city as illusory as her own dreams of wealth and independence.

The thought of becoming Lord Vanbrugh's mistress again was intolerable. She knew how he would treat her, delighting in her humiliation. And Henry, patiently toiling away in Shropshire, trying to restore her shattered ties with home – what would he think of her? If she went back to Lord Vanbrugh it would destroy everything Henry had worked for. Worse – it would expose him to his neighbours' censure as a gullible fool.

But Henry was not her only problem. Impossible as it seemed to betray his trust, it was equally impossible to allow Mr Yardley to be ruined, to lose Monksedge and Pembroke Street, to destroy all her hopes and schemes. There *must* be some other way out, thought Amaryllis desperately. There *must* be someone else she could appeal to for help.

It began to rain again, heavily this time. Great drops drummed on the roof of the carriage and streamed down the windows, obscuring the view. Up on the box, the driver muttered a curse and pulled his hat down to meet his upturned coat collar.

The cab continued its slow progress along an avenue, turned into a crescent and came to a sudden halt. Amaryllis, finding the window too streaked with rain to be of use, pulled it down and leant out to discover the cause of the delay. Ahead of them was a concourse of carriages and beyond, bright and vivid as a picture framed by the surrounding darkness, was the open door of a great house revealing an expanse of marble floor and a blaze of candlelight. A lady was stepping down from one of the carriages which had drawn up at the door. She moved towards the house, lifting her silken skirts out of the wet, while a footman sheltered her with an umbrella. She looked elegant and wealthy; her evening cloak was of heavy velvet and diamonds sparkled in her hair. Amaryllis did not recognize the thickset man who accompanied her, but the lady was Georgiana Vanbrugh.

At the sight of her, Amaryllis was visited by a sudden inspiration. There was one person she hadn't tried yet. One person who might assist her, not out of any sympathy for her predicament, but out of hatred for Lord Vanbrugh. She would appeal for help to Lord Mayo, the man whom Georgiana had been going to marry. Lord Vanbrugh had deprived him of a wife and made a fool of him as a jilted lover. She rapped on the roof of the cab, told the driver to return to Pembroke Street and sat back against the cushions with a satisfied look on her face.

Although the pavements were still wet and shining, the rain had ceased. Gentlemen lowered their umbrellas, cabmen took the sacking off their horses' backs and the street women reappeared, avoiding lamp posts and projecting ledges for fear of chance drips spoiling their bonnets. As the cab neared Piccadilly Circus there was a clatter of hooves ahead, a grinding crunch and another sudden halt. Amaryllis again put her head out of the window and asked the driver what was the matter.

'Accident up front, Miss,' he told her, gesturing with his whip. 'Barouche lost a wheel by the looks of it. We'll be a few minutes.'

Amaryllis sighed impatiently and was about to sit back again when she caught sight of a man she knew on the pavement. There was no mistaking him in the gaslight. It was Dr Dangerfield.

He saw Amaryllis at almost the same moment and stood motionless, staring at her, for so long that the street women nudged one another and a passing drayman made a ribald remark. It seemed to bring Dr Dangerfield to his senses, and he dashed across the street to the carriage.

'I must talk to you,' he said, wrenching the door open and getting inside. Amaryllis felt her heart thudding. After all these months he was beside her again, close against her.

'I shouldn't have left you like that,' he said. 'I've cursed myself for it again and again. Six months! I've been in torment – longing for you every single day!'

There was a jolt as the cab moved off at last and Amaryllis was thrown against him.

'You're so wonderful,' said Dr Dangerfield breathlessly. 'My darling, my lovely darling . . . ' He bent his head to kiss her. Amaryllis pulled him eagerly towards her. 'Your lips are like honey,' murmured Dr Dangerfield between kisses. His hands were pushing aside her cloak, feeling for her breasts under her dress. He seized her hand, kissed it, discarded it and then laid bare her breast. The carriage came to a halt, waiting to turn into Regent Street, and a gas lamp flooded the interior with light. To Amaryllis's frustration, Dr Dangerfield pulled the cloak back over her bosom and tore himself away with an exasperated oath.

'Not in here,' he muttered. 'Not where someone might see us. There's a place I know. Completely discreet.' He leant out of the window and shouted directions to the driver. The carriage moved off again, turning down Coventry Street.

Dr Dangerfield took Amaryllis back in his arms. Beneath the concealing cloak, his hands found her breasts. 'My golden princess,' he whispered. 'I love you, God, how I love you . . . '

But Amaryllis's mood had changed. Though her body still responded to his touch, her desire had ebbed a little. His exaggerated compliments jarred on her. She found them insulting. Did he take her for a fool? A sudden treacherous recollection came into her mind. 'I want you,' Lord Vanbrugh had said that morning with his usual unvarnished honesty. 'I'm sick of pretences anyway. I'll take what I can get.'

'I worship you,' Dr Dangerfield was saying, his mouth hot against her neck. 'I adore you. My dearest, my darling . . . '

The carriage came to a halt. 'Here we are!' shouted the driver.

'Thank God!' said Dr Dangerfield. 'Pull your hood over your face. No, let me do it. That's right. No one would recognize you now . . . '

The cab had drawn up outside a coffee house with the ambiguous sign 'Beds Available' in the window. As Amaryllis stepped down onto the pavement, the cab driver murmured, 'Done all right tonight, eh darling?'

Dr Dangerfield hurried her down a dark alley and they entered the coffee house by a side door. It was guarded by an old woman with fat white arms who sat at a desk with a cash box in front of her. After a brief exchange with Dr Dangerfield, she reached behind her for a key, eyeing Amaryllis appraisingly as she did so. Dr Dangerfield took the key and led Amaryllis, half running, up the stairs and along a shadowy corridor. At the far end, he opened a door and pulled her inside.

The room was furnished exactly like hundreds of others in London, let out for similar purposes. There was a double bed, a red plush armchair, a cheval glass and a washstand behind a screen. The bed was smooth and soft. Its banked pillows looked voluptuous in the dim light of the gas. Amaryllis found herself remembering another bed, its curtains worn into ribbons, its canopy topped by dusty plumes.

Dr Dangerfield gave her one quick pent-up embrace and

then put her to one side while he stripped off his coat. Watching his flushed, self-absorbed, fumbling haste, Amaryllis suddenly knew that everything had gone wrong. The nausea rose in her throat. Frantic to get away from him, she wrenched open the door and fled down the passage. At the street door, the old woman tried to bar her way, but Amaryllis pushed past her and ran out into the alley. There was a cab approaching. Amaryllis hailed it, got inside and collapsed in a corner, sobbing with relief. It was only then that she realized the truth. She had been deceiving herself all these months. She had never cared for Dr Dangerfield: it was Lord Vanbrugh she wanted.

Aghast, Amaryllis huddled against the stale-smelling cushions. Why did it have to be Lord Vanbrugh? Selfish, vile tempered, insulting and hateful. Amaryllis leant her hot forehead against the cool glass of the window. She ached with frustrated desire. She knew she had only to go to him and he would take her back again. But she could not do that. He'd treat her just as he had done at Vanbrugh and that was not what she wanted from him. Bella had been right all along. Whatever his faults, she found Lord Vanbrugh's frank declarations of lust infinitely preferable to Dr Dangerfield's artificial phrases and pent up desires. Their month together, bitter and resentful though it had been, had at least made hypocrisy impossible. Their relations had had an honesty more conventional couplings lacked. But now it seemed as if even honesty must be given up. If Lord Vanbrugh knew she wanted him, he would use it as a weapon against her. She had better guard against that; she was too vulnerable already.

Thirty-two

The weather was uncertain on the following morning and by the time Amaryllis reached Lord Mayo's house, a great black cloud was obscuring the sun. Since she was quite unknown to Lord Mayo she expected some difficulty in gaining admittance to his house, but to her surprise the footman not only let her in immediately but also agreed to take her card to Lord Mayo. He had been up very late on the previous night and he was still sitting at breakfast in an elaborate dressing-gown when Amaryllis's card was brought in. He gazed at it for a moment and then tossed it down on the table.

'Damned if I know who she is,' he said. 'What's she look like, eh?'

The footman smiled.

'Like that, is it?' said Lord Mayo. 'Well, we'd better have her in then. Tell her I'll see her at once, if she doesn't object to dressing-gowns.'

Amaryllis had no such objection. She found Lord Mayo seated behind an array of silver covers, finishing his breakfast with a bunch of grapes and a cup of black coffee. He was a youngish man, not yet thirty-five, with carefully curled blond hair, a blond moustache and features which would have been handsome had they not seemed rather too small for his face. He looked Amaryllis over appreciatively, but did not trouble to rise to his feet.

'Well now, Miss what's your name . . . ' He reached for her card. 'Vaughan, yes. Take a seat. Vile day, isn't it? Came in to get out of the rain, have you?' He gave a braying laugh at his own joke.

'I've come to see you on business,' said Amaryllis. 'I understand that you've had dealings with Lord Vanbrugh and that he's treated you badly.'

Lord Mayo's face darkened.

'In fact, you've good reason to dislike him?'

'Oh yes,' said Lord Mayo, 'I dislike him all right.' The first drops of rain began to beat against the windows. Lord Mayo pushed away his plate and lit a cigar. 'And what,' he asked between puffs, 'do you want with me Miss Vaughan?'

'I'm the woman on whom Lord Vanbrugh spent his sister's dowry,' said Amaryllis. Lord Mayo threw down his cigar and whistled. 'So you're the little lady who's cheated me out of a deuced chilly wife!'

'No, no,' said Amaryllis. 'I knew nothing about it. It was all Lord Vanbrugh's doing.'

'Yes, I knew I'd got him to thank for it. Georgiana's no jilt.' He picked up his cigar, stuck it into his mouth and lighted it again.

'A fellow doesn't like being made a laughing stock, Miss Vaughan. What's more the thing was damned inconvenient, by God it was! I didn't much fancy Georgiana, of course, but I had to get married to get my hands on my capital. All tied up till I walk down the aisle. My father didn't trust me and that's the truth of it. Dashed brute of a thing, isn't it?' Amaryllis did her best to look sympathetic. 'But you still haven't said what you want with me, Miss Vaughan.'

'It's rather a long story. You see, Lord Vanbrugh is trying to wreck my building development.'

'Is he now? And what's he doing that for?'

'Because I've refused to become his mistress.'

'I don't blame you there,' he said. 'The fellow's penniless. Even taken up picture dealing, so they tell me. Confounded common of him. So he's trying to ruin you, eh?' Lord Mayo gave one of his braying laughs. 'Bit of a lecher is our Vanbrugh. Ruled by his tail. Aren't we all? What do *you* say, Miss Vaughan?'

'I'd better explain more fully,' said Amaryllis. She recounted the salient facts as quickly as possible, uneasily aware of Lord Mayo's salacious eye upon her.

'Deuced interesting,' he said when she had finished. 'But what do you want me to do about it?'

'It's very simple. Just come round to Crewe Place and take a lease on a house. Purely nominal, of course.'

'People who buy from you are snobs, are they?'

'That's right. If they knew you'd taken a lease, they'd be so impressed they'd overlook the Vanbrugh Arms. They'd be able to tell their friends Lord Mayo had a house in their street. It would make *all* the difference.'

Lord Mayo stared vacantly out at the rain and then turned and said, 'Damn it, Miss Vaughan, I can do better than that! I'll come and have a look at the place and if it takes my fancy, I'll lease a house for a widowed aunt of mine! I've been wondering what to do with the old girl. I'll pay you for it too, all right. Just the job, isn't it? We'll see what Vanbrugh has to say about that!' and he gave Amaryllis a flashing smile, while outside the storm broke at last and the thunder rattled the windows.

Amaryllis thanked him, endured a lascivious kiss on her hand and took her leave, glad to escape him, even at the cost of a drenching on her way home.

Lord Mayo lived up to his promise. He appeared in Crewe Place on the following day, escorting an elderly lady in black, who seemed quite bewildered by her nephew's attentiveness. He spent a good hour sauntering about the site and then he declared that Crewe House was just what his aunt was looking for, bullied her into agreeing with him and signed the lease then and there. He stayed a few minutes longer, basking in Amaryllis's gratitude, and departed, gloating at the thought that he had got the better of Lord Vanbrugh at last.

House agents no longer bothered to send prospective buyers to Crewe Place but a few people occasionally appeared in response to Mr Yardley's advertisements in the paper, and shortly after Lord Mayo left a young couple ventured into the site office and asked to view. The young man's clothes seemed to have been chosen in the hope of giving offence to nobody and his wife's smart parasol only drew attention to her dowdy dress and bonnet. They introduced themselves as Mr and Mrs Wilson looking for a nice little family home and seemed rather flustered by the attention lavished on them.

By the time the Wilsons had seen over the site Amaryllis's head ached with tension and Mr Yardley, pale with nerves, tripped over the step as he led them into the office.

'Now then,' said Amaryllis, as brightly as she could. 'You've seen the properties. Is there any one you particularly liked?'

The young couple whispered together. 'Yes,' said Mr Wilson, 'we thought the one on the corner wasn't too bad, if it's still available. It gets more light than most.'

'Though the noise would be a drawback, Charlie. Being so near Saracen Street,' said his wife hurriedly. 'And we'd have to take a look round the neighbourhood, of course, before we signed anything.'

Her heart beating, Amaryllis produced her trump card. 'I believe the corner house is still available. It's a very nice property. Crewe House is the best, of course, but Lord Mayo has just taken that for his aunt . . . ' and she carelessly picked up the lease and then dropped it again, so that Lord Mayo's signature was visible.

Mr Wilson went pink with excitement. He and his wife whispered together. Then he said, 'My wife's still worried about the noise from Saracen Street. She prefers a more retired situation. Is the house at the other end of the terrace still available? Away from the street, I mean?'

Amaryllis suppressed the urge to hug Mr Yardley and dance round the room. 'Next to Crewe House?' she asked, as calmly as she could. 'Yes, that's still for sale. Not for long though. As you say, that *is* the quieter end.'

'No, well we'll have that one then.'

'I'm afraid I must ask you for a deposit,' said Amaryllis, chancing it, 'I could hold the property till this afternoon . . . as a gesture of goodwill. Another house I could reserve for a week perhaps, but this is in the most desirable situation. There are bound to be other offers.'

'No, no,' said Mr Wilson. 'This afternoon will be quite all right. I'll be off to my bankers at once.'

When the Wilsons had gone, Amaryllis and Mr Yardley sat

down and looked at one another.

'We've done our best,' said Amaryllis at last. 'If Lord Mayo wins over the Vanbrugh Arms we're saved. If not –'

'Oh, it'll be all right,' said Mr Yardley. 'Did you see the way their faces changed when you mentioned Lord Mayo? They didn't even ask about the gas supply.'

'They didn't want to know about the gardens either. Or the basements. And when I think how we sweated to make the staircases wider – they weren't even interested! We could have *stuck* the houses together for all they cared.' She laughed. 'You'll have to admit I was right about the basements. Can you imagine what the Wilsons would have thought of vaulted stone ceilings?'

Mr Yardley grinned.

An hour later, the Wilsons reappeared. Weak with relief, Amaryllis and Mr Yardley ushered them into the site office.

'We thought,' said Mr Wilson with a glance at his wife, 'that with a public house so near, a reduction in the price . . . '

'Out of the question,' said Amaryllis. 'We'll have no difficulty in letting the house at the stated price.' Seeing Mr Wilson hesitate, she added cunningly, 'If Lord Mayo has no objection to the Vanbrugh Arms I really don't see why anyone else should.'

'Very well then, I'll have it!' said Mr Wilson.

'Splendid! You've bought better than you know.' Amaryllis dipped the pen in the ink and handed it to Mr Wilson while Mr Yardley held the paper steady as he signed. Looking at their tenant's wavering writing at the bottom of the lease, they felt their spirits soaring. They were saved.

The Wilsons were the first of many. No sooner had they left Crewe Place than Mr Yardley went the rounds of the house agents with Lord Mayo's lease, and from that day on prospective buyers were again sent to view. The Vanbrugh Arms continued to be an embarrassment for another week, but since it was not deterring purchasers, Lord Vanbrugh gave in to the pleas of his tenants and had the façade dismantled. Coming back from Mr Linklater's house, where she had been to pay the first instalment of interest, Amaryllis saw that the Vanbrugh Arms had become a private house again and knew that her victory was complete. But the fact somehow failed to elate her and it was in rather a subdued frame of mind that she returned to Pembroke Street.

Once she had his signature on her lease and his deposit in her cash box, Amaryllis had no further use for Lord Mayo, and certainly no wish to continue his acquaintance. She'd hoped that he too had only been interested in getting the better of Lord Vanbrugh, but it was not to be as simple as that. On the very next evening, a carriage drew up outside Amaryllis's house and Lord Mayo got out, carrying a large bunch of hothouse flowers. Unwilling to offend him before his aunt was safely installed in Crewe House, Amaryllis told Bella to show him up and when he came in she accepted the flowers and reluctantly asked him to sit down.

Lord Mayo did so with alacrity. He lounged back against the cushions, eyeing Amaryllis appreciatively. There was a long silence which Amaryllis, growing hot and indignant under his gaze, made no attempt to break. Then Lord Mayo said suddenly, 'Confound it, Miss Vaughan, but you're a lovely woman! I don't know when I've seen a lovelier and that's the truth. What's more, I swear you know a thing or two! The moment I saw you, I said to myself, Mayo, you're in luck there, my boy!' With some difficulty, he extracted a velvet jeweller's case from his waistcoat pocket and sat balancing it between finger and thumb while he stared at Amaryllis.

'I expect you know,' he went on, 'that I'm not a poor man. I'm a damned sight better off than Vanbrugh, you can stake your life on that! Got a pretty little thing here you might like.' He opened the jewel case to display a diamond pendant. 'In return for services rendered, eh, Miss Vaughan? Come now, what do you say? Give a fellow a chance!'

Amaryllis sat stony-faced. Lord Mayo frowned. 'I hope you've not been wasting my time, Miss Vaughan,' he said. 'Because a fellow doesn't like that – not by half he doesn't. Vanbrugh's been a bit of a brute to you, hasn't he?'

'Yes.'

Lord Mayo fingered the pendant. 'You want to do him a

bad turn, I daresay. Well, I'll tell you this, Miss Vaughan. There's not a worse turn you could do him than to have a little game with me.' Amaryllis stiffened and he waved a finger at her. 'Now, don't try all that nonsense with *me*. I know the sort of woman you are; none better!'

'Lord Vanbrugh may want to make me his mistress – ' began Amaryllis icily.

'Yes, yes, but we needn't go into all that. I know what you're thinking. You could sleep with anyone, eh? And still infuriate Vanbrugh. But that's where you're wrong, Miss Vaughan. I fit the bill better than anyone else. You see,' said Lord Mayo, draping the pendant over his hand so that the diamonds sparkled in the lamplight, 'Lady Vanbrugh was a hot-blooded woman. She was down at Vanbrugh alone one summer. A damned convenient arrangement; my estates border Vanbrugh, you know. She took a fancy to me and Mayo's not the man to disappoint a lady. We always used that dusty old bed of her husband's. She made a point of it. That's the sort of spirited woman she was. It must have been twelve years ago, but Vanbrugh's never much cared for me since. Can't blame him really. Well, I ask you, Miss Vaughan, what husband ever did take a fancy to his wife's lover? Nice little revenge for you if you're willing. History repeating itself, eh?'

Amaryllis was about to tell Lord Mayo exactly what she thought of him when she was forestalled by steps on the stair. They reached the landing, the door opened and Lord Vanbrugh stood on the threshold. His gaze rested on Lord Mayo; then, with a furious look at Amaryllis, he swore violently and fell on his rival without even waiting for Lord Mayo to get up from his chair.

It was not much of a fight. The combatants were too angry to trouble themselves with rules and they panted and struggled and cursed one another like two drunken porters brawling over a bottle. Lord Mayo had the advantage of weight, but Lord Vanbrugh's jealous fury lent ferocity to his onslaught and a lucky punch delivered just as Lord Mayo tripped over a chair gave him the victory. Gasping for breath, Lord Vanbrugh dragged his semiconscious opponent to the door and heaved him down the stairs, casting his bunch of flowers after him.

Thirty-three

Lord Vanbrugh came storming back into the room, slammed the door and shouted, 'Mayo! My God – Mayo! Do you never stop? One man after another, in endless succession! Mayo!' he repeated in a voice of loathing. 'How could you, Amaryllis, how *could* you!' And he sat down beside her and put his head in his hands.

Amaryllis looked at him uncertainly. 'You don't think . . .'

'First my wife, then my sister, and now *you*!'

'You don't suppose I like him, do you? I've had to use him to protect myself from you!'

'You've said enough, Amaryllis. You couldn't insult me more if you tried!'

She stared at him, outraged. 'You think I'm his mistress. *Don't* you?'

'Of course I do! Do you take me for a fool?'

'Yes!' shouted Amaryllis. 'I was never anyone's mistress but yours. And look at the trouble that's caused me!'

He gave her a suspicious look. 'Then what was he doing here?'

'He wanted to make love to me.'

'Ah – I thought so!'

'– and I refused him!'

'You're lying. How else could you have got him to take a lease on Crewe House?'

'It wasn't hard! I just had to tell him it would anger you! He jumped at the chance. It was only later that he started to make a nuisance of himself – ' She broke off suddenly. 'Why the hell should I have to justify myself to you!'

Lord Vanbrugh could not think of a reason. He sat in unhappy silence, looking broodingly at Amaryllis. Aware of his gaze upon her, she felt a sudden acute longing for the warmth of his body against hers. Afraid he might read her thoughts, she said aggressively, 'It's none of your business *what* I choose to do! You've no control over my actions. How dare you come bursting in here – attacking my guest!'

'Your guest! Your seducer, more like!'

'I've a perfect right to see Lord Mayo, if I want. I've a perfect right to go to bed with him, if I want!'

In a fury, he seized her wrists. Instantly, her whole consciousness seemed centred on his fingers. Desire swept over her in a hot rush. Her heart began to pound, her breath came in constricted gasps, her blood surged thick and full. She stared at him, seeing her own emotions reflected in his eyes, as he too passed from anger to desire. His grasp on her wrists slackened, his fingers dragged along the soft flesh of her arms. She reached up a hand to his neck. There was a small soft hollow behind his ear; his hair was harsh to the touch. For a moment longer she delayed, tense and expectant. Then she reached towards him. He responded with desperate eagerness, straining her body against his, one hand grasping her breast. But her passion was too urgent for caresses. Sobbing with desire, she pushed up her skirts and pulled him down against her.

Afterwards, as desire receded, doubts returned. Lying there, drowsy and exhausted, Lord Vanbrugh murmured, 'You don't want Mayo, do you?'

Amaryllis was half asleep against his shoulder. She turned and kissed him languidly, her hand straying across his chest. 'What did you say . . . ?'

'Mayo. You don't want him?'

Amaryllis propped herself up on one elbow and looked at him indignantly.

'Of course I don't! What more proof do you want?'

He pulled her back against him, secretly delighted. With his free hand, he stroked her hair, smoothing the damp curls about her brow.

'This is a damned inconvenient sofa. I'm bruised all over. Remind me next time to use a bed.'

Amaryllis played with the edging of his shirt. 'There's one in there.'

'Yes, but you gave me no time to get to it. Besides, if you had, I should have remembered that I can't possibly afford you. How much is it this time?' His hand moved down to her breast. 'Reduced rates for old customers? And a further reduction because you wanted me almost as much as I wanted you. Don't bother to deny it. I won't believe you.'

'Perhaps I should pay *you*.'

'Yes, by the simple expedient of doing it all over again . . . '

Amaryllis reached up to kiss him, her hair falling over his face.

'I'm glad I chose tonight for my visit,' he murmured against her lips.

She drew back a little. 'Yes, why tonight? Did you know Lord Mayo would be here?'

'No, that was just a lucky coincidence.'

'Well, why did you come here then?'

He sighed. 'I hoped you wouldn't ask . . . I came here to threaten you. I was going to tell Henry Chesil you were still my mistress – unless, of course, you came back to me.'

'*What*!' cried Amaryllis, pushing his arms away.

'I warned you that time in Covent Garden that I wouldn't give up. Henry Chesil was all I could think of.'

'Of all the dirty tricks!'

'I know, I know. But I was desperate – at my wits' end.'

'I'm surprised your friend Cutler didn't have some nasty little scheme up his sleeve.'

'Yes, well, he did have a suggestion, as it happened.' Lord Vanbrugh's brow darkened. 'He wanted me to use force. He even offered to do the job himself. Beat you into bed with me – that's what he said. I kicked him out after that. There are limits.'

Amaryllis shuddered. Lord Vanbrugh looked rather ashamed of himself.

'I never liked the look of him. But perhaps I should have kept him on though. He'd have come in handy for Mayo.'

'Not him again!' said Amaryllis. 'Why can't you forget about Lord Mayo?'

'You know why.'

'You mean, because of your wife? But you didn't love her, did you?'

'No, of course not,' he said irritably. 'What's that got to do with it?'

'Everything, I should think. If you didn't love her, why shouldn't she amuse herself with Lord Mayo? It made no difference to you.'

'Damn it, she was my wife!'

'Well?'

'Don't you understand? He cuckolded me! Oh, it's useless to explain. You've clearly no idea what I'm talking about.'

'No, I haven't,' said Amaryllis. 'I think it's ridiculous to make such a fuss about it.'

'But she was married to me. I was supporting the woman.'

'She didn't bring you a dowry then?'

'Certainly she did. But once married . . . '

'It became *your* money. And your wife . . . '

'Had a duty to be faithful to me. I could have divorced her for adultery.'

'You were entirely faithful to her, of course.'

'Naturally I wasn't. For a husband, it's different. You know that perfectly well!'

'Why?'

'Because a husband's not going to foist any bastards on his wife as legitimate heirs. Or did you think it was men who gave birth?'

Amaryllis had forgotten about inheritance. She was silenced for a moment. Then she said suddenly, 'But she didn't, did she?'

'Didn't what?'

'Foist any bastards on you.'

'No,' he said grimly. 'I saw to that. I told her if she had a child, I'd ruin her; throw her out to beg in the streets!'

'You seem to have a habit of telling women that, when they won't do what you want. Would you really have ruined her?'

'Who knows? Perhaps, if I was angry enough. Anyhow the threat worked. That was all I cared about. I wasn't having Mayo's bastards at Vanbrugh – or any of her other lovers' brats for that matter.' He frowned. 'Forget Caroline. I don't want to think of her ever again.'

The next morning, Amaryllis woke in the half-light of a foggy day to find Lord Vanbrugh's place empty beside her and Bella surveying her from the doorway.

'Well!' she said. 'You've changed your tune, haven't you?'

Amaryllis sat up naked in bed, holding the covers about her. 'Where is he?' she asked.

'Gone home – and about time too!' Bella glanced around the room. 'I've never seen such a mess! Clothes lying everywhere and the parlour looks as if a bull's been let loose in it. That sofa will never be the same again.' She bent down to pick up a piece of underclothing and shook her head. 'I don't know! I despair of you sometimes. You wouldn't go to bed with Lord Vanbrugh to save yourself from ruin, oh no. We were all at our wits' end. And *now*, just when we've got the better of him at last, you fall into bed with him at the drop of a hat! Well, one thing's certain,' said Bella, looking hard at Amaryllis's flushed countenance, 'either you're in love with the man, or you've gone stark staring mad!'

'I'm *not* in love with him!'

'Oh, aren't you?'

'He's a hateful selfish brute, you know he is! Only an imbecile could possibly love him!'

'Well,' said Bella, 'if the cap fits . . . ' and she vanished into the parlour before Amaryllis's hastily flung pillow could reach her.

Lord Vanbrugh, meanwhile, was strolling about a picture gallery, feeling extremely pleased with himself. At last, after all these months, Amaryllis was his mistress again. What was more, his passion for her was reciprocated. He had had enough experience of prostitutes' pretended raptures to know that her response to him was genuine. Smiling to himself, he remembered how she had looked in bed this morning, her face flushed with sleep and her lips swollen with kissing. He had left her with intense reluctance, knowing that had she awoken he would have been unable to leave at all. But it was vital to remind one's mistress that she was not indispensable. Besides, he was still not convinced that desire for him and his money was Amaryllis's only reason for making love. He suspected some undergame. She had held out against him for so long when she could have staved off ruin by yielding. Why, then should she suddenly give way now? It was suspicious, but, try as he might, he could think of no explanation. Perhaps it would be best if he kept away from her for a few days. For three days, Lord Vanbrugh decided, trying to fight against the longing for her that was already threatening to undo his resolution.

Staring unseeingly at a large landscape, he began to plan Amaryllis's future as his mistress. He would take a little house for her in St John's Wood, one of the newer villas. She would keep Bella, of course, and one or two underservants as well. He would sell the Cuyp to help pay for it all. Gordon had shown a good deal of interest in it and was sure to buy if he lowered the price a trifle. But one thing he would absolutely forbid; there must be no more of this building nonsense. Amaryllis would have her hands quite full enough buying dresses and running the house for him. Besides, he wanted to find her at home whenever he took it into his head to call, not wandering round some grubby builder's yard. And he didn't like the interest she took in it all. It made her too independent of him.

Later that day Amaryllis, unaware of these plans for her future well-being, was sitting by the fire, trying to concentrate on the newspaper. She felt a certain pleasurable lassitude and was glad it was too foggy to go out. Before long, her thoughts wandered from the newspaper to the events of the previous evening and when she heard a carriage draw up outside the house she was so frightened that it might be Lord Mayo, or the police come to arrest her for his murder, that she was quite relieved when Bella announced that Mrs Saville was on her way upstairs.

'She looks as sour as a lemon about something. I knew

there'd be trouble before long.'

Georgiana entered the room slowly, her costly Indian shawl failing to hide the fact that she was several months pregnant. When Amaryllis had greeted her, rather warily, Georgiana enthroned herself upon the sofa. 'It is many months since we last met, Miss Vaughan. You will forgive the informality of this visit, I hope, since I am here in your own best interests.'

Amaryllis inclined her head unsmilingly.

'I know, of course, of my brother's attentions to you,' Georgiana went on. 'But until recently, I had paid no great heed to it. In the circles my brother frequents it is the fashion to go to extravagant lengths in the pursuit of women of, shall we say, a certain kind. But I'm now certain that my brother has another motive for his behaviour. I have no cause to love you, Miss Vaughan, as you are well aware, but for my brother I have even less regard. His treatment of you is despicable. I have come here to warn you against him.'

Amaryllis looked at her in surprise. 'What can you mean? I know Lord Vanbrugh wants to make me his mistress. I have always known it . . . '

'My brother, Miss Vaughan, is a jealous and vindictive man. He has never forgiven Lord Mayo for certain indiscretions with his wife. You will recall the revenge he took on both Lord Mayo and myself only last year.'

Amaryllis nodded.

'My sister-in-law's behaviour was always deplorable, of course,' said Georgiana. 'Lord Mayo was by no means her only lover. He was not even her only lover in Shropshire.' She hesitated for a moment, as if half reluctant to reveal the truth.

'Yes?' Amaryllis prompted her, ignorant of the storm about to break.

'One of her other lovers,' said Georgiana, 'her last, I believe, before her death, was another Shropshire neighbour – a certain Captain Vaughan.'

'My father!'

'Yes,' said Georgiana, 'your father. He cuckolded my brother and in revenge, my brother seduced his daughter. Pretty, isn't it?'

Amaryllis drew a deep breath. 'It's not true! It can't be!'

'I am not in the habit of telling untruths.'

'I don't believe it.'

'No? In my brother's world, Miss Vaughan, cuckoldry is the one unforgiveable sin. Where a man's honour is involved, he will behave like an animal.'

Amaryllis was silent for a moment. Then she said, 'It's not Lord Vanbrugh's part in the affair I find hard to credit. I just can't believe that my father . . . '

'Really?' Georgiana sounded amused. 'Men are all alike in these matters. If your father had been like mine, it wouldn't surprise you in the least. He was always bringing his mistresses to Vanbrugh.'

'Why didn't you tell me this before?'

'I didn't know who you were,' said Georgiana smoothly. 'Oh, I knew your name was Vaughan, of course, but it never occurred to me to connect you with Captain Vaughan of Monksedge. Why should it? I assumed Anthony had come across you in London somewhere. But I recently paid a visit to Vanbrugh and there I heard certain rumours . . . It was easy to put two and two together. Oh, have no fear, I was perfectly discreet.' She rose to her feet and said, 'I hope you've heard enough to convince you. I'll leave you to think it over. You can count on my help should Anthony prove difficult to detach. He can be distressingly obstinate at times.'

Thirty-four

After she had seen Georgiana to the door, Amaryllis went upstairs to the kitchen where she found Bella doing the ironing. A clean blanket had been spread over the kitchen table and a bowl of starch stood beside it ready for use. Amaryllis's nightgowns and underwear lay in a heap on a chair and the kitchen fire burned with a red glow, heating the flat-irons ranged before it. Bella had already lighted an oil lamp to resist the fog and the twilight. It shed a pool of yellow light on the nightdress she was ironing. She looked up inquiringly as Amaryllis entered.

'Time for your lamp downstairs, is it?'

'It's not that,' said Amaryllis, sitting down at the table. 'I want to talk to you.'

Bella picked up her iron, returned it to the row before the fire, chose another and flicked a drop of water onto it from her bowl. She watched with satisfaction as the water evaporated with a hiss. The smell of hot cotton filled the air as her iron began to move smoothly to and fro across the nightdress.

'I can't believe it, Bella, but Mrs Saville says . . . that my father was Lady Vanbrugh's lover.' Bella's iron was checked for an instant. 'It's not true, is it, Bella?' asked Amaryllis anxiously.

'Oh, it's true all right.' Bella turned the nightdress over and began to work on the front. 'It was many years ago, when you were a child. He was always visiting her at Vanbrugh, or coming up to London when she was here for the Season.'

'But how did you know about it, Bella?' asked Amaryllis suspiciously. 'You weren't even living at Monksedge then.'

'No. I knew Lady Vanbrugh in London.' Bella sprinkled water on an over-dry sleeve and steam rose from her iron as it moved across it. 'She called me in professionally, as you might say.'

'Professionally?'

'You heard me,' said Bella. She straightened herself and gave Amaryllis a long, hard look. 'I suppose, after all this time, you've a right to know the truth. You've stuck up for me against Cutler. But no telling anyone, mind. Least of all Lord Vanbrugh.'

'No, no, I promise.'

Bella returned to her ironing. 'I used to spend my summers travelling about the country. I had a pony and cart and a stock of ribbons for show. But it was herbs I was really interested in. I'd collect what I needed on the quiet, when no one was about. Then I'd go back home to London and stay there for the rest of the year, making the herbs into medicines and selling them to ladies who found themselves in an interesting condition and wanted to become – less interesting. You understand me?'

The fog outside seemed to have penetrated the room. The kitchen fire burned with a misty glow and the lamp cast a blurred and wavering light.

'An abortionist,' whispered Amaryllis.

'That's right,' said Bella. 'Anyone else would have guessed it long ago. How did you think I was making so much money? Taking in washing?' Finding that her iron had cooled, she returned it to the fender and took up a hotter one. 'I got to see things most people don't see, and I got to know things most people don't know. I was trustworthy. I had a name for it. They all came to me, the married women with lovers. They didn't dare go to some fancy male doctor who'd tell their husbands. Their maids would know the truth though. You can't hide pregnancy from a lady's maid. That's how I came to know Mary Canning; she was Lady Vanbrugh's maid in those days. We got friendly and we stayed friendly, even after she'd become a midwife. Mostly the midwives don't like us; we spoil their trade.'

Having finished the nightdress, Bella took up a goffering iron and began work on a frilled night-cap. 'It was Mary

Canning who took me to that great house the Vanbrughs' had in St James's Square. She led me up the backstairs to the bedroom. I can see it now. Lady Caroline Vanbrugh, sitting up in that great satin bed with her nightdress covered in lace and a cloud of hair down her back, as white-faced and desperate as any poor little drab of a serving girl I've helped out of kindness. Her fingers were thin and cold and they gripped my arm like a vice. "You must help me," she said. "I swore to my husband I was barren. He'd kill me if he found out the truth."

'Well, I did help her. I helped her that time and several times afterwards. That's how I came to know your father. He was the one who paid me when she'd spent all her pin money. They were both grateful to me in their way. They knew I could have blackmailed the pair of them, as easy as winking. But I never stooped to it, not once, not with any of my customers. Well, the upshot of it was, that when I decided to leave London I remembered Captain Vaughan and thought he might help me find a refuge, out of gratitude for the old days. I came to Monksedge and I asked for his help, which he gave as freely as he could. *He'd* not forgotten, even though Lady Vanbrugh had been dead four years by that time. He still mourned her, in his careless way, and he was glad to do what he could for me.'

Amaryllis stared at the fire. Then she asked anxiously, 'Did my mother know about it all?'

'I couldn't tell you. She may have guessed, who can say? She never took to *me*, that's all I know.'

'And Lord Vanbrugh?'

'Oh, *he* knew all right. He kept a pretty close eye on his wife's goings on, for all he didn't care twopence about her. She knew it too. She was terrified of him.'

'Then why didn't you *tell* me about their relationship, before I went to live with Lord Vanbrugh?'

'Because there was no need for you to know. It's all ancient history now. If you've any sense, you'll forget it.'

That night, Amaryllis was unable to rest. She sat up in bed and stared into the darkness. She must be mad to have slept with Lord Vanbrugh again; she was certainly mad to desire him. She was even cold bloodedly wondering if he was sleeping with her out of revenge – and this was the man she wanted to take as her lover. But that was part of his attraction. With Lord Vanbrugh she could be herself; she couldn't possibly behave worse than he did.

There was a patter of gravel against one of the front windows. Amaryllis went into the parlour and pushed the blind aside to peer into the street. Lord Vanbrugh's upturned face was just visible in the faint light from the gas lamp. 'Let me in, Amaryllis,' he whispered.

Amaryllis, secretly delighted, gave him an ungracious nod and then lit a candle and went downstairs to open the door. Barely inside, he pulled her hard against him. The candle went out and dripped hot wax on her nightdress.

'Look what you've made me do,' hissed Amaryllis crossly. 'Come upstairs – *quietly*.'

They had to feel their way in the darkness but when they reached the parlour Amaryllis relit the candle and put it down on the table.

'Not here,' said Lord Vanbrugh, coolly picking it up again and walking on into the bedroom. 'I'm not enduring the rigours of that sofa again.'

'How dare you!' said Amaryllis, her heart beating so loudly she felt sure he must hear it. 'What makes you think you can just wander in here at any time of the day or night . . . '

With an impudent smile, Lord Vanbrugh took off his cloak and began to strip off his jacket, while Amaryllis stood there accusingly, her hair haloed by the candlelight. His face softened suddenly. 'I was going to call at a more civilized hour, but the truth is – I couldn't keep away any longer.'

The next morning, Amaryllis woke to find Lord Vanbrugh's arms about her. He bent his head to kiss her and then said teasingly, 'I thought you'd never wake up. In the end I had to pinch you.'

'Well, I'm tired,' said Amaryllis, yawning. 'But since I *am* awake, I want to talk to you.'

He groaned. 'At this hour?'

'Yes. It's most important.'

'Oh God. The money. I was wondering when you'd get around to that.'

'Money has nothing to do with it! I just want to know why you made love to me – the truth, mind!'

'I'm sorry. I thought I'd been more than explicit . . . What other reason do you have in mind?'

'Revenge,' said Amaryllis, wishing that it did not sound quite so melodramatic.

He gave a shout of laughter. 'Revenge! Some revenge! You enjoy it too much for that! I agree I've a right to get my own back on you for your behaviour these past few months, but I'll find some more effective way of doing it.'

'Not revenge on *me*,' said Amaryllis. 'On my father. For sleeping with your wife.'

'Who told you about that?' he demanded, his amusement abruptly evaporating.

'Your sister told me, yesterday.'

'She did, did she?'

'Well? Are you sleeping with me out of revenge?'

'Don't be silly! Good God, it all happened ten years ago! Besides, you seduced *me*.'

'But you let it happen with astonishing ease.'

'Well, I was drunk . . . Oh God, let's not go into all that again! I want to know more about Georgiana. Why the hell should she start stirring up trouble all of a sudden?'

'Spite, I should think. She loathes you even more than she does me. She's with child, of course; perhaps it's had a bad effect on her temper.'

'With child? So that's what she's up to! The *bitch*!' He flung off the bedclothes and leapt out of bed.

'What are you doing?' cried Amaryllis.

'I'm going straight over to see Georgiana!'

Once at St James's Square, Lord Vanbrugh's temper was not improved when the door was opened by the butler who had once graced his own establishment; and he was further incensed by the sight of one of his former footmen hovering in the background. The butler showed him into the main drawing-room on the first floor and here, in spite of himself, Lord Vanbrugh was impressed by the transformation that had taken place. The room, so shabby when he had owned it, had been redecorated, but infinite pains had been taken to avoid any hint of ostentation. The furniture was new, but had had the gloss of newness miraculously removed, the carpet looked as if it had lain there for decades, the curtains had an air of aristocratic immutability and even the gilding on the pictures was of a duller gold than usual, as if gently breathed on by a London fog.

'Very good, Georgiana!' said Lord Vanbrugh, as his sister entered the room. 'No one would think it was first generation trade!'

'On the contrary,' said Georgiana, 'it's sixth generation Vanbrugh.'

'Talking of generation, why the devil didn't you tell me you were breeding?'

'Since you didn't see fit to inform me that you'd returned from Italy, I assumed the news wouldn't interest you.'

Lord Vanbrugh ignored this. 'It's Saville's, I take it?'

'Naturally.'

'I don't suppose there was anything natural about it! And *now*, Georgiana, you can explain what the devil you meant by telling Amaryllis Vaughan that I was sleeping with her out of revenge!'

'It was in your own interests. Your pursuit of that girl is making you the talk of London! You've made a fool of yourself over her for months! I thought it was time to put a stop to it, that's all.'

'You're lying, Georgiana. You don't give a damn about me. All *you* care about is getting your hands on Vanbrugh and the title, and you'll go to any lengths to do it! You're trying to get rid of Amaryllis because you've found out her birth's respectable. You're terrified she'll make me marry her and cheat that brat of yours out of a barony!'

'Well, what if I am! I've a right to defend my own! You're clearly besotted with the girl and you've been known to break your promises before now!'

'Well, I didn't intend to break this one! I hadn't the slightest intention of marrying Amaryllis. Good God, she's a whore! What kind of a fool do you take me for? But *now*, Georgiana, things have changed. You've meddled in my affairs once too often!'

'What do you mean?'

'Your vile behaviour has released me from all promises! I'm damned if I'm going to sit back and let my title descend to your brats! You can have your cursed dowry back! I'll get children of my own!'

'You can't!' gasped Georgiana. 'You *can't!* It's too late! I don't want the dowry. Stop! Where are you going?'

'To marry Amaryllis Vaughan!'

Thirty-five

When Lord Vanbrugh returned to Pembroke Street he found Amaryllis still in bed. She was sitting propped up against her pillows, drinking a cup of coffee. She looked up as he marched into her room and made a half-hearted attempt to straighten the sheets.

'Don't bother with that,' he ordered her. 'Get up and get dressed. We're going out.'

'Unfortunately,' Amaryllis said coldly, 'I'm rather busy this morning.'

'Yes, it looks like it,' said Lord Vanbrugh. 'Now get up, Amaryllis; there's a lot to do, I've decided to marry you.'

'*What!*'

'You heard me. Well – what are you waiting for? Get up!'

'I'm not going to marry you,' said Amaryllis bluntly.

It was Lord Vanbrugh's turn to look astonished. '*What* did you say?'

'I don't,' said Amaryllis, slowly and clearly, 'in the least want to marry you.'

'Oh God, you're in one of your difficult moods again . . . Don't be ridiculous, Amaryllis. Get up and stop wasting time.'

Amaryllis gave an exasperated sigh. Staying where she was, she put down her cup, reached for her comb and began to draw it through her hair.

'My patience is running out,' said Lord Vanbrugh threateningly. 'Keep me waiting much longer and I may change my mind.'

'I don't want to marry you,' repeated Amaryllis, still combing.

'Oh don't you! Why ever not?'

'Lots of reasons. Why do *you* want to marry *me*, if it comes to that?'

'To pay back my bitch of a sister, of course!'

'Yes. I thought it might be that. But I don't see how marrying me would pay back Mrs Saville. It sounds like cutting off your nose to spite your face.'

'Oh, I know what I'm doing, never fear! When Georgiana married Saville, I agreed to stay single so that her brats could inherit the title. But her damned interfering ways are beyond bearing! I told her this morning, as far as I'm concerned the agreement is void.'

'But I still don't see why you have to marry *me*. After all, I'm a fallen woman. Why not pick someone more suitable?'

'It's quite simple. If I end the agreement, I shall have to give Georgiana her damned dowry back.'

'Pembroke Street. I *see*.'

'Exactly, Amaryllis. Pembroke Street – which only you can bring me.'

Amaryllis laid down her comb, selected a strand of hair and began to twist it into a tiny plait. 'Yes,' she said thoughtfully. 'The marriage has its advantages from your point of view. I can appreciate that.'

'And from yours. You'll be a respectable woman again, Amaryllis – outwardly at least. With a little judicious bribery we should be able to conceal your past. If I marry you, you'll have a title, position, some standing in the world – and I'll make damned sure you behave yourself. You can make up your mind to that.'

Amaryllis loosened her plait and started another one. 'You think that to be Lady Vanbrugh would be a splendid thing. You say I'd have – what was it – title, position, standing in the world – '

' – Yes. A damned sight better than being a mere Miss Vaughan of very doubtful virtue!'

'Well, I look at it differently. If I married you I'd lead a dog's life and you know it! At your beck and call all day, forced to let you into my bed all night, I shouldn't be able to call my soul my own! And what's more,' cried Amaryllis in a burst of indignation, 'all my money would belong to you!'

'True to form, Amaryllis. Mercenary to the last. Don't be so silly. Of course all your money would belong to me. What do you think I'm marrying you for? The pleasure of your company? Now for God's sake stop talking nonsense and get dressed.'

'You haven't been listening to a word I've said! I've *told* you, about ten times, I DON'T WANT TO MARRY YOU!'

A dreadful silence fell. For a long moment Lord Vanbrugh glared at her. Then the storm broke.

'Then why the *devil* did you sleep with me!'

'Because I wanted to. Fool that I was!'

'Wanted to what? Answer me, damn you! Become my mistress? My wife?'

'Neither. I just wanted to sleep with you!'

Despite his rage, Lord Vanbrugh was genuinely taken aback. 'You mean . . . you didn't want any money for it?'

'No, of course not! That was only the first time. Before I had the business.'

'That's quite impossible!' he said categorically. 'Either you become my mistress, or my wife. Anything else is out of the question.'

'Oh it is, is it? And why is that? Because you won't be calling the tune, I suppose? Because you won't be able to order me around? Because you know I'll only stay with you as long as I want to and not because I have to.'

All this was so near the truth that Lord Vanbrugh grew angrier still. 'You dirty little whore! I must have been mad to offer you marriage. You'd be lucky to get into the local Magdalen! And where do you think you'll end up without a man to support you? Whining for charity in a debtors' prison or on your back in a dockland whorehouse where the sailors are too drunk to see what trash they're getting!'

'On the contrary! I'll end up a rich woman! *You're* the one who's heading for the debtors' prison! I've no intention of marrying you. You'd ruin us both!'

'What in hell's name makes you think you're so different? What makes you think *you're* special?' Lord Vanbrugh was black with rage. 'My God, *decent* women, let alone whores like you, would be only too thankful for an offer of marriage! You should be kissing my feet, damn you, in gratitude that I so much as *look* at you!'

Amaryllis gave a contemptuous laugh which did nothing to calm his fury. 'What sort of a fool do you take me for? I agree I'm not special. I'm not different. I daresay I'd have got married and been thankful like all the rest if *you*, Lord Vanbrugh, hadn't saved me from all that! You're the one who ruined me and you've only yourself to blame for what I've become. I'm a fallen woman now. I've tasted the sweets of freedom. Do you understand me? I'm my own mistress – I don't want to be yours!'

Lord Vanbrugh stared bleakly at her. He was conscious of a dead weight settling on his chest. At last he was forced to acknowledge his secret doubts and uncertainties. Amaryllis would never become the submissive mistress of his fantasy; he would never enjoy with her the comforting pretences his other women had offered him with such practised skill. It was time he faced reality. The chase was over and he would soon lose interest in the quarry. His face rigid, he walked to the door.

'Where are you going?' asked Amaryllis sharply.

'Away.'

'But . . . we can still be together, can't we?' she cried out in sudden alarm. 'It makes no difference! The money makes no difference!'

'Yes, it does. It makes all the difference. I want a mistress or a wife. What you suggest is – unnatural. I'll take no favours from you. I pay for my pleasures.'

'But don't you understand? I *want* to sleep with you! I don't need payment for doing what I want!'

But Lord Vanbrugh felt doubts overwhelm him afresh. For the first time in his life, he would have to come to terms with the needs of another human being. The prospect was too threatening to contemplate.

'My mistress, or nothing,' he said doggedly.

Amaryllis spoke as if every word cost her an effort. 'Then it's nothing.'

* * *

The weeks after Lord Vanbrugh's departure were the most miserable Amaryllis had ever known. Every night she cried herself to sleep and in the daytime she was so sullen and irritable that Bella declared she was impossible to live with.

But as time went on there were consolations. Henry's letters began to talk of her approaching twenty-first birthday, when Monksedge would be all hers at last. In London, work was steadily progressing on Crewe Place. Lord Mayo had been so anxious to avoid meeting the victorious Lord Vanbrugh that he had left London for a European tour, and in the haste of departure he had forgotten to tell his aunt to sell her lease on Crewe House. She had taken up residence a week later and lettings had become ever brisker in consequence. By mid-August, the left-hand side of the Place had been completed and the first tenants had moved in, enduring the noise and dirt from the building work in return for a temporary reduction in the rent. Then at last, in early September, the great day came when the last roof was completed on the right-hand side and a 'topping out' dinner was held for all the workmen.

'It's customary in the trade,' Mr Yardley had told Amaryllis. 'The house won't be finished, of course, but there's always festivities of some sort when the roof goes on. It's the last time all the workmen will be on site together. Then the masons and bricklayers will move on, since the structural work's completed.'

Amaryllis had rather resented the expense of a dinner and a half day's holiday but when she arrived at the Place for the topping-out ceremony she changed her mind. Everyone was present, washed and spruced up as much as was possible on a working day, and the site too had been tidied up for the occasion. Some of the buildings had been decorated with faded flags and a dining table had been set up on a patch of trampled earth and decorated with more flags and a pot of nasturtiums. Amaryllis's arrival was the signal for the ceremony to begin and everyone gathered in a solemn crowd in front of the end house, looking up at the roof where Silas was waiting, hammer in hand. A cheer went up as he nailed on the last ridge tile and there was a good deal of handshaking and backslapping which lasted until Mr Yardley suggested that they dine. He and Amaryllis sat in the place of honour at the head of the table while Silas sat at the other end, almost obscured from their view by two joints of cold roast beef and cold boiled ham, a pork pie the size of a cartwheel, a monster Cheddar cheese and enough loaves of the best white bread to stock a bakery.

At last, when even the heartiest eaters were beginning to tire, a shout of 'Speech!' went up and knife handles were drummed on pewter mugs. After a polite altercation with Mr Yardley as to which of them should begin, Amaryllis rose to her feet and lifted one hand for silence.

'Gentlemen!' she began, to roars of approval so loud that some of the residents came to their windows to see what the matter was, 'Gentlemen! I want to thank you all for your hard work over the past months. I'm sure you'll agree that Crewe Place is a job to be proud of! We've had our troubles but we didn't let them get the better of us, and I only hope we'll all work together again sometime in the future!' She sat down to loud applause.

Mr Yardley waited until the noise had died down a little and then he rose to his feet. 'I'd just like to second everything Miss Vaughan has said to you. And I've got a bit of good news that even she doesn't know about yet. Mr Linklater spoke to me this morning and he's offered us another development job on his estate. We'll take a look at it and if it seems a likely prospect it'll keep us all in work for another year!' Cheers drowned the rest of his speech. He sat down, smiling broadly, and in the excitement of the moment shook Amaryllis's hand so vigorously that it was sore for five minutes afterwards.

Smiling back at Mr Yardley, surrounded by the friendly faces of her workmen and conscious of the gleaming stucco of her new development behind her, Amaryllis knew that she had taken the right decision in refusing Lord Vanbrugh. She could never have sacrificed all this for a wearisome existence as his pampered and despised dependant.

An hour later, Amaryllis left Crewe Place and took a cab home. Pembroke Street looked almost welcoming in the summer dusk, which softened its harsh outlines and concealed its shabbiness. Smoke was rising gently into the darkening sky from kitchen fires, and at one end of the street an organ grinder was playing 'The Old Hundredth'. Contentedly, Amaryllis let herself into the house and began to mount the shadowy stairs. She had reached the first landing when she stopped abruptly, biting back a gasp of fear. There, standing silently on the stair, in exactly the place where she had first seen him all those months ago, was Cutler.

Thirty-six

'Surprised to see me?' said Cutler.

Amaryllis's first impulse was to run back down the stairs and out of the house. But she knew that she wouldn't get away. Her skirts would delay her.

'Where's Bella?' she demanded.

'Gone to Mrs Canning's, I made sure of that.'

Amaryllis's knees turned weak, her heart beat hard and fast. Cutler's cropped head and heavy shoulders belonged to a figure in a nightmare; there seemed nothing she could do but wait for his blows to descend. Then she remembered the advice Bella had given her after she had been accosted in the street. 'They want you to panic. They expect it. That's what they enjoy; seeing the fear in your face. Well, let them see it. It'll stop them giving you a knock-out blow like they would if you were a man. But don't let the fear take over. Don't let it paralyse your wits. In a fight, they're all you've got.'

Amaryllis gripped the stair rail hard, forcing a sense of reality back into her mind.

'Scared, are you?' said Cutler. His face, usually expressionless, began to flicker with triumph. 'Give me my money . . . '

From his tone Amaryllis knew that her answer would make no difference now. He was going to attack her, whatever she said. She delayed her reply as long as she dared, sizing him up with desperate care. He wore shirt, jacket and trousers – no hat to blind him with, no neckcloth to choke him. But no protective greatcoat either.

'I'll give you nothing,' she said, with a coolness that surprised her.

Cutler gave a sigh, almost of pleasure. His eyes were bright with the joy of hatred. 'I'll have to punish you for that,' he said quietly.

There was a long pause. Cutler seemed absorbed in scratching a stain off his cuff with one pointed fingernail. Amaryllis's hand clutching the stair rail was damp with sweat.

Cutler smiled suddenly, not at Amaryllis but at someone over her shoulder. 'Hello, Bella!' he said.

Amaryllis turned with a gasp of relief, only to find an empty stair, and at that moment Cutler's fingers seized her neck, forcing the breath out of her. For a second she was paralysed by shock. Then dimly, through the pounding in her head, she remembered Bella's instructions.

'Arch forwards, away from them. It's no good tearing at their wrists. Their arms are stronger than yours and they can strangle you in seconds. Arch forwards, at once. It loosens their grip and they can't choke you with one hand.'

Still clinging to the rail, Amaryllis threw herself forwards and sure enough Cutler's grip weakened. He muttered a curse and grabbed her by the shoulders, swinging her round against the wall with a crash that knocked the breath half out of her. Normally, such a blow would have left her sick and dizzy for minutes, but danger had strengthened her resistance and her mind stayed clear.

'Don't struggle,' Bella had told her. 'It's nothing but a waste of energy. Seize your moment, grab their balls, squeeze and jerk. Yes, I know you don't like the idea, but you can't use your knee, not in petticoats. Besides, the knee's slow and clumsy and you can't afford to miss. They'll murder you for sure if you try that trick and fail.'

Cutler was lunging towards her, his face intent and violent. Amaryllis clasped her hands before her, as if in terrified prayer. He rammed himself against her, pinning her to the wall with the weight of his body. His sour stench filled her nostrils and his hands again clutched at her throat, the pointed nails tearing her skin. Amaryllis knew that it was her last chance. She ground her heel on his instep, distracting his attention for the second necessary for her hands to flash downwards and grip and crush. With a groan of anguish, he fell away, doubled up and writhing with pain. He lost his footing, swayed and crashed backwards down the stairs until he lay still in a distorted heap at the bottom.

Amaryllis stood unmoving on the stair, shaking from head to foot and fighting back her nausea. Then knowing that she must get help, she went painfully downstairs. She could hardly bring herself to step over Cutler's unconscious figure, which barred her path to the front door. She was half afraid he was dead, and half afraid he was only shamming and would fasten his teeth in her heel.

She got past him somehow, shaking with revulsion, and reached the safety of the front door. Once out in the street she saw, with overwhelming relief, that Mr Yardley and Silas were coming towards her.

'We've come to talk over Mr Linklater's proposals . . . ' Mr Yardley's voice changed as he saw Amaryllis's pale face.

'Oh, I'm so thankful to see you!' she gasped, pushing the men into the house.

Mr Yardley saw Cutler lying on the floor. 'Who's this?' he demanded. 'What on earth's been going on? Are you all right?'

'Yes, yes, I think so . . . He's a housebreaker. He attacked me. He fell downstairs. He's not dead, is he?'

'Let's have a look . . . Silas, you go and fetch the police.'

'No!' cried Amaryllis, so frantically that they both stared at her. 'He's Bella's husband!'

Mr Yardley gaped at her. 'Bella's husband?'

'Yes, so we need to discuss – certain things.'

Mr Yardley rubbed his chin in perplexity. 'Well, I'd better take a look at him, at all events. Give me a hand upstairs with him, Silas.'

'He seems all right,' said Mr Yardley a few minutes later, when he had given Cutler a quick examination on Amaryllis's sofa. 'No bones broken – he's just knocked himself out. I suppose we'd better bring him round and see what he's got to say for himself.'

'I'd rather – I mean it might be better if – ' Amaryllis muttered, with a significant glance at Silas.

'I'll be just outside the door, if you want to be private,' said Silas. 'That way I'll be on hand if he tries to escape.'

It took several splashes of cold water before Cutler returned to consciousness but at last he opened his eyes and looked malevolently at Amaryllis.

'That's better!' said Mr Yardley, pulling him into a sitting position. As he did so, his hand came into contact with something hard and heavy in Cutler's jacket pocket. He reached into it and took out a leather pouch, filled with sand and weighted with lead at one end.

'So you're carrying a life preserver,' he said. 'The police will want to see this. Going to use it on Miss Vaughan, were you?'

Cutler muttered an oath.

'Don't waste your breath,' said Mr Yardley contemptuously. He turned to Amaryllis. 'If you'll tell me what's been going on . . . '

Amaryllis gave him a full account of her dealings with Cutler, to which he listened with growing disquiet. When she had finished he said, 'But why on earth didn't you tell me all this before? I could have helped you . . . And why didn't you go to the police? This man had broken into your house, frightened you, threatened you . . . '

'But Bella's his wife! He'd tell the police he was only trying to see her. I was sheltering her from her husband. They'd have had no sympathy with me.'

'Perhaps not – but sheltering a man's wife doesn't justify blackmail.'

'Yes, but it was only my word against his. And he'd have told the police how I came by Pembroke Street; you know he would. And then would they have believed me?'

'I suppose it would have been difficult. But this attack alters matters.' Mr Yardley balanced the life preserver on his palm. 'This is all the proof you need. He could be transported or even hanged. You've only to go and lay information –' He broke off, listening, as footsteps mounted the stairs towards them. The door opened and Bella stood on the threshold. Her gaze moved slowly from Mr Yardley, still holding the life preserver, to Amaryllis with her face pale and her hair dishevelled. Then it came to rest on Cutler, propped up on the sofa with a bruise developing on his forehead.

'Well!' said Bella. 'What's been happening here, then?' She

picked up a chair, placed it in the doorway and sat down as if to prevent any possible escape.

'You didn't punch him, did you?' she asked, frowning at Amaryllis. 'I warned you not to risk it . . . '

'No. I did everything you told me. He got that bruise afterwards, falling down the stairs.'

Bella smiled wolfishly. 'You *must* have taught him a lesson! I'm proud of you . . . Well, what's to be done with him now?'

'Mr Yardley thinks we ought to go to the police.'

'The police – yes, why not? Now we've got proof. Assault and housebreaking – that's transportation for life.'

'You bitch!' cried Cutler.

'Shut your noise!' said Bella. 'By rights it ought to be the drop.'

Cutler looked down at his calves as if he already felt the drag of the leg irons. 'I only wanted my rights,' he muttered savagely.

'Rights!' spat Bella. 'Oh yes, your rights! The *right* to steal all my money. The *right* to beat me black and blue. Snivel all you want. Now I've got the right to send you to the hulks and I'll show you no more mercy than you showed me!'

Cutler swore at her. He sat silent, thinking. Then he said triumphantly, 'No, Bella, it's not going to be as easy as that! You've forgotten your profession. Unless you want me to tell the judge all about it, the *hanging* judge, Bella, you'd better let me go.'

'They'd find you as guilty as me. You were my *husband*, remember. All the profits were yours.'

'I shouldn't care, though, should I? Better a quick death by hanging than a slow one in the hulks. No man my age gets out of those ships alive. The fever and the rats and the damp and the cold, they all kill you in the end – slowly and painfully. You knew that, didn't you, Bella? I'm not dying in those black pits. I go on the drop if I go at all.'

'He means it, curse him!' said Bella.

Amaryllis looked at Mr Yardley. 'But we can't let him go! I'd never feel safe again.'

'No, of course not,' he agreed. 'But if Bella – no don't tell me what she's done. I'd rather not know. But if we can't go to the police . . . '

'That's out of the question,' said Amaryllis hastily. 'They'd hang her for sure.'

'Why not send him abroad, then – to America perhaps?'

Amaryllis looked at Cutler. His face was swollen with rage. The veins in his neck and forehead bulged with blood. 'Yes, that's far enough. We'll send him to America.'

Mr Yardley hooked a hand under Cutler's collar and pulled him roughly to his feet.

'Silas and I will take charge of him,' he said. 'Some of the men can guard him till the boat goes.'

Cutler offered no resistance, but as Mr Yardley dragged him past Bella his face distorted with fury and he hurled a curseat her. Bella stared after him with a satisfied expression. 'It looks as if we've seen the last of him.'

Thirty-seven

When Mrs Gregory Saville arrived at Number Nine Jermyn Street one morning in late September, her appearance caused quite a stir among the men in shabby mufflers who were crowded about Lord Vanbrugh's front door and posted on his staircase. However desperate his lordship's financial position, however mountainous the debts they were waiting to collect, this lady was clearly rich enough to meet all her brother's obligations ten times over. Her bonnet alone must have cost fifty guineas and, when added to the cost of her jewels, her gown and the carriage and pair awaiting her outside, the total sum she represented was enough to make a debt collector's jaw drop. But there was more excitement to follow. An elderly man, who had been in the business forty years and had secured a good position out of the draught in consequence, no sooner saw the lady's face than he murmured, 'That's Gregory Saville's wife!'

The news spread like wildfire up and down the stairs and out of the front door into the street, where the latecomers were clustered.

'Saville could pay the lot and never miss it,' said the majority. 'He'll do it too. He's got to keep his brother-in-law out of prison. A few tears from the wife and we'll be paid in full.'

But those who had caught sight of Georgiana's face were less optimistic. It was hard to imagine those eyes filling with tears for her brother or anyone else.

Although Georgiana had looked at the duns with contempt, she was not ill-pleased to see them. They suggested that her brother's financial situation was even worse than she had hoped. The servant showed her into the sitting-room and told her that Lord Vanbrugh was still in bed but would be with her in a very few minutes.

There was no fire in the ill-swept hearth and evidences of neglect were everywhere. Piles of catalogues were heaped on chairs, grimy canvasses were propped against the walls, books lay broken-backed on the floor and an alarming number of empty bottles were ranged along the mantelpiece.

Georgiana sniffed disdainfully at the smell of stale wine and wood ash which pervaded the room, reached out a hand to ring for the manservant and then, with an impatient exclamation, crossed to the window and opened it herself. She retreated to a chair by the fireplace, sat down and picked up a book. It was an edition of Petronius, with extremely disreputable plates. Georgiana slammed it shut.

Eventually Lord Vanbrugh appeared. He was in his dressing-gown, dishevelled and unshaven. There were dark shadows under his eyes. He muttered a greeting and sat eyeing his sister distrustfully till his servant brought him a cup of coffee. Then he hunched himself over it and paid her no further attention. Georgiana waited until he had drunk enough coffee to revive him and then said, 'I heard you'd decided not to marry that girl after all, Anthony. I must congratulate you on thinking better of it. I'll even apologize for my interference. You were not as reckless as I'd feared and I freely acknowledge that I was in error.'

He laughed. 'Good of you! But I asked her to marry me all right. Don't think *your* opinion weighed with me. She refused me, thank God.'

'You can't expect me to believe that, but we'll leave it for the moment. I have something of far greater importance to discuss. I have come to make you an offer, Anthony. A generous one – in the nature of an olive branch after all our disagreements in the past. Both Gregory and I are concerned at your financial predicament. Matters are very serious, aren't they? I had only to look at the rabble on your staircase to realize that.'

'Get to the point, can't you?' growled Lord Vanbrugh.

'Very well,' said Georgiana, undisturbed. 'Gregory and I have talked about the problem and we have discovered a way to help you out of your difficulties. We've been looking for a country estate for some time but nothing suitable has yet come on the market. So Gregory's prepared to make you a handsome offer for Vanbrugh.'

Lord Vanbrugh's cup went crashing to the floor. 'Never!'

'Don't be absurd, Anthony. You're on the verge of ruin. You've no choice but to accept my offer. The position is clear. Either you sell to Gregory and preserve some small shred of credit for the family name, or Vanbrugh will be sold at auction by your creditors and Gregory will buy it just the same. It makes no difference to him but it makes a great deal of difference to you.'

'Over my dead body! You've already got the town house and the title. I was wondering how much longer you'd be able to keep your hands off Vanbrugh. But I'm not ruined yet!'

'And just how do you propose to keep your creditors at bay? You've no income, no credit, no assets . . . '

'I've my paintings.'

'Yes. Your paintings. It must be months since you last sold any.'

'I lost patience with it, that's all! I could sell some damn paintings tomorrow if I chose – and I shall, now you've given me a reason!'

Georgiana's self-control suddenly cracked. 'Oh for God's sake, Anthony! Can't you understand? There's no more *time*. Soon there'll be no Vanbrugh left for us to squabble over!' Real desperation sounded in Georgiana's voice. 'I went down to see it a while ago. There was damp everywhere. Another winter, maybe two, and it'll be too late. Already it'll take a fortune to make it habitable, and Gregory's prepared to spend one. He's got the money, Anthony, and you haven't. Why destroy Vanbrugh out of sheer selfishness?'

'I'd rather see the house razed to the ground than you as its mistress!'

Georgiana said no more. With a look of fury, she left the room.

* * *

Until his sister's visit, the duns on his staircase had caused Lord Vanbrugh little alarm. Born and bred in debt and existing permanently on extended credit, the spectre of bankruptcy had been at his elbow so often that it no longer had the power to frighten him into evasive action. His pursuit of Amaryllis had, almost imperceptibly, become the mainspring of his existence, and now that she was gone he had sunk into a lethargy. He had lost all interest in his picture dealing; it only reminded him that he no longer needed her purchase price.

But Georgiana's visit had made him realize that his bankruptcy would only mean his sister's triumph. He resolved to begin selling his paintings that very day. He wrote a hurried note to Mr Bentley telling him to promise his most pressing creditors payment by the end of the week and then he rang the bell for his servant and ordered his bath.

Half an hour later, another visitor mounted Lord Vanbrugh's staircase. But Bella's gaunt figure and plain black dress attracted none of the interest Georgiana had created, and when she muttered gruffly that she'd come for Lord Vanbrugh's laundry the duns let her pass without comment. At the top of the stairs she paused for a moment, listening. Then, without bothering to knock, she opened one of the doors and went inside.

She found herself in Lord Vanbrugh's bedroom. The bed was unmade, razors were laid out on the dressing table and in front of the fire Lord Vanbrugh was taking his bath. Luckily, it was a hip bath and its high back shielded its occupant from the door. Assuming Bella was his servant, Lord Vanbrugh paid no attention to her entrance and continued to wash himself. Unperturbed, she stepped forward and gave a harsh cough.

'What the devil!' exclaimed Lord Vanbrugh. 'Wait a minute. I know you, don't I? You're Miss Vaughan's servant'.

'That's right,' said Bella.

'Well, what do you want? And what the hell do you mean by bursting in here like this?'

'I had to see you. I thought your servant might turn me away.'

'Damn it, woman! Of course he would! I'm in my bath! And nothing Miss Vaughan has to say is of the least interest to me!'

'I haven't come from her. I'm here on my own account.'

Lord Vanbrugh's servant entered the room, carrying a can of hot water and a bath towel. On seeing Bella, he gave a horrified gasp and almost dropped the can.

'Stop gibbering, and get that woman out of here!' said Lord Vanbrugh.

Bella, a good six inches taller than the servant, folded her arms and stood her ground. 'I'll not budge,' she said, 'until you agree to listen to what I have to say.'

'Oh, for God's sake! It can wait until I'm dressed, can't it? Now get out of here and don't come back till I send for you!'

Half an hour later Lord Vanbrugh had bathed and shaved. He sat down at his breakfast table, poured himself a cup of coffee and told the servant to bring Bella in.

'Keep it short, for God's sake,' he said as she entered the room.

'I'll say what I've come to say. It's about Miss Vaughan.'

Lord Vanbrugh gave a scornful laugh. 'If she thinks she can come crawling back to me . . . '

'She doesn't know I'm here. In fact she hasn't mentioned your name since you left. I've come to see you because I know you love her . . . '

'Good God, what is this nonsense?'

Bella ignored him. 'I know you love her and from the way she's been behaving lately I suppose she loves you too.'

'You don't seriously expect me to believe you, do you?'

'Why not? It's the truth. She's been like a bear with a sore head since you left. Sulks, tantrums, complaints! I'm sick to death of it and I wish you'd go back to her and have done with it!'

'You're talking nonsense and you know it! If she was so fond of me, why didn't she become my mistress when I asked her?'

'She doesn't need your money. She's got enough of her own. And if she became your mistress she'd have to live in your house, under your thumb, and give up her business altogether, I daresay.'

'Well, of course. It *is* the usual practice.'

'No doubt. But how would you like it?'

'What I would like is irrelevant. A gentleman pays for his pleasures!'

'You mean a gentleman makes sure his pleasures do what he tells them. Well – I've said my piece. I'd better be going. Good day to you!'

Thirty-eight

As the landlord's gig bumped along the hill track towards Monksedge, Amaryllis looked at the familiar landscape with satisfaction. Beside her, Bella was too busy shielding the luggage from potholes to have time to spare for conversation and Amaryllis had her thoughts to herself. It was well over a year since she had last travelled along this track, and the contrast between the dispossessed girl and the woman of property was sufficiently sharp to bring a complacent smile to her lips. In a few minutes' time Henry Chesil would give her the title deeds and she could, if she chose, stay at Monksedge for the rest of her life, without the need to dig turnips for a living, as Bella had once predicted. She had done very well for herself, all things considered. If only Lord Vanbrugh . . . But she was not going to spoil her homecoming with useless regrets. Amaryllis straightened her shoulders and looked determinedly at the scenery.

She had always imagined herself returning to Monksedge in the height of summer, but now it was early October. There were dead leaves strewn over the muddy track and the bracken had turned to copper, though the gorse still flared yellow ahead of them, smelling like honey in the late afternoon sun. The gig breasted the ridge and Amaryllis leant forward expectantly as the well-remembered view came into sight. There below her lay the gentle Shropshire landscape, its low hills and secret, sheltered valleys overshadowed by the dark rampart of the Long Mynd. Amaryllis turned excitedly to Bella. 'There it is!' she cried. 'Look – there's the Long Mynd!'

'Well, what of it?' said Bella. 'Did you think they'd have moved it?'

Amaryllis gave her a reproachful glance but soon forgot her as the gig descended the track towards Monksedge. A couple of sheepdogs, barking frantically, bounded up to greet them as they turned the corner and accompanied them for the last few yards to the house.

It was all there, just as she remembered it: the black and white house, the crowded garden, the sundial half hidden by rough sheaves of Michaelmas daisies, and the apple orchard with geese foraging in the long grass.

Once the first bustle of arrival was over, Amaryllis sat with Henry and Maria in the parlour, drinking tea from the best Coalport china and listening, with only half an ear, to Maria's talk of linen and baby clothes. Over the rim of her cup, she surveyed the parlour furnishings, delighting in the thought that they all belonged to her, from the heavy walnut bookcase in the corner right down to the silver teaspoon lying in her saucer.

When Amaryllis had finished her tea, a servant removed the tray and Maria went to oversee the cooking of dinner, leaving Amaryllis and Henry alone together.

'You'll want your deeds, I expect,' said Henry. 'I have them all ready for you. These are the other papers and these are the keys in this wallet. Careful, it's a little heavy.' He handed them over half reluctantly, as if sorry to break the last chain linking him to Amaryllis. But Amaryllis was not interested in Henry's feelings. She took the packet he held out to her with more haste than politeness, pulled off the tape, spread out the deeds and was promptly absorbed. Soiled, greasy and written in the incomprehensible jargon of a country attorney though they were, she gloated over them, her loving fingers smoothing out the creases and gently tracing the cracked and crumbling seals of her long-dead predecessors.

The room was very quiet. Henry tried to concentrate on the gentle country sounds coming in through the open window; late bees droning among the Michaelmas daisies, sheep bleating on the hillside, a dog barking on the other side of the valley. But inevitably his attention reverted to Amaryllis.

'Maria and I will be leaving tomorrow,' he announced abruptly. Amaryllis looked up for a moment before returning to her papers.

'Oh, is your house ready then?'

'No, not for another month or two. But Maria and I will be staying with my father until her confinement. We'll both be happier knowing that Dr Simpson is only a few yards away . . . ' Realizing that Amaryllis was not listening to him, his voice tailed off into silence. He wondered when would be the best time to ask her if she would visit Chesil House. The invitation was sure to irritate her. It was hard to know how to phrase it tactfully. Better to wait, at all events, until Amaryllis was less preoccupied. But if he put it off for too long, he might never find the courage to begin. Painfully, Henry remembered his father's wrath when he had first broached the subject to him.

'Receive that woman in this house?' Mr Chesil had repeated incredulously, his chest swelling with indignation. 'Never! I wonder at you, Henry, for suggesting such a thing! A common prostitute in your mother's drawing-room! It's quite preposterous! No, really my boy, you've gone too far. It won't do. It will not do!'

'But father . . . ' began Henry.

Mr Chesil held up a podgy, protesting hand. 'No Henry. Enough's enough. That wretched girl is twenty-one. The trusteeship is over, thank God, and we can wash our hands of the whole business. I don't want to hear it mentioned again.'

'But father . . . ' Henry persisted imploringly, 'we *can't* wash our hands of it. Amaryllis will be staying at Monksedge and you *must* receive her here at Chesil House. Think of the gossip if you don't. It will all begin again. People already have their suspicions. If you don't receive Amaryllis they'll draw the obvious conclusions. And we'll all suffer from the scandal. The whole family will be disgraced!'

Mr Chesil stirred restlessly. 'Tarred by the same brush, eh? Hmm.'

Henry pressed home his advantage. 'The past is over now.

Amaryllis is a changed woman.'

'That's all very well! But she'll never be fit company for decent people and you know it. What you choose to do where Maria is concerned is your own business. I don't mean to rake up that old argument – you know my views by this time. But how can I ask Thyrza to receive a fallen woman in her own house?'

'She *is* her daughter.'

'Not any more! She's forfeited that privilege! Besides, there's nothing of Thyrza in her, thank God. She takes after her father, you can be sure of that. A very bad lot, Captain Vaughan . . . You're too soft on that girl, Henry. I'd hoped you'd forgotten that foolish – well, no more of that. Least said, soonest mended. But I'd hoped you'd forgotten.'

'Oh, it's not that.' Henry blushed uncomfortably. 'And I know, of course, that what she did was very wrong. But she was young, remember, and felt out of place here . . . '

'Through no fault of ours! I treated her like my own daughter! And *this* is how she repays me!'

'I know she's behaved badly, but in our own interests, we *must* treat her as if nothing has happened. Think of the shame and disgrace if we don't! Think of my stepmother's feelings and Maria's. And you're justice of the peace and a churchwarden!'

There was silence for a moment as Mr Chesil pictured himself sentencing the local whores to the house of correction while everyone sniggered behind their hands because his own stepdaughter . . .

'Very well,' he said irritably. 'Have it your own way! Though how I'm to explain it to Thyrza, I don't know.'

In the midst of these reflections Henry suddenly realized that Amaryllis was reading the final deed and brought his thoughts back to the present. His father had allowed himself to be persuaded, but would Amaryllis prove so easy to convince?

With a satisfied sigh, Amaryllis folded up the last deed and made a neat pile of her papers on the tea table beside her.

'Well, that's that,' she said complacently. 'Thank you, Henry, for all you've done. I can see you've looked after Monksedge beautifully.'

'Not at all,' said Henry, in some embarrassment. 'I mean – there's something more I want to do for you. I want to ask you to tea at Chesil House. You must come. It's important, Amaryllis. There have been rumours. People have been putting two and two together. But if it were known that you'd been received at Chesil House . . . '

'Everyone could *pretend* I was respectable.'

'Well, you want to be, don't you?'

Amaryllis considered for a moment. She had no wish to lead the life of a hermit at Monksedge. After all, how many people did she know in London? Mr Yardley, Mr Rugby, a handful of tenants and workmen; a chill contrast to the secure world she had lived in as a child and could live in again if she did as Henry suggested. This might be her last chance.

Amaryllis looked hard at Henry. 'I won't stand being lectured at!'

'No one will mention the past, I can promise you that. Maria will be present, remember, and she knows nothing of any – difficulty.'

'And I won't be left alone with my mother! She'll only cry and moan at me and it won't do a bit of good.'

Henry assured her that Mrs Chesil had no wish to see her daughter alone.

'Oh, very well then. I'll go if I must.'

When Amaryllis arrived at Chesil House on the appointed afternoon, she nearly went straight back home again at the sight of its prim brick façade. But Henry had been on the lookout for her and he ushered her up the path from the gate with such an anxious, conciliating air that she hadn't the heart to disappoint him. It seemed strange to cross again, openly in daylight, the hall she had last tiptoed through in darkness, dreading discovery at every step. It seemed stranger still to enter the drawing-room and find that, too, unaltered; the same furniture in the same positions, the stuffed pheasant still on the bookshelves and the backgammon board in the corner. But she had no time to look at it all. Mr Chesil was coming forward to welcome her with his familiar forced joviality, a flush rising behind his freckles and spreading down his thick neck. Behind him, Maria was exclaiming loudly at the elegance of Amaryllis's London gown, but her mother still sat at her embroidery frame, silent and withdrawn.

The servant brought in the tea kettle and the hot dishes and Mrs Chesil forced herself to make polite conversation, treating her daughter as if she had been any other visitor. But as soon as the servant withdrew, her face changed into a mask of disdain and she handed Amaryllis her tea as if she feared contamination from her touch. When the tea had been distributed, the sugar bowl was passed from hand to hand. In his agitation, Mr Chesil helped himself to three lumps and dropped them into his cup from too great a height, so that the tea splashed in his saucer. Mrs Chesil drank her tea as if it had been salted and avoided everyone's eyes.

Amaryllis knew that Henry could not be relied on in a social emergency and she tried desperately to think of something to say. London, Monksedge, all topics seemed fraught with dangers. Then, with a surge of thankfulness, she remembered Henry's new house. He had already told her all there was to know about it, but it would do her no harm to hear it again.

'How is the work on your house progressing, Henry?' she asked brightly. 'Do you think you and Maria will be moving in before Christmas?'

Henry answered her at length and Amaryllis reflected that she had forgotten what pleasure he took in explaining simple things in tedious detail. She found herself tracing the pattern of the carpet with her toe, just as she used to do in the old days. She was glad when Henry's explanation came to an end. But after that the conversation passed easily to other new houses in the district, to Mr Chesil's property in Hereford, to his sister's house in Shrewsbury. Amaryllis hid a yawn. She started to look at the clock and wondered how soon she could decently leave.

Mrs Chesil made no contribution to the conversation. She sat silent and still except for one occasion when Amaryllis's skirt brushed hers and she hurriedly twitched the material away. Her husband, however, was enjoying the talk; under its influence he became relaxed and genial. He was relieved to find Amaryllis outwardly unchanged and told himself that it would not be as hard to forget the past as he had feared. He could scarcely believe it had happened at all, with Amaryllis sitting there so neat and pretty and smiling so nicely at them all. He would push the uncomfortable fact that she was not what she seemed right down to the bottom of his mind and keep it there – and he'd see to it that Thyrza did so too, for all their sakes. His mind made up, he turned to Amaryllis and asked her how long she was staying in Shropshire.

'Not long. Another month at the most. I have business in London waiting for me.'

Mr Chesil was pleased that her stay would be so short. He reached out and patted his wife's hand encouragingly. 'In that case, I think we had better ask Amaryllis to come to our party next Saturday, Thyrza my dear.'

'Very well, if you wish it, William,' she replied submissively, without so much as a glance in her daughter's direction.

Thirty-nine

On the following day, Mr Bentley was climbing the stairs to Lord Vanbrugh's rooms with slow, reluctant steps. The duns had departed, pacified by the sale of a painting, but their absence did nothing to lessen the agent's anxiety. He thought nervously that if Lord Vanbrugh took kindly to his suggestion, then there might be hope at last. But if he took it the wrong way – ruin was inevitable. He paused on the landing outside Lord Vanbrugh's door and ran a finger round the inside of his collar. His livelihood depended on the outcome of this interview. He knew no one else would employ him as an agent. He was a good hand with accounts, he'd always taken a pride in his ledgers but he couldn't pretend to much flair for the job. And the Vanbrugh estate was a poor advertisement. He swallowed hard, summoned up his courage, knocked and entered.

Lord Vanbrugh looked up from a catalogue. 'Well?' he said ungraciously, 'what is it this time?'

'Financial matters, Lord Vanbrugh.'

'Oh the devil, not again! I thought you'd paid off the duns!'

'So I did, but they represented only the most pressing of your debts.'

'Out with it! Let's hear the worst.'

'The moneylenders are applying for a writ. *All* of them.'

Lord Vanbrugh turned pale. 'My God . . . ! Are you sure? I never thought . . . You told them I'd pay the interest, given a little more time?'

'Of course.'

'They'd heard it too often before, no doubt. And the paintings?'

'They were unimpressed. They told me they would have gone to law months ago, were it not for your connection with Mr Saville. But he's now given them to understand that he won't be involving himself in your affairs. They aren't prepared to wait any longer. You'll have to leave London immediately. The writs will be out by morning.'

'Leave London?'

'Yes. Tonight, or it may be too late.'

'And have I any prospect of returning?'

'None, my lord; unless . . . '

'Well?'

'Unless . . . ' Mr Bentley took a deep breath, 'you sell Vanbrugh to Mrs Saville.' Ignoring his employer's violent expletive he continued, choosing his words with care. 'I happen to know that Mrs Saville would still be prepared to purchase the property – at a sum more than adequate, in my opinion. The sale would have other advantages too, though not perhaps from Mrs Saville's point of view. You will remember the arrangement arrived at on the occasion of her marriage. In return for your agreement never to marry, Mr Saville waived all claim to your sister's dowry . . . '

'Yes, yes!'

'The dowry consisted of the four unencumbered properties in Pembroke Street, certain Shropshire rent charges, and Sargent Fields, a small piece of property on the outskirts of London. This is at present leased to a market gardening concern and brings in a comparatively low agricultural rent.'

'Yes, I remember it. It's out near Chelsea somewhere.'

'No, my lord. I think, nowadays, it would be better described as bordering Belgravia. Sargent Fields is ripe for development. Few properties in London can be more so. It would not be exaggerating to describe it as a potential gold mine.'

For a moment Lord Vanbrugh looked almost hopeful. 'That's all very well, Bentley, but you've just told me I'm ruined. I can do nothing except sit back and watch my creditors take the profits.'

'Not if you sell Vanbrugh to Mrs Saville – no, my lord, I *beg* you to give me a hearing! You can sell Vanbrugh, come to some arrangement with your creditors, tell them they'll be paid in full if they wait a little longer, and then invest the proceeds of the sale in a development scheme.'

'It won't do. I just don't have the cash. The mortgages will swallow up most of the money from the sale.'

'Very true. But there will be something. Not enough to satisfy your debts, but enough to invest in a development – if you do so in partnership.'

Lord Vanbrugh frowned suspiciously. 'What partnership? No one in their right minds would go into partnership with a man in my financial position. Least of all to develop land that could be seized by my creditors at any moment!'

Mr Bentley knew that he must proceed with extreme caution. 'A small building firm, anxious to make a name for itself, might be prepared to take the risk. Such a firm would not normally be given the chance to handle a project of this exceptional quality.'

'No. Nor be capable of doing the work,' said Lord Vanbrugh caustically. 'I take it you have a specific firm in mind?'

Mr Bentley cleared his throat and took the plunge. 'The firm is already known to us, my lord, and I have every reason to be satisfied with their work. Indeed it was one of their partners who brought the possibility of a development to my attention. He had drawn up quite a detailed scheme. I was very much impressed by it . . . '

'Well, get on with it, can't you? What's his name?'

Mr Bentley looked acutely uncomfortable. 'Mr Yardley, my lord.'

'What!'

'A very reliable man . . . ' Mr Bentley began feebly and then broke off, dismayed at the expression in his employer's eyes. He had expected him to be difficult, even angry perhaps; Lord Vanbrugh was always unreasonable where women were concerned. This was different. Mr Bentley was not a perceptive man, but behind Lord Vanbrugh's fury he sensed something akin to despair. He escaped from the room and crept forlornly away, comforting himself with the thought that Miss Georgiana might give him some sort of employment for old times' sake.

* * *

Left alone, Lord Vanbrugh sprang to his feet and began to pace about the room. Sargent Fields – so that was it! The whole thing was clear at last! He'd always known Amaryllis was playing some undergame. She'd wanted to get a hold over him, to make sure that her damned building firm reaped the profits from the development. But sending Bella to tell him she was in love with him was a cheap trick, even by her standards! What a fool she must take him for! No wonder she'd refused to become his mistress; she'd had her eye on richer pickings. She'd told him once he hadn't money enough to tempt her. Well, he'd never imagined for one moment that what Bella had said was true. He'd never been fool enough to believe Amaryllis loved him. Secretly, though, he knew that he had believed it and his desolate sense of betrayal was not made any easier to bear by his refusal to admit that it existed.

Lord Vanbrugh left London in undignified haste, by the night mail, but he found that Shropshire was not the best place to repress all thoughts of Amaryllis. No sooner had he set foot in the great, damp house, than recollections of the month they had spent there together crowded in upon him. Amaryllis's ghost was everywhere: wandering across the lawn as he took a walk on the terrace, sitting opposite him as he ate a solitary dinner, lying beside him under the dusty canopy as he tried, unsuccessfully, to sleep.

Again and again he relived their last night together, remembering her passion and trying to convince himself that in spite of everything she did really love him.

The next morning, unable to bear the house any longer, Lord Vanbrugh went out into his neglected grounds. He made a circuit of the park and then climbed the hill towards the obelisk which marked the boundary between his estate and Lord Mayo's land. The slope was steep and the October sunshine was hot on his back. Halfway to the summit he paused and turned to look back the way he had come. There below him, the roofs of Vanbrugh lay revealed in all their dilapidation. Missing slates were everywhere, birds' nests bristled from long disused chimney pots and a sapling had taken root in a sheltered corner behind the main pediment.

Lord Vanbrugh climbed on until he reached the ridge and

stood beside the obelisk. Below him were the roofs of Vanbrugh. To one side lay the sweeping curves of the main drive, green with weeds, to the other lay the lake and the crumbling façade of the temple. It would take a fortune to restore the estate and if it were not done soon it would be too late. The roofs would fall in, the lake would choke with reeds and it would all be his fault. He had better sell without delay. The thought of Georgiana's triumph was unbearable, but it would be just as bad to watch Vanbrugh pass, neglected and despised, into the hands of his creditors – and end up being bought by Georgiana just the same.

Lord Vanbrugh turned his back on his estate and gazed out across the sweet-smelling turf to Lord Mayo's lands. It was over then: he had lost it all. He was homeless and alone, betrayed by the one human being he had managed to care for.

He had been there for an hour when he saw a horseman cantering along the ridge towards him. As he came nearer, Lord Vanbrugh saw that it was Mayo. He expected him to turn away before he reached him but Mayo rode up and greeted him good humouredly.

'I'm not the man to bear a grudge, Vanbrugh. I like a good scrap as well as the next man. That's over and done with as far as I'm concerned and I'll tell you why.' He looked at Lord Vanbrugh with a certain malice in his eyes. 'That confounded girl has deceived the pair of us! Yes, you too, Vanbrugh! I came down here for the shooting and what did I find? The little whore's turned respectable!'

'*What* did you say?'

'Yes, I thought that would shake you,' nodded Lord Mayo. 'She's been here upwards of a fortnight staying in that old house of her father's. Received by her family, what's more. Tea at Chesil House; damned dull of course, but respectable – by God it is! I went to church on the off-chance of seeing her, and sure enough, there she was. Damned amusing, watching the vicar making up to her for the pew rent. My first thought was – put a stop to it! But then I said to myself, why spoil the fun?' He leant down from his saddle and gave Lord Vanbrugh a nudge. 'You and I, Vanbrugh, we know what we know, eh?' And with his braying laugh, he rode away.

Lord Vanbrugh stared after him, troubled and confused. Amaryllis had become respectable. It seemed incredible. But if it was true – *if* it was – then it was hardly likely that she was intending to ruin it all by becoming his mistress again. So perhaps Bella *had* been telling the truth. Perhaps Amaryllis really did love him. He felt as if he must be rid of this dreadful uncertainty.

Monksedge was thirty miles away and by the time Lord Vanbrugh reached the house the sun was close to setting. He dismounted at the gate and was about to enter the garden when Bella came round the side of the house with a basket of windfalls. She looked surprised to see him but she came forward to take charge of his horse.

'Where's Miss Vaughan?' he demanded.

'Out.'

'I must see her. It's urgent.'

'She's picking blackberries up over the hill there. It's not far, if you want to walk. Just follow that track till you see her.'

Forty

The path wound upwards for a little way over the shoulder of the hill. Then it descended through encroaching bracken fronds into a valley where a stream trickled along between banks of hazel and alder scrub. The place had a deserted air and the ground was hummocky and dotted with nettles.

Lord Vanbrugh followed the path until it petered out in a bramble patch; then he stopped dead, his heart beating uncomfortably hard. There, ahead of him, stood Amaryllis, her back turned towards him as she reached for a bramble spray, laden with fruit.

He clenched his fists till the knuckles whitened. Once he touched her, all would be lost. Telling himself she was sure to have cheated him, he managed to regain his self-control. Then he slowly relaxed his fingers and approached Amaryllis, pulling the bramble spray down into her hand.

She spun round, startled by his sudden arrival. A torrent of blackberries poured from her basket down into the long grass at her feet.

'Have you changed your mind?' she asked, as if their two months apart had never existed.

Lord Vanbrugh avoided her eyes. 'I've not come to talk about that,' he said roughly. 'I want to discuss your business proposal.'

'What business proposal? I made you none.'

'Don't lie to me. I don't suppose Mr Yardley came to see Bentley without consulting you. You want to develop Sargent Fields. Why bother to pretend otherwise?'

'I'm not pretending! If Mr Yardley came to see you, he did

so behind by back. I *told* him, quite definitely, that I'd have nothing to do with it!'

'You'd never pass up the chance to develop a site right next door to Belgravia. I know you too well to believe that, Amaryllis!'

'Oh, do you! Well, if the ground landlord were anyone else, I would develop it. But I'm not going to get mixed up with you again. I'd rather die!'

'Then why did you send Bella to my rooms with that maudlin little tale of unrequited love?'

'What do you mean? I never sent Bella anywhere!'

'You've a short memory! You sent Bella to tell me you were broken-hearted without me. In fact, as I was well aware, it was Sargent Fields you were pining for!'

Amaryllis looked at him in horror, her cheeks burning.

'You mean Bella – Bella told you that I . . . Then she and Mr Yardley must have – oh, it's *monstrous*! I'll never forgive any of you. Never!'

Tears of rage and humiliation poured down Amaryllis's cheeks. It was impossible to doubt her sincerity. Lord Vanbrugh's self-control melted away. He made an uncertain move towards her and then stopped and said, 'I want you; come back to me.'

Shock rendered Amaryllis speechless. She stood silent, the angry tears drying on her cheeks. Then, almost in spite of herself, she reached out her hand.

Lord Vanbrugh looked at it. He feared it might draw him into dangerous waters and hesitated, one last time, on the safety of the shore. Amaryllis made no further move towards him. She was conscious of a strange confusion of spirit. He wanted her; she knew she wanted him. Why, then, were they holding back? Slowly, she lifted her gaze to his, where he stood, awkward and uncertain, against the rusty bramble leaves.

Lord Vanbrugh took Amaryllis's hand.

They held each other close, cheek warm against cheek. Lord Vanbrugh looked at her with a new, half-wary confidence.

The strange element would not drown him after all. He drew a little away so that his gentle finger could outline the contours of her face. A thin rain began to fall, pattering down on the leaves and grass. They kissed each other softly, their hair darkening in the wet.

'I love you,' said Amaryllis. 'I wonder why I didn't realize it before?'

'I wasn't very lovable.'

'Neither was I.'

Lord Vanbrugh laughed. 'You still aren't,' he said, holding her tight in his arms.

'Well, you're just as bad. When I think of what I've had to put up with . . . '

'You didn't put up with it. That was the trouble.'

'Would you have loved me if I had?'

'I've always loved you . . . for at least a year. You were the one who kept making difficulties.'

'No I wasn't. You *would* keep bringing money into it. It only spoils things.'

'That's not what you said the first time we met!'

'I didn't love you then . . . You don't still want to marry me, do you?'

'No, no,' he reassured her. 'It doesn't seem to matter now.'

Amaryllis sighed 'I know you'll be impossible to live with. Me too – I'm just as selfish as you are. But you needn't think you can treat me the way you did at Vanbrugh!'

'I wouldn't dream of it. Not after the dance you led me . . . We'll have terrible fights.'

'I don't care – do you?'

'No. We always *have* quarrelled. I don't suppose I'll mind going on with it – in bed and out of it.'

He kissed her hard upon the lips.

'That's all very well,' said Amaryllis at last, 'but I've got my business to run.'

'So have I. Picture dealing – just as time-consuming as property development. And the sooner I start making some money, the better. There's a writ out for my arrest in London. If I can't pay my debts by developing Sargent Fields, I shall have to fly the country. In a word, I'm destitute.'

'Oh you are, are you? Then just how do you propose to finance your share of the investment?'

'I shall sell Vanbrugh to Georgiana.'

Amaryllis gasped. 'Sell Vanbrugh?'

He shrugged, with as much indifference as he could muster. 'I've really no choice in the matter. She's always wanted it and she'll give me a decent price – which is more than anyone else would. The alternative is bankruptcy, in which case she'd simply buy it off my creditors . . . I've really no right to hang on to it. Georgiana cares about the land. She'll look after it properly; far better than I ever did. She can afford to, after all.' He sighed. 'They'll tear down the ivy and scrub the statues and scythe the lawn. We won't recognize the place – not that I suppose we'll ever go there again.'

'Well, I do think you're better off without it.'

'I suppose so . . . It was always an incubus. Georgiana is welcome to it! Let it soak up Saville's fortune for a change. I'll concentrate on Sargent Fields. I hope it's going to be successful: I've no other prospect of paying off my debts.'

'Oh, don't worry, it's sure to succeed.'

'Well, I'm going to make damn sure my attorney crawls over every inch of your contracts. I've not forgotten that two thousand pounds.'

'Neither have I,' said Amaryllis tartly. 'You cheated me out of four hundred of them.'

Lord Vanbrugh tactfully let this pass. 'Georgiana will be furious if we make a fortune out of Sargent Fields. It was part of her dowry. Still, she's only got herself to blame and so I shall tell her. Not that she'll receive me, if I'm living openly with you.'

'You don't seem to mind very much.'

'No, it's one of the advantages of the arrangement.'

'It's all very well for you. No one minds if a man lives in sin. But what about me? I'll be ostracized by the whole of Shropshire!'

'Well, that's all to the good isn't it? They're dreadful bores and you know it.'

'But I don't want to spend the rest of my life on my own. No one will receive me in London either!'

'Nonsense. There are plenty of people in London who don't

give a damn. Mr Yardley for one. Stop making difficulties!'

Amaryllis still looked resentful.

'I do understand,' he said more gently. 'They threw me out of my clubs when I took up picture dealing. But I'll introduce you to people who are living in sin all over the place. You'll be all right. Or would you rather I went away and left you alone?'

'Of course not.'

'Good, because I've no intention of doing so.'

Amaryllis made a face. 'Oh well, I suppose I don't really want to spend the rest of my life being polite to the Chesils. I'll write and tell them what I've decided to do and promise never to see them again.'

Despite her words, she felt guilty about Henry. This was a poor return for all his months of patient effort on her behalf. But at least she would never again have to listen while he explained things to her.

'Never mind,' said Lord Vanbrugh. 'Would it help if I refused to develop Sargent Fields unless you lived with me? That would give you a sound commercial reason for the sacrifice.'

'No. I'm being silly, wanting to put the clock back. I burnt my boats that first night at Vanbrugh, and I'm glad I did.'

'Will you sell Monksedge?'

'Not unless I have to. They needn't think they're going to drive me away. I'll live in London, of course, but I'll come back to Monksedge when I can. I may have to mortage it though, to raise a loan for Sargent Fields.' She looked up at the darkening sky. 'It's stopped raining. We'd better go back to the house. Does Bella know you're here?'

'Yes. She told me where to find you.'

'Good, then she'll be cooking us dinner.'

Back at Monksedge, Bella was standing at the gate, arms folded, enjoying the evening air. She was about to go indoors and light the lamps when she heard voices coming towards her, raised in argument. Despite the deepening twilight, it was impossible to mistake their identity.

'Oh God, not bankers' stucco! No, really, Amaryllis, over my dead body! And a few classical details slapped on as an afterthought – I won't stand for it!'

'Oh yes, you will! Do you want to make money or don't you? The sooner you get one thing straight the better! If it sells – we build it!'

Bella smiled. Peering into the shadows, she saw them coming down the hill path, absorbed in their argument. Amaryllis swung an empty basket and Lord Vanbrugh walked beside her, his arm about her shoulders and his dark head close to hers. They had almost reached the gate before they saw Bella and fell silent. She looked them up and down and shook her head.

'Well,' she said, 'I've aired the sheets.'